for Judy
on your Birthday 2023
with love from
Dede.

A LATE FINDING

Other books by Lucy Beckett

Novels
The Time before You Die
A Postcard from the Volcano
The Leaves are Falling
The Year of Thamar's Book
In the Grieving of her Days

Non-fiction
Wallace Stevens
Richard Wagner's Parsifal
York Minster
In the Light of Christ: Writings in the Western Tradition

Poems
The Returning Wave

A Late Finding

Lucy Beckett

GRACEWING

First published in England in 2023
by
Gracewing
2 Southern Avenue
Leominster
Herefordshire HR6 0QF
United Kingdom

www.gracewing.co.uk

ISBN 978 085244 144 2

Typeset by Word and Page, Chester, UK

Cover design by Bernardita Peña Hurtado
Image © istock.com/Xantana:
The Gazi Husrev-beg Mosque in Sarajevo

For Deirdre

In the second century AD the Emperor Hadrian asked the philosopher Secundus, "What is a friend?" The philosopher replied: "A desirable title, an invisible man, a possession hard to find, encouragement in trouble, a refuge in misfortune, support in wretchedness, one who sees life, a man beyond one's grasp, the most valuable possession, unattainable good luck."

Translated by Teresa Morgan in her book
Popular Morality in the Early Roman Empire

To find. Not to impose. It is possible, possible, possible.

Wallace Stevens

Chalked on the wall of a New York subway: "Pray for me." Underneath in a different hand: "Sure."

CHAPTER 1

SATURDAY 13 FEBRUARY 2021

Once or twice in the dark, neither any longer dreaming nor yet properly awake, she wondered whether she'd invented him. Had she made him up because she needed him, as atheists say of those who believe in God? If she had, he would vanish like the wisps of dreams, and not be there in the daylight. As atheists say of God.

But invent means find. She used to say this to the children in her Latin classes, and enjoy watching them think it out. And in the morning he was still there, not, of course, here, in her flat, but there, in the little mews house beside the garage that kept safe a Bentley belonging to the Russian who lived, when he was in London, in three mews houses turned into a gold-plated folly, a rich man's pied-à-terre. Sometimes the Syrian caretaker who looked after the Russian's folly and had told Val about the gold taps would take the Bentley out for a spin—"The English call it a spin. I do not spin. I drive to the river and I drive back, quite straight"—and spend the rest of the morning washing the car with dedicated seriousness on the cobbles of the mews. Val's house belonged to the almost always absent Russian, who charged him a modest rent because he thought he was honest and reliable, which Clare was sure he was, and a Serb, which she knew he wasn't.

She had seen his house only once, the day before yesterday, because, when they met in the square, as they did on Wednesdays and Saturdays at three in the afternoon, there was frozen snow on the grass and it had been so bitterly cold that he said, "It is not possible for us to sit on our bench in this wind. It is an east wind, from Poland. I knew it well when I lived there. It is an old enemy. Will you come to my house and I will make tea for us? You have not seen my little house."

"Well—" Why was she doubtful? He had been to her flat twice for a cup of tea, a cup of coffee. They had been careful to sit at opposite ends of her large kitchen table and he had sent her up alone in the lift while he walked up the stairs. The Covid rules since Christmas had been very strict: visits were forbidden, what was called "household mixing" was forbidden, and people weren't allowed to meet even in the park for a walk. Unless they were in—a brand-new phrase for the pandemic—a support bubble. With some difficulty she had looked up the definition of a permitted bubble on a government website, and the pair of them, not of course that they were a pair, each living alone, and no more than near neighbours, had decided that it was well within what was allowed to turn themselves into a "support bubble". They could talk on the bench in the garden of her square, without being so far apart that they couldn't hear each other. They gave each other permission to take off the masks they wore against the virus, and it was within the rules even to meet indoors as long as neither of them belonged to any other bubbles. Both of them had just had their first vaccination. But in his house, which she knew to be very small? Would that be sensible? She had promised her daughter that she would obey all the rules. She would so much like to see where he lived..

"All right. Yes. Why not?"

She had her stick. He walked faster than she did, but, leading the way, he walked slowly, for her.

"Be most careful", he said when they reached the mews. "Muhammad yesterday washed the famous car and the water now is ice on the stones."

The cobbles were indeed terrifyingly slippery.

He stopped at a red-painted door in a whitewashed brick wall between the green rolled-down door of the Bentley's garage and a biggish window with a white orchid on the sill inside, and on either side of the orchid a scarlet cyclamen. In the sunshine and the freezing cold the whole effect was cheerful and a little Central European, like an illustration to a fairy story. This was just a swift impression. She had never been to Central Europe.

He opened the red door.

"Be careful", he said again. "There is a step down."

They were at once in what was clearly his living room. It was untidy but not dirty. A black cat with a white shirtfront and three white paws appeared and wound itself round Val's legs.

"My cat. His name is Ivan. I call him Ivitsa."

By this time, she knew that "Ivitsa" would be spelt "Ivica". Not that she was likely to be writing it down.

The cat jumped onto an armchair by the unlit electric fire and glared accusingly at the bars.

She looked round the room. There were books in shelves, wooden shelves of a basic flat-pack kind, from floor to ceiling on both sides of the fireplace, on the whole of the wall opposite the fireplace, except in the far corner where the steep, narrow stairs began, and, in lower sets of shelves, on the wall facing the window, which had a door at its centre. More books were in piles on the floor and on a deal table with a drawer, his simple desk, which stood at a right angle to the window. There was a landline telephone on the desk, and a laptop. As in Clare's much larger sitting room in her flat, there was no television. Either side of the fire was an armchair. One, with its back to the window, was shabbier than the other and clearly the one in which he usually sat. On the other Ivica was sitting with his front paws furled under his chest, silently complaining of the cold.

Val took off his coat, threw it across one arm of the old cane-seated chair at the desk, and knelt on the floor—something Clare couldn't easily do nowadays—to switch on the bars. One of the minor habits of old age, she ruefully recognized, was noticing how much or how little other old people could manage.

"So many books", she said.

He got back to his feet, a little stiffly and having to push hard on the floor with one hand, and smiled, spreading his hands wide in a gesture now familiar to her.

"Of course. Books are all of my life. But you know that." He waved a hand at the shelves. "Still I do a little buying and selling of books. A very little now."

3

He stepped towards her.

"Allow me to take your coat, Clare. If you will not be too cold without it."

She put her gloves in her coat pockets and let him help her out of her coat, which he put on the other arm of the chair at the desk. She took off her old sham fur hat, which nevertheless kept her warm, and put it on her coat.

"Please. Sit down near to the fire, while I make some tea. Or perhaps some coffee. Do you like Turkish coffee?"

"I don't think I've ever tried Turkish coffee."

"Really? The English are very—". He searched for the right word. "Conservative. Their tea, for example, with milk which I cannot understand."

"Because you are very conservative?"

He laughed. "Exactly. Why not?"

"Why not indeed", she said.

"But not to know Turkish coffee? I am used to the English but still they can surprise me. Even you surprise me."

"I'm so sorry."

He laughed again. "Do not apologize. Turkish coffee is thick and sweet, in a very little cup. Would you be brave to try it?"

"Of course, Val. It sounds delicious."

The kitchen, through the door between the lower book-shelves, was obviously the only other room on the ground floor. He went into it, leaving the door open, and started a process she could hear but not see.

For a moment, because of what he'd said about tea, she remembered Ayesha, the young Indian doctor so briefly her tenant last spring, who made her Assam tea in a way Clare hadn't ever grasped. Poor Ayesha. Early in the pandemic she had died of Covid in the hospital where she worked.

She shook her head, to banish the pain of the memory, and, before she sat down, looked more carefully at the room.

On the wall each side of the door into the kitchen were two framed pages of medieval manuscript, presumably repro-ductions. She went over, two steps, to look at them closely, first one, then the other. They must be pages from the same book. The lettering was in a script she didn't recognize, the

4

blocks of text surrounded by a border, first of very fine tracery, pale blue, then what looked like more lettering, larger and in gold, more blue tracery, more text in a thin band, and finally a wonderful decorated border, with stylized flowers, scrolls and whorls, scarlet, green and blue on what must have been in the original a fine parchment background, with gold leaf here and there. These pages were clearly European, clearly fourteenth or fifteenth century because of what they had in common with Books of Hours, so the writing, neither Latin nor Greek, must be Hebrew, or perhaps Arabic. She felt ashamed of her ignorance.

She turned. On the mantelpiece were two framed photographs. The larger was a faded sepia studio portrait of a handsome young man with a moustache, in a black suit, white shirt and black shoestring tie, looking down, not quite smiling, at a solemn dark-eyed, dark-haired girl sitting on a fragile chair, gazing up at him and dressed in a lot of white lace with an elaborate head-dress. His bride. She was holding a trailing bouquet of lilies and ivy, and beside her was a broken classical column with the plaster head of Pericles in his helmet perched on top of it. The picture—his parents, obviously, so some time in the 1930s—suggested calm, confidence, and middle-class prosperity. It was interesting that there was in the photograph no sign of any religious connection, yet Clare knew that Val's mother was Jewish, and that his father's mother was Catholic and his father's father Muslim. So the atmosphere suggested was modern, though the wedding must have taken place not far off a hundred years ago. She also knew that even the possibility of such a marriage was characteristic of the Sarajevo Val had described to her.

The smaller photograph was a black and white snapshot of a pretty young woman who didn't look more than 25, with two little boys, a toddler, perhaps three years old, holding her hand, his face serious like the face of his grandmother in the wedding picture, and on her other arm a baby of nine or ten months, beaming and waving a hand at the photographer, obviously Val. The woman was wearing a striped cotton dress and a simple headscarf tied behind her head. This must have been taken in the 1970s, when Tito was still alive and Yugoslavia was the most open, and probably the most cheerful, of all the communist countries in Europe.

She remembered that in the first conversation she'd had with Val, two months ago now, she had asked him where he was from, and he'd said, "I am a Yugoslav. Yugoslavia does not any more exist, but the word means only where the South Slavs live, and I am a South Slav." It had taken several more conversations before she understood why he chose to describe himself as a Yugoslav.

On the wall above the photographs there hung a large picture, probably also a photograph but this one in colour, of part of an exotic building she didn't recognize. She stood up to look at it more closely: the internal court or a large upstairs space of an apparently Islamic building, two storeys of slender columned arches in what was probably a circle, elegantly lit, with a pale marble floor, a large six-pointed star at its centre, and the roof a shallow dome of patterned, rather crudely coloured, glass. It was a beautiful space, except perhaps for the glass, and it looked oddly new, fresh and bright in the photograph.

She picked up the cat, which didn't object when she put him down in front of the fire, but folded himself neatly and went to sleep. She sat down in the less shabby chair, facing the window, the orchid and the cyclamen plants, and looked again at the picture of Val's wife and his sons. It recorded a happy family outing, unremarkable, and according to the little he had told her of his marriage, representative of what had been a happy family life. The toddler and the baby should now be in their forties, with wives and children of their own. Alas.

He reappeared.

"I am sorry, Clare. The making of Turkish coffee takes the time it does take. Another few minutes will make it ready. I hope you are a little warm by the fire? It is not a powerful fire."

"I'm fine, thank you. I'm sure the coffee will be very good."

He sat down opposite her in his armchair.

"You see, my house is small. There is a table in the kitchen, for two people to eat. And up the stairs is a bedroom, also a smaller bedroom, which was my bedroom while my friend was alive, and an even smaller bathroom. And there is a large cupboard which is useful."

"All you need, perhaps?"

He smiled. "All I need. Not all I would wish. I would wish a garden. There is a very small yard at the back of my house for a few pots of geraniums and a rose on the wall, so Ivica may go and come when I am out. He has his door in the kitchen door. Of course he travels to the bigger gardens. But he is a cat.

"There was always a garden when I was a child, my grandmother's garden, where she would grow even vegetables with her flowers. In Sarajevo when I lived in a flat I had no garden, and again in Wrocław there was a flat with no garden. That is why I offered to help the gardener in your square. You remember? Bill Atkins. When he died, the new gardener did not wish for help. But they said I could keep my key.

"So there is no garden of mine, though I can walk to Kensington Gardens of course, when we are allowed to walk, and always I can walk in the garden of the square, and sit on a bench. As we know."

He smiled at her, his blue-eyed smile. She smiled back.

"But I have lived in this house many years now, and it is quiet at night, which I very much like. Once, now a long time ago, I have heard a nightingale sing. From my bedroom window I can see some trees in the gardens of the big houses, the branches with snow in these few days, which there is not often in London. In winter there should be snow."

"Of course there should."

She felt again, as she often felt, talking to him, the distance, across which he had said that he would now never retrace his journey, between Central Europe and South Kensington. And not only because of Covid.

"What is the building in the picture, Val?"

"You cannot guess?"

"I suppose—is it a building in Sarajevo?"

"A building in Sarajevo, yes. This hall you can see is at the centre of the building where was my library. The building of my library before—before the great fire—and also after, because they have tried to rebuild it exactly as it was. Perhaps they have

7

succeeded, more or less. But the books—naturally the books, you know, almost all have gone for ever."

"It looks somehow Turkish? Was it originally an Ottoman building?"

"No. It is not old. It was not ever old even before it was shelled. It is not a real example of any kind of architecture. It was built in the 1890s. You understand: not long ago at all. It was supposed to look Turkish, or Moorish maybe, a romantic idea of Moorish imagined in Vienna. Like Mozart composing a Turkish march. It is a copy, more or less, of the ancient mosques of Damascus or Cordoba. It was to please the Muslim subjects of the emperor. It was the most grand building of the Habsburg times in Sarajevo. It was the city hall of Habsburg Sarajevo, and later it was the library, the National and University Library it was called. The collections were put there, together, some of the ancient collections, of the Muslims, the Jews, the Christians."

"I see. So your library, your books, were much older than this building."

"It was. They were."

He looked down, and then again towards her.

"But this building for a hundred years has been famous not at all for the library. It is famous because this building was where Franz Ferdinand and Sophie were received by the mayor and the officials of the empire—imagine, in their frock coats and their uniforms, here in the great hall—" He waved towards the photograph. "—on the day when the bomb had already failed to kill them. Up the stairs to the great hall Franz Ferdinand comes, and reads his speech, from a paper with stains of blood from the people injured by the bomb. After the speech they go, down the stairs, into the open car, to be shot."

She looked again at the photograph, the clean, empty space of the hall.

"Such a dreadful thing", she said, feebly.

"The most—" She saw him again searching for the right word. "—incompetent assassination in all of history. Except the first."

"The first?" Was he talking about the Romans? Julius Caesar?

"The first assassination in Sarajevo. On the day of the new

Bosnian assembly, properly elected you know, the beginning of real Habsburg rule after forty years of military Habsburg rule, a Serb boy called Varesanin shot the governor. He shot him five times and missed him each time and then he shot himself and did not miss."

"Goodness. Wretched boy. His poor parents. When did that happen?"

"In 1908. So short a time, that Bosnia was properly inside the Habsburg empire. And Varesanin becomes a hero for these young Serbs, for Gavrilo Princip and the others."

He looked across at her, perhaps to make sure she was following his story.

"Franz Ferdinand and Sophie come down the stairs from that picture, and get into their car. Half a dozen fanatic boys are scattered among crowds in the streets. These boys are like so many in the wars I saw, the wars of Bosnia so much later. None of them knows how to shoot straight or throw a bomb to hit the target. Princip himself was nineteen and he was waiting in the wrong place. The car was travelling in the wrong street. It was incompetent, yes, and it was bad luck, and also, yes, it was so dreadful. It was the assassination with the biggest, the worst, the most terrible consequences of any assassination ever. But the story shows—"

He stopped.

"The story shows?"

"I do not find the English words to say. How chance is all, is everything. Princip could have missed with his shot, as the others had done. The Archduke's driver could have taken the other road as he was told to. The government in Vienna could have discovered, quite easily I believe, that the Serbs in Belgrade were not responsible for the assassination. These boys were Bosnian Serbs, not Serbs of Serbia. But after all these chances, ministers in Vienna wanted to have war with Serbia. It was an opportunity, a chance, you might say—how difficult a language is English—for them to do what they had for years wanted to do. So there was war. So all the countries joined the war. So there were millions and millions of dead young men."

9

"Yes. So many chances. So many deaths."

He looked across at her, wincing.

"I am sorry, Clare. I forgot for a moment altogether the death of your son."

Clare's son Matt, a soldier in the British army, had been killed by a roadside bomb in Afghanistan nearly fourteen years ago. She had told Val of his death because several years earlier Matt had spent six months in Bosnia as part of a NATO stabilization force, sent to build whatever stability was possible on shaky foundations, and he had even been, briefly, to Sarajevo.

"No, Val. No. You mustn't apologize. We both of us have had—"

She looked up at the photograph of the girl with the little boy and the baby.

"Of course. We know. What do we know? Sadness. Always there is sadness, though the years come and go. There is love, so there is sadness." He was looking down at his hands, clasped in his lap as always when he sat and talked.

She made an effort to think of something else to say.

"I didn't realize", she said. This would do. Get him back to his books. "That your library was in such a new building. But the books, and the manuscripts? You have told me before—all the writings from different times in the city—"

"Ah. Yes. The building was new. It was a demonstration of Habsburg power, and also of Habsburg generosity to the subject peoples of Bosnia. Not all bad, Habsburg rule. Not at all. Did you know—of course you could not know—that all five mayors of Sarajevo in Habsburg times were Muslims? So not all bad. Like Ottoman rule. Not all bad either. Empires now in England are not permitted to have done any good things. It is true, naturally, that every empire did many bad things."

He smiled across at her.

"The building was new, yes, but, as I have tried to describe, the collections were old, very old and sometimes very precious, to me and to many scholars and students. For hundreds of years, almost five hundred years, there were different libraries in the city, and they became different collections in my library and in the Oriental Institute, which also was destroyed in the siege. I don't know how—"

Was he going to say "I don't know how to describe them"?

"Never mind, Val. Another time?"

"No. Now. While the coffee becomes perfect."

He leant towards her, his hands still clasped.

"I will tell you of one example. Only one. Have you heard of the Sarajevo Haggadah?"

She shook her head. "I'm afraid not."

Something in the word reminded her of David Rose, an old Jewish doctor, her friend for forty years, who had died in the autumn of 2019, before Covid was heard of.

"Is it some kind of Jewish book?"

"Good."

She smiled, a child in a classroom who had answered a question correctly. He didn't notice.

"Yes. It is a special Jewish prayer book for the Passover Seder. Everyone at the Passover meal reads a part of it. Because it is not holy, not the Tanakh, let alone the Torah, it is permitted for it to have pictures, pictures of people, which are not permitted in the texts of holy Scripture. Sometimes a Haggadah will have most beautiful pictures, and most beautiful decorations, like the Christian books of hours in the Middle Ages."

She turned to look at the pages of medieval writing on the wall behind her, but he was still talking, looking down at his hands, and she turned back.

"Because of the terrible persecutions of the Jews always, everywhere, or almost everywhere, almost always, and the burning of their books, there are very few ancient Haggadahs which have survived the centuries. Two are most famous, the Golden Haggadah, made early in the fourteenth century, which is safe in the British Library. You should go to see it, one day, when we are allowed to go anywhere. And the other, a little later, and not so rich or so expensive, from the middle of the fourteenth century, is the Sarajevo Haggadah. I would describe it for you, but—"

"O no", she said. "Was it lost in the burning of the library?" But he had said "is".

"Thank God, it was not. It was saved. Actually it was saved again. This book of the Jews has been saved more times than we even know. It was made in Spain, in a world—if you can believe this—where Muslims ruled but were happy to allow the Jews and the Christians to be also happy, because they had their synagogues and their churches and their schools, and their books, like the Haggadahs. Can you believe this? None of them was trying to destroy any of the others. Imagine. Then the Christian king and queen of Spain said all Jews and Muslims must go away or convert to Christianity or die. Some Jews brought the Sarajevo Haggadah to Venice—to the Ghetto no doubt, a Venetian invention, you know, the Ghetto—"

Shylock, she thought. Poor Shylock.

"And somehow it reached Bosnia and the Sarajevo library in the nineteenth century, perhaps with a Jewish family who knew that the Ottoman empire was still safer for Jews than most Christian countries. It was, it is, our most precious book, for its rarity. Not, actually, for its beauty. The pictures are simple, something like Christian paintings of the time in Italy, but these are made by someone who is not a very good painter. But it is a real book for real people, for the family gathered at Passover, for the children to see the story of the Exodus, the story of the Jewish people. The pictures start with Genesis and go on until the death of Moses.

"In Hitler's war in Bosnia the Nazis or the Ustasha were destroying everything Jewish. The synagogues, the Torah scrolls, the candlesticks, and then, we know, the people." He stopped, and looked at her across the sleeping cat, sorrow in his blue eyes. He looked down again at his hands. "All must be destroyed. The beautiful Sephardi synagogue—not so different from the great hall of the library—" He pointed to the photograph above the fire. "which was not yet the library, with galleries and a dome and a wonderful chandelier—was sacked and ruined and everything burnt, on the second day the Germans were in Sarajevo."

He paused, looked down for a moment, took a deep breath and went on.

"In the city when the Germans came the chief librarian was

a Muslim. His name was Doctor Korkut. He had been an imam in the Habsburg army in the Great War. Still in the library he was an imam. He saved from the Nazis a Jewish girl by pretending she was his daughter, and he saved the Haggadah also. It was very dangerous to carry this book out of the city. If anyone had found it Doctor Korkut would have been shot. But he was brave so he carried it away, and another imam in a village in the mountains where there was a small mosque hid it under his floor until the war was over. After the war Dr Korkot was arrested by Tito. He would not be a Communist. But he came back to Sarajevo and was again the chief librarian when I was young. I was his pupil in the library until he died, an old man, as I am now. I loved him." For a second or two he closed his eyes.

"And then—"

He stopped. Clare saw that he couldn't go on.

He looked at her, sad, closed his eyes again for a moment, and after a deeper intake of breath, stood up. With his hands on the back of her chair, so that she couldn't see his face, he said, "And then, fifty years later when there was again war, in 1992, boys, militia, *comitadji*, whoever they were, broke into the library to loot or destroy what they could. They left in the piles of rubbish on the floor the Haggadah. They had no idea what it was. A Muslim policeman found it and the chief librarian, another chief librarian so long after the Nazis, and he also was a Muslim, took it to the safe of a bank, an underground safe that no shelling could reach. This is why it is again, now, in the museum. This chief librarian was also my friend and by then my boss. His name was Dr Sijaric. After the burning of the library he was outside one day fixing plastic sheets to the wall to help protect what there was left to protect. A Serb threw a grenade. Dr Sijaric was killed. He was killed not far from where the great Valter was killed by a German grenade at the very end of Hitler's war."

"O Val, how dreadful. I'm so sorry." Then, to give him a question to answer, she said, "Who was the great Valter?"

"Ah. I forgot that no one outside Sarajevo has heard even the name of Valter. Vladimir Peric-Valter." He said this with a proud flourish. "Valter was his soldier's name. He was only a poor boy from a village. He was the organizer of the resistance to the Germans and the Ustasha in Sarajevo all through the war. He helped Jews escape when he could. He fed Jews who were hiding. He was almost the last to be killed as the Germans gave up the city and went away. When he died he was only twenty-five."

"How brave, Val, of him, and of your friend at the library too. What terrible times." She didn't turn in her chair to look at him.

He stood up suddenly.

"The coffee. I had forgotten. The coffee will be ready. I am sorry."

He went back to the kitchen and came out with a chair, a plain kitchen chair, which he put between the two armchairs, not too close to the fire. After another minute or two of clatter in the kitchen, a tap running, a fridge door opening and shutting, he emerged with a tray. On it were two small cups and saucers, blue and white patterned china, two glasses of water with ice, a copper or brass pot the shape of a hour-glass, with no lid and a long dark wooden handle, a kind of pot she had never seen before. Also a little plate with four squares of Turkish Delight, pale and snowy, and beside the plate two very small folded paper napkins. The arrangement of the tray had an ancestral formality. He put it on the chair, and carefully poured coffee into each cup from the copper pot.

"First you must have some cold water. It makes the coffee taste better."

She did as she was told.

"Now the coffee."

The coffee was thick, black and sweet, a little sandy. One tiny sip and she remembered that she had drunk coffee like this before, a thousand years ago when she was an undergraduate in Cambridge.

"It's delicious", she said. "And I have had it before. I'm not as ignorant as you thought."

He laughed. "Not ignorant. Not a word I would ever use for you. Only in this case without experience, you said."

"I had forgotten. Long, long ago, when I was a student in Cambridge, a place we went to sometimes for a good and very cheap meal was a Cypriot restaurant. A lot of lamb and rice. And then this coffee, like yours. And sticky sweet pastries with nuts and honey."

"Of course. Baklava. Everywhere baklava is made in what was the Ottoman empire. As Cyprus was, unfortunate Cyprus. When was this, that you were in the Cypriot restaurant?"

"1960, 1961. I remember the whole meal cost us three and six each. That's seventeen and a half pence. Another world."

This meant nothing to him. A stupid thing to say.

"1960. In Cyprus their war was over. Only it was never over. It is not over now. Were they Turks or Greeks, in your restaurant?"

She thought, but couldn't remember.

"I'm afraid I can't remember, if I ever knew." She closed her eyes and saw across candles in the little busy restaurant the smiling face of a waiter, his black moustache, his foreignness evident in that long-ago Cambridge where, apart from clever dons who were Jewish refugees from Hitler and the odd African prince being an undergraduate, there were very few foreigners.

"Turks, I think", she said.

"It would not matter. The coffee would be the same. Unless you spoke to them Greek or Turkish it would be difficult to tell the difference. As it is in Bosnia. Who is a Croat, who is a Serb, who is a Muslim? No one can tell by looking, and there everyone speaks the same language so in Bosnia it is even more difficult to know who is who, or who is what—and so it is even more mad when they kill each other. You know, in the wars, a man with a gun would say to another man, 'Are you a Serb?' 'Are you a Croat?' before deciding whether to kill him or not. Is that not mad?"

"It is mad. 'Are you for the King?' 'Are you for Parliament?' That must have happened in the English Civil War. As in any civil war, I suppose."

She took another sip.

"This is really very good, this coffee. Sustaining, somehow, and made all the better by the glass of water. How thin and miserable you must find the coffee I've given you."

"No. I am used to coffee in England. Yours is better than much English coffee."

To her surprise, in his sitting room for the first time, she suddenly couldn't think of anything to say. Usually they talked so easily. The wars, his experience and not hers, were an uncrossable space between them.

He sipped his coffee, and then his cold water.

"Have you been to Cyprus?" he said, politely filling the silence. She was grateful but careful not to show her gratitude.

"I'm afraid not. My husband—well, he always wanted to go to France or Italy for our holidays, so that was what we did. Lovely, those holidays were, in their way, but—Why did you say 'unfortunate Cyprus' just now?"

"You know where Cyprus is?"

She imagined a map of the Mediterranean, with Cyprus in the top right corner of the sea, pointing at Syria.

"Well, yes, more or less."

"Not far away from Bosnia, you understand. It is the same world, the Byzantine Mediterranean. There is pressure from the empire of Venice on Cyprus as there is on the Dalmatian coast."

She thought of Othello, sent to Cyprus to defend it against the Turks.

"The Venetians or the Genoese. They need the ports for trade. They quarrel with each other and Byzantium they despise, though Venice was once almost a Byzantine city. Venice conquers Cyprus. Constantinople falls, so the Ottomans come. But in Cyprus the Greeks, the Christians, have not gone, as in Ottoman Bosnia the Christians, which are here the Serbs, have not gone, and in Bosnia nor have gone the Catholic Croats who came from the north and the west. None of them have gone."

It was sometimes hard to tell whether Val was speaking of the past or the present.

"They still have not gone?"

"They still have not gone. The old empires came and they went, the Romans, the Byzantines, the Ottomans. Then more modern empires arrive, the Habsburgs in Bosnia, the British in Cyprus. There are fierce nationalisms which fill people with passion to escape from the empires, but the nationalisms mean hatred also. The United Nations or America try to sort out these divided places where once the people had a way of living side by side, like the Jews and the Muslims and the Christians in Spain. Once they were even friends, but now they are full of hatred. The powerful people who come in from outside try to stop this hatred, to mend these terrible breakings, but always they fail. From outside is made a partition. Show us a map, they say, and on the map they draw lines. They invent a constitution. We will have, they will have, shared power, divided power, power first for one people and then for the other, and so on and so on. The outsiders are pleased and then they go away. But the people of the country or the city cannot, or more exactly, they will not, make it work. In Cyprus it has been for a long long time as it is now in Bosnia: everything is shared and divided and not working. It has not worked in Lebanon—there is another example—and it has not worked in Bosnia. Does it work in Ireland, now, with Brexit? Of Ireland I do not understand what I read in the paper."

She opened her mouth. Not that she had anything sensible to say. But he hadn't finished.

"Because of all this I am in London. And because of such division, such lines on a map, your Cypriot family—it will have been a family—was sixty years ago in Cambridge. They are maybe still there."

"What a muddle—" She wasn't at all sure she had followed what he was saying. "What a terrible mess it all is. Why is there so much hatred when people used to be friends, neighbours?"

"Who can answer such a question? But I think when there were imperial cities ruling but far away, like Rome, Constantinople, Istanbul, Vienna, even some of the time London, it was better, not worse." She remembered something Hakim had said, about Ottoman Libya: "Istanbul was not oppressive most of the time, and it was so far away that hardly anyone in Cyrenaica or Tripolitania had ever been there." Something like that. Hakim, a refugee like Val but very different, was a young Libyan scholar she had helped to reach London, years ago now.

Val stood and picked up the copper pot.

"A little more?"

"Please."

He poured a little more into each of their cups.

"Always we make coffee in such a pot. It is called a *cezve*. So always we make only small amounts of coffee. it is better so. You should have a sweet, always a sweet with coffee, if there is a guest."

She had never liked the look of Turkish Delight. But she couldn't not try it.

"A little water first", he said.

The sweet was quite different from what she had expected, sugary, yes, but light, with the sugar an insubstantial dusting, and a gentle taste of lemons and almonds.

"That's good. Thank you, Val." She finished her piece of Turkish delight, took one of the little napkins and wiped her mouth and her sticky fingers.

"I'm so glad I came. It's lovely to see where you live."

Was that too much?

He said, "I am also pleased", but without looking at her, so perhaps not. She finished her coffee.

"Can I ask you something else?"

"Anything, Clare. Please."

She turned in her chair to look at the wall behind her.

"Those pages of manuscript—I suppose they are magnified? They're very beautiful. I don't recognize the script—is it Hebrew? Or perhaps Arabic?"

"The script is Hebrew, very finely written. Arabic script is very different, you know, but there are other connections. I will tell you. The pages are not magnified. They are reproductions, good ones, but reproductions, and that is their true size. These are from very big books. An old Hebrew Bible written in books like these, codices they are properly named, is most rare: the Jews always have preferred scrolls, at least for the synagogue."

"Are they pages of your Haggadah? The Sarajevo Haggadah?"

She enjoyed the phrase as she said it.

18

"O no, by no means. The Haggadah is much smaller, smaller than a quarto book, and it is quite different, with its pictures of the Old Testament stories, as I tried to describe. The Haggadah pictures are family pictures, almost pictures for children. Compared to this book, these books I should say, because there are three volumes, the Haggadah is primitive. These are pages from the Lisbon Bible, a wonderful thing, which is in the British Library also, a thing more beautiful, actually, by far than even the Golden Haggadah."

He looked at her carefully, she thought to see if she were still interested, decided she was and went on.

"In these days in the British Library they have a miraculous machine, I don't know its name and naturally I can't even imagine how it happens, it is very digital and I am not, but you can see in the Library exhibition these books, the Golden Haggadah and the Lisbon Bible, and the machine allows you to turn the pages so that you don't have only two pages to look at but you may look at all the pages from the beginning to the end. Not that you really turn the pages, but you see as if you turn the pages. It is too difficult to explain but it is miraculous."

"Perhaps we might go to the British Library when Covid is all over and things are open again? And you would explain the precious books for me?"

Too much again? No. Surely not.

"Of course, Clare. It will be my pleasure. Have you been, have you never been, to the exhibition rooms in the British Library?"

"No I'm afraid I haven't. When my—I used to go to the Kensington museums, specially the V and A, but of course I haven't been for a year because of Covid."

When my friend David Rose was alive, she had been about to say, but of course Val knew nothing of David Rose, and she was not going to talk to Val about David. Ever, probably. She didn't want to explore why not.

"The Victoria and Albert Museum. Where you went with your friend, Dr Rose."

It wasn't fair, she thought, ridiculously she realized, that he'd read her book.

"Yes", he said. "I have been there several times. It is an easy walk. But I find it is a very confusing museum."

"Well, yes. I can understand that. It is a mixture, certainly." A mixture she loved. Never mind.

"So tell me about the Lisbon Bible", she said, withdrawing a little.

Books, after all, were his profession. It's always all right to ask people to talk about what they know best.

"It is not so old as the Haggadahs. We have for it an exact date, which is 1482, and even we have the name of the scribe who did the wonderful writing."

She liked the scholarly "we".

"He is called Samuel ben Samuel ibn Musa. An interesting name, you see. He is obviously Jewish, but his name is arranged like an Arab name. Why? Because the Jews and the Arabs had shared so much in the past history of Spain, and also Portugal. Most of Spain and Portugal had been Muslim lands for hundreds of years and the Muslims had great—great respect for the Jews. At the same time the Jews had learnt much from Arabic designs and calligraphy. Look at those pages carefully—"

He stopped and spread his hands.

"Clare. I am so sorry. I am talking to you like a teacher to a student. This is not good. I am sorry. If possibly the pages interest you, I should have said."

"Of course they do." She stood and turned to face the framed pages.

"Are you sure?"

She smiled at him, beside her now, as he smiled back. "Yes, I'm sure", she said.

"Good. Then look. You will know, in Islam, it is not permitted to draw people, or animals, or, almost, even flowers. So Muslim artists have always been skilful with patterns and lettering. These pages are pages of Holy Scripture which the Haggadahs, as I told you, are not, so here the Jews agree with the Muslims, and look how well they use patterns to frame the text, and lettering in gold in the frame also. Nothing could be more—" He bent his head as he stood beside her, searching as so often for the right word. "—more elegant than the blue filigree of the background to the gold lettering. Is 'elegant' the right word?"

"'Elegant' is a good word, but perhaps 'delicate' is better? The filigree—that's certainly the right word—is as delicate as very fine lace."

"Thank you. Let us say 'delicate' for the filigree. But that's not all they did in this workshop. There are also Christians in fifteenth-century Portugal where the Hebrew craftsmen are making this book, and the Jewish painters have seen the books of hours that the rich people treasure, with their bright colours and complicated borders, painted in Florence or Antwerp or Bruges. So, because craftsmanship is always a competition, they expand the rules a little to add these flowers and leaves in their patterns, and more gold, and even here and there—" He pointed at the elaborate border at the bottom of one page. "—a bird, you see, among the flowers."

She leant forward, to look.

"A bird, yes—lovely, almost camouflaged among the flowers. The work is extraordinary. I've never seen anything like it."

The work. She knew this was the right word. Her nanny, seventy years ago, used to use it about very fine needlework, smocking perhaps, or embroidery so perfect that the separate stitches could hardly be seen. "Look at the work in that, Clare."

"I have those pages here—they are prints from the British Library—because they are for me a picture, a memory, of what was Sarajevo, my city. The Jews make a Bible, their Bible only, naturally, the Old Testament as Christians say, and it would not be as it is without the work, the workmanship—which is a fine English word—of the Muslims and the Christians who surround them. Fourteen years after they are making these books, all the Jews and all the Muslims are told in Portugal that they must leave or become Christians or die. It is Portugal following Spain, after so long, after so many centuries. When they are ordered to go away, the Jews come to the Byzantine world, which is now Ottoman because it is not long ago that Constantinople is conquered. This means that the Jews in Sarajevo, like the more important Jews in Salonica, were Spanish and Portuguese Jews and their language was Ladino and they were neighbours and even friends for hundreds of years with the Muslims and the Christians, even with the Catholics. It was not very different from how Spain and Portugal had been, and it was still so even in the Yugoslavia of Serbian kings after the Great War."

When his Catholic and Muslim father had married his Jewish mother.

"Serbian kings?" She had never heard of kings in Serbia.

"They were bandits turned into kings, with parliaments, or supposed parliaments, to fill the space left by the end of the empires. They ruled, not well, what they called 'the Kingdom of Serbs, Croats and Slovenes'. No Bosnia, you understand, in the name of the kingdom of Yugoslavia because they did not count the Muslims. Bosnia had more Muslims, so Bosnia was neglected and so was Sarajevo. The city was no longer important. But these bandit kings did not much disturb the people, the mosques, the churches, the synagogues, of my city. Still the people were mixed together. They were peaceful friends, neighbours in the *komšiluk*. There is no English word for this. No word but perhaps sometimes the thing?"

She wanted to ask him what the word meant but she saw she shouldn't interrupt him. All this history was his, was him. Perhaps he had not often, even not ever, explained it in England?

"But in Hitler's war the Nazis and the Ustasha suddenly came, and nothing Jewish was safe, no—".

He stopped. She knew he was going to say "no people", as he had just managed but now couldn't.

She said nothing, again, while he regained his grip on what he was telling her.

"My library, with Muslim care as I told you about the Haggadah, did survive Hitler. But it did not survive Radovan Karadzic, a Bosnian himself, and Slobodan Milosevic in Belgrade pulling his strings like the strings of a puppet."

His voice had risen: Clare had never before seen, in their quiet conversations in the garden and in her flat, this furious sadness. He'd told her about the shelling of the library several times, more often than he'd talked about what had happened to his family, but he'd told the story calmly, as if describing a grief lived through and overcome. The grief was not overcome.

"I will find something for you to see. A moment."

He went upstairs. She heard him go into what was obviously the bathroom, and a couple of minutes later pull the plug of the lavatory. She heard him in another room open a drawer and half a minute later shut it. He came down with a plastic folder of photographs. He put it on the table by the window, shook the half-dozen or so photographs part-way out of the folder, riffled through them and took one out. He gave it to her.

"Look."

A black-and-white photograph, A4 size, of the charred and crumbled arches of the hall in the picture over the fireplace, the arches, open to the sky, ruined and flaky, standing in piles of rubble, chunks of stone, pieces of metal, plaster shaken from the walls leaving patches of bare brick, glass everywhere, ash and more ash, ash like snow fallen from the sky. No book could have survived the fire that delivered this desolation. She looked up at the picture over the fireplace, and back at the photograph in her hands.

"You see?"

"It's terrible. Really terrible. And why?"

"I have tried to tell you. But there is no reason to be told. It was destruction for the joy of destruction. People who are able to destroy only destroy. That is what they do. What they did to Sarajevo. As you know. The Bosnian Serbs destroyed their own city because they wanted every Muslim, every Croat, to be dead. Why? Because Slobodan Milosevic had lied and lied about the past and present of Serbia, of Yugoslavia, of Bosnia-Herzegovina and Kosovo, and enough people had believed his lies to believe that they were fighting in a noble war like the Serbs who had fought the Ottomans long long ago, and lost. Now at last they would win. To persuade enough people to fight for the Greater Serbia that they promised—you see, like Mr Trump and Make America Great Again—they had to lie most of all about the Muslims of Bosnia. The Muslims of Bosnia, entirely harmless and peaceful people like my grand-

23

father, like my wife and all her family for hundreds of years, had to become fundamentalists, Islamists, terrorists, the enemies of all the world. Nothing could be further away from the truth of the lives lived by the Muslims of Sarajevo. It was the same lie Putin told about Chechnya. He bombed and killed the Chechen people and said they were terrorists when the terrorism in Russia had been done by the KGB, by Putin himself. And now, look, now Putin is trying to kill Alexey Navalny, the man who told the truth about the so-called terror attacks of the Chechens."

He's right about Trump, she thought. Look at what happened in Washington last month. Lies, violence and wrecking, which could have been much worse. But she said nothing, not wanted to deflect him.

He leant forward, wanting her, she thought, to pay particular attention.

"The cruelty and destruction in Chechnya was like the cruelty and destruction in Bosnia, but here in England Bosnia and Chechnya are both forgotten. They were famous for a few moments, for terrible things that were done, and by now they are places that were not known before and are already forgotten."

He sounded very like Hakim telling her of the horrors inflicted on Libya by the Italians, and by everyone since 2011 who had stoked the civil war.

"O Val, I'm so sorry—I mean, I'm so sad for you, and for everything you've lost."

"You are very kind, Clare. Kindness does make up for very much, and your kindness—it is like the kindness of the old *komšiluk* of my city once upon the time. Perhaps even—I can't explain in English."

"It's all right. You needn't try to explain", she said, suddenly nervous of what he might be trying to say. She thought again of David Rose. "Some things are better left undefined." But that was after decades of friendship, whereas Val she had known for two months, a little less than two months.

"I should try, I think."

He turned away from her and from the pages of the Lisbon Bible on the wall, and picked up the tray with the coffee pot, the cups and two pieces of Turkish Delight left on the saucer. He took the tray into the kitchen and came back at once.

"It's time I went home", she said. "My daughter often telephones me on Saturdays at about five, and I should be in when she rings or she will worry."

"Sit down one moment, before you go. As the Russians sit, before a journey."

She smiled. "It's not much of a journey, back to my flat." But she did sit down.

"A Russian would now say nothing. Long ago it was a moment for a prayer, for a safe journey. But I want to say, to try to say, that your kindness has brought me back."

"Back?" Would this help him or not?

"I find I am able to—it is possible for me to receive your kindness. This possibility is something I would not have believed. So I am back, somewhere that was closed to me after I left Sarajevo, was closed all the time in Poland, and then was closed, again and more, after my friend died, something I thought would never open to me again."

"I'm so glad, Val. You know, these things are given to us from time to time, and it's—well, it's lucky if we are able to take them. Now I really must go home."

A sentence of Augustine's came into her head. She remembered it often. "God wants to give us something, but our hands are full." Of course she didn't tell him this.

She stood up, not very briskly because the old armchair was low, soft and awkward to get out of. He stood before she managed to, and picked up her hat, which he handed to her, and then her coat off the chair by his desk. He helped her on with her coat, exactly as a polite stranger in a train or a waiter in a restaurant might have done.

He put his own coat on and then, while she pulled on the gloves she had stuffed in her coat pockets, took her stick from where she had propped it by the door.

"Here is your stick. It is very good but I shall come with you to the end of the mews because of Muhammad's ice."

He didn't take her arm but walked close beside her, ready to stop her falling in case she slipped on the cobbles. She took

25

good care not to, and her ancient boots were still pretty sound on ice.

When they reached the street, with her flat almost in sight on the other side of the square where the tall houses, like the pages of the Lisbon Bible, were patterned by the filigree branches of trees, still with snow along them because it hadn't thawed all day, she stopped, so that he did too.

"Thank you, Val. I've so much enjoyed the afternoon."

"It was my pleasure for you to come to my house."

After a short pause when she failed to say goodbye and leave him he said, "Shall we meet on Wednesday? In the square?"

"Yes, of course. I'll see you then. And thank you again."

It would be Ash Wednesday, but she couldn't go to Mass, wouldn't have the black cross of ashes on her forehead, because of the Covid rules. She remembered Ash Wednesday last year, not long before the first and most stringent Covid lockdown. Mass as always. Ashes as always. It seemed a long, long time ago. She must prepare for Lent nevertheless, and say nothing to Val about the day.

She smiled, and, as she turned to walk away, he gave her as a signal of farewell his brief bow of the head. When she looked back after walking a few yards towards the square, he hadn't moved but stood watching her, as if, it absurdly occurred to her, he thought he might never see her again. She waved. He waved in reply, and, as if he'd been waiting for her to turn and wave, disappeared into the mews.

CHAPTER 2

SATURDAY 13 FEBRUARY 2021

She walked on, crossed the road to the railings of the garden, and unlocked his gate, not his at all of course, but she thought of it as his because it was on his side of the square. As she locked it behind her she looked back, but even the entrance to the mews was now out of sight.

She walked slowly along the path under the trees, round the outside of the grass that was still covered in frozen snow. Between the path and the wrought-iron fence, black and grey against the snow, were the sticks, the unpromising-looking twigs, of the shrubs and the rose bushes that would in May and June be covered in leaves, fresh green leaves before the mildew or the blackspot came, and flowers. May and June seemed impossibly distant. Would the pandemic be over by then? Would Hakim have come back from Hadrian's Wall? Hakim. What would he think of Val? This was an important question.

Some snowdrops had appeared in two or three places at the edges of the shrubbery, but looked as if the flowers, on the point of coming out, had thought better of it and retreated into greenness. There were a few untidy footsteps in the snow and the first stage of a snowman, a snowball rolled along, leaving squashed grass in its track, until it it was almost a foot across and then tipped onto its flat side. No one had bothered to roll the next layer. Perhaps the children had wanted to go home because their hands were cold.

When she reached her gate, the gate almost opposite her house, she stopped and looked back: nothing of Val or his house was visible but what she saw from the gate looked different, though she had known these railings and this gate and this garden for more than forty years, and nothing had changed much. Nothing at all had changed today, but now she knew his house, exactly where it was and how it felt to her, outside and inside, and that was a change.

Into the house, up in the lift, into her flat, gloves, coat, hat, taken off and put in their usual places in the little space inside the door that did for a hall. She had to sit down on the stool there was just room for to take off her boots and put on slippers instead, her cosy sheepskin slippers that Carrie had given her. In the kitchen she half-filled the kettle and switched it on because she always did. She looked at her watch. Nearly five. She stretched a hand towards the radio to turn on the PM programme, and then didn't. She had to think, or at least sort out what she felt, which was a kind of thinking. She was afraid she had in Val's house felt too much, would be feeling too much now if she allowed herself to.

Too much for what? That was a question that also needed answering.

She put off both the thinking and the feeling until the kettle boiled and she had made some decaff tea: probably she shouldn't have accepted Val's strange and delicious coffee. Coffee at any time after lunch stopped her falling asleep when she went to bed, and she became angry and sad about almost anything or almost nothing when she couldn't get to sleep. Then she would have to get up and start again, with camomile tea and an escape-from-real-life book, usually Wodehouse.

As she shut the fridge after putting milk in her tea the telephone rang. She looked, this time, at the kitchen clock. Penny.

But it wasn't Penny.

"Clare?"

"Hakim, how lovely to hear you. How are you?"

She sat at the table with her tea and the telephone, pleased to hear him, also pleased that after all she didn't have to think yet.

"I'm very well, Clare, thank you. I thought you would be in the flat now because your daughter telephones on Saturday afternoon, doesn't she?"

"Usually, yes, she does."

"But an hour ago you were out. I was surprised."

She'd forgotten, again, to set the message machine on the telephone.

"I was, yes. I went for a walk, in the snow. Is it very cold up there too?"

"Very cold, and there is plenty of snow, with the sun shining, but also a terrible wind. The wind is colder than any wind in London. I had to come into the city today, to collect some things, and the cathedral looked very beautiful from the other side of the river. I walked across the bridge to look back. It is the best view. The cathedral is even open. I was surprised. I went in. There was no one there almost, perhaps six people in that great, great building. I thought of you Clare. That is why I called you, to see that you are well."

"I'm very well, thank you, Hakim. Isn't it astonishing, the cathedral? It's almost my favourite."

"Which is your favourite one?"

"Ely. You won't have seen Ely. It's not far from Cambridge. A miraculous church. It was once an abbey, with monks, as well as a cathedral, in a very small town. Actually Durham was too, a monastery I mean. But how are you getting on, Hakim, with the work? It must be difficult in the middle of winter, and such a cold winter too."

"I love it, the work, the cold, the beautiful hills, no people coming. The site is closed. The museum is closed. But I may work. I love all of it. It is wonderful. It is—how exactly to say this?—"

He sounded like Val. Foreigners her friends always seemed to be. Even David had been a foreigner though he was born in England.

Hakim's English was much more ambitious than Val's.

"It is like a mirror, a reversal, a reverse maybe, of a site where I did some work a long time ago. I was a student and there was still Gaddafi. We were many miles south of Benghazi, almost in the quite empty desert. There was also a frontier town, very far from Rome, from civilization, from the sea." When Hakim said "the sea", he always meant the Mediterranean: Libya is a long east-west strip of the north African coast and then a thousand miles of desert. "It was a town for legionaries and their families, their slaves, their cooks, their baths, their teachers for the children, everything the Romans always made sure that they had, wherever they built a garrison town. Also their clay jars and pots"—he laughed—"for olive oil and wine and fish sauce, that they had to have for civilized meals far in the desert or far in the northern hills. Like Vindolanda on the Wall, my frontier town in Cyrenaica was far as the Romans thought it useful or necessary to go. In that country also were not many people, and the people were too poor to pay tribute, and there was nothing valuable for the Romans to take. They were right about Scotland and wrong about the Sahara, but the Romans didn't know about oil, wicked oil. They had only beautiful, harmless olive oil."

No wonder the university had asked for him back after his lecture. He was in himself the ancient Mediterranean, even on the telephone, even on a February afternoon talking from Durham to London.

"So what do you mean, the reverse?"

"Well, you can imagine—here is the far north instead of the far south, the cold and the rain and the hills instead of the sand and the rock and the heat of the desert. Everything green, or even white when it has snowed, instead of everything burnt red. As different as it could be. But the Romans obey their orders and make the correct bricks and do the correct calculations and build the same everywhere."

"O Hakim it is good to hear you. I'm so glad you're enjoying yourself up there."

"Something I must tell you, Clare. There is a church here. I thought you would like to know this. There was no church in my town on the edge of the desert."

"A church? How do you mean?" She stupidly thought of a little village church in the wilds of Northumberland.

"A Roman church."

"What?"

She remembered the ruined Byzantine churches in Cyrene and in Apollonia, the Greek and Roman site on the Libyan shore which meant so much to Hakim, and where she had delivered a talk about St Augustine and the African church for the cruise passengers. Hakim had been listening to her talk, though she hadn't noticed him.

"A real church. A Christian church, but not like the ancient churches in Libya. Here there is no memory of a Greek temple or a Roman basilica. This church is small and simple and only low walls are left. In the summer they found parts of a chalice, made of lead, with Christian symbols cut into it, a boat, for example, with a sail and a cross for the mast, like the church to carry people over the sea. Now the senior archaeologist is sure that the building where they found it—it is the oldest chalice anyone has found in Britain—was a church. Fifth century. Sixth century. Maybe the Romans had gone, maybe not all of them had gone. Who were these Christians? Perhaps Anglo-Saxons had arrived. Maybe not yet. Very interesting, don't you think, Clare?"

She was thinking, quickly, of the centuries. In the fifth century Augustine was alive, in North Africa, not far from the Sahara Hakim had been talking about. He died in 430 when the Romans, whatever that meant, probably only the officials and the army, had already left Britain. By the end of the sixth century Irish monks had come to Iona and one of them, Aidan, early in the seventh century, had arrived in Lindisfarne and was converting pagan Northumbria to Christianity. So whose was the church on the Wall in this gap between the Romans and the church of Aidan and Cuthbert, Cuthbert whose tomb was in the cathedral Hakim had visited today? Perhaps Hakim and the Durham archaeologists he was working for would find out.

"I do. Of course I do. As interesting as could be. Fascinating to wonder who made the church and when—"

She stopped because it had struck her that he was talking too much

"Are you lonely up there on the Wall in the cold, Hakim?"

"Lonely? No. It is better than London, although I miss the flat and the garden of the square. But Ayesha I remember more happily here, far from where she died. And even—"

And even he has met another girl, she thought, finding while she made that guess that she didn't mind at all that he hadn't said he missed her. Why would he, when she was still here, and he could telephone and find her at the kitchen table? And if he had other fish to fry after the miserable loss of Ayesha, then hooray for youth and vitality and everything about him that was so winning. Including the black patch over his lost eye.

Hakim Husain was the young Libyan archaeologist she had met on the cruise, the comfortable expensive cruise paid for by Penny and Charles, that she had joined in 2009, when she was recently widowed. She had met him at Cyrene where he was being an exceptionally articulate and brave—he had even mocked Colonel Gaddafi—guide for the cruise passengers. Five years later she had helped him leave what was by then the very dangerous Libya, and last summer he had been living and working in her flat for the second time. In May he had managed with great difficulty to get out of Libya through the chaos of the fighting and shelling, and then all the Covid restrictions, to England—he worked in the department of Greek and Roman antiquities at the British Museum—and when he was safely back in London he had been writing a scholarly report on the state of the major Roman and Greek sites in Libya after ten years of civil war.

He had been in Libya for several weeks, risking his life for what he always called his stones, and he had lost his eye in a mortar attack. While he was away, his girlfriend Ayesha Gupta had come to stay in Clare's flat in the early weeks of the pandemic: her landlady had thrown her out because she was a doctor and therefore, the landlady decided, too dangerous a tenant. Ayesha, brave and good, just qualified or even not quite qualified, had volunteered for the Covid wards and had died of the virus at the beginning of May.

The loss of Ayesha, and his absence when she died, had haunted Hakim for months. But after he finished his report, the Museum, in October, when most of the Covid rules had been relaxed, had sent him to the university in Durham to give a lecture on the archaeological crisis in Libya. At Durham they had liked his lecture (or probably him) so much that they had asked the Museum to lend him to them for the academic year, to help with the new finds at Vindolanda, a complex military and civilian site just south of Hadrian's Wall, and he had been delighted to go.

So she had lost him again, after only four months of him living in the flat as he had done for rather longer when he first arrived in London now nearly seven years ago. But Northumberland, sealed off as it quickly became because of renewed Covid lockdowns, wasn't Libya, even if two thousand years ago it had been, according to him, more or less the same, and she was happy that he was loving the work and also loving the north. She had been a little worried that his name and his Arab appearance might set off bigotry and careless insults so far away from London: the people in the north-east had voted heavily for Brexit in the referendum, nearly five years ago now. Cynical encouragement of xenophobia from politicians in London had no doubt encouraged them to think they were voting, among other things, against immigration, of which they had very little experience. Might they think Hakim an unwelcome immigrant, a sinister Muslim, even a terrorist? But, as far as she could tell from his occasional telephone calls, all had been well and he hadn't run into any unpleasantness, let alone aggression. "The English they speak here I like, though it is not easy to understand after the English in London."

"Have you made some friends?" was all she said now, the question parents ask after a child has been in a new school a week, even a day.

"It is not easy", something he often said, "to talk to many people because of the Covid rules, the masks and the distance. But a couple of students have been allowed to come to help, as long as we all stay outside, and that is good."

Ah, she thought, but asked him no more questions.

"And you, Clare", he said. "Are you all right? Are you very careful, with the mask and the distance, in the shops for example?"

"I'm very careful, I promise. I've had one dose of the vaccine, which is good, though they keep saying old people like me mustn't feel liberated straight away so I'm still doing nothing. Almost nothing. But even in London, where it's been very bad since Christmas, the virus is beginning to get better, slowly, so perhaps by the spring things will feel almost normal again."

She wanted to ask him if he would be coming back to London at some point to check in with the Museum, but she didn't. Her children, and her granddaughters, had never liked it when she asked them questions about their plans, and she was used to treating Hakim as one of the children.

"At least", she said, to keep the conversation light, "the old are allowed to go to the food shops this time. I don't have to depend on Mr Clements to get my shopping and my paper. He disliked the *Guardian* so much he had to summon all his Blitz spirit to collect it for me."

Even after years in England, Hakim wouldn't have understood what she had just said.

"He didn't like me living in your flat, did he?"

Or perhaps he would.

"Bother Mr Clements", she said.

Mr Clements was the grumpy caretaker who cleaned the stairs, sorted the post, kept an eye on the venerable and not wholly reliable lift, and had shopped for her and some old people in other flats during the first lockdown. He read the *Express* and had been a keen Brexiteer.

"I will see you soon, Clare. Now I must go. I have to get a train and then a bus and then another bus to get back to the Wall."

"Goodness, how complicated. I'm so glad you rang, Hakim, and glad to know you're still enjoying yourself in the frozen north."

"I am. I am. Goodbye, Clare. Take care until I come back."

"'Bye, Hakim. You take care too."

After his earlier telephone calls from Durham or the Wall, she had felt desolate, as if he were much further away than he was, and might never come back. But this time, as she finished her tea, she found she was smiling. It was good to hear him sounding cheerful and happy, and if he had met a girl, perhaps an archaeology student helping at Vindolanda in the freezing cold, that was good too. He shouldn't pine too long for Ayesha, any more than he had pined too long for the girl in Libya who had been killed during the fighting that surrounded the end of Colonel Gaddafi, the girl with whom, in the last months of peace in 2011, he had swum in the sea at Apollonia where the green marble columns of the ancient churches still stood.

But she knew that it was because of something in her, not because of something in how he'd sounded, that she wasn't feeling sad about his absence. To be honest, to be exact, it was because of Val.

She got up and switched on the kettle. More tea. Before the kettle even boiled the telephone rang again.

"Mum—"

"Hello, darling. How are you?"

"Who on earth have you been talking to? I've been trying to get you for hours. Well, quarter of an hour, anyway."

"I'm so sorry, darling." She knew that Penny, in Yorkshire since Christmas because her husband Charles, a Tory MP, was, or had been, working from home, had practically nothing to do. "I was talking to Hakim."

"O, him. I thought he'd gone."

Penny disapproved of the whole idea of Hakim, though she'd only met him once. Her husband disapproved even more. "Bloody Muslims. Can't trust them an inch. Any of them. I wish your mother had more sense."

"Well, yes, he has. He's on Hadrian's Wall fussing about the Romans."

"I suppose if he's gone, that's why you were talking to him."

"More or less, yes."

"Never mind him. Are you OK, Mum? Doing your mask and social distancing and all that? I do wish you weren't in London. The virus numbers have been so bad for weeks."

"It's been very bad, I know, but it's all right if you're careful, and I am careful, and doing practically nothing. You know that. Anyway the numbers are beginning to go down. And I've had a vaccination, last week. I told you."

"Only the first shot."

"Much better than nothing. In any case, I'd rather be at home than anywhere. I think all old people are happy being at home in the winter. Like Badger."

"Badger? How do you mean, badger?"

"O come on, Penny. Badger. In the Wild Wood."

"O that badger."

Second childhood, she's thinking, Clare could tell.

"Mum, are you sure you're all right? What day of the week is it?"

"For goodness' sake, darling. I'm not losing the plot. Not yet. It's Saturday, the thirteenth of February 2021, and I'm perfectly all right thank you very much. You really needn't worry about me. How are you and Charles? Is he zooming in to the House of Commons all the time?"

"That's all been a bit of a nightmare as a matter of fact. The whole Zoom thing. We have very unreliable broadband in the village and the boy from some snazzy firm Charles found who came to fix it seems to have made it worse rather than better. About twelve he was."

"Probably just the right age for fixing the broadband."

"O Mum. Charles gets furious with computers very quickly. So he's in London most of the time at the moment, getting into the House as much as he can. His secretary organizes the Zoom when he can't go. I'd rather stay here. At least I can ride every day though there's been no hunting. Politics seems to have more or less packed up anyway. All anybody ever says anything about is the virus."

Of course, Clare thought but didn't say. They're lucky to have the virus to blame for everything so they don't have to mention the horrors Brexit is producing and the worse horrors to come. And the opposition, no doubt for reasons of their own, don't mention them either: it's no good sounding too furious about Brexit if their priority is winning back the old Labour seats that voted Tory for "Get Brexit Done", another promise founded on a lie, a bit over a year ago.

"And Carrie Symonds", Penny went on. "They complain a lot about her. Charles says she's a menace and will do for Boris in the end. I'm sure he's exaggerating. But honestly, talk about twelve. It's ridiculous having her there, pretending to be the First Lady, something we've never had thank goodness."

How Penny would love to be married to the Prime Minister, Clare thought, unkindly she knew. The chances of Charles becoming Prime Minister, however, were, mercifully, zero.

"And I wish she wasn't called Carrie."

Penny's elder daughter was called Carrie. She had been in

Nepal for eighteen months, first helping to rebuild a village destroyed in an earthquake, then teaching English, now helping with Covid in the high mountains, along with her American boyfriend. Clare missed her very much.

"I know. It's tiresome, isn't it. Do you think she's really called Caroline, like Carrie?"

"I've no idea. Wretched girl. But I do feel quite sorry for her, however annoying she is. Boris is all very well, and I'm all for him as a politician, but he's hardly house-trained is he?"

"He's getting a bit old for the retriever puppy performance. I will say he's had to grow up a bit over the virus."

She and Penny had this kind of rambling, gossipy conversation every Saturday. It was a reasonable way of keeping in touch.

"Anyway, Mum—" Penny had done her bit for the week. "I hope you're not getting too lonely down there. At least Hakim was some company." This was generous of her.

"No, darling. I'm not lonely a bit. I'm pretty used to living by myself by now, and there are always books."

"Books? But Mum, really, books aren't much company."

"O yes, they are. In fact, that's exactly what they are."

Since Ayesha's death, and specially since Hakim had gone to the north, she had spent more of her days reading than she had probably ever spent before, even when she was an earnest undergraduate. She had taken out of dusty shelves classics she hadn't read for decades, the longer the more satisfying. *War and Peace* she had read when she was fifteen, soon afterwards deciding that *Anna Karenina* was much better, and soon after that deciding that Dostoyevsky was much better than Tolstoy. But *War and Peace* had kept her going for the whole of October, and she had enjoyed every page, even what she dimly remembered as the boring bits about history and generals making less difference than they thought.

Pointless to say any of this to Penny who probably hadn't read a single proper book since she left school.

"Do you remember kindly giving me for Christmas Barack Obama's book about being President?"

"Did I? O yes, you asked for it. I vaguely remember."

Penny had ordered it; Amazon had sent it.

37

"It's so interesting. I'm half way through it and enjoying it very much. He writes beautifully and he's really good company—so, you see, books can be. Company, I mean."

"If you say so, Mum. American politics—I don't know—hard to follow, I should think. But I'm glad you're liking the book. I must stop chatting. I've got my online bridge club at six."

"Of course, darling. We'll talk again next week."

"'OK. Of course we will. Bye, Mum. Lots of love."

Penny. She and Charles hadn't been exactly in favour of Trump, but they hadn't been horrified when he won in 2016, and hadn't been enthusiastic when Obama won either of his elections. It was hopeless talking to them about politics: Brexit, which Charles swore he'd wanted all his life but which Clare knew he'd only noticed as an issue because of Nigel Farage, had been the last straw.

One of the reasons she so much missed Carrie was that Carrie and she agreed about politics, which was cheering considering that Carrie was twenty-three and both bright and sensible. Penny's younger daughter Daisy had chosen to go to university in Vancouver. She had come home briefly in August, when it was allowed, but hadn't been seen since. She wasn't interested in English politics, or, come to that, any politics anywhere, though, as far as Clare could make out, the courses she was taking seemed to include every fashionable topic under the sun. Perhaps she cared about climate change. That would be a start.

Clare got up from the table, rather stiff, and put the kettle on again. She knew she was supposed to think, now that she had talked to both Penny and Hakim, and now that no one else was likely to telephone.

She made another mug of decaff tea, and while it was getting strong enough to taste of something, she went into her sitting room and looked out of one of the windows at the square, the garden, towards the beginning of the street which had in it the narrow opening, wide enough for the Russian's Bentley, of Val's mews. The winter evening was dark, but not properly dark. The street lamps shed pools of light on the pavement, and the leafless trees of the square were motionless, every branch with its icing of snow as if etched, just visible against the faintly orange glow of the dark sky, never properly black in London. The frozen snow on the grass shed its own eerie light.

What was it that she was supposed to think about? And "supposed"? Where did this sense of an obligation, almost of a duty, come from? From inside herself, obviously. The old Catholic phrase "examination of conscience" came into her mind—and she remembered with some sadness that she hadn't been to Confession for almost a year, because of Covid—but examination of conscience wasn't quite right, wasn't exactly the reason for the need to think that she'd felt so strongly when she first came in.

The truth, that was what she was after, the truth of her afternoon with Val, in his house for the first time, and what she had felt then and was feeling now about it, about him. Could feeling be set to one side so that the truth could be reached? Of course it couldn't. Facts could be reached, but she had known almost all her life that facts and the truth were not the same. What she had felt was essential, necessary, to any account of the afternoon. Sometimes she was sorry rather than pleased, let alone proud, that, last year, David's death first of all and then the pandemic, her acute fear for Hakim in Libya, and Ayesha's death, had turned her into a writer.

Now, somehow, she couldn't just fall back on the reassurance of her ordinary conversations with Penny and Hakim, particularly Hakim, so positive and cheerful, and pretend that her afternoon with Val meant nothing, or nothing much.

She returned to the kitchen and her now strong but cooling mug of tea, and took it to the end of the table where her laptop lived, leads coming from a tangle of cables on the floor and also from her printer stowed on the seat of a kitchen chair. She had only the vaguest idea of which lead meant what and didn't dare unplug her laptop to take it into another room, let alone outside the flat. What if the battery ran out or she couldn't plug the leads back correctly? "It's brilliant you've got a laptop, Gran. You can take it into the square and do stuff in the sunshine." Carrie had been replaced by Hakim as her stand-by IT consultant: she hoped to goodness nothing would go wrong while he was on Hadrian's Wall.

She opened the laptop, checked for emails, found none, and set up a blank page. Then she shut the lid and sat absolutely still for a few moments with, perhaps, a prayer.

It must have been more than a few moments—perhaps a prayer had morphed into a doze—because when she sipped her tea it was undrinkably cold. So she tipped it into the sink and rinsed out her mug, polishing away the tea-stains with a washing-up sponge.

But she knew, then, what had happened that afternoon.

It was the house, everything about it, the photographs, the old armchairs, the books everywhere, the framed manuscript pages, the plants on the windowsill, of course the coffee, that added up to Val's place, his, unique in the world. And she hadn't even seen his kitchen.

She realized that every night, when she prayed for the souls of all the people she had loved or been closely bound to who were dead, and these, by now because she was old, were nearly all the people she had ever loved or been bound to, she remembered them in a place, each of them in his or her place, as different from each other as the people themselves were.

She remembered Matt, her son who had been killed in Afghanistan, here, in the flat, as a toddler whose passion was tractors, and much later as the soldier who left the flat to go to Sandhurst carrying a suitcase and an ironing board, kissing her goodbye before Simon drove him away for his first term as a cadet. She remembered her father in his little flat in Hampstead where he lived as a widower and, with Clare beside his bed, died so quietly that she had to be told by the nurse that he'd gone. Her mother she saw always in the house in Yorkshire where she had grown up and Clare as a child had gone for holidays, the house where Clare's cousin now lived and where her mother would come in from hunting, like Penny years later, muddy and cheerful, throwing down her bowler hat, her crop and her white string gloves on the table in the hall. And Simon, her husband of more than forty years, she thought of in his study at the far end of the flat, surrounded by bookcases and facing a map of Yorkshire which he didn't much like, sitting at his big untidy desk, often on the telephone with his chair tipped back and his feet on the desk, a pen in his hand writing something that she knew might have nothing to do with whoever was on the other end of the telephone call. Simon working; Simon writing; Simon talking.

And so on, through her Yorkshire grandparents, remembered in the same house as her mother, and her Czech grandparents, killed by the Nazis, whose names she knew but who could not be remembered because she had never known them or their house, their place. Her old nanny she remembered pedalling away at her sewing machine in the nursery of her childhood, while the Light Programme played hymn tunes on an organ from Nanny's favourite, Sandy Macpherson's "The Chapel in the Valley". Then her more recently dead, all with the places she remembered them in, David in his tidy little house in South Kensington or across a table from her in the café of the V&A; dear, good Ayesha coughing and coughing in her bed in the flat before the paramedics came to take her to hospital.

She let the list tick through her mind, as it did every night in her prayers before she got into bed. Almost every night someone on the list would for no obvious reason become vividly present to her so that she really was remembering him or her before God. Now, she stopped the list before she got to the end, to David and Ayesha, because she understood what thinking of it had shown her.

It had shown her that Val as a person in her life had changed from being someone she hardly knew, someone she had met less than two months ago and had been pleased to talk to on a bench in the square on Wednesday afternoons and sometimes on Saturdays because she was talking to no one at present, to someone who counted in a different way because she had seen his house, had spent an hour in it with him, and now he and his house, his place, would always be as one.

She knew him better. Perhaps that was all there was to it.

When he'd come to her flat, had he felt anything like what she was feeling now? He'd done this twice, when it was raining and their bench couldn't be sat on, for a cup of tea, or coffee, she couldn't remember exactly. It must at least once have been coffee, which he must have found miserably unlike his own, because of what he'd said about it, which was no doubt just politeness. His politeness, though different, was almost as unfailing as Hakim's.

But he hadn't seemed particularly interested in where she lived. She was, in other words, over-reacting, over-interpreting, finding much significance where there was hardly any. She smiled, thinking of Simon. "There you go again. Mountains out of molehills aren't in it." But Simon was before she had written anything except her long-ago little book on St Augustine, which wasn't much of a success and which no one now had even heard of.

What, she wondered as she often had, would Simon have made of the book that had, by a miracle she still thought, been published in September when she had finished writing it only at the beginning of June? He would have been pleased that he hardly appeared in it: it had been a book about widowhood rather than marriage, and he would have seen the point of the distinction. But, with his allergy to exaggeration and his conviction that women, even reasonably intelligent ones, always exaggerated their own responses to almost everything, he would have shut the book impatiently and often, with an implied if not voiced "for heaven's sake".

And Penny? She had, naturally, given a copy to Penny, and sent one to Daisy in Vancouver and one to Carrie in Nepal, which, weeks later, had, for a wonder, arrived. Daisy thanked her grandmother politely but thereafter showed no sign of having read the book. Carrie loved it, and emailed enthusiastically, above all impressed that she had managed both to start and to finish it and, it seemed to Carrie, to get right things she remembered herself. "Well done, Gran. You're a very accurate writer." Penny had been thrilled to recognize herself in the first few pages—no one in the book, except public figures, had been given their real name - and then hadn't, Clare was certain, read far enough to discover what kind of book it had turned out to be. Clare had promised her that there was nothing in the book to cause any upset to Charles's parliamentary career, as there wasn't, and Penny had taken her word for it. Charles's parliamentary career, in any case, was non-stick, unimpressionable plastic, Teflon as people used to say about Tony Blair. Charles was an obedient back-bencher who voted as instructed and had never in his life had an idea of his own; having been chosen by the dozen local figures who ran the constituency Tory party, he was safe in his very safe seat for good as far as Clare could see. Unless there were skeletons in his cupboard, to come clattering out at the hands of the *Sun* or the *Daily Mail*. Very unlikely: Penny had never seemed anxious about pretty secretaries and pretty secretaries were about as far from the straight and narrow as Charles's imagination was likely to have led him. Financial shenanigans? Favours in return for party donations? Cash for questions? Also unlikely: Charles had never been important enough.

Her book had been little noticed. She and the publisher had posted off a number of copies. She'd enjoyed this. The book had a beautiful picture of Hakim's stones at Apollonia on the front cover and she liked to think of it giving pleasure as the jiffy-bag was opened. There had been three sympathetic reviews and a dozen or fifteen letters and emails, kind, appreciative, and seeing the point, in varying degrees, of what she had tried to do, from friends and people she knew less well but had thought might enjoy it. That was about it, and some dozens of copies had even been sold. This hardly counted as a literary success. Nevertheless she felt somehow justified in making the considerable effort that had produced the book.

And it had delivered Val to her.

Looking back, over only two months, she must try to discover what his appearance in her life actually meant, Simon's sceptical ghost notwithstanding.

CHAPTER 3

TUESDAY 15 DECEMBER 2020

One surprisingly sunny day in December, more like late autumn than winter, she had been sitting on a bench in the garden of the square reading the *New York Review of Books*. She was wearing mittens because it wasn't exactly warm, her very old second-best winter coat (she had only two, and had had them both for twenty or thirty years, not because she was too poor to buy a new coat but because she didn't need one and hated shopping for clothes), and a wool headscarf, black with red, orange and yellow flowers that Carrie had told her made her look like a Russian babushka in a student production of a Chekhov play. That was fine.

She noticed, slowly, that someone was standing in front of her, not close, in fact the recommended two yards away. She looked up and was for a moment startled to recognize an old man, not exactly a stranger but someone she didn't know. She'd seen him in the garden a number of times, on a bench on the far side of the lawn, usually, in the summer, asleep, though sometimes reading a book or a newspaper she didn't recognize, He looked always a little scruffy, as if he needed someone to look after his clothes. She remembered thinking that perhaps his wife had died, and also how much less comfortable he looked than the black cat with white paws who often slept in the sun on his or another bench. It was seeing him now, in the mask everyone was meant to wear against Covid 19, waiting for her to notice him, that, for no particular reason, had given her a slight shock. She put down the *New York Review*.

"I'm sorry", she said, only because it was something to say.

He bowed his head a little, with politeness and a distinct foreignness.

"Excuse me, please", he said. "May I ask you a question?"

"Yes, of course."

44

"I think you are Mrs Wilson. Am I correct?"

"No. Absolutely not."

"But I was sure—"

Then she understood.

"O I see", she said. "Have you come across my book?"

"I have read your book, indeed. I found it very interesting, and sad, of course, but most interesting, when I have seen you so often in the garden. I have also seen your friend, the young man, Mr Husain. Or perhaps he also has another name—you call him Mr Husain in the book."

"But how on earth did you find out about the book?"

"The caretaker of your house. You have called him Mr Clements."

"Mr Clements—but—" She was going to say that Mr Clements had probably never read a book in his life. Instead she said, "How does Mr Clements know that I've written a book?"

"Mr Clements knows everything."

"Well—that's extraordinary." She couldn't make it out.

"You gave a copy of your book, I believe, to some old people who also live in your house, and they said to Mr Clements that you had written a book about living in the square. Mr Clements thinks you will make the square famous."

She laughed, mostly with relief. There seemed to be nothing alarming about this old man, or about how he had heard of her book.

"I'm afraid it won't. Not enough people are likely to read it, I'm sorry to say. But are you a friend of Mr Clements? Do you live in the square? Why don't you sit down?"

She put a hand on the seat of the bench, which was long enough for three people to sit on.

"Thank you", he said, and settled himself at the far end of the bench. "I do not wish to interrupt your reading."

"O, that's all right. It'll keep."

Would he answer her questions? Perhaps she shouldn't have invited him to sit beside her?

"Mr Clements is not my friend but I have for a long time known him. I used to do some gardening in the square for Bill

Atkins. If you have lived here for a long time, as your book says, you perhaps remember Bill?"

"Yes, I remember Bill very well. I have lived in the square for more than forty years."

"Bill and Mr Clements used to go to the pub together after work and sometimes they invited me to go to the pub with them."

"I see."

This sounded fine. Had he forgotten her second question?

"So do you live in the square?"

She was annoyed at herself for the "so", an irritating mannerism which she knew she had caught from the people on the radio who started with "so" when they began any answer to any question, or indeed began any question.

"O no", he said, looking round the square at the tall houses with their imposing front doors at the top of flights of steps.

"No. I live, I have lived now for almost fifteen years, in a little house in a mews, the mews—perhaps you know it?—a short distance along that street."

He pointed at the street, a street with pretty early nineteenth-century houses, which joined the square almost opposite the windows of her flat.

She was surprised. The mews houses in the neighbourhood were bought and sold, she knew, for hundreds of thousands of pounds, more probably millions by now, and he didn't look prosperous enough to live in one.

"I am a tenant only", he said, picking up the surprise she hadn't expressed. "I came to London fifteen years ago, to visit a friend, an old friend from my home. When I arrived I found he was ill and I stayed with him until he died. He was the tenant of the house, and the rent is low—That is why—"

He stopped, not needing to explain any further the reason for him living in a house he obviously couldn't afford.

"When Bill died the committee of the garden allowed me to keep my key. I am so thankful for my key."

He looked at her, along the bench, and smiled, a wonderful blue-eyed smile which transformed his face.

She wanted to ask him where he was from, more precisely where he had come to England from, fifteen years ago, but couldn't see how to ask him tactfully, without a faint suggestion, which was the last thing she wanted to imply, that he didn't belong in this London square, with its solid Victorian prosperity. She found she was looking round the square as he had looked.

"You would like to know my country, where my home is?"

She was impressed by his intuition, which reminded her of David, dead now for fourteen months. She missed him every day.

"I would, yes. Your English is very good and I can't guess from your accent—"

Was this polite? She had a peculiar sense that she was losing her bearings. Was he Russian, Polish, a Jew perhaps, from central Europe like her father? But he wasn't in the least like her father. Nor, actually, was he at all like David, who was a German-Jewish doctor born in London.

"No. I have not lost my accent. Now I will never lose it. I am too old."

He smiled at her again, disconcerting her as if he wanted her to guess his nationality and knew she would guess wrong.

From nowhere there slid into her mind the memory of Kent leaving for exile in *King Lear*. "I am too old to learn."

"I came to London from Wrocław", he said, as if letting her off the guessing game. "Do you know the name Wrocław?"

"No. I'm sorry. I'm afraid I've never heard the name before." What he had said was "Vrotsuav". She couldn't even picture how it might be spelt.

"No one in England has heard of Wrocław. It is a city in Poland, an important city with a most complicated story. It used to be a German city called Breslau—do you know the name Breslau?"

She shook her head. She was doing very badly.

He laughed, for the first time.

"You must not worry. Also no one in England has heard of Breslau. At the end of Hitler's war Stalin and Churchill drew a new map of the east of Europe. Poland, the whole country of Poland, was pushed many many miles to the west, so that it lost its east parts to Russia and Ukraine, and was given new west parts which had been German before. Breslau, which to the Poles is Wrocław, was the important city in this new part of Poland. Many Poles already were there in any case. Before Frederick the Great this was the Holy Roman Empire, Habsburg Silesia."

Silesia: a third name she didn't recognize. She was trying without success to visualize on a map what he had just told her.

"Breslau had suffered very much from the Russians at the end of the was because Hitler said it was to be a fortress city. Of Sarajevo he said the same. But now it is a good Polish city."

"Goodness, how complicated."

His explanation meant almost nothing to her. She felt ashamed of her ignorance both of what happened at the end of the war and of Frederick the Great. She felt ashamed particularly because reading her book had clearly led him to assume that she was properly educated, decently informed. He couldn't have guessed that she knew very little about the eighteenth century, the only period in European history that she actually disliked. Was what he'd said about Frederick the Great something to do with the Partition of Poland? She didn't ask, for fear of sounding as stupid as she felt, and promised herself to look at Simon's old Times Atlas when she went back to the flat. She needed an actual map. Maps she loved. She was good at the Mediterranean, good at Hakim's North Africa, very good at maps of the classical world. She had been able to draw maps of the great Greek and Roman battles since she was at school, Salamis, Plataea, Lake Trasimene. But she was very bad at eastern Europe. Germany, Poland, Russia: a vague sense of their borders was all she could summon up, and she did know that they had often changed.

She pulled herself together.

"I'm so sorry", she said. "I was trying to imagine—You are Polish then?"

"No. I am not Polish. I was for ten years in Wrocław because I left my country when it was not possible for me to stay there. I had wished to go to Germany because I did know German, but it was difficult and instead I found a job in Wrocław. Poland, you understand, after Communism had gone, wanted very much to be part of an older Europe. Refugees like me, who had some knowledge of languages and of books, they were pleased to give some work to. I did not know Polish. I thought it would be easy for a Slav who knew Russian to learn Polish, another Slav language. I was wrong and I had to work very hard. But the job was good and the people of the city were kind. Most of them were kind. I do not look Jewish."

"O. Is that still difficult? Even now?"

"In Poland it will never not be difficult, I think. More difficult, naturally, in the countryside than in the towns."

She had to let that go.

"And your English?" she said, for a harmless question.

He still hadn't said which country he came from.

"I knew some English when I came to London. From books, and also from some English and American soldiers and some other people who tried to help us in my country. When I came here, I learnt more English quite quickly. It is easier to speak than Polish. Easier, I should say, to speak badly. To write it is terrible because of the mad spelling. Polish spelling is terrible in a different way, but it is not mad. I am a south Slav. My country is Yugoslavia, which means the place where the south Slavs live. I should say my country was Yugoslavia because now it does not exist."

He had slipped her this answer to her original question as if he were ashamed of it, or perhaps nervous of her reaction.

"I see."

She didn't. She didn't even know what the parts of Yugoslavia were called now. She did some quick mental arithmetic: if he had spent fifteen years in London and ten, before that, in Poland, he had left Yugoslavia in 1996. She wished she could remember in which year her son Matt had been posted to Yugoslavia, and where he had been. She wished she'd paid more attention to what he'd told her and Simon, though it hadn't been much, when he came home on leave.

"That means you were there, in Yugoslavia, through the war in the 1990s?"

"It was not one war. There were different wars, three wars, one war and then the next war. Yes. I was there. I left because of what was done in the wars. I am a librarian."

She didn't, then, make the connection between the last two things he'd said, because she didn't know enough, hadn't paid enough attention to the news at the time.

"I'm so sorry", was all she could think of to say.

"You are kind. Thank you. But—"

He stopped and bent his head, looking down at his hands clasped together on his lap. He was sitting upright on the bench, his back straight, his knees together. She thought that before this she had only seen him asleep, or sitting sideways, reading, in the garden. Perhaps she was wrong. Perhaps she had also seen him gardening with Bill, years ago. She couldn't remember.

Suddenly he raised his head and looked at her, his eyes clenched, anguished.

"But English people do not know—how can they ever know—what a war in a country, inside a country that is supposed to be united, a single country, can be for the people who live in that country? How there is hatred where once there was, what? Not hatred, not perhaps love either, but ordinary living from day to day without killing or fear. English people have no memory of how this ordinary living turns into hatred and destruction and death."

"Well, I suppose that's almost true, at least since the seventeenth century. There were several bouts of civil war in the Middle Ages: people wanting to be king, other people wanting to stop them. In the seventeenth century we had a more serious civil war. Again it was about who was to rule the country but there were other things at stake, not just this man or that man in power. There were a lot of battles, a lot of deaths. The king was convicted of treason in a court, and executed. But all that was long ago, beyond memory of course."

Except in Ireland, she didn't say. Cromwell in Ireland. William of Orange in Ireland. War in Ireland in the 1920s. The Troubles. Unforgotten.

"In a court? I did not know that. The king was tried and executed? Not assassinated? That is remarkable for the time, I should say. For any time maybe,"

She knew she was in schoolma'am mode. Would she bore

him? Perhaps not. She went on, leaving out Cromwell and King Billy.

"But not at all long ago there was more or less a civil war in Northern Ireland. It ended twenty years ago but it had lasted years and years. It wasn't as bad as the war, the wars, in Yugoslavia, I'm sure, but it was bad enough to kill many people and for people to be afraid of their neighbours. It is over but there is still the possibility of trouble, and Brexit is making trouble more likely."

"Have you been to Northern Ireland?"

"No, I haven't."

Matt, in the army, had been sent there too. The lawless streets of Derry. She remembered how shocked he'd been by the atmosphere of tension and distrust, by what was being done, and by what people were afraid might be done, by so-called paramilitaries and by soldiers too, in what was supposed to be part of the United Kingdom, part of his own country, but, again, she couldn't remember much of what he'd said.

"You do not know, then."

He sounded almost aggressive.

"No. I'm sorry. I suppose you're right." Why was she conceding anything to this total stranger? Because she liked him? And now she'd made him angry. She saw him swallow the anger because he wanted to go on talking to her.

"I think ", he said, "Northern Ireland was a mess at the end of the British empire, with the wrong lines drawn on a map. Is that correct?"

"More or less. Though it was also—"

She was going to say that it was more complicated than that, and a much older story, but he went on.

"The Irish were subjects for a long time in the British empire. But the English have never been subjects in any empire ever, so there is much that they do not know."

"Well, yes. You're right about that. Though I don't suppose many English people think much about the empire nowadays."

"The black people do, from the slave islands in the Caribbean. The people from India do. Africans do. How is it possible for them not to think about the British empire?"

He leant forward earnestly, so that he had to look up at her, sideways and up, with his blue eyes. "And the English themselves, they may not think, but they know without thinking that they must be right and good because always they were the imperial power. If you win, if always you did win, you must be right. That is what they know. Might is right. The triumph of the will. It is what drives all empires. Ask the Romans. Ask Mr Putin."

She hoped this wasn't so. Was it? She had never thought of this before, but she saw he had a point, at least.

Now he couldn't stop.

"In my country", he said, "we have very much experience of empires, very long experience, but never did we have experience of being the imperial power. We have been subjects always. Until after the Great War we were subjects, of one empire or another. Then we were told, we, the south Slavs, the Yugoslavs, that we were free, that we could be our own country, But except when Tito ruled, we have made only a mess of it. We cannot manage by ourselves. Yugoslavia has come into pieces and outside people have told us we should be this little country and that little country, when we were better as Yugoslavia, and maybe even better in one empire or the other. But Britain, which was the imperial power of imperial powers, and also always part of Europe as you can see in the museums and the galleries"—he swept his arm in the general direction of the Gloucester Road—"thinks it cannot manage except by itself. If it is not a ruling power it must be a subject power. Subject to Brussels. It does make no sense but it makes Britain do Brexit", he said, bitterly. "So now there is dislike for people like me who are here because the European Union made it possible for us to come here."

"O dear. I do hope not. Not dislike, I mean." She knew how weak this sounded.

"Worse than dislike. Go home, people say, in a shop, in a pub, since the Brexit referendum. And even in this year, when Mr Johnson promises to get Brexit done—as if this country could sail away from Europe into a great ocean of freedom - there is a fear of foreigners from Europe which for many years in London I did not find."

Now she bent her head, ashamed.

She sensed him remembering that he didn't know her at all, and that she might profoundly disagree with him.

"You did not like Brexit?" he said. "You did not vote for Brexit?"

She raised her head to meet his question, his anxious look. She smiled, shaking her head.

"Certainly not. You've read my book. I was horrified, miserable, at the referendum result. And I've been miserable and angry about it ever since. It's a terrible thing we've done to ourselves, and also to the EU. Nothing and no one made us do it, and it was entirely unnecessary, entirely a matter of political ambition, a few cynical politicians who wanted power and encouraged and used the worst instincts and prejudices of the people who read the Sun and the Daily Mail to get it."

"They wanted power and they got it. If people do want power enough, often they do get it. Like Slobodan Milosevic."

She felt ashamed again because she couldn't remember— wasn't Milosevic the leader of Serbia who had died while he was being tried in The Hague? Or was that someone else? How ignorant she was. She was sure, at least, that Milosevic was a Serb.

"You're not Serbian, then?"

"I could be a Serb who thought Milosevic a wicked man who was responsible for many thousands of deaths. I could be a Serb who disagreed with Milosevic. But actually, no, I am not a Serb. My friend who died in my house six months after I arrived in London was a Serb. But he had left Yugoslavia long before anyone had heard the name of Milosevic. He knew only from England, from here in his little house, what Milosevic made of Serbia, what he made to happen in Bosnia, in Sarajevo where we both were boys, in the same school. And if he had not died, he would have been as sad and as shocked as I was by the Brexit referendum, as you also were."

She knew she didn't know enough to grasp all this properly. And he still hadn't told her what he was, only that he was a Yugoslav who wasn't a Serb. She had no idea of the right question to ask him.

Again, he understood without her saying anything.

"I am a Bosnian."

Matt had certainly been in Bosnia.

"Bosnia was where the war, the wars, were at their worst?"

"That is correct. I say I am a Bosnian. You will perhaps think you know what that means, what a Bosnian is. But you will not know how many possible things a Bosnian may be."

Again, she had no idea what this meant.

"No. I'm sorry—"

"Listen a moment." Then, "Are you too cold? he suddenly said, thinking perhaps that he was keeping her outside too long on a winter afternoon.

She smiled again.

"No. Not at all. Please explain."

"I am eighty-one years old. I was born in the spring of 1939, in the days of peace. My father's father was Muslim. My father's mother was Catholic. My father himself was neither Muslim nor Catholic though sometimes he went to Mass to please his mother. And sometimes he would stop in the street at the call to prayer."

He looked at her again.

"You are Catholic. Are you shocked?"

"Certainly not."

"'Who knows where God is?' my father said to me when I was a small child. 'Better to hold on to what you have been given.' I think he said this to me, but it may be that he said it to my grandmother and she told me."

"His wife, my mother, was a Jewess. Her parents, and even more her grandparents, were good faithful Jews. But none of these parents and grandparents hated each other. Not at all. They lived, all of them, in Sarajevo. They were Slavs, all of them, called Yugoslavs since the end of the Great War which was the end of the empires to which all the people called Yugoslavs had belonged, then or earlier. You would not be able to say, from looking at any of them, or from listening to them talking, my parents, my grandparents, the others of my family, whether they were Muslim or Jew or Catholic. So what am I? Who am I? I have hidden among the religions always."

54

He had said all this looking down at his clasped hands. Now he looked at her, and smiled.

"You are surprised?"

"I'm—well—I have to admit it's all difficult to understand. I thought these differences, in religion, were so important?"

"They are now, because of the wars, not because of religion itself. How religious were the fighters in Northern Ireland who fought and killed for the IRA or their enemies? I can't remember the letters for their enemies but they were Protestants, weren't they, because the IRA were Catholics. It was said to be because of religion, for two different kinds of Christianity? Not so? But the boys who shot people and threw bombs? There is not, is there, much religion in shooting people and throwing bombs. The same was in Bosnia. I am I with one label. You are you with a different label. So I hate you. If I can, I will kill you. Where in this is a mixture person like me? The Nazis had a word for me, a *Mischling*, a mixture person. Partly not Jewish and partly Jewish. So to be killed. Partly was enough."

"I see. Or rather, I don't see. So difficult it must have been. I still feel confused, even when you explain."

"Of course you are confused. I am myself confused, some people would say, looking at me, or hearing this description from the outside. You must be confused, they would say, in this confusion of different religions, different histories. But, you know, I am not confused. Fused, perhaps, but not confused."

He looked delighted with this skilful piece of wordplay.

"Or not confounded", she said, in a more exact Latin spirit, but this flummoxed him. He'd probably never heard the word.

"I'm sorry", she said. "I think I do understand. You are who you are, and each of them, your parents and grandparents were who he was, who she was, with none of them under attack from any of the others. This was what you meant, what you were saying, about ordinary life, people living with differences that were just that, differences. Without hatred."

"With love. Even with love. As it was for my parents. And then—"

She saw he couldn't talk about the wars. A phrase from how people think now in England came into her mind: "identity politics". Wasn't he, sitting beside her on a garden bench, a living refutation of what was meant by "identity" in that phrase?

She went back a bit to ask him a question.

"How much did they care about religion, your parents and grandparents? Or was religion for them only a matter of tradition, different traditions, that they thought of as part of the past?"

"As people do in England?"

"Yes, most English people do, I'm afraid. Though many Muslims, some Jews and some Christians still take religion seriously, in what they believe and in the habits of their own lives."

"As you do, don't you?"

This was on account of the book, though his direct question, accompanied by a direct look from his blue eyes, was a question no English near-stranger would have asked.

She liked the directness.

"Yes, I do. I'm a Catholic, as you said, and I go to Mass. When I can. Not now, of course. You will have seen, in the book."

"Yes. Good", he said. She didn't mind this either. Perhaps he only meant that she turned out to be very like Clare Wilson in the book.

"And your complicated family?" she asked.

"My Catholic grandmother and my Jewish grandmother were both serious in their religion. The grandfathers were not so serious, and both my parents not serious at all. All this my grandmother, my Catholic grandmother, told me. She was alive, you see, to tell me. Only she."

This raised questions she couldn't ask.

"I think", he said, "that the time when my parents were young, after the Great War, was not a serious time."

"I expect that was true in many parts of Europe. Not in Russia of course."

"For Sarajevo it was a bad time. For all of Yugoslavia it was a chance for agreement and instead disagreement was worse and worse. Communism was not too bad. There were quite a lot, you know, of Communists in Bosnia. Fascism was much worse. The Serbs quite liked Hitler. The Croats very much liked Mussolini. Bosnia was between all things, as always it has been, since it was between Latin and Greek, the old Roman empire and the new."

"Goodness", she again needed a map.

"Your parents?" she said.

"My father was a little bit Communist, then more Communist after Hitler invaded us. My mother I think was not political. She loved her parents and she loved Sarajevo. But then—"

She found she was wanting to return his confidence in her by telling him something about her own family, which wasn't as unconfused as he probably thought, though he knew from the book, if he remembered, that her father was a Jewish refugee from Prague.

But he suddenly stood up. Standing in front of her where he had been standing when she first noticed him, he said, "It is becoming too cold. I should go back to my house. I hope—" What did he hope?

"I hope I have not talked for too long", he said.

"Not at all, not at all", how inadequate and English this sounded. "I am so pleased to have met you."

"I hope I may talk to you again, here in the garden, one day?"

"I hope so too."

"Goodbye", he said, with his little bow of the head, and he set off, briskly for his age, on the gravel path that took him round, under the trees, to his side of the square.

After he had disappeared she sat, entirely still, for a few minutes and wondered what had just happened. She refolded the *New York Review of Books*, of which she had read only half of the first article, and went back to her flat where, automatically, she made a mug of tea.

She found herself standing at the sitting room window, with her mug hot in both hands, looking down at the garden—the bench they had been sitting on, beside the path to her left, was hidden by shrubs—and finding it difficult to believe that she had had such a long conversation with someone who was, still,

57

a total stranger. She didn't know his name, any more that he knew hers although he had correctly—"Am I correct?"—identified her as the Clare Wilson of her book. Neither of them had thought to ask the other's name, nor chosen a moment to volunteer his own, her own. Yet they had exchanged so much, more, in some ways, than she had exchanged with anyone since David's death. Hakim was different, because he was like one of the children. So was Ayesha, whom she had known for such a short time but loved, again as if she had been one of the children, or grandchildren: Ayesha was only a year or two older than Carrie. Hakim was much younger than Penny, or than Matt would have been, a few years older than her grandchildren.

She sat down on her usual armchair and sipped her tea. She was, as she often said to Penny, entirely used to being alone; she didn't mind being alone; indeed, she often consciously enjoyed being alone. Even when Hakim left to go to the north, missing him was tempered with some relief that she was again by herself in her flat, with no one else to worry about, feed, iron shirts for. But she realized, to her surprise, that her encounter in the square had made her feel lonely—feeling lonely is not at all the same as being alone—as she almost never did.

She wanted to tell someone about her conversation with the old man in the square, to see what someone else, a sensible person who knew her well, would think. Was this ridiculous? Was what ridiculous? Wanting to tell someone about what had just happened? Or what had just happened itself? Probably both were no more than a result of not having enough in her life, of Hakim having gone, of the Covid lockdown having made it impossible all year to see anyone or go to Yorkshire which she longed to do, of her granddaughters being on different continents, both as far away as could be. Evidently she was after all a gullible old woman who had allowed herself to be picked up, like a sixteen-year-old in a cinema queue, because she had long ago forgotten that one was supposed to be cagey towards unknown men with flimsy excuses for making contact. But had he seemed at all alarming? No he hadn't, not for one moment.

What would Penny say?

She knew exactly what Penny would say. "Honestly, Mum, whatever next? You do realize you'll be eighty next year? You can't go on collecting dodgy foreigners like stamps. It's not safe for one thing."

"Really, Penny. It's nonsense to describe Hakim as a dodgy foreigner—you know it's nonsense. And I may be extremely old but I'm not dotty: this man in the square didn't strike me as remotely dangerous. Just lonely."

That was it; he talked as someone talks who hasn't for too long had anyone to listen.

"Well, there you are. You felt sorry for him. You need to watch out, all by yourself at your age. Charles would be horrified."

"I'm sure he would. Charles was horrified by the very idea of Hakim. Don't you remember? Bound to be a terrorist, he said. And what harm has Hakim ever done anyone? Me or any of the rest of you? Absolutely none. In fact now he's a recognized British Museum authority on Roman frontier provinces."

"Well, if you say so. Whatever that means, it sounds respectable enough. But this chap is obviously much weirder than Hakim. He's old, for one thing. At least Hakim's young and has a proper job. I think you ought to be very careful, Mum. You shouldn't tell him anything about yourself or where you live."

"He knows where I live because of Mr Clements."

"Bugger Mr Clements. He should mind his own business. What was he thinking of, telling this man about you?"

"He told him about my book."

"O that. Don't say Mr Clements has read it?"

"No, of course he hasn't. But the man I met in the garden has."

"So he says. Mum. Did he talk about money at all?"

"About money? Certainly not. You don't understand, darling. It was a friendly conversation between two old people that began because of my book."

"Are you sure that wasn't just an excuse—to start a conversation, I mean? He might have been planning it for weeks."

"No. I'm not sure. But if it was, an excuse I mean, it doesn't matter."

59

"O, Mum, for heaven's sake—suppose he's a crook who wants to get into the flat to burgle it?"

"I'm sure he isn't. Sometimes, you must remember, people are just as nice as they seem. Anyway, even though I'm ancient, I can manage my life myself, thank you very much."

This was an imaginary exchange, though Penny was predictable enough for Clare not to have had to work her imagination very hard to put it together. All the same, Penny's warnings, which she had invented as she sat drinking her tea, must have been somewhere in her own head, invented or found. She smiled, at herself.

Since there was no one to talk to about the man in the garden—David would have listened, and delivered a sensible view—she relaxed into her ordinary evening routine, the PM programme, news about the coronavirus, how many deaths, how many new cases, the six o'clock news, half an hour of silence to write something before *The Archers*, and then a little cooking and a basic supper which she always looked forward to because by then she was hungry. And usually she sat in her armchair by the fire with the book she was reading, at the moment *Middlemarch*, which she hadn't read since she was young, hadn't enjoyed then and wasn't enjoying now, until bedtime.

But after supper this evening she went into Simon's study and pulled his heavy old *Times Atlas of the World* out of its bottom shelf. She carried it to the desk, left clean and tidy by Hakim who had been working in here until he left for the north.She found Yugoslavia, one country then, with Bosnia marked as a region within it but without boundary lines. She looked back at the date of publication. 1968, it said, Second Edition. It must have been a wedding present from someone: what a good present. But it wasn't much help on Yugoslavia now that the country had fallen to bits. There was Sarajevo, in mountains in the middle of the region called Bosnia. She gazed at it, seeing only that it was in the middle of Bosnia, in the middle of Yugoslavia, in the middle, probably of the province the Romans called Illyricum. Between Rome and Constantinople as the man in the garden had said. But then?

She wished she had a good historical atlas. There had been one in the library of the school where she taught for twenty years. Out of reach now, in a number of different ways.

She looked for the city in Poland where he'd spent ten years. At least this edition of the Atlas was produced after the Second World War and would have eastern Europe as redrawn by Stalin and Churchill. She failed to find Wrocław in the index because she didn't know how it was spelt. Eventually, with eastern Germany and western Poland spread out over two huge pages, she found Wrocław—so that was the spelling—and then only because it had Breslau in brackets and smaller print under the name. Another city in the middle. She saw how it had been in Poland and was now in Germany. A city on a river she had never heard of, the Oder, that rose in Czech mountains and flowed through Poland and northwards through Germany not far from Berlin and reached the German coast of the Baltic. A city with hills to the south, and to the north the great flat European plain, green on the map, that stretched from Holland to Russia. She closed the atlas and put it back where it belonged.

Seeing his places, his history, these two cities, on maps was somehow reassuring, even if she knew nothing whatever about either of them.

The conversation on the bench stayed with her, worrying her less and less. Before she got into bed, she prayed as she always did, standing at the window of her bedroom with the curtains pulled to behind her, closing her eyes or looking out at the trees in the square. She added him, her nameless acquaintance, to her list of the living for whom she prayed every night, and by the morning their conversation had become something that simply interested her and that she hoped might be continued in due course. Or this was how she had decided to describe it to herself.

Perhaps she would see him again after Christmas.

CHAPTER 4

15 DECEMBER – CHRISTMAS DAY 2020

In a little more than a week's time she was going away for Christmas, as she always did, to stay with Penny and Charles in the Yorkshire village where, in a larger house now lived in by her cousin's son and his family, she had in her childhood and adolescence spent part of almost every school holiday. It had been her grandparents' house, her mother's home, and she had all her life loved everything about it, most of all the country close by which could be walked to, and further away the moors and the steep dales that intersected them, with sheep-cropped turf, little streams, ancient stone walls and bracken, which once could be ridden to—there had always been horses and ponies, and still were—and, now that she was an elderly visitor, could be driven to in a car. Five or six miles away, too far for her to walk these days, was the quiet churchyard among woods and water, a couple of miles from any village, where Matt was buried. She would visit his grave when she was staying with Penny and perhaps take him some holly and ivy, better than chrysanths from a shop, which would look bedraggled as soon as it rained. Matt had always loved Yorkshire too, and the army had brought him back from Afghanistan, so that they had at least been able to have a proper funeral.

Penny and Charles were in Yorkshire for the whole of the parliamentary recess. In theory Charles, in his constituency for longer than usual, was keeping in touch with his Westminster office by email and telephone and holding constituency surgeries on Zoom. In practice, no doubt, his PA in London was faithfully fending off almost everything that sounded like work. And Clare suspected that in Yorkshire the constituents most likely to need help, with changing benefits or whether it was allowed during Covid to call a telephone engineer when British Telecom said it wasn't, or whether they really had to pay for

62

their television licence, were the very ones least likely to have a computer. So being given an email address or a website in a recorded telephone message would muddle them even more than their problem was muddling them already. Not the sort of thing Charles bothered to imagine.

The plan was that she would go up by train to York on the day before Christmas Eve and stay until the day after Boxing Day. A Christmas relaxation of the Covid rules for five days had made this plan possible, and she was looking forward, as a child looks forward to something known and predictable, to four nights in Penny's pretty and comfortable spare room and three whole days in which she could walk out of the village into the woods and on one day borrow Penny's car to visit Matt's grave and even drive up to the edge of the moor. She had done all this at Christmas last year. That visit seemed many years ago, in the ordinary world before Covid. At bad moments in the lockdowns, she had wondered if she would ever again see Yorkshire. But she would after all, very soon, for four nights and three days over Christmas.

Less than a week before Christmas the government cancelled the five-day relaxation of the rules. No one in London was allowed to meet anyone not already living with them, let alone to travel anywhere, and Penny on the telephone from Yorkshire said she was relieved.

"I really wasn't happy about you coming on the train, Mum, with so much virus about in London. Much better for you to stay safe in the flat for a bit longer."

Was Penny worried about her, perhaps catching the virus on the train, or worried about them, catching it from her if she brought it from London? The fact that people who felt perfectly well could both have and pass on the virus had made for paranoia about infection all over the country.

She understood that Penny and Charles wanted to steer clear of a disease that could be very nasty, even dangerous, whatever one's age, but she did wonder, not for the first time, what the point was of keeping the old, who would die anyway before long, alive but separated from their families so that they might as well be dead. Her disappointment at the cancelling of her days in Yorkshire, promised and looked forward to, was as childish as the expectation had been. She told herself, again not for the first time, that compared with so many old people living by themselves she was extremely lucky and ought to be grateful to God. She was well, and she liked reading books, and she had her key to the square garden, where she had even met a stranger to talk to. Once. Quite enough to be grateful for.

She could even write, peacefully at her kitchen table, taking words, phrases, sentences, whole paragraphs out and putting others in or, often better, not, and enjoying every day the wonders of her laptop. Or she would be able to write again one day, when there was anything to write about.

All the same, having prayed her way the night before through the vigil Mass she should have been at in the little, unbeautiful Yorkshire church where she had married Simon, she woke on the morning of Christmas Day feeling bereft. She knew she should be able to deal with what was nothing more serious than being deprived of a treat. She was certainly too old to be feeling this sorry for herself. She couldn't go to Mass because all the places in the church in Kensington Church Street, where for decades she had been to Mass, had long been reserved by people who had known they were going to be in London. Penny rang to say Happy Christmas, which was fine, but when Penny told her there was snow on the ground in the village, she cried. Penny didn't notice.

She remembered, or thought she remembered, the snowy Christmases of her childhood in Yorkshire; even if there had been only one or two when it had really snowed, there had been in them a magic she had never forgotten.

In London it was cold, frosty, sunny, Christmassy enough, but there wasn't any snow.

After she'd had some coffee, she opened her laptop and found emails from both her granddaughters. Penny must have told them she was still in London. Carrie knew she would never risk taking her laptop to Yorkshire. Daisy in Canada, if she thought at all, probably assumed she had a smartphone and could get emails anywhere.

Daisy only wished her a Happy Christmas and asked her if

she remembered the fun they'd had in Yorkshire last Christmas when she and Daisy together had decorated the tree with some ancient lights and baubles Penny kept in a cardboard box. *Mum and Dad will be sad not to have you for Christmas.* Not very, she thought. *Sorry not to be coming home this year. Hope to see you soon.*

Carrie, who knew her grandmother much better, had written:

Poor Gran. How miserable for you not to be allowed to go to Leckenby after all. I know you love being there. Do try to have as cheerful a day as you can. It's a shame Hakim has gone for the moment—but at least without a man in the house you're not having to cook. All the same you should give yourself a treat for lunch, something you really like but usually think is too expensive. And I bet you're reading a book you're properly enjoying.

I do hope to be back in the summer when all these rules and regulations have faded away. I'll bring Bill with me—he hasn't been home to the US for eighteen months either—and you must meet him. I think you'll like him.

> *Happy Christmas Gran*
> *Love you*
> *Carrie*

She was puzzled by the appearance of Bill: she thought Carrie's American boyfriend was called Paul. The young, she thought.

Reading this email for the third time, she missed Carrie painfully. Carrie would have helped. She could have described the stranger of ten days ago to Carrie, and Carrie would have said something like, "Ask him to tea, Gran. I'll give him the once-over and see if I think he's OK." But Carrie was in the Himalayas, and Clare couldn't possibly send her an email saying that she'd met an interesting old man in the square and didn't know what to do.

As she thought this, she realized she was making a ludicrous fuss about nothing. For a start, there was no need to do anything. She'd spent half an hour ten days ago talking to someone she hadn't properly met and whose name she didn't know, and that was that. This is what comes of not having enough in your life. Perhaps I am going dotty, as Penny is always afraid I am.

She felt sheepish, now, almost ashamed, because she had gone back to the garden at about the same time every afternoon since, and more because she had been increasingly disappointed each day that he wasn't there, though most of those days had been too cold or too wet or both for any sensible person to be even outside.

And now it was Christmas Day and the sun was shining, sparkling the frost on the grass in the square.

She got up from the kitchen table where she had been checking the emails on her laptop. There were only the two from Carrie and Daisy. She opened first the fridge and then the store cupboard to see if she could see some treat, as recommended by Carrie, that she could have for lunch. She found a jar of quite promising-looking French pâté which someone, probably Carrie herself, had brought her from an expedition abroad: the kind of thing you buy in the Gare du Nord while waiting for the Eurostar to be called. Perfect. She put it in the fridge to get cold enough to have on hot toast with some salad for lunch.

She had decided that later she would watch the Christmas Day Latin Mass in the Jesuit church in Farm Street. With help from Hakim she had discovered how to find the Farm Street livestreamed Mass on her laptop, and nowadays she watched it every Sunday, It was very different from the much plainer English Mass she was used to, but she liked the Latin and the silences, which reminded her of how Mass was when she was a very new convert in the early 1960s, just before the changes to the liturgy. She had thought at the time, although, as a classicist, she was sad herself about the Latin, that the old Catholics who made a tremendous fuss about the changes, some of them actually leaving the Church altogether, had failed to understand properly what the Mass really was. Now, decades later and as old as they had been, she was less sure of the theology, less sure of everything, than she had been then, and more sympathetic to them: it must have been at the very least a shocking loss, of the long familiar, of the words and laden silences of all their lives, of a formal beauty and restraint that was at the core of the Mass however complicated or simple the surrounding church. She had been put out herself, though no more than put out, by the changes a few years ago from plain undistinguished English for the Mass to more elaborate, less English English that included one or two hideous and probably heretical phrases: "that we may merit to be coheirs to eternal life". Augustine would have had a fit. And "Drink this cup", not English at all, jarred every time she heard it. You might as well say, "eat this plate".

Watching the Farm Street Latin Mass, she liked also the elaborate foreignness of the Jesuit church, full of statues and mosaics and gilding, rich stained glass and a richer red and blue and gold roof, which, although of course it was Gothic Revival not Gothic, almost had the atmosphere of a church abroad, in Italy say, or France, where you might be pleased to creep in at the back of a church when Mass happened to be being said. Sometimes, on their holidays, she used to find her way, through a small door in a much larger one, taking care to close the door behind her without banging it, into such a church early on a Sunday morning with the widows of the neighbourhood in their black clothes with their rosaries, leaving Simon asleep in some hotel room, and joining him later for breakfast. The church would always be colder than the holiday morning sunshine outside. In Venice or Perugia or Roman Arles, where Hakim would so love the stones, or even Paris, it had been a way of not being a tourist for half an hour.

Paris: she remembered going, years ago, to an early morning Mass in Saint-Germain-des-Prés, her favourite church in the city and the one that felt the oldest. Later in the morning she had walked to the *quais* with Simon to look at the *bouquinistes'* stalls, and in one of the beautiful grey streets leading to the Seine they had met a distinguished-looking elderly man walking towards them. As he passed them he tipped his hat to her and smiled. "Who on earth was that?" Simon said. "I've no idea. He was at Mass this morning." She had never forgotten him. Thinking of him now she thought civility, civilization, politeness, polis, the Greek for city: where had it all gone? But perhaps, really, it hadn't, or at any rate not all of it. And the man she had talked to in the square: hadn't he had a little in common with the man in the grey street between the Boulevard Saint-Germain and the Seine?

Nevertheless she longed for the country, for Yorkshire, where she should be.

She tried to concentrate enough, to pay enough attention, for watching the Mass at her kitchen table to become as much as possible like being present, sitting, standing, kneeling, in a church. But it wasn't the same, not at all the same. On weekdays, instead of watching a livestreamed Mass happening somewhere else, she read with care the readings and prayers for the day in her Missal, thought through them and the connections between them as best she could, and felt at least near to the rhythm of the Church's life, while missing acutely being there, in a church, on her knees, looking up at the altar, for the heart of the Mass, the Eucharistic Prayer, seeing in her mind's eye beyond the priest at the altar St Augustine saying the same words, offering the same bread and wine, and beyond him Jesus at the Last Supper. "This is my body."

As the Christmas Mass was ending, not long before midday, the telephone rang. Penny again? Surely not. Hakim calling to say Happy Christmas? Hardly.

"Hello."

"Clare? It's Michael."

Her cousin, in Yorkshire. In his house they would all soon be having lunch, Christmas Day lunch.

"Shut up, you two." The sound of children quarrelling subsided a bit. She heard them still arguing as they left the room, and then the slam of the door.

"Happy Christmas, Clare. Sorry about the racket. I just rang to say how much we're all missing you. I can't remember you not being here for Christmas, and we were looking forward to seeing you."

"You're very kind, Michael. I'm so sorry not to be there but it just couldn't be helped. Whether Boris Johnson really knows what he's doing is another matter entirely, but we do have to do as we're told."

"Of course we do. How are you getting on, Clare? Are you well?"

"I'm fine. Don't worry about me. Give my love to Sarah and the children, and wish them all a Happy Christmas from me. And thank you so much for ringing."

"Lovely to hear you. 'Bye for now."

"Goodbye, Michael."

A nice fellow. He was an old-world Tory squire, a JP, the MFH, county councillor, chairman of this and that in the neighbourhood. She disagreed with him about all kinds of things, and he no doubt thought she was practically a Marxist, but he was solid, reliable and very family-minded—his father, several years dead, was her first cousin so she wasn't even his aunt—all of which counted for a great deal.

At nearly three, telling herself that if she wanted to catch the last of the sun she should go out, and resolutely thinking of nothing but how cold it was going to be, she put on her coat, a scarf, her old fur-lined boots, her sham fur hat and warm gloves, and went down the stairs, because it was good for her to ignore the lift.

As she unlocked the gate in the wrought-iron fence of the garden, she saw he was there, on the bench, wearing a black mask, reading a book. She briefly panicked, almost turned the key back to lock the gate, thought for a moment that the only sensible thing was to vanish before he noticed her, and then pulled herself together. She heard in her head, as she often did, Simon's voice saying, "Let's not exaggerate".

She locked the gate behind her, put the key in her pocket and her hand back in its glove, and walked towards him neither fast nor slowly, telling herself she mustn't look too pleased to see him.

He looked up when she was ten yards away, closed his book, stood up, bent his head in his little bow as she approached, and said, "Good afternoon, Mrs Wilson, and a happy Christmas to you."

She smiled at the "Mrs Wilson" and let it go.

"A very happy Christmas to you too."

She sat down at the far end of the bench, as he had done

ten days ago, so that there was a respectable social distance between them.

He sat again, looking at her, she thought, as if she were a friend he hadn't seen for a long time, as if he were searching for signs of change, of aging, even perhaps of sadness. Then he pulled his mask down to under his chin and smiled. She hadn't forgotten his smile.

"And so we are both alone at Christmas. But to be alone is not unusual for me, and not unusual for you also?"

"Well, most of the time it's not unusual at all. But I don't think I've ever been alone at Christmas before. I was meant to travel to Yorkshire, in the north, to stay with my daughter and her husband, but—"

"But now no journeys are permitted. This is sad for you and also for your daughter."

He looked at her with kindness in his eyes.

"The stay in Yorkshire was what you told in your book, of last year's Christmas?"

She kept forgetting that he'd read her book: the fact that he had both read it and paid attention—perhaps he had re-read it after meeting her? - meant that he knew much more about her than she knew about him. She had, after all, met and talked to him once, only once. For a moment she thought it wasn't fair. But whose fault was it that the book existed?

"That's right. You've read my book very carefully."

"I read it slowly, because of my bad English, but carefully, yes, and in these days I have read it a second time."

There. She couldn't reply to this. He asked her a question, she thought to help her.

"Would your granddaughters also be with their parents, there to see you, at Christmas in Yorkshire?"

"No. Neither of them is in England. They're still at opposite sides of the world, partly because of their lives, what they're doing, but partly because they're stuck where they are on account of the Covid rules about travel. I wouldn't have seen them at Christmas even if I 'd been able to go to my daughter's."

She wanted to ask him if he had any grandchildren but one thing he'd said in their first, their only, conversation stopped her, though she couldn't remember exactly what it was. She had gathered that he had no family any more. That was all.

"I do not have a family", he said. "A family I did have, in my own country, my own city, but now I have no family."

"I'm so sorry. What—why—?" Damn. She saw she shouldn't have even begun a question.

His head was bent, his hands clasped in his lap.

"I cannot tell you. One day it is possible I can tell you, but not today."

One day, he had said. This meant—but she didn't allow herself to get as far as thinking through what this meant.

He raised his head, looked at her and said, "The names of your granddaughters—or maybe the names you have given them in your book—are Carrie and Daisy. Is that correct?"

She smiled, partly because they didn't know each other's names, yet, and it didn't matter.

"That's right."

"In the book they were in Canada and in Nepal. Are those countries where they are now?"

"That's right. How clever of you to remember. Daisy is a student in Canada, in Vancouver, as far away as can be. She seems to love Canada. Her sister's a couple of years older—but you'll remember that too from the book." She thought for a moment. "Carrie, Caroline really, is nearly twenty-four, and yes, she's still in Nepal."

"That is very far away also, and more difficult than Canada. Why is she still in Nepal? She was helping poor people, no? She is not climbing Mount Everest?"

She laughed. He was making this easy for her.

"Certainly not. Carrie is very good. She's working for—" She was going to say "an NGO", but realized she'd forgotten what the initials meant in time to say, "a charity. She went to Nepal originally, in the summer before last, to help rebuild villages ruined in the earthquake that happened five or six years ago. I can't remember exactly when, but thousands of people were killed. She loves the people and the mountains and so she stayed to teach some English in the village schools. Everyone everywhere wants to learn English still, however

71

badly England behaves. I suppose really because of America. It's like Latin was once. The language of power. Anyway, she was coming back in the summer and then she couldn't leave because of the pandemic, and now she's helping the people in the mountains to cope with all the difficulties."

She saw a wistful, almost dreamy, look in his eyes.

"You are very lucky to have such a granddaughter. But maybe she is very lucky to have such a grandmother."

She blushed, hoping he hadn't noticed. She wanted to say, "That's ridiculous, you don't know me at all." Instead she said, "Carrie has always made up her own mind about everything. And she's a kind girl."

"Exactly", he said.

She couldn't answer this.

He sat still for a moment, looking down at his clasped hands, and then raised his head, looked at her with serious eyes, and said:

"Are you afraid of the coronavirus?"

He said the word very precisely, in his foreign accent, as if the word itself had become a familiar of his mind.

She thought about his question, with the unexpected feeling that she hadn't thought about it before.

"Yes and no."

He laughed. "The English are good at 'yes and no'. *Sic et non*, like Abelard in the Middle Ages."

"Really? But Abelard wasn't English, was he?" She had the dimmest memory of Abelard and Heloise, a tragic love story; she couldn't remember when or where they lived but they must have been French.

"Not English at all. He was a scholar, a philosopher, a great man for argument, in twelfth-century Paris. He wrote a book called *Sic et non*, which the theologians thought was very dangerous. It is the sort of book that in communist or fascist countries is banned. You can't have yes *and* no in such countries. Only yes *or* no. Totalitarian: altogether yes or altogether no." He smiled, and went on, "I am sorry. We do not need to think of Abelard. I asked you about the coronavirus?"

There, again the precision. Now she tried to answer properly.

"I ought to be afraid of it. A young doctor who was staying with me at the beginning, in April, was working every day on the Covid wards at the hospital in the Fulham Road. She caught the virus and two weeks later she died. So I saw—Well, I saw how quickly it can overtake a person, and she was young."

"Ach—"He raised a hand to his mouth. "I remember, from your book. Ayesha, such a brave girl. I should not have asked the question. I am so sorry. That must have been very unhappy for you, and very frightening also. You could very easily have yourself become ill."

"I could, yes. Oddly enough, I wasn't frightened then. It was all too sudden, and too sad. The saddest thing was that I couldn't see her after they took her to the hospital, and the poor girl was by herself in a foreign country. You'll remember all this too. Her mother was dead, her father was thousands of miles away, and her boyfriend, young Hakim who you've seen in the garden, was in Libya and we couldn't reach him. I'm sure the doctors and nurses in the hospital did their best, as she'd been doing herself, looking after dying patients, but all the protective stuff, the mask and gloves and overalls—you can't see even if a person is smiling. It's not like someone you love holding your hand."

"No. It is not. But if a person is already alone—"

His eyes had darkened.

"It would be better", he said, as if it were a conclusion he had already come to, a familiar thought, "to die quickly I think, a heart attack, a stroke. That would be better. Like your friend, Doctor Rose."

David's death, of course in the book. A blessing no doubt for him. She also remembered what this stranger had told her about how he came to live in his house in the mews.

"And your friend", she said, "how did he die?" Should she have asked this? But his friend had died many years ago, so probably he could talk about him.

"It was slow, until in the last weeks it was quick. By then he was in hospital. But it was cancer, his illness, so I could not take, excuse me, I could not catch it from him. I would not become ill because he was ill. This meant that there were no

73

masks or gloves when he was still in the house. He did have pain, but there were many drugs. A nurse did come to the house, in the morning and in the evening, to help me. It was difficult, yes. But maybe it was not so bad as the coronavirus, when one cannot breathe."

"Yes. We must be careful, both of us. But soon we shall have the second vaccine because we're old, and then we'll be safer."

"It is reasonable to be afraid of an unpleasant death, do you think? But it is not reasonable to be afraid to die, to be afraid to be dead, when I am old already, as you say? Do you think?"

There was a plea in his voice.

She felt a kind of weight that she should try to lift, or try to help him to lift.

"I think you're quite right", after a minute she said. "It probably isn't reasonable to be afraid to be dead. But it's not easy to be reasonable about our own death, or really perhaps our own dying, even when, or perhaps specially when we're nearly at the end of the time we've been given."

He was looking as if he hadn't quite understood this. She struggled on.

"It's the not knowing that's difficult, isn't it? Not knowing when, or how, or whether, if it's the virus or horrible cancer, we will manage to be brave enough, when there is a lot of pain, or when it's difficult to breathe."

She watched him thinking about this.

He shook his head. "No", he said, and she saw that this didn't fit with the question he thought he'd asked her.

"Brave enough for what?" he said. "For who? Who will care, who will know, if we are brave at the end?"

"We will know. That's why perhaps we should practise."

"No one can practise to die."

"No. Not exactly practise to die. But we can practise accepting, accepting being old, being unable to do things we could do when we were younger, above all accepting loss because loss happens." She thought of Matt, and how many years it had taken her to accept his death, not to be angry every time she remembered what had happened to him, the amateur roadside bomb in Helmand province. The folly of the government

74

keeping soldiers in Afghanistant long after the people who had organized 9.11 had gone, and neglecting Afghanistan because of invading Iraq. Neither need have happened. As the years had gone by and things in Afghanistan had got worse rather than better, Matt's death seemed more and more nothing but loss, waste, his seriousness and funniness gone pointlessly into absence. But what good was it, to Matt or to her, for her to be angry, with wars and governments, with Tony Blair and President Bush and the war on terror going on and on and making so many countries more dangerous, when Matt was safe with God? This she tried always to hold on to, and mostly succeeded. Then she thought again of David, his death a loss but a gentle loss, of an old man who had died so quickly he could have known nothing. And he also was safe with God. Lucky David. Blessed David.

She wanted to say, "We can practise putting things into the hands of God because we aren't ourselves strong enough to carry them", but she didn't dare. She didn't know him well enough. The word "God" might push him away from her for good, so that this might become the last as well as only the second conversation they ever had. Really, she told herself to try to remember, she didn't know him at all.

"Death happens. Is that what you mean? If there is no one left"—he looked at her steadily, his blue eyes intense—"if there is almost no one left—I am sorry—to know us, to understand who we might be, who we have been, then our death only happens. It does not matter. Is that what you would say?"

She didn't have the confidence to pick up and hold on to the implication of what he'd said, it seemed by mistake, and apologized for, so she answered his last question.

"No. I would never say that our death doesn't matter, because that would be like saying that our life doesn't matter, our years and days and hours, however many of them we have forgotten, and what we are, how what we have been in all those years has made us what we are—we know that they matter, that we matter, don't we?"

Why couldn't she say things more clearly? But perhaps he had understood.

"Do we know this? Do you know this? I did know this once. I used to be sure. When I had work that needed to be done, then I was sure. I cared too much, maybe, for my work in Sarajevo but I could not doubt that the work did matter. Even in Wrocław, though I was not important in the library, I had only what was left of the German library to care for, but I knew that my work did matter, that there had been too much loss before, in Wrocław and in Lwów. Even in London the work I did was not important but to me it did matter. When I first came, after my friend died, I was lucky to be given a job in a bookshop where they sold books in many European languages. I had enough work every day for me to think I was needed. Now—I am old, of course, and I am not needed, by anyone, so—if I die of the coronavirus, if I cannot breathe and I am afraid, it will not be important to anyone. Will it?"

She wanted to say that it would be important to her, but she couldn't. If she was ever going to be able to say such a thing, and perhaps she wasn't, it was much too soon. So—God?

He said, "You did say, didn't you? 'however many of them we have forgotten'. What did you mean when you said this? If we have forgotten what we have said, what we have done, most of all what we have thought and not said, then all these things are altogether forgotten. Not so?"

That was exactly like her father. "Not so?" Because it was almost German.

"Well, perhaps not."

She tried to remember exactly what he had told her about his complicated family, with the three religions, Judaism, Christianity, Islam. There had been huge chasms between them and sometimes, including now in some places, which seemed to include his home since the wars, murderous hatreds across the chasms. But he had told her how the differences between them had not been a problem in the Sarajevo of the past. And not because nobody cared any more: hadn't he said that both his grandmothers, one Jewish and one Catholic, were serious about religion? So he had been brought up with at least a sense that for some people God was there, was essential to their lives, had not been killed. "God is dead and we have killed him" was what, with a note of victory, of triumph, her nice, kind, clever but entirely secular husband Simon had thought. Did this old man with a past she'd hardly begun to understand agree with Simon? Perhaps she couldn't go any further, talking to him, without finding out.

"Do you believe", she said, "that God, the God of Jews and Christians and Muslims, is real, is there somewhere, somehow, and knows us, each of us?"

He spread his hands wide apart, as if welcoming someone. He had known, she could tell, that this was where their conversation was leading. That was a start.

Then he smiled and said, "Yes and no."

She smiled back.

"But—", she began.

"I am sorry. The question is serious. Not a question for a joke or for an answer too clever, as Abelard was. Yes, sometimes, on some days, I do believe that God is, that God is there, as you say. On these days, when I start, like every day, being quite sure I do not believe, I cannot all the same make myself believe that the people I loved, I love, have gone, altogether gone. My wife, my boys, my father who I do not remember clearly, my mother who I do not remember at all, my grandmother, who I loved and who was disappointed by me: have they gone for ever into nothing as if they had never lived? If God is not real, they have gone, like the flame of the match a person blows out when he has lit his cigarette. For two or three seconds there is a flame, then, for another second, a scent of burning, then nothing, a little piece of wood, like the bones of a man or a woman, or the ash they give you after a person has been cremated, to be thrown away. I did not know what to do with the ash they gave me after my friend was burnt at the crematorium, which is a horrible word. It is in my house because still I do not know."

He looked at her, but not as if he were expecting her to answer.

"I cannot believe this, that the ash, the blown-out match, is all. So this is *Sic*. This is yes. There is somewhere where is God, where the souls of the dead rest in peace. But most days, *Non*, no. Most days it is too difficult to believe. I have read the books that show that it is not rational to believe that God is real, that we are better because we have left God behind in the past where people were ignorant and uneducated and believed in God to make things seem more fair, more just, when nothing is just and nothing is fair. Most days I agree with these books."

"I do know how difficult it is."

He seemed not to have heard this.

"Look at the world. It is not just. It is not fair. People are cruel and greedy and lazy and other people suffer and have to leave their homes and die, in wars and not in wars. Look at Syria now, and Yemen. Children are dying of hunger. Britain, a rich, rich country,"—he raised his arm in a wide gesture that took in the settled prosperity of the square and the Gloucester Road and Prince Albert's museums beyond—"says it cannot afford to send food into Yemen to save the children from dying while it is selling aeroplanes to Saudi Arabia for much money and Saudi Arabia is using those aeroplanes to bomb the hospitals and the villages in Yemen."

He looked across the space between them with pain in his eyes, and went on:

"In Sarajevo there was a hospital for old people. The Serbs shelled it. The old people who were still alive were frightened and some were mad and they were taken to a school for little children where the chairs and tables were too small for them and then the Serbs shelled the school also."

"How horrible", she said. Again he couldn't stop.

"It is not surprising that people have always wanted God to be there so that somewhere there is justice."

Something had happened to his English. He was speaking more fluently, more correctly, than usual. Was it because he'd thought about all this before? He must have, of course, either by himself, or with his friend who had died. Or with someone else. Again she thought she must try to remember that she had talked to him only once before. She didn't know him, at all.

"There were terrible things also when I was a child but I could not, I do not, remember them. I had not seen them, or maybe I had been too young. I could not remember my mother and her parents being taken away. And my father—I do remember him laughing and joking and throwing me up in the air and catching me. He smelt of cigarettes. But he was somewhere in the mountains when he was killed and I was already with my grandmother. She protected me and taught me so that when I was young I did not bother to think about God. I accepted God and did not think. No *Sic et non.* First one, you could say, and then the other. My grandmother went to Mass on Sundays and taught me to say prayers by my bed at night and sent me to a nuns' school to learn to read and write, and the nuns told us all about God and Jesus and the Virgin Mary. 'She will look after us', they said. 'Every prayer to her is answered.' So I believed. Yes. *Sic.* But once I was old enough to go to the Gymnasium I did leave God and Jesus and the Virgin Mary behind with the nuns. I could see that the prayers to the Virgin Mary were not answered. Also I knew that the Catholics, the Croats, had helped the Nazis to murder the Jews. So they were not even good. I could not say to my grandmother this, any of this. But my friends and I, we did not care. It did not seem important to ask the question. So I did not believe. *Non.* This was the 1950s. Do you remember the 1950s?"

"Yes I do. I was at school too." She had been far too deep in the classics, in Virgil whom she loved even more than she loved Shakespeare, and in struggling to get her Greek up to the standard of her Latin, to bother about God. She thought of herself as too grown-up to believe in God, and said to the other girls in her class that she was an atheist, which sounded impressive and might have shocked them if they had ever heard the word before.

"Perhaps it was a little the same in England. The war was over, the Germans had gone—I know that there were never any Germans in England—and the empires had gone a long time ago, at the end of the Great War. Not yours but ours. We were fortunate. If we had believed that God was there, we would have thanked God that we had Tito and not Stalin. Things were getting better. Even my grandmother, who had many things to make her sad, told me I was lucky to be alive now. She told me how good it was that Tito, unlike Stalin, unlike the Soviet communists, did not turn the churches into museums or close the mosques. He did not like religion and he said he would remove it from Yugoslavia but he did not do it, at least in Sarajevo. As a boy he was a Catholic, like me. The synagogues had gone, of course, with the Jews."

He stopped. She scarcely breathed. After a pause when she feared he couldn't go on, he said, "With my mother. And her parents. I must have met my Jewish grandparents. I was a baby, a little boy, two or three. I do not remember them."

She might have reached out a hand to him. But he was too far away, at the other end of the bench. Probably just as well.

"The Germans left only ashes where Jewish buildings and Torah scrolls and books had been. As the Serbs left only ashes where my library had been. Ashes like the ashes of the Jewish people who were burnt when they had been gassed. I don't know where they took them. My grandmother after the war did try to discover. There were officials. There were some lists. But it was not possible."

He stopped, and looked at her, she thought to see if he had said too much, if he was upsetting her, or perhaps boring her. Was she even still awake?

"I'm very sorry", he said. "I talk so little in my days that now I talk too much."

"No. Not at all. It's a terrible story, all the way back to when you were a small child. Really terrible, and I'm so sorry. But I'm glad to listen." Was this all right? "Your country is a world I know almost nothing about. Please go on."

"Are you sure?"

"Please."

"If you are glad to listen, as you say."

She smiled and he said, "You are kind to me."

He took a deep breath. "So", he said. This was an old German beginning, not the current BBC mannerism. Her father also used to use "so" in the same way. "So. Full stop." was how it sounded. Like "Not so?" with its question mark.

"So. After the nuns there was the Gymnasium. The Habsburgs, you understand. A proper German kind of education they had left us. And the Habsburg Gymnasium was for all the religions. It always had been since it was given to the city. No one even asked. That was old Sarajevo."

He sighed deeply, without looking at her, took another long breath, and went on.

"And all we wished, my friends at the Gymnasium and I myself, was to be modern, to watch American films, to hope that one day we would be able to wear blue jeans like James Dean. He was dead very young—somehow we admired this. Why? Who knows? Do you remember the films of that time? There was a film called *Rebel without a Cause*: we wanted to be free and wild and fall in love on the streets like James Dean in Los Angeles. But Sarajevo was not Los Angeles. By no means. It was sad perhaps, after the war, but it was not wild, and not modern. It was what the French call correct. We were very silly, rebels without a cause indeed. And also I remember, quite different, there was *High Society*, the film I liked best. I watched it three times in the same week: Grace Kelly and Frank Sinatra and very rich people and—what was his name? The other singer?"

"Bing Crosby." They had shown the film on a Sunday night at her boarding school, and she and a hundred other teenage girls had thought it the most romantic thing they had ever seen.

"Exactly. This was even more silly. You understand? Blue jeans and chewing gum, and at the same time trying to be charming the girls like Frank Sinatra by the swimming pool. How did we have time to think about God?"

"Most adolescents at any time don't think about God."

"Is this true? I expect you know. You were a teacher, Mrs Wilson, weren't you? I learnt from your book."

"I was, yes."

"Students, not boys in school but students at university, think about God, or some of them do. I know this from books. I did not. I was a student in Belgrade. When I was eighteen, nineteen, I can't exactly remember, my friend Vladko and I decided that Sarajevo was provincial—this was one of our favourite words for what was boring, what was home, you understand we thought we were very sophisticated, very French, though we knew nothing about France—so we should escape. I should escape my grandmother and her wanting me to go to Mass on Sundays. Vladko wanted to escape his parents because they argued with each other about what Vladko should do, should be, and he wanted to be a painter which they thought was stupid and he would not make any money. There was no art school then in Sarajevo, so we went to Belgrade. Vladko became a student at the Belgrade Arts Academy and I started as a law student at the university. My grandmother wanted me to be a lawyer like my father, and I had no idea of my own what to be. But the law was very dull and difficult, and I loved books, not law books but real books, so after one year I changed to a literature course, which very much worried my grandmother. I read German and some Russian literature, in German, and then I found I could afterwards be trained to be a librarian, still at the university in Belgrade."

"And God?"

"Still no God. Not even the question about God. This was my fault. I was busy, so I was too lazy to ask the question. Busy or lazy. They can be the same. Also it was the fault of Belgrade. You have not visited Belgrade?"

"No. I'm afraid I haven't been to anywhere in Yugoslavia."

"It is too late now, too late for Yugoslavia. Possibly it is also too late for you?"

"Much too late. I can't imagine going abroad now. Airports I dislike very much and they're bound to be worse than ever because of the virus. And Brexit, wretched Brexit."

"Certainly it is too late for me—to go back. Back is where no one can go. Is not this true?"

She felt the chill of this. But he returned them to ordinary memory.

"In any case, Belgrade always was a difficult city; for me now it is nearly all a bad memory only. There was, for two months, a very pretty girl."

He smiled and shook his head.

"For two months only."

"One doesn't forget", she said.

"Never mind, as the English say. They don't mean never mind anything. They mean don't mind any longer, what it was that you once did mind. Ach—"

He shook his head again, and regained his grip on his voice.

"Belgrade is old, a very old city, a Roman city. It has been in too many wars. Only the Serbs are its history since the Romans, and the Serbs have been in and out of empires and foreign rule, Byzantines, Hungarians, Ottomans, Habsburgs, more Hungarians, and always Russians shadowing all the others as if they would wish the Serbs to be Russian. The Serbs didn't like to be in the Byzantine empire. They didn't like at all to be in the Ottoman empire: their most famous battle, which they write about and sing about and make political speeches about for ever, was not a victory but a defeat, by the Ottomans, a long, long time ago. And least of all they liked the Habsburg empire, which had occupied Serbia a few times for a few years over the centuries but Serbia was still outside it even when Vienna had been waiting for so long to replace Istanbul. In 1918 it was too late for Vienna and so Serb princes and kings and assassinations went on until Hitler, and then there was Tito and communism. The Serbs, so often beaten, have been proud and fierce through all this subject life—what is the English word? Subjection. That is the word—since they came from wherever they came from, central Asia no doubt, and now they are Christian nationalists of a very cruel kind."

"They've always been Christian, surely?"

"They have always been Christians, yes, since they were pagans converted by missionaries from Constantinople. The Serbian Church is itself alone, very proud, not liking to obey anybody who is not a Serb. It never liked to accept any Greek authority, or any Russian authority—and now the Russian patriarch is naturally much more powerful than the Greek one in Istanbul—and still they do not. The Serbian Church, more than Tito's socialist government, when I was a student made Belgrade not friendly to Jews or Catholics, and I was half a Jew and partly a Catholic, and even more unpopular partly a Muslim, and now it is far worse. The Serbian church put itself alongside Milosevic for national unity and power, as the Russian church has put itself alongside Putin who pretends to be a faithful Christian."

"I had no idea—"

"I am sorry. Why do I tell you all this, and on Christmas Day when you are a good Catholic?"

"When I should have been to church, I know. I did follow a Christmas Mass on my laptop. It's not the same but it's better than nothing."

This wasn't what he'd meant when he apologized.

So she went on, "It's all right. Everything you're telling me - it's so interesting, because I had no idea—"

She couldn't say exactly what she had no idea of, but it didn't matter. He couldn't stop now.

"I tell you this to show that when I was a student in Belgrade God belonged to the Serbian church and was nothing to do with a young student from Sarajevo who was trying, and failing I must say, to learn the law, and then trying, and now succeeding at least a little, to read many books in the languages I knew and even could learn. This was enough. I stayed away from all religions."

She looked at him. She could see he wanted her to respond. She thought for a moment.

"I think you mean you stayed away from churches and mosques. And I don't suppose there'd have been many syna-gogues left in Belgrade after Hitler's war. But what about the books you were reading? In my long life I've often found that something in a book has made me stop and think—think about God, perhaps, and whether only God can make sense of some-thing I've read which is describing something I've known or partly known myself."

She had put this clumsily. She saw him trying to under-stand properly what she had meant to say, and muddled into an unnecessary complexity when the point was simple.

He thought for a minute and then he said, "I was reading so many books when I was young. But you are quite right. I do remember—in one book—I think what you say is called in Arabic *Taqwa*. It is a Muslim word for knowing God is there."

He sat absolutely still, his head bent, his eyes closed, for so long that she wondered whether he had fallen asleep. Then he raised his head, looked at her, and said, "Did you read *Doctor Zhivago*, all those years ago when you also were young, when both of us were young?"

"Yes, I did. When I was still at school. Wonderful, it was." Into her head came the music of the film, Julie Christie's face in a fur hat, the rats flopping out of the room where Zhivago found her in the country. She shook her head to banish all this. He was remembering the book, not the film.

"I read the book when I was a student in Belgrade. I have not thought of it for many years, but what you say—the questions and the answer—something like what you say, I remember now, I think I remember."

She was surprised.

"Was it allowed, in Yugoslavia, the book? There was such a fuss in Russia about Pasternak and the Nobel Prize, wasn't there?"

This was all a dim memory from so long ago: she wasn't sure what had happened.

"More than a fuss", he said. "It helped to kill Pasternak. The Soviets persecuted him over the prize so that his spirit was broken. Two years later he died. But Tito was not censoring books by enemies of the Russian state, enemies of Stalin. Not at all. In his way he had been an enemy of Stalin himself. And we knew, some of us who were studying literature knew, that *Doctor Zhivago* was defending us, each of us one by one, against not only Stalin but Tito also, against Communism which counts people in hundreds of thousands, not one by one. First I tried to read the book in French. But then there was a German translation which was easier. The real, Russian, book came only later."

He thought again.

"Boris Pasternak was a Jew, you know, a Jew who is moving towards believing, what exactly? Believing that Jesus, a Jew like him, was also as Christians say, the son of God? Perhaps he was truly the son of God?"

As the centurion said at the foot of the cross, she thought and didn't say.

"And if he was, if he is, everything is changed. Do you remember that there are signs in the book of this?"

"No. I'm afraid I don't. I read it a very long time ago, probably not very carefully."

She wished she could forget the images and, worse, the tune, from the film. She wished she'd paid more attention to the book all those years ago. But it didn't matter because still he couldn't stop talking.

"Zhivago is not a Jew. But one of his friends is a Jew. His name is Misha, yes, Misha. Misha Gordon. As a boy he has all the difficulties that Jews have, everywhere, and also in Russia. There is a place in the book where Misha says that Jesus offered very quietly a new kind of world where there are no nations but only persons. The offer was so quiet that almost nobody did hear it, and lots of Jews, lots of Christians have ever since the time of Jesus never heard it. I am not certain that Misha in the book says all this but he does say that Jesus, if people had noticed what he was saying, would have changed everything. I have never forgotten this because it seemed so important when I read it. And it seemed to account for—to make reasonable and good—the way my family and many people in Sarajevo treated each other, not as parts of nations but as persons. Do you understand?"

"I think so. Now, yes, I understand. I'm afraid I didn't notice in the book what you say about Jews and Christians."

"One Jew. That is the point. Or two perhaps. Misha and Pasternak. At the very end of the book, after Dr Zhivago is dead, Misha Gordon is still alive and he and another friend—I do not remember his name—are in Moscow, with a book, and the book is Zhivago's book, the book we are ourselves reading at this moment, and they have a kind of hope for the future because of the book."

She had forgotten that too. The book inside the book. Like hers. She smiled but he didn't notice.

"I'm afraid" she said, "I remember mostly the love story—I was very young when I read it, fifteen or sixteen—and also I do remember the horrors of the civil war in Russia. There. Another civil war. The worst kind of war, as you said the other day, when we first talked."

He nodded and gave her a long look.

"Yes", he said. "Our first talk."

He nodded gently and then shook his head more vigorously,

to banish some thought?

"Do you remember the poems?"

"The poems?"

"Dr Zhivago's poems."

"O, I see. No. I'm sorry. I don't remember any poems in the book."

"They are printed at the end of the book, or so long ago they were. They are called 'Zhivago's poems' so that we should think they are the poems Zhivago wrote when he was lost in the snow, in deep Russia, in a house with only Lara. So it was the best time of his whole life. The poems are very beautiful. To hear how beautiful they are you need to read the Russian. Are you able to read Russian?"

Again she had to remember that they were still almost total strangers.

"No. Not a word, I'm afraid. I don't know even the alphabet."

"Why would you know Russian? Never mind, again."

He smiled.

"The poems, you understand, or some of the poems, are Christian. You will see, if you look at them, although only in English. The last is the best. It is called 'Gethsemane.'"

"Really?"

"Really. I wish I could remember the poem to say it for you. Most of it is the story of Gethsemane. Jesus is in the garden. He is afraid. His friends are asleep. People come to arrest him. But the end of the poem is a miracle. Death and resurrection of course. And Jesus becomes the judge in glory, the Pantocrator high in the dome of an Orthodox church."

She felt ashamed.

"I wish I'd paid more attention when I read the book. But I wasn't a Christian myself in those days so I probably wouldn't have noticed the poem." Actually she would, she knew, have dismissed the Christian poems and anything else suggesting Christianity in the novel as not for her, no longer interesting, part of a world intelligent, educated people had left behind with childhood because nowadays it belonged only to people like her Nanny, who had taught her to kneel by her bed and say her prayers and used to take her to Sunday School in the church at the end of their road in Kensington. A clever, arrogant, opinionated schoolgirl: that's what she was when she read *Doctor Zhivago*. A child who knew quite a lot for her age but almost nothing about anything that matters.

"Do you have a copy of *Doctor Zhivago* in your flat? Probably you have very many books."

This was a guess, based on his reading of her book, an accurate guess.

"I do have many books, yes. But *Doctor Zhivago* after all these years—I'm not sure."

"Will you look for him, when you go home?"

She smiled.

"Yes, of course I will."

"You know", he said, standing up. "It is soon dark, and it is too cold. You are cold by now, Mrs Wilson?"

She shifted, realized she had been sitting still all this time, and realized how cold and stiff she was. She leant heavily on the arm of the bench to stand up.

"Yes. It's cold, and getting dark, as you say."

Should she or shouldn't she invite him for a cup of tea? She said, without even deciding, "Would you like to have a cup of tea in my flat? It's just across the road."

He looked at her with surprise, and pleasure she thought, and smiled his thanks.

"Thank you, Mrs Wilson. You are kind to invite me. But—"

He pulled his mask up over his mouth and nose.

"But it is too soon, I think. We should follow the rules today, yes?"

He seemed suddenly, again, a stranger, and his accent had returned.

She was both disappointed and relieved.

"Yes. I'm sure you're right. Another day, perhaps?"

"Another day, yes. Thank you. And thank you for your listening to me. It is my Christmas present."

His little bow, and he was walking away across the frosty grass.

She looked at her watch. Almost an hour, they had been sitting on the bench. No wonder she was cold. And he hadn't even had any gloves, or a hat. At least he had a scarf that looked warm though it had seen better days. An expression of Nanny's that meant what it said. Perhaps there was no one to give him a new scarf for Christmas.

And "too soon"? Too soon for the coronavirus? Or too soon for what?

CHAPTER 5

CHRISTMAS DAY 2020

Back in her flat, grateful for the warmth which she felt gradually thawing her stiffness and coldness after she had with some difficulty taken off her coat, hat, scarf, gloves and boots, the boots particularly hard to pull off.

She was getting old, she thought, waiting for the kettle to boil. She got stiff more quickly, and cold more quickly, than she did even quite a short time ago, and it took her longer to recover from both. What would she do if she found she actually couldn't pull off her boots? Wait, obviously, till she thawed? Buy new boots, with a zip? Carry on, in other words, as long as she could.

Old, yes, but also stupid?

She had invited to tea, invited to come into her flat and sit at her kitchen table, a man whose name she didn't know and who she had talked to today for only the second time. Penny would have been horrified. But she knew by now that he was who he said he was, that he could be trusted, that he wasn't going to look round her flat for what he might steal, or ask her for money.

How did she know? She knew.

But at the same time she was grateful to him for saying no to her invitation. He was right: it was too soon. But if they met again, talked again, in the garden of the square, perhaps once or twice more, it would be all right, it would be natural and not awkward in any way, for him to come to tea. Tea, so useful, so English. Not a drink, not a meal. Just tea.

It had indeed been getting dark when they'd left the bench. Now, at just after four, it looked from indoors completely dark outside. With her mug of tea in her hand she closed the curtains in the kitchen, in the sitting room, in her bedroom, and stood still in the middle of her bedroom wondering where in the flat she might have kept, unlooked-at for decades, the copy of *Doctor Zhivago* she'd read when she was still at school. Not in here. There was an old bookcase in her bedroom where she kept the classical texts of her long teaching life, Homer and Virgil and the Greek tragedies, Herodotus, Thucydides, three or four of the easier dialogues of Plato, the other Latin poets children were sometimes set to read, Catullus and Horace, and the Ovid she had always avoided when she could, some Caesar and Livy and Tacitus, some Cicero speeches. There they were, in Greek and Latin and English translations, with, sticking up from their pages, a forest of slips of paper marking passages for one reason or another. Many of these slips of paper had a word or two visible, written in the red ink of the schoolteacher. How much of all that these books represented would the children she'd taught, now no doubt parents if not grandparents themselves, remember? A little perhaps might be remembered by most of them, a few scraps of ancient history, a dim sense of something conjured up by a name: Plato. Tacitus. That was all one could hope for. But a few more of them might perhaps remember, if not much that was specific, the atmosphere of fate and loss and doomed beauty in Virgil or the elegance of Horace's sharp little poems or the intellectual crackle of listening to Cicero brilliantly holding forth in court (or, as she used to tell her classes, reading the brilliant sentences he might have delivered in court on a good day).

She knelt down to take out her old copy of Thucydides in Greek and her old brown and white Penguin Classics translation by Rex Warner, such a help with the seriously difficult Greek. "Clare Feldmann September 1957" was written inside, by her, aged fifteen, in unfamiliar handwriting. A folded piece of paper fell out of the book: a copy, made by her on some long-ago Xerox machine that could do only purple lines, of a map of the battle of Sphacteria. A few boys from those classrooms of twenty or thirty years ago might remember the map, as she had always done, and be surprised to discover years later, as she had been, that Navarino Bay was also where the French and the British had sunk the Ottoman fleet in 1828 to help the Greeks. And if they did, so what? As Simon had been too kind to say, though his attitude to her work always implied the question.

As for her, the Battle of Navarino was one of the very few things she remembered about the crumbling of the Ottoman empire in the nineteenth century. She must ask him, her new friend—was this the right phrase? Possibly. But can you think of someone as a friend when you don't know his name?—to explain more about Yugoslavia and the Ottoman empire. Hadn't Yugoslavia been invented because the Ottoman empire had collapsed after World War One? Was that what he had already more or less told her? Or had she got that all wrong?

She looked again at the map in her hands. The faded purple outline reminded her of all the exam papers she had typed, laboriously to avoid mistakes, and Xeroxed for her classes. How remote and strange that pre-computer world of type-writers and purple ink seemed now. She folded the map and returned it to the place it had come from in her *History of the Peloponnesian War*. The Penguin Classics of her child-hood she had loved and collected, brown and white for Greek books, purple and white for Latin. She still had all those she had bought. On the back of *The Peloponnesian* War was a small round price sticker. Three and six. Then she put both books back in the shelf and, with a considerable effort, holding on to the bookcase with one hand and pushing hard on the floor with the other, stood up. Kneeling on the floor had almost become something she could no longer do.

Doctor Zhivago wasn't going to be in her bedroom. He cer-tainly wasn't going to be in Simon's study, with the economics books, the sociology and politics books, or the neat pile of his own reference books and archaeological journals that Hakim had left on the little table beside the desk. Meaning that he would come back.

Might it be somewhere in the shelves in the sitting room? Perhaps.

As she peered at the shelves, she found she remembered the look of the book: the dust jacket was blue and yellow in squares or rectangles, with a black and white photograph of Pasternak on the back. Max Hayward and someone else, whose name she'd forgotten, were the translators. What a weird thing memory was: she can't have thought of *Doctor Zhivago* for years and years, and yet somewhere among the tangle of a million tiny connections in the brain, which she didn't understand at all, was this clear picture, when she needed it. No wonder someone as intelligent as St Augustine had found the memory a wonder to be explored fifteen centuries ago. And wasn't it a mystery no better understood now than then?

Where was the wretched book? And was it likely to have kept its dust jacket all this time, sixty-three years? She couldn't find it anywhere in the sitting room, though she looked as carefully as she could along all the shelves. Perhaps it had lost its dust jacket; she couldn't remember anything at all about the binding of the book.

Penny's room. That might be the answer. She had at some point decades ago when Penny was a teenager who never seemed to read any books except best-sellers by Jilly Cooper and Joanna Trollope—their books regarded as tosh by Clare who had never read any of them—sorted out some great but easily readable novels to tempt Penny into raising her sights a bit.

Penny's room was very cold, with the unfresh smell of a room no one had been into for a long time. There was no point in turning on the radiator, which anyway probably wouldn't work. She might have opened the window if she hadn't known it was even colder outside. She did close the deplorably dirty curtains: she should take them down and wash them. One stuck. She tugged at it and as it shifted a dead spider and two dead flies tangled together fell to the floor with a faint tap. She must try to remember to wash the curtains.

The room had for years been a store room for old stuff vaguely awaiting possible great-grandchildren: a folded-up playpen, a cot taken apart, a high chair, Penny's rocking horse and a dolls' house Daisy at four had much loved. All these things were left from Penny's and Matt's childhood, practically antiques now, though there was a pushchair from the days when Carrie and Daisy were toddlers. And, yes, once she'd pulled the pieces of the cot into the middle of the room and leant them against the rocking horse, there was the bookcase, only a yard wide, with three shelves. On top of it was a wooden

Fisher Price clock which Penny's godmother had brought back from New York in, probably, 1970 when Penny was one. You wound it up with a big wheel at the back which a small child could manage and a picture with numbers revolved slowly at the front while the musical box inside played "The clock stopped never to go again when the old man died". She wound it up, and it worked still, as perfectly as on the day it arrived. No baby or toddler she had ever had in the flat had failed to enjoy this clock, and none had stopped it working.

The books. She put the clock back and knelt to look, on one knee this time, to make it easier to get up. The top shelf held girls' books from the past. She had enjoyed them more than Penny had. They were mostly American, *Little Women* and the three that followed, *What Katy Did* and the rest of them, *Anne of Green Gables* and a few more. One or two English stories, *The Secret Garden*, *The Children of the New Forest*. A lot of pony stories, Penny's favourites, and a few school stories filled the middle shelf, but there—this was what she'd hoped to find—on the bottom shelf was a mixed collection of really good but not difficult novels she had moved there out of the over-crowded shelves in the sitting room, hoping Penny might be tempted to try something of real quality. *Emma* and *Pride and Prejudice* as small hardbacks, Oxford classics she had bought herself when she was at school, then a number of Penguins, *The Great Gatsby*, *A Passage to India*, *Cider with Rosie*, *The Pursuit of Love*, *Animal Farm*, some Maigret stories, a little notebook-sized edition of *A Shropshire Lad*, hardback copies of *Le grand Meaulnes* and *The Leopard* and, yes, at the end of the shelf, Russia: more Penguins, *The Captain's Daughter*, *The Cossacks*, *Fathers and Sons*, *Home of the Gentry*, some Chekhov stories, *One Day in the Life of Ivan Denisovich*, and, last in the row, a dull red hardback without its jacket, *Doctor Zhivago*. All the books were very dusty. Those on the bottom shelf, she was pretty sure, hadn't been touched since she put them there more than thirty years ago. She was pleased to see them again, and pleased with her choice, specially her choice of the Russian novels: no daunting whoppers hundreds of pages long, but wonderful books, all of them. Anyone of sixteen or seventeen who read his or her way through the books on this shelf would be well set up as a literate person.

Then she realized that the phrase shouldn't be "would be" but "would have been": didn't her choice of these books now belong to an unrecoverable past?

She saw how all of them, if Penny had ever opened them— when? In the mid-1980s—would have struck her as hopelessly old-fashioned. And as for Carrie, a bright girl born at the end of the twentieth century, with starred A-levels and a good degree, she probably wouldn't have known the names of any of their authors. Except for Jane Austen, though even the famous moment of Colin Firth and the wet shirt on the television had happened before Carrie was born.

Kneeling by the bookcase, very cold again, she felt break over her a wave of sadness that brought tears to her eyes and to the back of her throat. These books, nothing more than an almost random collection of books she loved and had, one day long ago, chosen to put in here hoping that Penny might read one or two, represented so much to her: her own adolescence, her learning to read properly, with attention and imagination, discovering the people in these books, their lives and places, the ways they talked and felt. To her, and to how many others, in this brittle new world? Only to the old. She read the *Observer* every Sunday, because she always had and because the news and comment part of the paper was always interesting, often impassioned in a way she found thoroughly sympathetic, and the articles usually well written. But every Sunday it took her more and more pages of the Review section of the paper, twenty, twenty-five, thirty pages, to reach anything, usually a normal book review, which she could even understand, let alone get anything out of.

The sadness that had washed over her like a wave was now withdrawing back and back: she could hear the drag of the pebbles on the beach. In the incomprehensible world of 2021 these poor old books were no more than relics, stones and broken shells, old bits of wood, drying seaweed, left on the shore by a rapidly receding tide. She thought of Matthew Arnold on Dover beach and his "melancholy, long, withdrawing roar", the "eternal note of sadness" of the end of something. The end of faith. That was what Arnold was mourning.

He hadn't been right about that. Faith had survived. When did he write the poem? In the middle of the nineteenth century. Almost two hundred years ago now, and faith had not died, though many people wished it had and more and more people, at least more and more people only Christian because belonging to no other religion, entirely neglected it. But whatever this little shelf of books represented had died, or had almost died. Hadn't Matthew Arnold hoped, even expected, that "the best that has been said and thought" would sustain the soul and replace the no longer believable constructions of faith that the receding tide had broken, carrying the debris far away into darkness? Wasn't there once a kind of liberal consensus of confidence that this would be so? Hadn't she herself, the arrogant teenager who said she was an atheist, thought that some imprecise combination of personal relationships and beautiful writing was all that was needed to see a person through the problems and sadness of life, of which, at sixteen, she had not the slightest experience? Was this what this little row of books she had, in vain, put temptingly in Penny's room represented? If so, was knowledge of them well lost?

Absolutely not. Why not? She decided to see later whether she could answer this question.

With considerable difficulty—even kneeling on only one knee was no longer a straightforward proposition and again she had to hold on to the top of the bookcase with one hand, though it wobbled, and press hard on the floor with the other to get herself upright—she stood uncertainly, regained her balance, and then had to bend down, one hand still on the bookcase, to extract *Doctor Zhivago* from the bottom shelf. She opened the curtains before turning out the light and took the book, which suddenly seemed very precious, into the kitchen, warm and friendly after the bleakness of Penny's room, and sat down at the table.

She blew at the dust on the top of the book's pages, but her breath wasn't enough and she had to get up, open the book and clap it shut, producing a little cloud of dust, and then clean the whole book carefully with a slightly damp washing-up sponge. The dust came off in lumps and she threw away the sponge. Inside the front cover was, again, her own signature: Clare Feldmann 1958. It was a handsome volume, now that she could see it properly, bound in red cloth and with the author's own signature, B. Pasternak, written in gold across the front cover, in western, not Russian, script. She held the book for a moment in both hands, looking at the signature. What had her new friend said? (This, she realized, was the second time she had thought of him as her friend: was she getting herself used to the phrase?)

He'd said that the Russian government's fury about the Nobel Prize had helped to kill Pasternak. They had broken his spirit and he had died.

Poor Pasternak. She found herself saying for him, in her head, the prayer she said always when she heard the news of a death. May the souls of the faithful departed through the mercy of God rest in peace.

The old man on the bench—she was determined to maintain some distance when she thought about him—had remembered more than she had about Pasternak, but then he had lived for years in a Communist country even if Tito and Stalin had fallen out. What he'd said had brought back a dim memory of what had happened. Pasternak had been awarded the Nobel Prize and the Russian government had said that if he went to Stockholm to receive it he could never return to Russia. So he refused it. Was that it? She thought for a moment. Who was running the Russian government in—she looked inside the book - 1958? 1958 was the date of the book appearing in Italy, and in English in England. That was only five years after Stalin's death. So Khruschev was ruling Russia, Khruschev who had invaded Hungary with tanks a couple of years earlier, and closed again all the churches Stalin had re-opened to encourage patriotism in the war. Khruschev was by no means the teddy bear he liked people to think. What you got for telling the truth, and telling it well, in Russia, was punishment and perhaps death. This was how it was sixty years ago, and how it had been when Dostoyevsky was sentenced to death and at the last minute reprieved and sent to prison instead, and this was how it was now: journalists and politicians who had exposed his lies Putin had had poisoned, strangled, shot. He had killed that very brave girl, Anna Politkovskaya, who had told Russia and the world the truth about what Russia was doing to the Chechens. First she was poisoned and when she survived that she was shot. Hadn't he just almost killed Alexei Navalny, with the terrifying poison that had almost killed two Russians in Salisbury and actually killed an English woman who had nothing to do with Russia? Alexei Navalny had written a book to demonstrate that Putin had organized terror attacks in Russia to justify the destruction of the Chechens, falsely presented as Islamist terrorists. As the worst Israelis call the Palestinians. And the Chinese the Uighurs, to justify, to make appear acceptable to the War on Terror west, treatment of human beings which was actually dreadful.

The world.

She put the book down on the table and turned to the last pages.

Yes, here were the poems, "Zhivago's Poems", forty pages of them, and yes, the last—the very last was a different translation of one of the poems printed earlier—was called "Gethsemane". It wasn't a very long poem, fourteen four-line verses. Most of it was a vivid retelling, with exact detail, of Jesus's agony in the garden, his friends too tired to stay awake, and then, at his arrest, his rebuke of Peter, and his acceptance of the suffering and death ahead. But the last two verses, even in English which, as an old hand at trying to translate poetry, she knew was muffling the Russian, she had to read over and over while what Christ was saying resonated for her.

> "You see, the passage of the centuries is like a parable
> And catches fire on its way.
> In the name of its terrible majesty
> I shall go freely, through torment, down to the grave."

He could not avoid his fate, which, with him freely accepting it, would change the significance of the whole of time. She read the four lines again, and this time she heard behind Christ's words Tamino's magic flute play as he walked through the fire. She shook Mozart out of her head and read the lines once more, just his words, over silence.

Then came the last four lines, the lines of Easter:

"And on the third day I shall rise again.
Like rafts down a river, like a convoy of barges,
The centuries will float to me out of the darkness.
And I shall judge them."

There. Christ Pantokrator, as the old man on the garden bench had said, the almighty ruler of everything, of all time.

Just now, kneeling on the floor by the bookcase, she hadn't shed the tears that came because she saw that these books, these much loved books she'd chosen for Penny to read all those years ago, were no more than forlorn relics of a world of feeling that had passed for ever as a tide that would not turn went out. Now the tears poured from her eyes.

What was she crying for? Who was she crying for? For the world which had not listened to Christ, not then, not ever, which did not listen to him now. For him with his passion, his death, always ahead of him, in every Mass. She remembered something she had always known and had forgotten for decades: Pascal had said of the scene in the garden of Gethsemane: "Christ is in agony until the end of the world." He is to die. Death is waiting for him. This is my blood which will be shed for you. And you will pay no attention, will let my blood fall to the sand of the desert and dry and disappear.

She got up from the table, pulled open the dresser drawer in which she had kept tissues for decades, since Penny and Matt were messy toddlers, and cried more.

She was crying also, she realized with a kind of relief, because she was relaxing a tension, letting go an emotion that she hadn't wanted to recognize, let alone name. Something to do with her heart. Something to do with finding company and comfort that she had no idea she so much needed, on what she had supposed would be a calm, solitary Christmas Day: she was after all far too old to mind, much, the disappointment of not being in Yorkshire for Christmas. It wasn't that she needed distraction—Pascal had been very fierce about distraction—or needed to be cheered up. It was more than either, different from either.

What had he said?

"Thank you for listening. It is my Christmas present."

Her tears, that had almost stopped, started again. He was lonely. Perhaps he had been lonely for years. And she—she must have been lonelier than she realized, since Hakim had gone, since Ayesha had died, but really, because they were so young, since David died, more than a year and a half ago. Company, another person to listen, to hear, to pay attention to, to receive attention from.

There was a phrase at the back of her mind. There. Got it. I and Thou. What was that? A little book her father had been keen on, years and years ago, a book about the difference between relating to someone as a person, thou, to be addressed, and relating to them only as he or she, which might as well be it. The second person, opposite the first, with connection. Or the third person, separate from the first, without connection. She had read the book, a present from her father, when she was maybe sixteen, at the time of *Doctor Zhivago*, and she was sure she hadn't really understood it. But she remembered that she gathered from it that only by practising real I—Thou relationships could we begin to understand something about God, the ultimate and eternal Thou. Or was it that God is the eternal I, and each of us is, perhaps, to God, Thou? That, surely better, must have been the point.

Looking back, she was surprised, and pleased, that her father, a thoroughly secular Jew who to her knowledge had never, since he reached England as a young man fleeing Hitler, been near a synagogue, had so much liked a book about God.

That little book—now she remembered the author's name, Martin Buber, Jewish, perhaps German because the book was called *Ich und Du*, wasn't it?—must be somewhere here in the flat. It was a drab, grey, small paperback, not a Penguin, about the size of *The Shropshire Lad* she had just seen on the bottom shelf in Penny's room. She remembered what it looked like but not where it was. She was certain she had never thrown it away.

She looked round the kitchen, idiotically. Of course it wasn't in the kitchen. And she wasn't going to look for it now, more kneeling, more getting cold and stiff. Perhaps tomorrow.

Ich und Du: so much better in German because *du* was still what friends and lovers and parents and children called each other, and Thou was not. As for *I and You*—perhaps the point couldn't be made at all in current English.

Of course, she smiled through what was left of her tears as she realized, she and the man in the garden, had they been talking in German, were still a long way from the point of calling each other *Du*.

She mopped her face, blew her nose, and got up to put the tissue in the bin. As she sat down she took *Doctor Zhivago* from the table and opened it at the beginning. Before she found the first page she realized that she knew what the first sentence would say. This was like hearing the opening chord of a familiar symphony before the orchestra had played it. "On they went, singing 'Eternal Memory.'" It must have been more than sixty years since she had read this sentence on this page, and somewhere in the mysterious depths of her mind it had been waiting all this time.

She closed the book. What she must do was read it again, as someone who was now old, someone who had loved and lost a good deal, because all those years ago she 'd been too conceited, too sure of what she thought, simply too wrong, to read it properly. She must find the place where Zhivago's friend Misha, the Jew, said that if only people had listened to Christ, the nations, the quarrelling murderous nations full of hatred and bitterness, would have dissolved into persons, one by one. One by one in the hands of God. That they had not listened was exactly the cause for her tears just now.

And the shelf in Penny's room of favourite books from her youth? They were not a cause for tears, whatever anyone else thought or didn't think of them. Weren't they rather a cause, even now, for grateful celebration? There was in all of them

still, because there always had been, some truth, some goodness, some beauty. She thought of the beauty of the writing in
Gatsby, and in Laurie Lee's descriptions of the deep country
of his Gloucestershire childhood; she thought of the truth and
goodness in the accounts of the old, mourning change and loss
in the 1860s, in both *Fathers and Sons* and *The Leopard*. These
were no more than examples, ultimately no doubt fleeting
examples, of some, only some and only relative, presentations
of fragments of the absolute qualities of God, caught in a net
of language that belonged to a time that would pass, but some
was not none, and what was relative had its value precisely
because it could be placed in relation to the absolute truth and
goodness and beauty that are, that is, only in God. This was why
Matthew Arnold had been wrong. He had wanted to replace
the absolute with the relative, if he had succeeded, the relative
would not have increased its value but altogether lost it, so that
it would indeed have become only debris on the beach.

After all, *Doctor Zhivago* had been one of those books she
had chosen, and there in the poem her friend in the garden had
remembered was a shining fragment of the truth. She turned
the pages back to the last paragraph of the novel, before the
poems.

Just as he had said, the long and mostly desperate story
ends on a note of hope and happiness, with two old friends,
one of them Misha Gordon, sitting quietly with the book that
"seemed to know what they were feeling, and gave them its
support and confirmation". It must have been his memory of
this that chimed with what she had happened to say about
hearing traces of God in what one might be reading.

She closed *Doctor Zhivago* and bent her head, sitting at her
kitchen table on the evening of Christmas Day, as she tried to
put together in her mind, her memory, what it was that had
turned the sadness of that withdrawing tide into some kind
of achievement of calm and faith that wasn't new for her but
distantly familiar.

Then she remembered. It was Augustine, as it so often was
when she tried to reassemble something she had learnt, who had
explained to her, long, long ago when she was writing her little

book about him, that value which was relative was still value. It was all in *City of God*, that enormous formidable book, so much less formidable than it looked once you started reading it, like *War and Peace*, she thought, with a smile at how much Tolstoy would have disliked the comparison. She had read *City of God*, all of it, because when she was writing about St Augustine she felt she should. A great deal of it of course she had forgotten, but she remembered how clear it had been about retaining what had been good in the this-worldly empire in which he had been brought up and in which so much was bad because driven by greed, ambition and the craving for power. He had called these motives, constants in human nature, collectively *libido dominandi*, lust for domination, and lust for domination was exactly what Nietzsche had recommended, calling it the will to power. What else had driven Donald Trump and Boris Johnson? According to Augustine turning towards God should mean turning away from the priorities of the pre-Christian earthly city, which the Romans had built and fostered and admired because "they had no other city to praise"—she had never forgotten the phrase—although there had been solid and virtuous achievements in their earthly city, as there always would be, since we cannot choose not to live in it, only not to love it, or not to love it most. And Augustine acknowledged all that had been good and useful about his own education in the grammar and rhetoric that had made him one of the great writers of the world, and he knew the value of Virgil and Cicero and the Greek philosophers in their patchy and partial relation to the whole truth which they could not know. He had thought all this through, in a way that was fresh, brave and entirely characteristic of him, so that he allowed, for example, Virgil, whom he and Clare, she had always known, had loved in the same sort of way, and Plato, whom neither Augustine nor Clare knew well enough, their necessarily incomplete sense of God, the relative beauty of what they wrote, instead of consigning them to oblivion as "pagans".

When she had understood this, so long ago, she had thought it too obvious to be remarkable, which meant that she hadn't really understood it at all. What Augustine had done, in this book, was to hold in honour for the future "the best that had been said and thought", as Matthew Arnold put it, so that in classrooms down the centuries, in monasteries and cathedral schools and universities, and even in the schools where she herself had taught, the good things of the world he had inherited should be sustained and valued properly, that is in relation to the truth and goodness and beauty of God.

Good. She was pleased to have pulled herself together enough to have arrived at some kind of calm after a day that had upset her ordinary calm, her ordinary balance.

Nothing much had happened. She had met, for the second time, an elderly foreigner who lived nearby and, two old people each alone on Christmas day, they had talked for an hour or so in the increasing cold and the gathering dark, and their conversation had been, as well as sad because his life had been sad, warming, cheering, a little confusing, but surely that should be all? Nothing much. Nothing to rattle her, or, she hoped, him. That was how a sensible person would see it.

She took *Doctor Zhivago* to her comfortable chair in the sitting room, switched on the electric fire though the old radiators had made the room quite warm anyway, and started reading with her tartan picnic rug over her knees. This was the first winter she had thought of this ancient rug, unearthed, like *Doctor Zhivago*, from Penny's room. She'd had it dry-cleaned and it was as good as new, cosy and consoling like a hot water bottle. Paintings of old people, and descriptions of old people in novels, often had them with blankets over their knees. Now she knew why. Mr Woodhouse no doubt sat in his armchair by the fire with a rug like hers to keep him warm. Not that she would fuss like Mr Woodhouse, even if there were someone to fuss to.

She read a couple of pages: the little boy at his mother's funeral, his confused, fatherless childhood, an old monastery, a freezing blizzard. All this made her feel even warmer, even more comfortable. And how good to be back in Russia. After *War and Peace* all through the autumn, she thought she should re-read a long, demanding English novel. So she had started *Middlemarch*, an old Penguin she must have read when she was young. She had got about a quarter of the way through, wasn't enjoying it because she couldn't like any of the characters, and found George Eliot's strenuous effort to make sense of a world without God deeply unsympathetic. She was relieved to find she could decide she needn't go on with it, on account of *Doctor Zhivago*. She had very rarely stopped reading a book she hadn't finished. Just choosing to do this, because of her friend in the garden, gave her a sense of liberation.

She read for an hour and a half. No one telephoned: Christmas Day, so once Penny had rung, no one else was likely to.

Then she made herself scrambled eggs on toast and cooked some frozen spinach which, with some butter and nutmeg, was good enough. She made a mug of camomile tea to take back to the fire and the book. Before she settled down again she took *Middlemarch* from her bedside table and put it in its place in the sitting room.

Bedtime. Bath. Hot-water bottle. Prayer.

As every night, she stood in her dressing gown, with the curtains closed behind her, and looked out over the square, tonight as cold as Russia. No snow was actually falling but the ice in the air was almost a sound. She took her rosary out of her dressing gown pocket. After the Our Father, which sometimes she had to say quietly to herself several times until she could focus her concentration, and before the list of people, living and dead, mostly dead now, for whom she prayed every day, she always said a decade of the Rosary. Only one decade. It was a habit she had formed years ago and liked because it took her through the life and death and resurrection of Jesus with the immediacy of imagination, and that was good. She had been glad when Pope John Paul II had added the five luminous mysteries to the old fifteen of time immemorial: they gave her more of Jesus's life, and more moments of beauty not yet scarred with suffering.

Paintings she loved had helped, so that for many of the mysteries she remembered always the same painting because it took her deeper into the scene, the moment, that had, after all, actually taken place. Tonight she had reached the crowning with thorns.

It was Christmas Day but she never changed her loyalty to the order of the events remembered in the Rosary: she was able to think of Jesus as the baby in the manger even as she thought of his Passion. Simultaneity, she had read somewhere, was a mark of Christian belief.

There had been, the night before, while it was Christmas Eve and she might have been setting out for Midnight Mass, the pain and fear of the scourging, in her mind's eye Jesus tied to a Roman pillar about to be flogged by a soldier whose whip is raised to strike. Impossible not to wince at the blow to come, perhaps especially because Jesus and the column and the soldier with the whip are at the back of the painting in a white, open hall, while larger and nearer the onlooker are three richly dressed men standing in a strange stillness and paying no attention to the torture of Jesus. This was a Piero painting, a small astonishing painting she had seen once in Italy long ago. And tonight she had to look at, to inhabit, the pain, worse than fear, of the crowning with thorns, in her memory of a more astonishing painting: Fra Angelico in his monastery in Florence imagining Jesus in a white robe with a white blindfold over his eyes, sitting on a pretend throne with in his right hand a stick and in his left hand a ball, the pretend sceptre and orb they had given him to make fun of him, while around him, because he can't see, mockery comes from nowhere and everywhere, a face with no body spitting at him, hands coming at him, plucking at him, terrifying, one holding another stick. The blood from the thorns trickles down his forehead. If he moves the thorns will pierce more deeply. Every twenty days, she reached this moment in her recitation of the Rosary, and each time she felt Jesus's suffering, his passion, what is being done to him, most acutely because of the mockery and the blindfold as well as the smarting from the thorns.

"Jesus is in agony until the end of the world", she remembered again.

After her ten Hail Marys and her Glory be to Father, which recalled her to the resurrection, she wound her rosary round her hand and prayed for all her dead, most intently for Matt and David Rose, also for Simon and her parents and others loved and lost, and then for the living, Penny and Daisy, Carrie in Nepal, Hakim at Vindolanda, and—well—her friend in the garden. It didn't matter that she didn't know his name. Known to God, she thought, as she gave him and his loneliness and the sadness of whatever had happened to his family, into the safekeeping of God, the God of his Jewish mother and his half-Muslim, half-Catholic father, the God he occasionally believed to be there, somewhere.

She turned back from the cold Christmas night to her bedroom with its soft lights, at her bedside and on the dressing table. It was warm, and as familiar and comforting as could be—she had changed nothing in it since Simon died and she had taken his clothes and a few other things to Oxfam—but tonight it looked somehow different, as everything else did.

Looking vaguely at the long, low bookcase against the wall opposite her dressing table, she remembered that somewhere, with the small Bibles, the Authorized Version her godmother had given her when she was eleven, a scarlet and gold miniature version of the Bible made for the Queen at the coronation, and the little blue Jerusalem Bible of about thirty years ago, the Book of Common Prayer she'd had at school and the old Roman Missal someone had given her when she became a Catholic, there was—what? She looked at the shelf. She couldn't see the books properly; they were too far from either of the lamps in her bedroom. But she knew that here there was something she had thought of earlier this evening. Yes. *I and Thou*, the little grey-beige paperback. Here, in writing different from the teenager's signature she had found in Thucydides and *Doctor Zhivago*—as an undergraduate she had affected Greek e's, to look more classical, and had kept them ever since—was her name again, Clare Feldmann. The date was 1961, and beside it, proudly, Cambridge. The English translation had been first published in 1937, and this copy belonged to the tenth impression, 1958. This was remarkable: no short dense book of this kind by a Jewish philosopher could these days possibly run into ten impressions. Had the war made the book popular? Or news of the Holocaust after the war? Had Buber survived the Holocaust?

She saw she had marked lots of passages with pencil lines in the margin. When she read a few of them she also saw that she couldn't then have understood what Buber was saying, and probably couldn't understand him properly now.

She discovered a slip of paper, a torn off piece of the lined yellow paper she had affected at the same time as her Greek e's but long ago given up, between two pages towards the end of the book. She sat on her bed to read it. The writing, hers, was in ink that had faded, unsurprisingly, over, perhaps, sixty years.

He that loveth not knoweth not God; for God is love. Herein is love, not that we loved God, but that he loved us. No man hath seen God at any time. If we love one another, God dwelleth in us.

And under the lines "1 John 4.8": she was always careful with references.

So long ago, when she was beginning to think about becoming a Catholic, and knew almost nothing about almost everything, she had perhaps understood something, even a good deal, of what was said in *I and Thou.*

She crossed the room to her dressing table and, just before she switched off the lamp, caught sight of herself in the mirror, the old mirror in a painted frame that had sat on her dressing table since she got married. She looked old and untidy in her dressing gown, white-haired, her neck, always covered with a scarf when she was dressed, stringy above her nightdress, her face so lined now, sunk as all old faces sink, better with spectacles than without, verging on Miss Havisham. She thought of the spider's web in the curtains in Penny's room. But she smiled at the mirror as if thanking her undergraduate self for the Christmas present she had just found.

She put the book and its slip of paper on her bedside table, on top of *Doctor Zhivago*, got into her warm bed, switched off the light and went to sleep.

CHAPTER 6

SUNDAY 23 MAY 2021

No, she hadn't invented him. He was real enough to become both closer and more mysterious to her as weeks and then months of the winter went by.

To match the anxiety and fear the pandemic was putting so many people through, the winter of 2021 was long, cold and grey; most of the rest of February had been both colder and wetter than usual nowadays, with a good deal of frost even in the middle of London. March had produced occasional moments of warmth, but April was particularly unpleasant, cold, gray and dry, the daffodils coming out reluctantly and the tulips very late. May so far had been wet, very wet, and still cold. There had been nothing to lift the spirit in a spring that didn't properly arrive.

Many of the rules to minimize the spread of the virus had been relaxed as more and more people had been vaccinated and fewer and fewer of those who caught it were getting seriously ill and dying. But things, all the same, didn't feel normal. Everyone was used, now, to wearing a mask in shops and people were still mostly keeping to the distance between one person and another that had become a habit over more than a year. She and Val agreed that, athough they had both had the double vaccination, they shouldn't go anywhere, separately or together, on a bus or a tube, because they were old and still felt vulnerable. They didn't wear their masks when they talked to each other, and were so relaxed these days that they had almost forgotten to regard themselves as a self-defined "support bubble".

She had several times thought, when remembering to be grateful to God, that it was an odd, and a so good, consequence of the regulation and isolation imposed by Covid that the disaster of the pandemic had brought closer together two old people each living alone who otherwise might have got no further than one conversation in the garden. She had no idea whether Val, in the first months of the pandemic, had seen as few people as she had—there was so much about his life that she didn't know—but now, she knew, he was as grateful as she was for the chance, or, actually, the gossiping of Mr Clements, an unlikely agent of fate, which had brought them together, and then for the rule which had invented the support bubble.

During their third or fourth afternoon on the bench in the garden she had asked him his name. He smiled his wonderful smile—she thought that if she'd met him when he was five years old she would have known him by his smile—and said, "So, you have asked me what is my name. I thought, will she ask me? I have thought that maybe you liked not to know my name as if I am a character in a book you are writing and you have been waiting to imagine a name for me."

As if she had, really, invented him.

"Well, perhaps. After all, you do think of me as Clare Wilson, which is a name I imagined."

"And that is good. We are in a kind of story, is it not so? A story of which we do not know the end. Like a life, any life. I hope you will keep Clare Wilson as your name. For me at least your name?"

"If that's what you prefer, then of course."

Was he going to tell her his name, or not?

Again the smile.

"My name, my only name because actually I am not in a book, or perhaps not yet in a book—"

This time it was she who smiled.

"—is Valerijan Radic. Valerijan has an extra j in it, after the i an English person would expect, because of Serbo-Croat spelling. And Radic has a c at the end, with an acute accent, which in England I leave out. Valerijan is not a rare name in Yugoslavia. But in England it is. In the bookshop where I had my job they called me Val, like St Valentine who does not exist but whose name they know because of St Valentine's Day, which is invented for makers of cards as Hallowe'en is invented for makers of sinister disguises. You see how well I have learnt England?"

"You have learnt England very well." Had he? She wasn't sure.

"Also in the bookshop they called me 'radish' because someone thought it was funny."

"Childish, the English can be, very often I'm afraid. Look at St Valentine's Day and Hallowe'en. They are instead of real saints, real feasts, don't you think? Like Bonfire Day."

"Bonfire Day?"

"The fifth of November. In London you might not have noticed it, I suppose, though there can be fireworks in the distance. Gunpowder, treason and plot. On the fifth of November in 1605 some Catholics had hidden barrels of gunpowder in the cellars underneath Parliament. They were going to blow up the king and the parliament. They were discovered. If the plot had succeeded it would have been the most terrible, the most brilliant, terrorist attack anywhere before 9.11. So it is remembered with bonfires that celebrate the discovery of the gunpowder in time to save the king and parliament. Sometimes the bonfires burn figures of Guy Fawkes, the leader of the plot. Children used to make these figures they were going to burn, and collect money. 'Penny for the Guy', they'd say. They are anti-Catholic bonfires."

"Really? Even now?"

"Even now, though most people probably don't remember the story and don't know for how long Catholics in England were blamed for everything bad, the plague, the fire of London, and on and on."

"And the Irish are Catholics?"

"The Irish. Exactly. Poor, so bad; Catholics, so worse. It's always been said that in London after the war, when I was a child, people to do labouring jobs were badly needed but lodging houses had notices in their windows saying, 'No Irish, No Blacks, No Dogs'. I don't know that this is true but I can believe it."

"That is horrible."

"Yes."

"The English and religion. That is another topic."

Not for today. They left it for another time, and she said, "But what about Valerian? Does St Valerian exist? If he does, I'm afraid I've never heard of him."

"Actually there are four people called St Valerian. Maybe there are, there were. I would be a little doubtful about all of them."

"Four saints called Valerian—goodness. What do you know about them?"

He laughed.

"Not very much, because there is not very much to know. The best of them, the most definitely fixed in history I think, is a North African bishop, a martyr in the fifth century."

"O, I'm glad."

He looked surprised.

"You are pleased? Why does this please you?"

"Because once, a very long time ago, I did some work on the North African bishops of the late Roman empire. I was going to write a book, but then I got married and there was never time to do the work."

"But St Augustine? He was a North African bishop and you did write a book about him?"

"I did. Later. I'd forgotten I'd told you—No, of course, it's in my book. Now I come to think of it, the bishop of Hippo who wanted Augustine to succeed him, and manoeuvred him into being a priest so that he could be the next bishop, was called Valerius. Not Valerian, and he wasn't a martyr. Perhaps St Valerian was a friend of Augustine's, or even an enemy. He had plenty of both, friends and enemies. I don't remember Valerian's name, but there were so many of those Roman bishops and I've forgotten nearly all their names. But what about the others?"

"The others are even further in the past, so what is known of them is even less certain. There was an early martyr in Gaul and another in Rome. And nearer to my home there was a bishop of Aquileia, an ancient city on the Adriatic Sea, a very important city before Venice was thought of."

"Yes, I do know about Aquileia, though not about its St Valerian, or any of your saints called Valerian. Lost in the mists is where they are, the mists of late antiquity. Isn't it a lovely phrase, 'late antiquity'? It always sounds sad because it suggests things were going to get worse, which they did. So your name is a name from late antiquity, a distinguished name to have. Much better than Valentine."

"There was also an Emperor Valerian, but he was not a good example of my name."

"I haven't heard of him either. What happened to him? When was he?"

His smile.

"He was earlier than your late antiquity, and he was more bad than sad. I don't remember exactly when he was. About 250 or 260 I think. Certainly before Constantine was emperor; also before Diocletian. He lost an important battle against the Persians and they took him prisoner. This was not good for the reputation of Rome."

"No. I'm sure it wasn't. And then?"

"He died in Persia."

"Never mind him. More agreeable to be able to choose between four saints than to be called after an emperor who lost battles."

"Quite right. And also the emperor Valerian was a persecutor of Christians, though he was not the emperor for long enough to be a famous persecutor like Nero or Diocletian. By the way, Diocletian was a most interesting emperor. He saved the empire and was a great persecutor of Christians, but did you know he was a Croat peasant from first to last? For me he is a man from nearby. So is Constantine who was born in Nis, in Serbia. Some things have not very much changed. You know the word *comitadji*?"

"No. Yes. You used it when we talked before. What does it mean?"

"It means a band of fighters under a leader. Not a real army. They were an invention of Constantine, the *comitatus*, a band of local fighters to help the Roman army. We have them still."

"Well—of course."

"These Balkan emperors, Diocletian and Constantine, they are interesting because they were between, you see, between Rome and Greece, east and west, like Bosnia."

113

"Like you?"

Another smile.

"Like me."

Back to history.

"Constantine was made emperor in York", she said. "So to me as well he's a man from nearby. But Diocletian—I don't know much about him, apart from him persecuting Christians. He's a bit early for me. Or a bit late if you think of the Roman history people learn in school. If they learn any Roman history. The tetrarchy: wasn't that his idea? What happened to him in the end?"

"Ah—so good, his end. He retired, like Charles V, emperor of the world, or Pope Benedict. People with much power do not often do this. There has to be a constitution to make them go away from power. Look at President Trump, and his riot two weeks ago. That was like Rome at its worst. But the constitution did win. Who knows how narrowly the constitution did win? Diocletian invented a new constitution for Rome, the tetrarchy as you say. He set up the empire's future he thought—it did not last of course: the tetrarchs quarrelled—and he retired to his grand house at Spalatum on the Adriatic, now it is Split, where he looked after his garden."

"You're always telling me things I didn't know, which I do like—which I do very much enjoy."

"Are you sure? You are not just kind to listen?"

"I am sure, really."

"You must tell me to stop, to shut up as you might say if you were not too polite, if I am talking too much. If I am boring, which in England is a great sin."

"You're right. It is. And you're not. Boring, I mean. Not boring at all."

Silence. A silence she saw he couldn't break. So she said, only to break it for him, "Roman emperors then. Which is your favourite?"

He laughed.

"I don't know. Most of them were a bit terrible. Some of them were only terrible. Hadrian was very good. Justinian was good. But I think any librarian would have to say Marcus

Aurelius. We are told he was very good, partly by himself. In every library in every language are copies of his Meditations. I wonder do people read them? Is he maybe one of the books people have and do not read? I think so."

He smiled again.

"But there were many Christian martyrs when he was emperor. I have the idea that the St Valerian who was martyred in Gaul was one of them."

"Some people", she said, "have written that Marcus Aurelius may not have known about the martyrs, or perhaps even he admired the Christians he heard about." This was something she did know, or anyway had come across somewhere.

"This is what the English call 'wishful thinking'. Not so?"

"Perhaps."

Then she caught hold of something that had been just out of reach in the maze of her memory.

"There is something else, something I wonder if you've heard of, that's called Valerian. I've just remembered it. It's a fine plant about a foot high or more with red or perhaps dark pink flowers, a tough, cheerful plant. Once it's got going, probably in a garden, it'll grow anywhere, in a wall, at a roadside, anywhere it can find a place."

He looked at her for a long moment.

"Anywhere it can find a place. That is good."

The expression in his eyes was becoming familiar: it meant, yes, you are right to think there is more to what I have said than its obvious meaning. And, as often with him, she had to change the subject.

"Like the Christians before Constantine", she said, wildly she knew. "Even when they weren't trying to kill them, or take them prisoner to be victims of gladiators or lions in the amphitheatre, the officials of the empire were suspicious of them because they wouldn't worship the emperor. But they grew, they flourished, like valerian, anywhere they could find a place." She saw in her mind's eye valerian flourishing under the stone walls of cottage gardens in a Yorkshire village street.

"You know them well, Mrs Wilson, don't you, those early Christians? They are almost your friends?"

"I used to know some of them, only a few. But I don't know them well enough any more, I'm afraid—look at your saints, the four Valerians I had forgotten or never known. And"—this was an easy swerve—"please, now that I know your name, you must call me Clare."

"Clare, yes. I will try. It is like Du in German or Tu in French, is it not? So strange at first, it needs some practice. But I will try. And you will call me Val, which sounds quite English."

Again she had to pull them back to information.

"Let me tell you an extraordinary thing about Marcus Aurelius. There was a new discovery, only made in the summer of last year, just the other day in fact. Hakim told me about it when he was still in London. He told me that a metal detector person—"

Mr Radic—she must get used to thinking of him as Val—looked blank.

"I'm so sorry. A metal detector, or perhaps a metal detective is what he should be called"—she knew they liked to be called "detectorists" but thought the word too ugly to be uttered—"is someone with a machine that tells them if there is metal under the earth." She demonstrated by putting her fists side by side and waving them searchingly over the unpromising gravel path in the garden of their London square.

"I understand."

"This metal detective found an almost perfect bust of Marcus Aurelius buried in a field in Yorkshire, not far from where my family live. It's very small, a bronze bust, obviously a portrait of Marcus Aurelius, and with it—perhaps someone was making a votive offering of some kind—were several other bronze pieces, including a little horse. And they weren't even found where there seemed to have been a building, a villa or a temple. Interesting, don't you think? So far away from Rome. Though York was an important legionary garrison for centuries, and a town called Malton, even nearer to my family's home, had a military camp and a civilian settlement, a smaller version of York, for the same centuries. Very early there were Roman towns, begun as soon as the Romans arrived in the north. And a little later there were villas in the countryside, farms and comfortable houses for the officers and their families. They had hot water and bathrooms, very nice in the winter in Yorkshire. Perhaps they retired from the army, and looked after their gardens like Diocletian."

"Ah the Romans", he said, putting his hands together as if to clap. "We have them in common, don't we? They were everywhere. Near Sarajevo the bombs and explosions of the wars brought to the surface of the earth many coins and pieces of Roman pots, and pieces also of armour, and maybe bronze portraits of Marcus Aurelius." His smile. "There were too many things that were found, and the city was too chaotic because of the fighting, for them to be examined and recorded as they should have been."

"Of course. Archaeologists need some peace and quiet." She thought of Hakim at Hadrian's Wall, still in Northumberland in the bleak winter but in the blessed silence of no tourists, examining and recording. Perhaps there was a pretty archaeology student helping him. She smiled and said, "Hakim was very cross that an amateur with a detecting machine and not a proper archaeologist had found the emperor."

"You think of Hakim often, Mrs Wilson, excuse me, Clare. Not so?"

"I do. I'm fond of him, you know."

"Yes. He is a fortunate young man."

When she got home that afternoon—it was some time towards the end of January and a mild, cloudy day, but she hadn't written down the date—she remembered bits of this inconsequential conversation, perhaps the most important bits, though they had talked of this and that for nearly an hour. It had been easy, and most agreeable, and after it she soon got used to calling him Val, as, equally naturally, he called her Clare. It was two or three weeks later that he asked her to tea in his house because it was so cold, and she went.

And now it was past the middle of May, though the spring was still disappointing, and she had seen him, and talked to him, and visited his house for coffee several times as he had visited her flat for tea, and still he was mysterious to her, opaque, as David hadn't been, or Hakim, so it wasn't only because he came from a part of the world, and a language, of which she had known nothing. Perhaps it was mostly because she hadn't known him when he was young, and that age and loss and desperate times had accustomed him to a wariness that was more than the courtesy of distance between two old people taking care of each other's feelings. Whatever it was, his reticence delighted rather than depressed her, perhaps because it implied some kind of future for them that wasn't entirely predictable. There was more to learn, of him, of them, if nothing else.

Of their many conversations, rambling and inconsequential as they mostly were, she remembered that one, in the garden in January, more clearly than most because it was when she learnt his name. She also sometimes remembered that when she got home and looked up valerian, the plant, on the internet, she discovered that an old English name for it was "all-heal".

CHAPTER 7

SUNDAY 23 MAY 2021

She hadn't seen Penny since the November lockdown began. They had been in touch: Penny was good about remembering to telephone regularly. She hadn't, or she hadn't yet, told her about Val. What, in Penny's terms, was there to tell?

Today was Pentecost, though she had been to Mass only by following, as usual, the Latin Mass in the Jesuit church in Farm Street, and she was actually going to see Penny and Charles, who had asked her to Sunday lunch in Barnes. They wouldn't be aware of Pentecost, and probably didn't know or had forgotten that it was long familiar in England as Whitsun. Now it wasn't even attached to a Bank Holiday: Whit Monday had been abolished on account of its unpredictable date. Easter Monday might well follow it into oblivion, as fewer and fewer people had a sense of Easter as anything beyond chocolate and a holiday weekend. "Why not call it the first weekend in April and have done with it? At least everybody would know where they were." This was only too likely.

She thought of St Cuthbert and St Wilfrid and the Synod of Whitby and tremendous arguments over the date of Easter. Northumberland and Yorkshire in their Anglo-Saxon glory days.

Penny was sending a minicab to pick her up at half past twelve.

At quarter past she was sitting, ready in her coat because it was still so cold outside, thinking not for the first time that she should pay more attention to the Holy Spirit. The homily at Mass had been a really dull letter about climate change from all the bishops to English and Scottish and Welsh Catholics; the phrase "our countries" appeared in it more than once: a tiresome nod to identity politics. This was obviously a letter written by a committee, its second priority being not to offend anyone. Of course it was important that all people everywhere, therefore all British Catholics, should acknowledge the scale of the climate crisis and resolve to do whatever they could to help protect the earth from more damage, but an ordinary Sunday would have been a much better moment for the bishops to say so. Pentecost, such an astonishing story, was surely a day for reflecting on, even reflecting, the miraculous scale of God's communication with human beings in the Spirit as well as in Christ. And wasn't it also a day to thank God for the wonder of the Church and its survival, but at the same time to acknowledge with shame and sadness its shocking flaws, the arrogance and self-indulgence and greed and cruelty of some of the priests and people, now and down the ages, who were of the Church but not of the city of God? Whatever they may have smugly assumed. Augustine's *corpus permixtum*: she remembered how pleased she had been long ago, as an inexperienced and badly informed new Catholic, to find Augustine, with his usual inspired common sense, explaining that the Church will always be a mixture of people, good, bad and indifferent, and that it couldn't and shouldn't be identified with the city of God. Not enough people, century after century, had paid attention to this, or even properly understood it.

She prayed at her kitchen table for the Holy Spirit's help in what she would try to say to Charles at lunch.

Yesterday she'd had an email from Carrie in Nepal.

Hi Gran,
I do hope you're still OK, sticking to the rules and all that, and staying WELL.
It's terrible here now. I think we all felt Nepal had got away with it even up to a few weeks ago, because of the mountains or the simple life or the travel bans everywhere. But now it's come in from India with a vengeance and people in the villages where I live and work are dying before they can reach a hospital—they can't afford to get to a hospital because they're miles away, and they couldn't afford what they'd have to pay if they did get there. Anyway, even if they could pay, the hospitals don't have enough doctors and mostly they don't have any oxygen at all. Imagine.

Up here we've given up school and told the children to stay at home. All the NGOs are working together, mostly to talk to people, to explain about washing their hands all the time and wearing masks and strictly staying away from anyone who's ill, but it's really difficult even trying to persuade them to do the simplest things. They all gather round to look after anyone who's ill because they always have, specially old people who are much the most likely to die, as they are everywhere.

People are very scared now. Weird rituals and sacrifices come out of the woodwork if people are frightened enough and it's hopeless trying to say clustering round a bleeding hen or a goat is the very last thing they should be doing, just because of the clustering—people close together breathing each other's breath.

Of course what the whole country needs is vaccinations but there aren't any vaccines, or hardly any. We haven't seen a single one up here. You can't blame India for hanging on to all their vaccines, and all their oxygen too, with so many people dying, but how can anyone make a vaccine in Kathmandu? They've always had canisters of oxygen in Kathmandu for people climbing Everest: you can imagine how far they're likely to go when it comes to saving people's lives.

It doesn't help that the government is even more of a shambles than usual, so the other big countries that might help, China and Russia, with India paralysed by the virus, can say 'Why don't the Nepalese get a grip and do something to help themselves?' But the politicians aren't the ones who are dying. Probably they're getting vaccines on the black market from India for huge sums of money.

I've written all this, a bit more calmly, in a letter to Dad. Not as long as this. Attention span limited, to say the least. Surely the British who keep saying how brilliantly they've done with the vaccinations and how many spare vaccines they're got, 70 million I read somewhere on the internet, could send a couple of million to Nepal for the old people here? This is one of the poorest countries in the world and it's desperate for help. I've asked Dad if he can raise it in the House of Commons. What are MPs FOR if not for doing something really good at a time like this? But I know there's not much hope. Look at what's hap-pened to DFID—abolished by this government and now there are dreadful cuts in the aid to poor people all over the world. There are NGO programmes here that are going to have to stop, just stop, letting people down, pregnant women, girls training to be district health workers, teachers struggling with no books, not even coloured pencils for the children, all sorts, just having to be told there's no more money. I don't think Boris Johnson cares two hoots about anything except himself.

Mum says you're going to lunch with them tomorrow. Can you have a go at Dad about Nepal? It can't be beyond even this ghastly Brexit lot to simply decide to send spare vaccines to countries without any. Can it? You're so good at putting things clearly, Gran, and minding about the right things—he might even listen to you, and after all I have been here for nearly 2 years so I can really see what's going on. That ought to mean something to him?

Look after yourself. I still hope to get home and SEE YOU before too long,

> *love you lots*
> *Carrie*

Poor Carrie. Good Carrie, in the thick of the worst of the pandemic, bravely trying to do whatever she could. And she must be all too likely to catch the disease. She would be sensible and careful. She was young and strong, yes, but Ayesha had been young and strong. Carrie wasn't a doctor or a nurse: perhaps she didn't have to get close to people who were very ill, dying. Yet if people were dying in the villages without doctors and nurses, Carrie might well be helping to look after them in their houses.

But whatever danger she was in—and she would never make a fuss about that—she had given Clare this task, this responsibility, to talk some sense, some altruism, some principle, into Charles. Almost certainly a completely hopeless project.

At twenty-five past twelve she went carefully down the stairs, as usual ignoring the lift. Her mini-cab, a couple of minutes early, was just stopping at the kerb. The driver, an elderly Indian in a turban, got out to open the car door for her.

Every time she saw an Indian she felt a fresh pang about Ayesha and her death: had she taken as much care of her as she could have?

He looked at the notepad on the seat beside him, and then turned to look at her.

"You wish me to take you to Barnes, ma'am?"

"That's right. Thank you." She told him the address. "It's very easy to find. Not far from the church."

He set off round the square. "You have been to this address before, ma'am?"

"O yes. Often. It's where my daughter lives."

"But you will not have made this journey for many months, because of these lockdowns?"

"You're quite right. I haven't been to Barnes for a long time. A year and a half, I suppose."

"I see. You will be surprised by the roads we must take."

"Really? Why?"

It crossed her mind for an instant that he might be going to take her a way that was longer than necessary to push up the fare, but as quickly as it had come she banished the thought.

"Because, ma'am, Hammersmith Bridge is closed now for many months, so we must go down to Putney and up again to Barnes through much traffic. The river, you know, does not flow straight."

Of course. She'd read about Hammersmith Bridge more than once in *The Guardian* and then forgotten all about it. Carelessness, incompetence, political failures, buck-passing, and now no possible way for people living in Barnes to cross the river without driving miles in the wrong direction one way or the other. Then she thought, They'll be being driven mad by the closed bridge. They've asked me to lunch because they want to sell the house and live in my flat. They want me to live in David's little house in South Kensington. So convenient for them that he left it to me. How am I going to cope with that as well as vaccines for Nepal?

After so many months alone, and only her gentle conversations with Val breaking and cheering her solitude, she felt a kind of panic. She didn't want to see Penny and Charles, she couldn't face arguing with them over where she should live and where they wanted to live, and she had no idea how she could fulfil the promise she'd made, even if only in her head, to poor Carrie and her Nepalese villagers. She leant forward. She was going to tap her friendly driver on the shoulder and ask him to take her home. She was within sight of eighty, after all. She could always say she wasn't feeling up to going out to lunch. An old friend, a splendid woman who at eighty-three had suffered a catastrophic stroke and eventually died, had said to her years ago, "Once you're past seventy-five you can always say you're not feeling up to it. Covers anything or nothing."

She should wait until he had to stop at a traffic light. When he did, she lifted her hand and he said, "Are you all right, ma'am? There is something wrong?"

She sat back, leaning into the comfortable seat.

"No, no, I'm fine. Thank you. I was—feeling a little sick. I'm perfectly all right now."

"I am sorry. I will drive most carefully."

"Of course you will. Don't worry."

"Would you like me to open your window a little way? For some fresh air you know?"

"That would be kind. Thank you."

She couldn't avoid the issue of houses for ever. She couldn't let Carrie down. And she couldn't—she could but she mustn't— let herself be such a coward. Do not be afraid.

She thought. Or perhaps prayed.

The driver after a few minutes said, "Are you feeling better now, ma'am?"

"Much better, thank you."

As the car came out of the built-up streets and began to cross the open spaces of Barnes Common, with trees in new leaf, the grass green from all the rain of the last few days and weeks, and even some weak sunshine—a spring day, in fact, though more like March than May—she realized what she had to do. It was so obvious, and after all so simple, that she was surprised it had taken her so long to see it. Also it was bracing and encouraging to be out of the flat, out of the square, almost, for five minutes, in the country, and she let it calm her fears.

On the other side of the Common she said, "Do you know where the church is?"

"Yes, ma'am."

"The street is on the right after the church, and the house is half way along on the left."

He parked in a space two cars away from Penny's front door.

"Is this close enough, ma'am?"

"Yes, that's fine."

She got her purse out of her bag.

"The gentleman who made the booking has arranged the payment, ma'am."

That was good of Charles.

"O I see. Well—"

She found a five pound note, and gave it to him

"You've been most kind. Thank you. And I'd just like to say—" She hesitated. Was this tactless, a mistake? But she'd started—"that if you have family or friends in India I'm so very sorry for the terrible time people are having there."

"It is terrible, yes. My cousin and his son have died in these last weeks. But my wife died here in London in May last year. She was a nurse. So in England also we know what it is, the Covid and the loss."

"I'm so sorry." May last year, when Ayesha died. "How dreadful for you."

Then she added, because it was true, "They will not be forgotten."

"Thank you, ma'am."

She took her stick and her bag and walked to Penny's house. At the door she pressed the bell, heard it ring inside, and turned: he hadn't started the car and was watching, perhaps to make sure she was all right. She waved. The door opened. He waved back, and drove away down the street.

Charles stood in the doorway, looking slightly put out.

"Clare. How lovely to see you. We haven't seen you for far too long. How are you? Who was that you were waving to?"

"O that was just the minicab driver. He was a nice man. Thank you so much for paying for that, Charles. I'm most grateful."

"Come in, come in. Penny's in the kitchen. Let me take your coat."

It was very warm in their sitting room, though there was only a rather tired arrangement of expensive artificial roses, dusty silk, in the fireplace.

"Awful weather isn't it? I don't think we've ever had the heating on at the end of May before. Would you like a drink, Clare? Some sherry before lunch? A gin and tonic seeing as how it's Sunday?"

"No thank you, Charles. I'm fine."

"Some elderflower with ice?"

"Yes. That would be lovely. Thank you."

He made her a glass of elderflower cordial, soda and ice, and poured himself a gin and tonic.

He sat down opposite her.

"So how have you been, Clare, all this time? Keeping well, I hope, vaccinated and all that?"

"O yes, they've been very good, very efficient. My GP practice is excellent."

"That's the stuff. Boris's great success story, the vaccination roll-out."

"Of course."

This wasn't the moment to start an argument about Boris Johnson, what he'd done or not done, what the NHS had managed with or without his help or hindrance.

"And you and Penny?" she said.

"O yes, vaccinations all round, and we've been OK all through. Penny's been mostly in Leckenby—well, you know that—and I've only been in London when I've really had to be. Barnes, you know—But that's a subject we'd better come to over lunch."

She'd been right.

Penny came in, a Laura Ashley apron Clare had given her years ago over her jeans and cashmere jumper. Clare stood up to greet her.

"Mum—how lovely to see you. I think we're allowed a hug nowadays aren't we?"

Penny, after the hug, held Clare by her shoulders to look at her properly.

"You have done well, Mum. You look exactly the same and we haven't seen you for months. I don't know how you do it."

"That's very kind of you, darling. Actually of course I look older—how could I not, when I'm getting so ancient? But perhaps after a certain point a bit more white hair and a few more lines don't make that much difference. One of the good things about old age is that nobody actually looks at you."

"Rubbish, Mum. You look great. You really do. And it's clever of you not to have put on weight. Almost everyone's got fatter in lockdown. Nothing to do but eat."

"O well, I—"

"Talking of which, lunch is ready. Would you like to come and carve, Charles?"

They went into the dining half of Penny's cheerful sunny kitchen with its French windows, shut, into the garden.

"We ought to be having lunch on the terrace at the end of May but it's much too cold. Sit down, Mum."

Clare saw a joint of beef on the counter by the stove. She hadn't eaten what the papers call red meat for a long time. She wished it were a chicken.

"Not too much for me, Charles, please."

"O nonsense, Clare. I bet you haven't had a proper Sunday lunch for months. Good for you, roast beef. Good for anyone."

She wanted to say, "Well then. Why is your government doing in our beef farmers so that Boris Johnson can show off his Australian deal as Global Britain and encourage the Americans into a deal that will be even worse?" She had read a furious piece in the *Observer*, this very morning, saying that hill farmers in Scotland, therefore also in North Yorkshire, therefore some in Charles's constituency, were going to suffer from this Australian deal, and quite likely would have to go out of business, for a tiny economic gain for the country. Prices guaranteed for fifteen years. What is fifteen years on land your family has farmed for a century? Two centuries? Another, even more furious piece in *The Observer* had raged against the government's decision to cut the aid budget, depriving, exactly as Carrie had said in her email, the poorest people in the world of the simplest, most necessary, help. And all to save a tiny proportion of government spending. Which of course wasn't the point. The point was to please the Tory press and the right wing of the Tory MPs and the new Tory voters in Brexit constituencies who didn't like foreign aid because they didn't like foreigners.

But she must keep her powder dry. She heard Simon's voice in her head: "If you want to win an argument that really matters, timing is everything."

So she said, "Thank you. This looks delicious." when Penny put too loaded a plate in front of her.

They ate in silence for a few minutes, Charles and Penny each with a glass of wine, Clare with her elderflower.

"Well done, Pen. The beef's just right."

"Good. You never quite know, with beef—"

"Have you heard from the children lately?" Clare said.

This was to see where, if anywhere, Charles had got to on Nepal.

"Daisy's fine", Penny said. "She still seems to be enjoying herself in Vancouver though they've had virus restrictions and rules like everybody else. She wants to come home for a bit in the summer but she doesn't know yet whether it'll be possible what with quarantine and tests and everything, there as well as here."

"How much longer has she got, in Canada?"

"One more year anyway. She says she wants to do some extra degree and stay another year after that."

"I can't see anyone turning Daisy into an academic", Charles said. "I dare say she'll get bored with all the peculiar stuff she's learning. Trendy this and trendy that. Then perhaps she'll come home and get an ordinary job and maybe even find someone to marry. Time we were grandparents, Penny and me."

He smiled at Clare.

"Great-granny Clare. That would suit you a treat, wouldn't it?"

"I would enjoy that, yes." The last time she had thought about babies was when there seemed to be a promising future for Hakim and Ayesha.

"What about Carrie?" she said.

Charles and Penny looked at each other.

"Carrie's OK", Charles said. "We wish to goodness she'd come home, but she says it's difficult at the moment with so much Covid in that part of the world."

"Would you like some more, Mum? Another roast potato? Go on—I know you like them and I bet you never bother with roast potatoes when you're all alone in the flat."

"No thank you, darling. I've eaten too much as it is."

"Rubbish", Charles said, getting up with his plate in his hand. "You eat like a bird. I'm going to have a second helping anyway. Penny?"

"No thanks. I've made a rhubarb crumble, Charles. I don't suppose you ever have a hot pudding either, Mum?"

Charles sat down with more food on his plate.

"No of course not. Can you imagine?"

"While we're on the subject of the flat", Charles said, his mouth full. "I suppose it took you hours to get here?"

No logic in his transition, but he'd made it. The BBC had a new posh word for this kind of move. Segue, that was it. But she must concentrate.

"A bit longer than it usually does, yes, because of the bridge being closed."

"Enough time for you to make friends with that Paki driver."

"He was a Sikh. He wore a turban."

"Same difference."

"His wife died of the virus."

"Probably refused to be vaccinated. There's a lot of that, you know."

"She died last year, in May."

Charles and Penny had never known about Ayesha, staying in the flat, and then, so soon, dying of the virus. There had been no point in telling them then, and there would be even less now.

Penny cleared the plates, put bowls in front of Charles and Clare, and got her crumble out of the oven.

"Dear old rhubarb crumble", Clare said. "This looks perfect, darling."

"Anyway", Charles said, as Clare was pouring cream on her pudding. "You'll have seen what a total pain in the neck the bridge is being for Barnes. Takes forever to get anywhere north of the river."

"How long do you think it'll be before it's fixed?"

"God knows. Six years, last I heard."

"That's totally ridiculous. Surely—" She thought of Matt and him saying once how quickly the army could throw a bridge over a river, even a bridge that tanks could cross. Better not mention this to Charles.

"Bloody Labour politicians, that's what it is. Hammersmith and Fulham, Labour council. Then the Labour mayor of London—that Muslim fellow, I expect he's a hero of yours, Clare—sitting on his hands doing precisely nothing. And Richmond, our council this side of the river, Liberal Democrat. What do you expect?"

"What about the Prime Minister? He talks about a bridge between Ireland and Scotland. You'd think he could bang a few heads together and get a bridge over the Thames sorted out?"

"He's got one or two things on his plate at the moment, you may have noticed."

"More crumble, Mum?"

"No thank you, darling. Delicious, it was."

"Cheese?"

"No thanks. A lovely lunch, but enough."

"Coffee?"

"Coffee would be nice." It might keep her awake tonight, but never mind. She needed it. Do not be afraid.

"Go back to the sitting room with Charles. It's more comfortable in there. I'll do a bit of loading and bring the coffee in a minute."

"You see, Clare", Charles said when they had settled again in their armchairs, leaning forward with clasped hands in front of him, his earnestness indicating that they'd reached what had been the point of asking her to lunch. "The bridge has just been the last straw."

"How do you mean, the last straw?"

"Penny and I've got to the point where we've about had

living in Barnes. This house has done us very well all these years, but with the girls gone and Penny wanting to spend most of the time in Leckenby it's much too big for us now. Not to mention expensive to run. And now Barnes has become a nightmare for getting to the House or anywhere in the middle of London on account of the bridge."

She said nothing.

"At the same time we've been thinking—Well, isn't your flat getting a bit much for you nowadays, Clare? It's surely bigger than you need and the outgoings must be quite steep?"

"I'm very attached to my flat. Old people, you know, Charles, don't necessarily want to move out of where they've always lived just because they've got a bit too much space."

"We're only thinking of you. How much easier it would be for you, surely, to be somewhere smaller?"

"It's not difficult, my flat. You can hoover the whole flat in half an hour. And I can see of course how well it would suit you and Penny if you sold this house and moved into it. So handy for the tube. Gloucester Road gets you anywhere."

Penny came in with the coffee on a tray.

"Mum! It's nothing to do with the tube. Or the bridge for that matter. It's just that we worry about you rattling around in that dear old flat, with all Dad's books and stuff still there, and loads of junk from when Matt and I were children. Wouldn't it be nicer to clear it all out once and for all, decluttering you know, all the rage nowadays. And wouldn't you really be happier in David's little house which he so kindly left you? Cosier, and easier altogether. Don't you think?"

She put down the tray on the Habitat glass coffee table, a wedding present which had miraculously survived, and poured coffee into three cups.

"Sugar? No, of course, you don't."

Clare took her coffee and looked down at her cup for a minute while Penny gave Charles his.

"Listen, both of you. I don't want to leave my flat. I think you actually know that. It has been the background to my life for so long that, now that I'm old, I don't want to shut the door behind me because it would be shutting the door on almost everything I remember." And, she didn't say, shutting the door on my afternoons with Val, in the garden, or in his house, or in the flat. And Hakim was likely to need his bedroom and Simon's study, when he came back to London; she didn't say this either.

In the silence she sipped her coffee, very hot, strengthening, very different from Val's coffee, thick, sweet and consoling.

"But Mum—"

Clare lifted her spoon, surprised at herself.

"If there were no other way for you to sell this house and to move closer to Peter Jones and the House of Commons, I might feel morally bound to let you have the flat. After all, you and Carrie and Daisy are the only people I have to leave, or give, anything substantial to."

She could tell Charles was suspicious of this. Let him suspect whatever he liked.

"But, as you say, there's David's house. It's a nice house, worth an absurd amount of money now. I'd intended to keep it for Carrie. But who knows when she'll be home, and whether she'll want to live in South Ken, soon or ever. So if you want to sell this house and can deal with getting rid of the tenants in David's house—I've no idea how easy or difficult that might be—you can have it, if you'd like to live in it."

"Goodness, Mum—do you really mean that?"

At the same moment Charles said, "This is a very sudden decision, Clare. Are you sure you've thought it through?"

She laughed and sipped some more coffee.

"If you mean have I talked to lawyers and the bank and all the rest of it, no, I haven't. But I've always thought that David leaving me his house, such an extraordinary thing to happen, was a stroke of luck neither I nor any of you deserved. But there it is. And this seems the most sensible thing to do with it, if you want to leave Barnes after all these years. This house'll be worth a lot by now I should imagine, and Hammersmith Bridge won't be closed for ever, so you'll be able to sell it for a fortune and put Carrie and Daisy on—what do they call it on the wireless?—the housing ladder, when they come home and need flats or whatever. Knowing her, Carrie'll probably want to live in the East End anyway."

"You don't think you might change your mind?" Charles said. "You do have a tendency to—"

"Charles." Penny said, implying "for goodness' sake shut up".

Penny, Clare could see, was angry with her mother and taking her anger out on Charles.

"I only meant—", he said.

"I know exactly what you meant, Charles", Clare said. "Could I have a little more coffee, darling? It's awfully good."

It must have been the coffee that was keeping her courage up.

"You meant that I'm impulsive, reckless, decide things, do things, without considering all the ifs and buts that should make a sensible person hesitate. But, you know, I'm actually quite careful. I've known for some time that you—both of you, but specially Penny—would like to live in my flat. And why shouldn't you like the idea of living in it? It's a jolly nice flat. I've never lived in David's house but I know it's also nice, and I imagine it might suit you quite well.

"I've no idea how complicated it would be to get the tenants to move out. Not very in the case of the American who rents the main house; I think the lease was set up with six months notice on either side—I've got a copy of it of course—and it's only a year and a half since David died. Mr Steinberg, he's called, he runs a little gallery in Walton Street and he doesn't even live in David's house himself." There's a young boyfriend, lazy but harmless, living in the house, she didn't say. Whether or not he was still there, she didn't know. Mr Steinberg faithfully paid the rent.

"Mr Parker in the basement has lived there ever since David retired and turned his surgery and waiting-room into a flat. He's perfectly OK though he's not very friendly. He works in the City. He's reliable, he looks after the garden, always pays the rent and doesn't make problems. But he's lived there for at least fifteen years and David did want him to be allowed to go on living there, though I don't think he made any kind of legal commitment to him. So that might be more difficult. But no doubt you'll have people, Charles, lawyers and so forth, who could deal with Mr Parker for you if you wanted the whole house, which I expect you would. There's probably some way of paying off a tenant you want to get rid of, and if you sell this house you should have loads of money."

"But Mum", Penny said. "Hold on a minute. We haven't even thought about David's house, have we, darling?"

"Well—"

Oddly enough, Charles was less good than Penny at fudging the truth.

"I think Penny's been rather picturing herself in your flat," he said, "her childhood home after all, where she lived all her life till we married."

"The flat would need doing up, of course. It's terribly old-fashioned, Mum. I've wondered for years why you don't do something about the kitchen. No one has kitchens like yours any more."

"Exactly", Clare said. "I like my kitchen as it is, thank you very much. With a proper table to sit at, eat at, even work at, which I often do."

Penny had probably been looking for months at advertisements for shiny new kitchens.

"Work?" she said. "O, your book you mean. You're not writing another one are you?"

"Why not?"

"Perhaps it's time to retire, Clare", said Charles, who hadn't read her book but was backing up Penny. "Retire and downsize. After all, time marches on."

Charles's parents had died years ago. His two sisters had coped with their old age and their deaths. She saw he was doing his best to obey Penny's instructions. Poor old Charles.

"I know I'll be eighty next year", she said. But I'm still capable of doing this and that"—even making a new friend, she didn't say—"and I don't propose to stop until I have to." Stop living, she thought. "I need my kitchen table. And I don't need the kind of kitchen you see all the time in the colour magazines: islands and granite and barstools, nowhere to put cookery books or the wireless or a comfortable chair. And costing as much as a house used to cost not long ago."

Penny stood up, gathered the coffee cups and put them on the tray, took it to the kitchen, came back and sat down again.

"What about the rent, Mum, the two rents, from David's house?"

"I managed perfectly well without them while David was alive, and actually I've mostly just left them in the bank. There hasn't been anything to spend money on since the pandemic started. Apart from everyday boring stuff there's only been the train fare to York for Christmas that went west with going to Leckenby. So I've saved the rent. Useful perhaps for when I need looking after which one of these days I may well. That's another thing: it'll be nice to have the flat if I do. If I need to be looked after I mean. Plenty of room for a carer. And there aren't any stairs in a flat which for the very old is a good thing."

"You've made up your mind, haven't you?"

"Yes, darling, I'm afraid I have. I'm sorry, but there it is."

She looked across the glass coffee table at Penny, who was glaring at the floor, with a cross down-turned mouth familiar to her mother from all her life.

She heard Simon saying, long ago, "Stubborn as a mule when she's set on something. You know where she gets it from? Her mother."

"Simon—you can't say that—I—" She had been going to say, "Don't I always let you have your way?" Over schools for the children, holidays, all sorts of things. Then she realized he had a point, which was why she remembered what he'd said. And wasn't she being, now, as stubborn as a mule?

"Don't worry", she said. "I won't live for ever. If I conk out, which I easily might—look at David—or if I lose the plot and have to go into a home, you'll have the flat anyway, and one or other of those things is bound to happen before too long. Meanwhile—well—I really don't want to live anywhere else."

Penny neither spoke nor moved.

"Come on, Pen. It's fair enough, you know. If Clare wants to stay in her flat, then she must stay in her flat. And her offer of Dr Rose's house is very generous, very generous indeed."

"It's a poky little house. I remember going to the surgery as a child. Dark. Down area steps."

135

"That was because the surgery was in the basement. On the other side of the house it isn't even a basement. Mr Parker's sitting room, which used to be David's consulting room, opens into the garden. A pretty garden. Anyway, you really can't decide against it until you've had a proper look at it, and Charles too, of course. It's actually a lovely house, not big but with a lot of charm, and in the very nicest bit between Kensington and Chelsea."

"Poky", Penny said.

"We'll certainly go and have a look at it, if the tenant won't mind", Charles said.

"He won't mind. Let me know when, or if"—Penny was still looking mutinous—"you'd be able to go and see it and I'll have a word with him, with them, since there are two of them. I should probably go and talk to Mr Parker properly. I don't want to rattle him by suddenly asking if you can look at his flat. Let's hope he's thinking of retiring—he must be about old enough by now—and going to live in the country because he's fed up with lockdowns. Apparently there's a lot of that happening."

"That's very kind, Clare. In fact you're being extremely kind altogether and we're most grateful. Aren't we, Penny?"

Silence.

But so far, so fairly good. Now or never.

She sat forward in her chair, as Charles had leant towards her to talk about the flat.

"Charles, there's something I want to ask you while I'm here."

"Of course. Any time, Clare."

She could see that Charles thought his assignment from Penny had gone reasonably well.

She thought, for a moment.

"You're an MP and your party has a huge majority."

He laughed, a little. "I'm not sure I like the sound of this."

"I gather we have 70 million spare vaccine doses we don't need, or don't need in the foreseeable future."

"Do we? As many as that?"

"We've done brilliantly with vaccines, I do realize, but don't you think it's time we started sharing what we don't need with the poorest countries which are having a truly dreadful time? I don't know how much Carrie has told you about Nepal, but the situation there is desperate, with thousands of people dying, and we could help, at once, by sending a plane with enough vaccines at least for the old people. Couldn't we? You know they have nothing in Nepal, no money to buy vaccines and no way of making them, and India can't help them because the virus is killing so many of their own people. What do you think?"

There. The case. Quite quickly and crisply made, she thought.

Charles got up and went to stand in front of the fireplace with his hands behind his back as if he were about to make a speech.

"I've heard from Carrie too. Yes. And yes, Nepal is poor and it's next to India where Covid is quite out of control—what can you expect in a huge backward country like India? But I can't wave a magic wand for Nepal, Clare, however much I'd like to help Carrie's friends. There's such a thing as government policy. I don't decide it any more than you do. The cabinet gets all the scientific advice and they decide, or the PM decides, what's best for the country. This country. That's what he's elected to do. I imagine Nepal's pretty far down the list of his priorities."

"I'm sure it is." This was not the moment to embark on the topic of Boris Johnson's priorities. "But isn't that exactly the point? Nobody here's likely to care much about Nepal unless they happen to have been there for a very expensive holiday, or perhaps served with the Gurkhas, but it's one example of a place where if we wanted to we could do something to help, something not difficult to do, and not even very expensive, which could save hundreds and hundreds of lives. In the mountains where the earthquake damage hasn't yet been properly repaired—you know that was why Carrie went there in the first place - they've got no doctors, no oxygen and no vaccines. We can't send them doctors or oxygen but wouldn't it be perfectly easy to send them vaccines? Anyone, Carrie for instance, can do vaccinations with half an hour's training. Then, if the old people get the virus at least they won't die. You could make a good argument out of all this, couldn't you?"

"Clare. I don't think you understand. I can't raise Nepal, just like that, in the House."

"Why on earth not? Isn't this just the sort of thing back-benchers are for?"

"Not unless they want to stay backbenchers for ever", Penny said. "Really Mum, you can't be bothering Charles with a little thing like this when Boris is fighting a global pandemic."

"It's not a little thing if you're choking to death in a Himalayan village. And if this government were really fighting the pandemic in a global spirit they'd see that the rich countries have got to share the vaccines with the poor countries or Covid will never end. It only needs the rich countries to join together and produce the money for the world to be fairly vaccinated. It's totally possible but—"

"You've been listening to Gordon Brown" Charles said. "Or reading him in your wretched *Guardian*. Haven't you? I'm sure he's doing his best but Gordon Brown's a busted flush, don't you see? He's part of the past. Everything's different since his day."

"You mean the Tory party's different, don't you? Well, Gordon Brown could still be right, couldn't he?"

"Mum, please. Poor Charles. It's Sunday. I think he deserves an afternoon off, don't you?"

"Look, Clare", said Charles, looming from his actorish height in front of the fireplace and paying no attention to Penny. "Compared to most countries we're very generous with aid—"

"Charles, how can you say that? We used to be. Not any more. Tony Blair invented the point seven per cent. David Cameron and Mrs May carried it on. Boris Johnson said he would and now he's ratted. Abolishing DFID, making aid part of foreign policy so we only help wretched people if it benefits us, cutting aid to desperate places just when they need it most because of the virus, and now refusing to send to the poorest and most terrified people vaccines that we don't need, that will go off and be useless if we keep them too long—it's all dreadful, Charles, really dreadful, and I'm ashamed of it, all of it."

"Well. You and your left-wing friends may be ashamed but most people in this country are proud, proud of Boris, proud of the vaccination roll-out, proud of us for standing up to Europe and doing our own thing. Our vaccination roll-out's been better than anything any of the EU countries have managed, have you noticed?"

"O Charles. If you still think Brexit is so brilliant, have you asked your constituents whether they want their lives ruined by a deal with Australia that will let in cheaper, nastier beef and lamb produced from badly-treated animals? Not to mention worse horrors from America which are sure to follow? Have you forgotten that you represent farmers?"

Damn, she shouldn't have complicated things by reacting to Charles's boasting. How stupid. She clenched her fists in irritation that she'd given him an open goal.

"O, I see. It's all about Brexit after all", he said. "I might have known it. Brexit's over, Clare, in case you haven't noticed. It got done, as Boris promised. And mostly as a result of getting it done the government, I'm here to tell you, is very popular at the moment. Look at Hartlepool in the by-election the other day: used to be a solid Labour constituency, solid Labour candidate, worthy front-line doctor through Covid, but anti-Brexit. Beaten hollow. And you know perfectly well my constituency voted for Brexit in the first place. And my vote went up in the Boris election in 2019. So there you are."

For a moment Clare said nothing. She was furious, mostly with herself for letting the discussion slide into Brexit when it needn't have been deflected from sending vaccines to Nepal, but partly with Charles for being, as always, so pleased with himself for nothing more than being carried along in Boris Johnson's slipstream. But was there any way to use her fury to help Carrie? It was evidently no good, either to Carrie or in general, to say, "You lied to the farmers before the Brexit vote. You're lying to them at the moment, though they're beginning to see through the lies. And no doubt you'll go on lying to them until they're done for."

Instead, she got a grip on herself, took a couple of deep, calming breaths, and said, "Don't you think it would be rather splendid if you stood up in the House, next time there's a debate or questions about the virus—there won't be a debate about aid because lots of MPs, including plenty of Tories, I notice, are shocked by what the government's doing to it—and just produced some figures about how many people have died in Nepal and how many people have been vaccinated, and then how many spare vaccines we could send without us suffering at all, to a country that can't make vaccines and at the moment can't get them from anywhere?"

"I don't think you understand—", he began.

"Understand that it's difficult to get a question in—yes, I do understand that—or understand how difficult it is to deviate from the party line? But don't you see? You'd be a hero, Charles, if you managed this. The press would pick it up. Even the Tory papers would go for it. 'Backbench MP pleads for virus-sharing': that couldn't be unpopular with anyone."

Charles stood in front of the fireplace with his head down. Thinking? Unlikely, but possible.

"And imagine"—this had better be her last shot—"how pleased and proud Carrie would be if you actually managed to make a difference, to save some lives on the other side of the world."

She had nearly said something more about the Gurkhas, and owing gratitude to Nepal, but remembered in time that Charles thought the Gurkhas were something to do with the imperial past, so any debt he recognized would be the other way round.

"It's no good, Mum", Penny said, recovered at least a bit from her sulk. "Charles has to stick to what he's supposed to know about if he's going to get anywhere in the Party. Which certainly isn't Nepal. The Northern Powerhouse is supposed to be his thing."

A dead duck, Clare wanted to say, like Levelling Up, but didn't.

"Anyway, you know how Carrie exaggerates. Of course the virus is extra bad in such a poor country, but it's the sort of thing people like that are used to, isn't it?"

Clare was feeling a little faint or she might have snapped at Penny. Too much coffee probably. But she was also very angry.

She hadn't talked to Charles for more than a year. He was her son-in-law. He was an MP. She wasn't going to let the cuts to the aid budget go. The second piece in that morning's paper came to her rescue.

"Listen, both of you, specially Charles since you've been elected, after all, to take a careful and responsible view about what the government is actually doing. Never mind the northern powerhouse, whatever that is or will ever be beyond a slogan. And never mind Brexit—you wouldn't have thought I would ever say that, would you?"

"So it isn't Brexit that's the worst thing ever suddenly?"

"It's bad, certainly it is, whatever all you Brexiteers and the Prime Minister keep saying. Look at the mess in Ireland. But worse, even worse, is ruining our reputation for generosity and reliability across the world by making these cuts, which mean slashing programmes people have been relying on, for clean water, for malaria drugs, for girls' education, clinics at the back of beyond, care for pregnant mothers—many of these things will just stop because of how the cuts have been done. And with all the other rich countries giving more rather than less aid because of the pandemic, how does it look to the rest of the world that we're doing all this real harm for what is actually, compared to what the pandemic has cost us, a small amount of money?"

She wished Charles would leave his podium position in front of the fireplace—he looked as if he should have a Union Jack behind him—and sit down. Perhaps treating her like a tiresome heckler at a political meeting was good for his confidence.

"If it's such a small amount of money, Clare", he said, "How can losing it be such a disaster for these places?" He nodded and grinned, pleased with his debating point. "Eh? Answer me that."

Her son-in-law could be so infuriating that she wondered, not for the first time, how she had all these years remained more or less on speaking terms with him.

"Charles! Where's your imagination? The good a small amount of money can do in a desperately poor part of Africa, or Bangladesh, or Nepal come to that, is off the scale different from the good the same amount of money can do in Barnes or even in Barnsley. Surely you can see that? And another thing. If it's a small amount of money compared with everything else the government is spending, has to spend, then saving it wasn't the point of making the cuts, was it?"

"What do you mean? Of course it was the point."

"No. It wasn't. The point was to please the Brexiteer MPs and the Tory papers and the hooray nationalists we seem to have more and more of—none of whom have ever liked the aid budget—and to demonstrate to the famous red wall voters that the government can be tough on foreigners. Wasn't it? Like the Home Secretary is tough on foreigners. Because Brexit was really about keeping people out."

"Look, Clare." His voice was taut.

At last he left the fireplace and came to sit on one arm of the sofa, too close to her armchair, so that he was still making her look up to him.

"Please, Charles", Penny said. "Don't be too hard on Mum. She hasn't had anyone to talk to for months, you know."

"I think your mother can look after herself perfectly well", he said, not looking at Penny, but she had lowered the temperature of the discussion.

"The thing is, Clare", he said, in a more ordinary voice. "You have to accept that there's all sorts of things about politics the ordinary man in the street, or woman in the street, can't begin to understand."

"Like the fact that politicians mind more about what's good for the party than what's good for the country? And more about what's good for the next election than what's actually, really, good? I think even geriatric *Guardian*-readers like me can understand that."

"You can't say that, Mum."

In a way she was glad to see that after all these years Penny would rally to Charles's defence if she thought he was being attacked.

"Well, I can", she said. "Because in this case it's obviously true."

"Of course it isn't true. It's nonsense, socialist nonsense. We can't afford to help everybody in the world when the pandemic has cost us such a huge amount of money. Anyone can see that. And Brexit—I know you hated it because for some peculiar reason you like foreigners better than poor old Brits who've had to put up with far too much immigration for years—Where was I? Yes. Brexit was all about the good of the country, standing on our own feet instead of being bossed about by Brussels. There is such a thing as sovereignty, you know, getting back control of our own country, whether you believe in it or not. That's what Brexit was about. The good of the country."

"It was about the good of one section of the Tory party from start to finish. And David Cameron being terrified of Nigel Farage. Well, look at them now, the Brexiteers and the ones who became Brexiteers to get into the cabinet, running the country less efficiently and less honestly than any government I have ever known in my long life."

At the same moment Clare said, "You can't say that, Mum, when they're doing the vaccinations so brilliantly", and Charles, getting off the arm of the sofa, said, "That's enough. I must go and do some calls. There's no point talking to your mother about politics, Pen", and left the drawing room, slamming the door behind him.

After a silence, broken only by the sound of Charles slamming his study door across the hall, Clare said, "O dear. I'm so sorry, darling. It was sweet of you to ask me to lunch, and lovely to see you after such a long time, and now I've made Charles really angry, which I shouldn't have done, and achieved nothing for Carrie, not even a promise that he'll think about it. And I've probably made things difficult for you later."

"O never mind that. You know and Charles knows that you'll never agree about anything to do with politics and there we are. It's like Charles and Carrie and politics. They can't agree about anything and I just have to put up with them arguing."

"You can always fall back on the dotty old lady excuse. No need to take any notice of anything someone as ancient as me might say."

"Don't be silly, Mum. If Charles really thought you were dotty he wouldn't get so cross."

This was uncharacteristically astute of Penny and she was no doubt right.

"Anyway, there are more important things in life than politics."

"Of course there are", Clare said, though she thought that sometimes there aren't, and also that the things that are always more important than politics had been beyond the scope of Penny's attention all her life. Her fault no doubt, for not fighting Simon hard enough over a Catholic school. At least if she'd been to one Penny might have grown up with a sense that the great questions do need asking.

"The flat would have been nice", now she said. Ah. This was definitely more important than politics. "But of course Charles is quite right, if you want to stay in the flat, you must."

"Thank you, darling. I expect it won't be for too long."

Clare suddenly felt exhausted. Sleep seemed a good idea, death not a bad one.

"You mustn't say that, Mum."

"Why not? It's true."

She felt her face sagging from tiredness, but managed to say, "Anyway, I ought to be getting home. Do you think you could ring for a taxi, or one of your nice minicabs?"

She thought Penny might offer to drive her home. When she didn't, Clare was relieved.

"Of course, Mum. I expect you need your afternoon nap."

Penny stood up, took her mobile out of her pocket, pressed a few buttons and asked the minicab to come. "On Mr Roberts's account. Thank you."

"Five minutes, Mum."

As Clare got, stiffly, out of her armchair, Penny said, "I'm sorry, Mum. I expect I shouldn't have thought it was so obvious, about the flat."

This, from Penny, was quite handsome.

"I suppose I assumed you were bound to see it like me. But you don't, and there it is. It's very kind of you, as Charles says, to offer us David's house, and we'll go and see it and have a think. Apparently it's a very good time to sell houses.

Everybody wants bigger houses, and proper gardens, because of being stuck in flats through the pandemic, so it shouldn't be difficult to sell this house. And we'd be much luckier than most people, wouldn't we, still not having to buy another one."

Perhaps that would make David's house nearly as good as the flat in the end.

"Well, darling. See what you think. Both of you. You might see what the girls think too. There's always email."

"They're so far away. I don't suppose either of them thinks much about us, or Barnes, or anything to do with home. Daisy used to be fond of this house. She might be sad if she never sees it again. Carrie couldn't wait to get away when she started at uni, even though she could easily have lived here."

"Carrie likes my flat I think, even though it's in such an impossibly incorrect part of London. Maybe I'll leave it to her in my will—then she could have it in the end, even if you and Charles want to live in it when I die."

"Mum, you mustn't keep talking about dying. You're doing really well for your age. I'm sure you'll live for years and years."

"I rather hope not, I must say. My generation is the one that's been so well looked after by the NHS and brilliant medical science that we're all living longer and longer. Very likely longer than we really want. And it's a sensible idea when you're old to keep the prospect of death in view, don't you think?"

"I think it's a bit morbid. And if you're well, surely it's good, to be living longer, isn't it?"

"Of course it is. Yes. I don't mean to complain. Not at all. I'm lucky to be well—and—lucky to be alive in lots of ways, I know. Life's still interesting, that's the great thing."

"Good for you, Mum."

The doorbell rang.

"There's the minicab." Penny sounded relieved.

Slowly and awkwardly and with Penny's help Clare put on her coat.

"Goodbye, darling, and thank you so much. Do apologize to Charles for me, won't you?"

But in the car on the way home, this time driven by a silent black man, West Indian or African, she was angry all over

145

again. Not so much because of Penny and the flat, ordinary family stuff and Penny behaving exactly as she had all her life when she failed to get her own way, but because of the impermeable carelessness of both Charles and Penny about the people dying of Covid in Nepal, when it was perfectly possible and not in any way outrageous to do something to help them. And they'd cared even less about the people in other desperate countries where those trying their best to improve their lives had been suddenly deprived of resources without which they could do nothing.

She remembered, as she had several times, what Val had said about the British: never having been part of anyone else's empire, never having been invaded since 1066, they still assumed a kind of superiority which justified any degree of national selfishness. We had taken, in the eyes of the rest of the world, a considerable step away from this ingrained complacency when we got so many rich countries to agree to contribute point seven percent of GNP to helping the poorest. When was that? She couldn't remember but knew it was when Tony Blair was Prime Minister. Perhaps it was Gordon Brown's idea; after all it was Gordon Brown who had managed to get all the rich countries even including Russia and China to unite enough to deal with the financial crisis that had been America's fault. So the point seven per cent might well have been him. In any case, those were the good days of Clare Short at the Department for International Development. And, as she'd said, pointlessly of course, to Charles, the commitment had been stuck to since. Until now. The Department had been junked, and the point seven per cent was being junked too. Complacency, national selfishness, arrogant recklessness as to trust and reputation, back in control. "Take back control", she thought bitterly. The Brexit slogan. For this?

So that people would die.

By the time her minicab crossed the Cromwell Road and turned into the square, she had almost forgotten most of what had happened at lunch and was lost in a daze of despair with the government, which was sure to last at least another three years. By which time she might well be dead.

146

She came to when the driver opened her door to help her onto the pavement.

"Thank you. I'm so sorry", she said, for no reason except that she had not been paying any attention to him or the journey.

She opened her bag.

"The fare is on the account of Mr Roberts", the driver said, not as kindly as her Sikh of the morning.

"O, of course."

She gave him, in any case, the other five pound note she had in her wallet, and he thanked her with a nod before getting back in the car and speeding away.

She felt too tired for the stairs: usually nowadays she walked up, with the idea that it was good for her, her hand just above the banister in case she tripped but not using the banister to pull herself up. Mr Clements's lift was working properly, which it didn't always. At last, with the door of the flat shut behind her and her coat hung up, she was glad, so glad, to be home.

While the kettle boiled she walked round the kitchen table, touching things here and there, the wireless on the dresser, the geranium struggling a bit in not enough sunshine on the windowsill - Val had brought it last time he came for tea—the old brown teapot she hardly ever used but couldn't throw away, the *Observer* crossword, always easier than the *Guardian*'s, finished on the table. She had been out for less than three hours and it was as if she had come back after months away. But then, she hadn't been out to lunch for fifteen months so perhaps just that had been a kind of shock. And if Penny had had her way, she would now be looking at her kitchen as if she were about to leave it, to lose it for good. If she had agreed to what Penny wanted and moved into David's house, her kitchen wouldn't have lasted a fortnight beyond her leaving it: Penny would have spent a lot of money turning it into something quite different.

The kettle boiled. Decaff tea, though after all that coffee it was probably too late to save her night.

At least she'd been strong enough to see off the plan which Penny had no doubt been brooding on for so long that she'd persuaded herself it was bound to come off.

Had she spoilt Penny, the wilful child who liked to get her own way and often did? Perhaps she had, partly to make up for always finding Matt so much easier. Simon certainly had: Penny amused him because she was so different from him, as she was, except for her stubbornness, also from Clare. He was not amused when she married Charles, but for Penny's sake had made the best of it and when the girls were small children he had loved them as much as she had herself.

Well, Penny had had a pretty easy time. She'd never done a day's proper work since she married, unless organizing fund-raising events for the hunt or the Tory party counted as work, and Charles had followed a standard path, from the City into the House of Commons, respectably if not with notable success. Perhaps Penny could do with a bit of grit in her life.

She sat down with her mug of tea and suddenly wished, acutely, that she had someone to talk to about the day, about Penny and Charles and the flat and David's house, and how useless had been her attempt to get Charles to imagine that he might do something about sending vaccines to Nepal. She could tell Carrie that she had failed, but that was all: Carrie was so far away and in the middle of real sadness and some danger. She wouldn't be surprised that Clare had failed with her father but she was bound to be disappointed.

David would have understood it all, and David was dead.

There was no one else to tell. The story of her day was a story set in England and set in privilege. Hakim, had he been here in the flat—how she wished he would come back—was too young and too foreign to understand. And Val? Val was also too foreign, and he was too old. She couldn't complain to Val about Penny and Charles, not only because he wouldn't be able to imagine what she was talking about but because it would be disloyal to them; they couldn't, by now, help being who they were, and thinking how they thought or failed to think. And she couldn't grumble about her family to someone who had lost his wife and both his sons and had no one left to love.

One day, perhaps, she would get him to talk about what had happened to them: so far he hadn't wanted to, or perhaps he hadn't been able, to. And she had only the vaguest idea of how he'd lost his parents, so long ago.

His mother and her parents, none of whom he remembered—she thought of the trusting face of the Jewish bride looking up at her new husband in the photograph on Val's mantelpiece—had, she knew, been taken away from Sarajevo, where most Bosnian Jews lived, respected and appreciated for hundreds of years, by Nazi or Ustasha soldiers. How had it been done? Had they tried to escape? What became of their house? Perhaps Val didn't know the answer to these questions, any more than she knew what had happened to her Czech Jewish grandparents. Even her father's escape, by himself, from Prague just before the start of the war she knew almost nothing about because he never talked about it, even when he was dying and she was looking after him. He had talked, then, three or four times, about his childhood, about how his father, a maker and restorer of beautiful furniture, had made a wonderful sledge for him and his sister, and how in the Christmas holidays they had played for days in the snow. In the summers there had been holidays with grandparents in a village in the Tatra mountains. He had told her that his sister, a couple of years younger than him, had died when she was eight years old, of diphtheria, and that he hadn't been allowed to see her when she was ill but had gone with his parents to her funeral. "Her coffin was so small." This was the only time he had ever said to Clare that he had a sister. "She was called Clara. When you were born I wanted to call you Clara, for her and for Clara Schumann, but your mother said Clara sounded too foreign so we settled for Clare."

After her father's death she had asked David about diphtheria, which she'd never heard of. "A cruel disease, quite common once and very contagious. It killed mostly children. Horrible swelling of the throat. You never hear of it now: one of the great vaccination successes."

Poor little girl, choking to death in Prague in the 1920s, of a disease that vaccination had since wiped out.

She sat at the table sipping her tea. Vaccination: her random remembering had led her back to the people who could be saved in Nepal and weren't going to be, certainly not by the Tory government, and also to what she had read and heard of the crazy, or wicked, campaigns on the internet which frightened people who had no sounder sources of information into refusing vaccinations which could stop the epidemic reaching them. She hated the phrase "culture wars", and much disliked the signs that some of the issues deeply dividing Americans into groups of people who couldn't hear or listen to each other were arriving in England, particularly arriving in universities, but at least "anti-vaxxers" were here not, or not yet, a mob of rabid right-wingers as they were there, identifying themselves as supporters of Trump, enemies not only of democracy but of common sense, certain that the presidential election had been stolen and that vaccination was a conspiracy designed by the powerful to weaken or harm them.

What a world. She did so miss David, though she was glad that he had been spared even knowing about Covid 19.

The telephone rang. Penny, hoping she had got home safely?

"Is that Clare Wilson?" an unfamiliar voice said, a woman's voice.

"Yes it is." She tried to sound non-committal without actually saying no.

"Good afternoon Clare. I hope you are having a nice day."

"No I'm not. And you're a cold call. Goodbye", she said, and pressed the red button on the telephone to end the call.

She sat with the telephone in her hand for a few minutes, the world seeming more hateful, more isolating, more difficult to negotiate than ever. Then she put the telephone back on its stand, pulled her laptop towards her, and wrote an apologetic email to Carrie saying she had done the best she could with Charles, got nowhere, and wished she could think of anything else she could do to help with vaccines for Nepal.

Do keep safe, darling. And if you can find a way to come home before too long, that would be wonderful.
I'm fine, just as usual, ticking over OK.
    Much love
      Gran

Then, because it was comforting, to have the laptop open in her warm kitchen, and to feel the keys under her fingers, she pulled out the drawer immediately in front of where she always sat to work. It was a shallow drawer under the table top so she had to fold back the tablecloth to open it. It had in it some envelopes, some postcards saved from expeditions to museums and galleries in case anyone deserved to be sent one, a few stamps and pencils, and, stuck with little blobs of Blu Tack to the inside of the drawer on the left where she could easily see it a slip of paper which said in her writing: "Instructions to icon painters: Make the sign of the cross. Forgive your enemies. Say a prayer."

She did all three, realizing as she did that poor old Charles was who he was and not actually an enemy, and Penny was still less an enemy. And her prayer was for Val, that he should be well and as happy as possible.

Then she started to write a first draft of what she remembered of her day.

CHAPTER 8

SATURDAY 3 JULY 2021

She sat at the kitchen table in her dressing gown with tears pouring down her face. After a few minutes she got up, sniffing and swallowing her tears, took her glasses off and felt her way to the drawer where she kept the box of tissues. She mopped her eyes and her cheeks, blew her nose, wiped the tears from her glasses with another tissue and put them back on, but was still crying when she turned off the *Today* programme which had returned to the subject of tonight's football match in Rome. She sat down again, took a deep shaky breath, and sipped her tea which was still hot. Consoling tea.

She shut her eyes and found she was saying to herself not the prayer for the dead which she so often said for Matt but "God be merciful to me, a sinner". Why? Because by now she should have learnt patient resignation to the loss of Matt? Perhaps.

What she had just heard, what had made her cry because it had shocked her into memories that were more vivid than the familiar surroundings of her ordinary Saturday morning kitchen, was a news recording from twelve years ago. 2009, they'd said, two years after Matt's death. A BBC journalist was reporting from Camp Bastion, the British base in Afghanistan. He was watching the coffins, three coffins, of soldiers killed, as Matt had been killed, by a roadside bomb. The coffins, with their flags, were being slowly carried between lines of their comrades onto a plane which would fly them back to Brize Norton; afterwards they would be buried at home. As the cargo doors of the plane were shut, a bugler sounded the Last Post.

She and Simon had watched that scene on the television what seemed like over and over again. Different soldiers, whose names she hadn't registered, their parents, their widows, their children, perhaps this morning listening, as she had been listening, while boiling kettles, getting the milk out of the fridge, looking at the clock so as not to be late for whatever the children were doing on Saturday morning, to the *Today* programme.

For all the soldiers killed in Helmand there had been the same silence. and then the Last Post. Simon liked to watch the television news. Now she never turned it on. The films of desperate refugees in camps in Libya, Hakim's Libya, or of bulldozers and fire destroying the Amazon jungle, or of glaciers crumpling into the sea, or of soldiers in sand-coloured kit crouched, as Matt had crouched, behind stones and smoke in a sand-coloured desert in Afghanistan: any of these, all of these, gave her nightmares. The wireless news was better, fewer pictures to haunt her dreams and more substance, more discussion and criticism.

Her memories had substance, they had pictures and they had feeling: they were part of her soul. At the kitchen table with her eyes closed she was back in the rain at Matt's graveside in the quiet churchyard in Yorkshire, the little church by a beck, so remote that there was no village anywhere near, as a bugler sounded for Matt alone the Last Post that she had just heard again from the Afghanistan of years ago. As she stood there with Simon and three soldiers and Penny and Charles and the vicar, with behind them perhaps twenty or thirty Yorkshire relations and friends, she knew she would never get used to the loss of Matt.

She had understood, because she had been following the story for days on the wireless and in the paper, that the Americans and therefore also the British were going to pull all their remaining soldiers out of Afghanistan. She had heard diplomatic but none the less angry generals, both British and American, complaining, if not in so many words, that the politicians had made a mess of the whole enterprise, this war that had lasted twenty years, except for the success at the very beginning when the Taliban had been defeated and the horribly effective fanatics who had planned and delivered 9.11 were chased out of the country. And now, this morning, there were politicians—at least, there were two Tory MPs who had been soldiers in Afghanistan—who were equally angry, and miserable too, because it was impossible for the British to stay and support the Afghan army if the Americans were leaving. We haven't enough of an army left. We have no international clout left, after defence cuts and Brexit and the aid cuts she had fallen out with Charles over.

Wasn't there going to be, at last, a vote in the House of Commons on the aid cuts, next week? The week after? There were rumours of a Tory rebellion. Would there be enough rebels actually to defeat the bill and restore the aid budget? Almost certainly not, with such a huge Tory majority. Would Charles be brave enough to join the rebels? No chance. Not only would Charles never vote against Boris Johnson but, as she had seen at that awful Sunday lunch in Barnes, he had no sense, no feeling, for what was disastrous about the cuts.

But now, today, for all that the Prime Minister—it still jarred even to think of Boris Johnson as the Prime Minister— so often boasted about "global Britain", here were these Tory MPs who had served in Afghanistan saying we are actually too weak to take a line of our own and leave some troops to help the Afghan army, to help the people who helped us, and the people in general, anyone, girls in school, women journalists, teachers, judges, who all this time had been promised support against the Taliban, and were already being picked off by them. Bombs attached to cars. Snipers in the street. And fighters more sinister than the Taliban, belonging to an Afghan version of IS, had a few days ago killed mine-clearers working for the Halo Trust. She thought, as everyone no doubt did when they heard any news of the Halo Trust, of Princess Diana in mine-clearing kit somewhere in Africa. The brave men she'd admired, the men who saved lives by finding and dealing with mines in terrible countries with wars still going on, had been in Afghanistan respected and protected even by the Taliban.

One of the MPs on the Today programme was most anxious about the fate of interpreters who had been brave enough to work with the British army for years: how was it going to be possible to get them out, to get them and their families to safety? And, knowing the government's hostility to all refugees and particularly to Muslims—Brexit hostility—what would become of them if they did manage to leave the country?

There had been, she remembered, a photograph of Matt and his soldiers in Afghanistan, smiling in the desert, like a school team photograph, with for some reason a dog at Matt's feet. At the end of the first row, smiling like the others, was their Afghan interpreter, nearly as young as the soldiers, perhaps about the same age as Matt. Of course she couldn't remember his name but she did remember Matt saying when she asked about him, "He's a terrific star. We couldn't have coped in the villages in Helmand without him."

Years ago, the photograph was taken: might it still be in the flat? And where was he today, that interpreter? With, probably by now, a wife and children and elderly parents, like her, to be looked after? Would someone be making the effort to rescue them from danger? Would there be time and opportunity? Could they be found, wherever they were, if the Taliban were determined to kill them?

Another thing she had never forgotten was the wild, wonderful landscape of mountains and desert and rock that you saw on the television pictures, and in a few other photographs Matt had shown her and Simon, and the noble and beautiful faces of the Afghan people. Why couldn't the outside world have left them alone instead of invading their country and then abandoning them, as the Russians had done, as the British had done several times in the nineteenth century? And now, having invaded the country again in 2001, we and the Americans were about to abandon them again. Shame was what she felt, almost every day, about Boris Johnson's government, and today more than ever because of Matt.

Could she find that photograph? Would it have the interpreter's name on it? She couldn't remember whether or not the picture had a line of names at the bottom. Where might it be? She looked, absurdly, round the kitchen as if the photograph might be in here, in a drawer, on a shelf. Was it in Matt's room? No. She had cleared Matt's room soon after his death, to make it a spare room with no reminders of him in it, a room later for Carrie occasionally, for Hakim when he first arrived, for poor, good Ayesha, for Hakim again. In Simon's study? Possibly. She had never taken everything out of the drawers in his desk. Later she would look.

She got to her feet. Time to pull herself together. She had stopped crying. She got another tissue from the box, blew her nose firmly, and stood looking out of the kitchen window at the dreary backs of the houses in the next street, Victorian and newer than Victorian, and beyond them the cutting where the District and the Circle Line trains have trundled towards High Street Kensington for a hundred and fifty years.

As she was looking at all this without seeing it, she asked herself, as she often had before, how much of this grief, after so long, was more than her feeling sorry for herself? Where was Matt in her tears? God be merciful to me, a sinner. She turned back towards the kitchen and then went to her bedroom to get dressed. She had a lot to do this morning. As she got out clean underclothes, new tights, her favourite shirt, a skirt instead of trousers for respectability, and a black cashmere cardigan, her best, she let her useless grief turn into useless fury with the politicians whose decisions had sent Matt into those hot rocky deserts where he had been an easy target for the Taliban.

The Americans, President Biden, in this respect following President Trump who had made a deal with the Taliban that left out the Afghan government, had decided to pull all American troops out of Afghanistan before the anniversary. In just over two months it would be twenty years since 9.11, the reason for invading Afghanistan, which then had seemed an obvious and necessary thing to do since the attack had been planned and organized there. Not by the Taliban, who had been allies of America not long before, helped with arms and cash against the Russians, but by rich Saudis led by Osama bin Laden. She remembered Hakim's explanation of Saudi fundamentalist Islam, of which she'd known almost nothing at the time. Brutal Saudi Arabia: she thought of the horrifying murder of the sixty-year-old journalist Jamal Khashoggi, killed and cut up in the Saudi consulate in Istanbul on the orders of the Crown Prince.

And now? Afghanistan now? There had been twenty years of a war that had lately become again more cruel, more terrifying for the people in the mountains, in the villages, even in the streets of Kabul, specially if they were women with education, prominent positions, identifiable cars. All this time there had been Afghans killing each other, and the Taliban killing (many fewer) British and American soldiers. She knew, because she had often heard both generals and politicians saying so, that through these twenty years there had also been serious and expensive efforts to improve the country, and that these had certainly done a great deal of good. Afghan schools were better, especially for girls. Afghan hospitals were better. Afghan soldiers were better trained. Possibilities for women to work and contribute to Afghan society had expanded and many impressive women had become lawyers, even judges, doctors, journalists, politicians. Hence the recent murders of several of such women. And how much of this actual progress, particularly the fairer treatment of girls and women, was likely to survive what was about to be the triumph of the crowing Taliban, was more than doubtful. It had been because of 9.11 that we were there, and it was because of the twentieth anniversary of 9.11 that we, towed both in and out by the Americans, were leaving. Probably we shouldn't have been there nearly so long. But surely we shouldn't now be leaving?

Thinking it through all over again as she got dressed had dulled both her grief for Matt and her anger. She thought of the suffering of so many in Afghanistan. The long disaster had been terrible for thousands, hundreds of thousands of people, people one by one, parents, children, boys with guns, old people in despair. And the disaster was now most likely to get worse.

Dressed and reasonably presentable, she brushed her hair— it would be good to wash it later in the morning if she had time—and saw in the mirror that her face was still a mess from crying. It would after a bit return to normal, not that that was anything, nowadays, to write home about.

She went back to the kitchen and put on the kettle, the simplest of all comfort habits, and the most English—she smiled at the thought, and its refutation of Penny's theory that she behaved like a foreigner—waited till it boiled, poured down the sink her half-mug of cold tea and made a new one. She knew she had a list to make and shopping to do, but before she started on all that she needed to think properly about Afghanistan. For Matt. She left the wireless unturned-on, poured milk into her fresh tea and sat down in a different chair, at the end of the table where her laptop was attached to its tangle of flexes.

Obviously she was no more than a newspaper-reading, BBC-listening old widow who knew only what she had collected from the most ordinary sources of information. But she knew enough to think that, however persistently dreadful the hatreds and cruelties that had kept Afghanistan in an almost permanent state of civil war since the Russians invaded it more than forty years ago, it couldn't have been sensible for first President Obama and then President Trump, and now President Biden to announce to the Taliban that they were going to be left to get on with reclaiming control over the country by one date and then another date. This, however popular it no doubt was at home in America, was surely presenting the Taliban with nothing more complicated than the wait for a guaranteed victory. The mothers of American soldiers who would come home would be pleased. The mothers of American soldiers who had been killed were probably crying in their kitchens like her. Did anyone think of the mothers of Afghan soldiers, or the mothers of children killed by landmines or by American drones as they played outside their houses?

But the long miserable story was even worse than the desertion at its end of people who had trusted the Americans and the British to make sure that the Taliban would never return to power.

Perhaps it was Iraq that was the worst part of the story, as the generals were now saying. Some of them, or some of their predecessors, had no doubt told Bush and Blair all those years ago that invading Iraq would be a terrible mistake, probably not legal, and certainly a dangerous distraction from what had been begun, and had already been promised for the future, in Afghanistan. To this advice, which must have been given, the president and the prime minister had paid no attention. What was done in Iraq immediately following the presentation to the world of a great American victory had been catastrophic: thousands of Iraqi soldiers sacked but let loose with their guns; looting and destruction in Baghdad—she remembered Hakim's misery over what had happened to the national museum—and other ancient cities; sectarian rivalries and hatreds deliberately stoked from outside; and over it all an American occupying regime that seemed to have no idea what it was up against and was surprised that people were not delighted to greet it. Were the Iraqis likely to have forgotten the Americans' shooting from the air thousands of fleeing soldiers in the first Gulf war—shooting defeated soldiers as if they were targets in a video game—or the Americans' killing from huge tanks more thousands of Iraqis, who had been ordered to defend trenches like the trenches in Flanders in 1915, and ploughing their corpses into the ground so that they were discovered only months later?

And while Iraq was turning into a deadly shambles, out of which, among other things, would emerge ISIS, Afghanistan became increasingly difficult to control, increasingly deadly, because no one in America or Britain was giving it the attention and the resources it should have had.

So all of it, this recent terrible history, was why Matt was killed in 2007, his life half lived. She was and always had been angrier with the politicians in London and Washington than with the Taliban fighters who had put together the bomb that blew up his inadequately armoured jeep. Who were they? They were true Afghans, of the mountains and the desert, young men accustomed to violence and misled by an Islamist ideology that, according to Hakim, had little in common with real Islam, and they were trying to free a country badgered and bullied by empires since Cyrus and Alexander the Great. They were not interested in democracy about which they probably knew almost nothing, and which, in the world of Trump and Boris Johnson, it was easier and easier to despise. And now they were again the victors, so that freedom, for many many Afghans, freedom to go to school, to read and write as they liked, to listen to music, to choose to wear a veil or not, was going to thin and fade, again, for who knew how many years?

Young men had always died in wars. Wars had always been projected, planned, promoted, by powerful people who were not the young men who died. When had the mothers of the young men who died ever felt that a victory justified the death? Perhaps the defeat of Hitler had allowed the mothers of the shot-down pilots, the drowned sailors of the Atlantic convoys, the young men who had died of fever or Japanese torture in Burma, the tank crews who had burnt to death in Normandy, to feel that the sacrifice of their sons had at least resulted in a freer, more just, and more hopeful Europe, or half of Europe when the Iron Curtain, so soon, had come grimly down.

She read through what she had just written. Who for? When for? She had no idea. But it had been comforting to write it down. Why? How peculiar the process of writing actually was.

She knew there were thousands, millions, of people in the country who felt and thought as she did about all this, and not just the *Guardian* readers mocked by Charles. All those thousands, millions, and more millions entirely unaffected by Afghanistan, had voted against Brexit—everyone always forgot that almost half the people who voted, never mind those who didn't, had voted against Brexit—and now, she imagined, they felt as helpless and as despairing as she did. The orderly, peaceful, increasingly united Europe of the last forty years had been damaged, disrupted, even broken, by us, the UK, even against the votes of the majority of people in Scotland and Northern Ireland, doing something entirely unnecessary for which its keenest defenders had so far produced not a single sensible justification.

She saved what she had written, shook her head and shut her laptop. That was it, for today. Real stuff had to be done.

She looked at the kitchen clock. Nearly half-past nine. She felt like making a hot water bottle and going back to bed. But she must try to forget the world and Boris Johnson and Matt's interpreter whose name probably wasn't on the photograph even if she could find it, and concentrate on lunch.

Why had she ever thought it was a good idea to introduce

Hakim to Val at a meal when she had, of course, had to invite Hakim's girlfriend as well? It was going to be more complicated than she felt she had the strength to cope with. But she couldn't say she wasn't feeling up to it, that wonderful all-purpose excuse, could she? The meeting of the three of them would have to happen some time. So it might as well happen today. Do not be afraid.

Shopping, cooking, making the table look nice, buying some flowers for the sitting room: most of this she could do on automatic pilot and it would help her confidence to feel in command of it all. She hoped Hakim and Emma would arrive before Val.

It was six weeks ago, six weeks tomorrow in fact, that she'd had lunch in Barnes with Penny and Charles, the lunch that had ended in one of the worst rows she'd ever had with Charles. She hadn't seen him since, though Penny a couple of times had come to the flat for tea and seemed reconciled to the idea of moving into David's house at some point in the future. The plan had become vague. She herself had been to talk to Mr Parker in the flat and had found, to her great relief, that he was thinking of moving out of London to share a house with a friend in Suffolk. "The pandemic has taught us how much we can do from home, so why not work from the country?" A guardian angel had arranged this, she couldn't help feeling; she almost felt guilty, as if she had actually prayed for Mr Parker to want to move. Meanwhile the picturesque Mr Steinberg had been warned, by Charles's lawyer, that he might before long be given six months' notice to move (or to move his boyfriend: Charles and the lawyer weren't aware of how Mr Steinberg organized his life, and didn't need to be) out of the main house. Apparently he'd taken this reasonably well. And Penny, after one visit to the house—"a nice boy let me in and made me a cup of coffee, though the chap downstairs wasn't very jolly"— had got her imagination to work on plans for knocking the whole basement into one glamorous modern kitchen. There was plenty of scope for an island and lots of granite, and even, presumably, a table to eat at. "We could make a French window instead of the ordinary window", so that the room would be a miniature version of their kitchen in Barnes. "Like a New York house, you know, Mum. You go in through a door sort of under the front door and on the other side of the house it's the garden".

She had spent only a couple of days in New York, decades ago, with Simon on their way to an academic conference at Princeton. They had stayed in what she remembered as a quite grand hotel, "midtown" she thought that part of Manhattan was called, so she had no idea what Penny was talking about. She did know the door into what used to be David's waiting room. "It sounds lovely, darling. I'm sure you'll do it beautifully."

After this peaceful and positive conversation about the plan, Penny had gone back to Yorkshire and her horses. She and Charles would put their Barnes house on the market in September and see what happened.

Clare had been glad to tidy this issue away as more or less settled because the rest of her life seemed to be anything but.

Three weeks ago, in the middle of June, Hakim had come back from Hadrian's Wall. He telephoned a couple of days before, saying he would appear at teatime on Tuesday, and then, characteristically punctual, he appeared on Tuesday at half past four with a bunch of sweet peas in one hand, his familiar old suitcase in the other and a large black computer bag over his shoulder.

As she opened the door of the flat he leant forward and kissed her on the cheek.

"Clare. It is so very good to see you."

He put the sweet peas in her hands, and shrugged off the shoulder bag, which he propped by his case on the floor.

She almost couldn't respond. He had never kissed her before and she'd been expecting his familiar, and never not moving, hand to the heart and bow, which was how he had greeted her when he first emerged from his flight to Heathrow from Cairo seven years ago, and how he had always greeted her ever since.

"Hakim", she said, after a moment. "You're back. You look really well."

He looked better than she had ever seen him, somehow both older, better set up and broader-shouldered, and at the same time younger, his face, with his piratical black patch over his lost eye, happier and more open than when he'd set off for the north in the autumn, still thin and sad after Ayesha's death and his absence when she died.

And then the kiss.

A girlfriend, a freer, less careful love affair, must be the explanation.

"So do you, Clare. You have kept yourself well through all these difficult times. That is very good."

He looked down at his luggage.

"May I please stay in the flat for a few nights?"

A chill, nearly a shiver.

She managed not to say "Only a few nights?" Instead she said, "Of course, Hakim. Your room is just as you left it and the study—"

Even this was perhaps too much. Never, she remembered David saying years and years ago when Matt was thinking of joining the army, let the children see that you think you can't manage without them. In the first place they'll feel crowded by your feelings, which isn't fair on them: they'll have quite enough to do coping with their own. And in the second place you can manage without them perfectly well.

"I'll put these in water. Lovely, they are. Thank you."

"I remember you like them, the sweet peas."

He must have walked from the tube station, with all his kit, to the flower shop in Gloucester Road.

A few minutes later as they sat at the kitchen table, he with his peppermint tea, she with her decaff ordinary tea, and a plate of chocolate digestives between them, she said, "So how are you, really, Hakim, after all this time? Will you be going back to the Museum straight away?"

She knew she had asked the second question to put off as long as she could the answer to the first.

"Yes, of course. I shall be there tomorrow. I will be pleased to be back. I should have been back sometimes during the months I was on the Wall, but Covid made it not possible. I am most thankful, grateful I should say, to them that they allowed me to go to Durham for all the university year. They did not have to allow me to go there, and I must thank them for the time I have been away. And also I must make a good report of the work I have done. There is much at Vindolanda that will interest the Museum I know. Some complicated redating may be necessary, and not only for Britain."

Roman Britain, naturally. The Roman empire was where he lived: he had grown up among what he called his stones, the stones of Cyrenaica, mostly actually Greek, where she had first met him.

"That sounds like months of work." Had she kept a note of hope out of her voice? But "a few nights"?

"It will take much time, yes, but it is so interesting. It is possible I may be allowed—once the restrictions of Covid are finished—to travel to Arles to compare, to consult, that is the correct word, with the very excellent Roman museum there. You know, in Arles, as well as the famous sites there is Constantine's own palace? When it is possible maybe even I will travel to Rome."

"I see. That sounds like plenty of exciting work for you. And—"

She couldn't avoid the question any longer.

"And what about you yourself? How are you? How have things been all this time?"

"I am very well, very well."

He took a biscuit from the plate and ate it slowly. Perhaps he too was nervous of his news?

He finished the biscuit.

"Clare". He put his hands flat on the table, one each side of his mug, and looked straight at her. "I have a friend, a girl-friend. She is English. She has a degree in archaeology and she has just finished a postgraduate year of study."

He stopped. This was very stiff, impersonal, as if he were recommending her for a job.

She wasn't surprised, either by the girl's existence or by Hakim's formality.

"Let me guess", she said. "She's been studying the Roman frontier."

He laughed. Because he had got over the most difficult bit?

"Yes, of course. She and another student were helping at Vindolanda. She could be a good archaeologist. She did not complain in the very cold weather. Also she has—" He looked down, searching for the right word. "She has a feeling—what is the English word?—a sense, an instinct—that is the word, an instinct—for what something does mean, even a very small fragment. She has been clever to work in her holidays on some city sites, in Chester, in London, where there is building to happen so always there is very little time for the archaeologists before big machines will pour concrete into the site and nothing will be found ever again. This is good experience, a good training for instinct and for quickness. How much she is interested in the history of the empire, in who the Romans were, I am not sure."

He smiled. "Archaeology under the pressure of time, not enough time, is not like finding Marcus Aurelius in a Yorkshire field, peaceful and quiet, not at all."

He was giving her permission to laugh, to help both of them.

"Hakim. You're jealous, aren't you? I know the fellow who found Marcus Aurelius was only an amateur, very annoying for professionals, but think how exciting it must have been. What a thing to find. Almost two thousand years and there he is, one of the good emperors, and there weren't many of them, in a Yorkshire field. Found by pure chance. Never mind. He was found. That's what matters, isn't it?"

"Of course. You are right, Clare, as always you are. I am—in love with her, you see."

There. He'd said it. Now she couldn't answer.

"Ah", she eventually said. "I understand. Well, that's wonderful." This was the best she could do.

"Is it?" He looked at her as if he were actually asking the question, even hoping for an answer.

"I think it is wonderful", he said, "and then I am not sure. Here in your flat I am not sure, because of Ayesha. Ayesha was—We would have been married if—if I had not—"

"Hakim. You are not to blame yourself. Nothing that happened was in any way your fault. I said this often last year and it's still true. Ayesha would have volunteered to work for the

Covid patients anyway, even if you'd been in England. You know she would. And the fact that she caught the virus and died was terribly bad luck. Nothing else. Lots of doctors and nurses caught it and died in those awful months at the beginning, but many many more didn't catch it or didn't die."

"But—" She could see he didn't know how to go on.

He picked up another biscuit and immediately put it back on the plate.

He looked at her again, anguish in his one eye.

"Would she think me to be not faithful to the memory of her because now I have a girlfriend? And this—"

She thought he was going to say, "and this is different", but she didn't dare help him in case she was wrong.

"Listen to me a minute, Hakim. Ayesha would be nothing but happy for you if you are happy now. Remember how it was. When you found Ayesha, which was so good for both of you, you knew that Samira would be pleased for you, and wouldn't think you had forgotten her, didn't you? You told Ayesha about Samira, didn't you? And you were sad together for her, for her young life lost, and you knew she would have wished you and Ayesha nothing but well. Why isn't this—"

He interrupted because, she could see, he had thought of the parallel and dismissed it.

"But it was not the same. Much more time had gone by. For Ayesha, with Ayesha, I was a man not a boy. I was in another country. Everyone in my family was dead as well as Samira. Now—look."

He looked himself, round the kitchen, the dear old kitchen. He had lived here twice for months and months.

"Here is your flat, it is the same, you are the same, Ayesha is almost still here."

She waited for a minute or two, almost praying for what to say.

"Think about her", she said. "Remember her properly, who she was, what she was like."

He was looking at her, for help, his lips pressed together, to stop himself saying anything, or perhaps to stop himself crying.

She tried again.

"Ayesha was a very sensible girl. She loved you. Of course she did. And if wretched Covid had never happened, you would have got married as both of you wanted, with the blessing of her father and even with the terrific Indian wedding in Assam she imagined. And I expect, as the children's stories say, you'd have lived happily ever after. She died loving you and you didn't let her down, not in any way. She completely understood why you had to go to Libya, what you felt you should do to help to protect your stones. She knew your work was in you, was you yourself, just as her work was in her, was being a doctor. What you must understand now, thinking about her, is that she would never have wanted you to live for the rest of your life in mourning for her. All alone. She wouldn't have wanted that."

"I failed to protect her." He had listened. But had he heard what she had tried to say? "And in protecting my stones I have also failed."

Desolate, he sounded. But there was relief in his voice: he had found something else to talk about.

"Clare. May I make for myself some more tea?"

"Of course you may."

"And for you?"

"No. No, thank you."

He got up, switched on the kettle, left the kitchen to go to the cloakroom near the door of the flat, came back looking more himself as the kettle boiled, and made another mug of peppermint tea. He didn't wait to take the teabag out but sat at the table again, holding the hot mug in both hands.

"When I was in Libya last year I could do almost nothing but watch the dangers and see the damage of the fighting. I did report on what I saw. There have been other reports more recently. Things are worse now, more out of control, especially in Cyrenaica. People are building cheap new houses close to the ancient stones of Cyrene: tombs and pavements and buildings no one has excavated ever will be lost under concrete and the archaeologists—there are a few there and they have to carry guns now—are given no chance, no time, to see what may be under the earth. The builders—what is the word?

167

Yes—the developers. They do not care. This is not London or York or Lincoln. There is looting. The developers make money. They are not interested in antiquities. But the looters are. The looters also have guns, my friend the head of antiquities in Cyrenaica has written. The looters bribe the builders or terrify them with their guns, and statues and mosaics are arriving in salerooms in Paris and New York. These are precious stones which belong in Libya, which belong to Libya, not because they are valuable—which is why the salerooms want them— but because they are precious to the life, to the history of my poor country. When it is allowed, when it is possible, I should go back there. But—"

He stopped. She knew what he was going to say.

"But I would be leaving Emma. It will be—for how many years? We have no idea how many—too dangerous to take her with me. And then it may be like Ayesha. I left her in London and when I had gone she died."

He bowed his head over his mug, cupped in his hands, as if he were praying. Perhaps he was.

She stood up.

"Hakim, you are worrying about too many things at once."

He didn't move.

"Bring your tea next door and sit in a comfortable chair. Then we can begin to sort all this out."

He did as he was told, as she knew he would, and when they were sitting opposite each other in the sunny sitting room with the old low table in front of the fireplace between them, she said, "You know I understand what you feel about Cyrene, about your stones. And you know you can't go back for now, not until it's possible to do some real good there. The time will come. Of course it will. Look what Cyrene and all the other sites have been through over centuries and centuries. They'll survive. You have to believe that they will. There will be peace. The tourists will come back, like me on the cruise, and the world will help Libya tidy up the stones."

"Maybe", he said, without confidence.

"You have to be patient, and work away at what you can do and are so good at."

He shook his head sadly, but when she said, "I want you to tell me about Emma", he looked at her and smiled.

"I told you—"

"No you didn't. You just described a clever young archaeologist with two degrees."

He laughed. "You are right. Again. I will try."

He sipped his tea.

"She is very beautiful. Also she is very English. Perhaps I do not know her very well. Ayesha and I—we were foreigners together, also Muslims together, so we were not foreign to each other. When I am with Emma I understand that I am a foreigner in England in a way I have not known when I am with you. Is this strange?"

"Not at all strange. I'm old, and half foreign myself you must remember, and I've known all sorts of people." With a curious pang, she thought of Val. How well did she know him, really? "Emma is young and perhaps she has mostly, so far, known only other English people."

"She had a boyfriend in Durham for a year, before I met her, and he was English. She says he was quite boring. I think I understand this."

What could she ask him that was easy for him to answer and would tell her more?

"Where did she go to school?"

"She was at a London school, not far from here I think. It is quite famous."

"St Paul's perhaps?"

"I think St Paul's, yes."

This meant a prosperous family as well as a bright girl.

"After her school she was a student in Durham. She had learnt Latin at school, and history and English, she said. But she thought archaeology would be easier to study. And when she started to study she enjoyed to learn. There are good teachers in the university."

"Have you met her parents?"

"I have met her mother and her stepfather. They came to Durham last week, to see her. They live outside London now, near Oxford I think. They were driving to Scotland for a holiday. She said they would like to meet me. She told them about me. I don't know what she told."

"How did it go, when you met them?"

He looked surprised. She realized what a hopelessly English question this was.

"Were they friendly? Were they keen to find out who you are, what you do?"

He thought.

"Emma's mother was friendly, yes. She asked me about working in the Museum. Is it an interesting job, my work? Are there nice people in the office? How long do I expect to stay in London?"

"That sounds all right." More or less all right.

"The stepfather was not so friendly. He looked surprised when Emma and I first went into the dining room of the hotel for lunch. They both stood up and kissed Emma. Her mother shook my hand and smiled when Emma said, 'This is Hakim.' He looked surprised before he shook my hand, as if it was not easy for him. I think perhaps Emma had not told him about my lost eye and my patch." He put a hand up to his face and slightly adjusted his patch.

Had she told them he was a Libyan, an Arab, a Muslim, a foreigner? Surely she must have? If not, she might be clever and a promising archaeologist but she didn't have much common sense.

"The stepfather asked me where is my home. When I said Libya, he said, 'That's Colonel Gaddafi isn't it?' I said Gaddafi was a dictator, very cruel and very mad, and he was killed in 2011. He said it must have been terrible since then. He said something like 'That's the problem with dictators. You bump them off and then you have a shambles. Like Saddam Hussein.' I suppose in a way he was right. But when he said, 'No wonder you're over here. Sensible chap', I understood—I'm not sure what I understood. Maybe he was thinking that I should go home soon. Maybe he is right."

"You shouldn't go back to Libya soon. Certainly not. You know that. And poor Emma, only worrying about you if you did."

"Would she worry? Maybe. She doesn't know very much about Libya. She knows that it was there I lost my eye because of a mortar shell. But it was too complicated to explain."

What kind of a girl was this, really?

"Have you met her father?"

"Not yet. He does live in London, so maybe I will meet him. I don't know. Emma has not said. He is very generous to Emma and her brother. He bought a flat for them, somewhere north of the City, east of the Museum. Is there a place called Hackney?"

"Yes, there is. It used to be a poor part of London but I believe it isn't any more. Nowadays, according to the papers, it's full of people like Emma and her brother living in expensive flats made out of old buildings."

He didn't notice her sharpness. She regretted it at once.

"Emma hasn't lived there yet, because of Durham and her master's degree. Her brother—he is older—has lived there. He was working in the City so it was convenient for his job. The flat is empty because he has gone to New York for the company he works for. This is a big bank, an American bank I think. But now Emma has finished the degree and she has found a job, a good job, in London, she will live in this flat."

"What sort of job has she found?"

"It is a job in antiquities in one of the important salerooms in London."

"Sotheby's? Christie's?"

"It is Sotheby's I think. I have told her she must be very careful to check how Greek and Roman antiquities have reached a famous London saleroom. What I told you about looting in Cyrenaica is very serious. And the wars in Iraq and Syria have given the opportunity for looting to more people, now to many many people. What happened in Palmyra I cannot forget. Where are the stones hidden by Khaled al-Asaad before they executed him?"

"That was so terrible, Hakim. I remember how upset you were at the time."

He looked at her across the table and his mug, surprised that he wasn't thinking at that moment of Emma.

"I don't want Emma to be dealing with the criminals who sell carvings and mosaics that are stolen, that they know quite well are stolen."

"I don't think you need worry: she'll be too junior for some time, I'm sure, to be making decisions of that kind. They'll be expecting her to learn on the job."

Could she, without upsetting him, sound a little doubtful?

"She's done awfully well to get such a good job exactly when she needs it. Or been very lucky."

"Lucky, yes. I know she has been lucky. But she deserves this luck. She has studied enough, and also has enough practical experience, to be good at the work she will have to do. She had, I'm sure she had, good recommendations from the department in Durham. And she told me a friend of her father's is an important person in the saleroom, which was helpful for the job."

"I expect it was."

Silver spoon, the whole story. Emma's world was not going to be straightforward for Hakim to negotiate.

"How old is Emma?" she said.

"She is almost twenty-three."

"She's still very young", she said. And you're thirty-six, she didn't say, which they will probably think too old for her. Thirty-six. Matt's age when he was killed. "But it sounds as if she's got her life very well organized."

"She has even a car, which was good in Northumberland when it became not so cold. We made a bubble to go together in the car sometimes, to other sections of the Wall, maybe to a castle."

Val, she thought again, grateful that he was her generation, her age. Her bubble friend. Neither of them had a car.

"Her car won't be easy to cope with in Hackney."

"When she comes to London she will leave her car with her mother and stepfather. She told me they are all right to have her car. It is a big house, I think."

She mustn't, must not, be sour when she hadn't even met the girl.

"Do you know what her father does? What his job is, I mean?"

"Not exactly. She says he works in the City—that means banks and money, doesn't it? maybe like her brother—but she doesn't know what kind of work he does. He has another family with three small children, but Emma does not very much like her stepmother so she does not very often see her father. Her stepmother is much younger than her father, not many years older than Emma."

"I can imagine. Poor girl. She must have had quite a difficult time, growing up."

"Not so difficult I think. She was happy at school, and as a student in Durham. She is I would say a happy person, which is one reason—"

"One reason that you love her?"

"Of course. She does not know to be sad, to be afraid. It is strange to me, but it is beautiful also."

The British. She remembered what Val had said months ago, about the British being always sure they're right because never have they had to cope with being invaded, occupied, oppressed by foreigners.

What could she ask him that wouldn't upset him but would tell her a little more?

"Is she a kind girl?"

"Kind?" Surprise again.

Talking about this girl she hadn't met, she felt the gulf, the uncrossable space, of foreignness between her and Hakim, even though he had said it didn't exist, as she'd rarely felt it before. As she'd never felt it when they talked about Ayesha.

"Yes, of course she is kind. She has been most kind to me. As kind as you have been for these years. But also it is different—how can I explain?"

She laughed.

"It's all right, Hakim. There's no need to explain. Of course it's different. She's your girlfriend."

"I know what has been her kindness that I can tell you. She found a cat, in the winter, a little cat, starving and cold. It belonged to the farm where she stayed, close to the Wall, but nobody wanted it. She gave it warm milk and it was better and slept on her coat. She took it back to Durham. I think she tried to keep it in her student flat but someone left the window open and it disappeared. She was very kind to this cat."

"Did she look for it when it disappeared?"

"I think she did try. But in the streets of a city it is difficult. The cat was lost. So then she was a little sad." He smiled.

The British are kinder to animals than they are to people.

She looked across the table at him, and smiled back.

"Thank you, Hakim, for telling me about Emma. Would you like to bring her here, perhaps for tea one day when she gets to London? I'd love to meet her."

"Of course. I have told her about you, that you have been so good, and that without you, without your help, I would not be in England now, I would not have my job at the Museum, I would not have been able to work at Vindolanda, I would not have met Emma. So she also will be thankful, grateful I should say, to you."

I doubt it very much, Clare thought but didn't say.

"Bring her as soon as you can, if she would like to come." They stopped talking about Emma. At supper she let him tell her all about Durham and Vindolanda and how Roman Northumberland was, how little seemed to have happened there since the Romans left except for a good deal of fighting and raiding between the Scots and the English. "Have you heard of some robbers called the border reivers? Hundreds of years of raiding and burning. No fine building, only thick stone barns and short towers, one gang against another. Like the militias now in Libya. The Romans were for such a long time forgotten. As in Libya also."

She loved hearing him talk, after nine months without him, and it wasn't until the morning when he was about to leave for the Museum that he said: "It is so good to be again here in your flat, Clare, and so good to see you. But I shall in some days, or a week or two weeks, I am not sure exactly, be able to stay with Emma in her flat."

I know, she didn't say.

"Yes of course, Hakim. Have a very good day at the Museum. They'll be pleased to have you back."

CHAPTER 9

SATURDAY 3 JULY 2021

Ten days later, actually eleven days later because it was Saturday, a week ago, Hakim and Emma came to tea.

She had told Val that she couldn't see him that day: on Saturdays, now that the Covid restrictions had been relaxed, they always walked, if it wasn't raining, up to Kensington Gardens, as far as the Albert Memorial, sometimes further. They had decided it was good for them to walk, rather than just to sit, though if there were an empty bench somewhere on the way they would sit for a while. They talked little on these expeditions. They enjoyed each other's company.

"I can't do our walk on Saturday, Val" she had said on Wednesday when she was having coffee and Turkish Delight in his house, Ivica, who was now used to her and even apparently fond of her, sitting on her lap. They took it in turns, on Wednesdays, to have each other to tea. "I'm so sorry. Hakim is bringing his girlfriend to meet me."

"Ah", Val said. "That will not be so easy for either of you."

"O, from what I've gathered from Hakim, I don't think it'll be a problem for the girl, just coming to see an old lady who's been nice to Hakim."

Val's blue, piercing look.

"I was meaning to say it will not be easy for you or for Hakim. He will very much hope that you will like his girlfriend. No?"

She smiled. "You're right." So like him, to be right about this. "I'll do my best."

She hadn't told Val much about Emma. She hadn't, ever, told him much about Hakim, but he had from her book a fair impression of how he was and how she felt about him. She couldn't describe to Val her anxieties about Emma: they were, as she seemed to keep finding about all sorts of things nowadays, incommunicable to a foreigner. How she wished

David hadn't died. Though, if he hadn't, would she have made friends with Val? Honestly? Probably not. If Carrie would only come home she could describe to her what worried her about Emma and she would understand, or more or less understand. Then she smiled to herself: Carrie's assumptions about the Emmas of this world were even firmer and less tolerant than her own.

Years ago, about twenty years ago though she couldn't remember exactly when, Matt had had a girlfriend for more than a year, which for him was a long time, though, being a soldier, he was away for much of the year. She was called Sophie. Clare couldn't remember her surname. Matt must have been about thirty. Sophie was a good deal younger. Clare had a vague memory that she was a teacher, or a basic child-entertainer more likely, in an up-market nursery school in Chelsea, the sort of establishment where the children were fetched by nannies or au pair girls who gossiped on the pavement till the children emerged. Sophie's job, Clare had thought at the time, was like Princess Diana's before she married Prince Charles. She was small, pretty, blonde, and obviously sexy. She flirted with Simon, who basked in the atmosphere she created: so did Matt who clearly enjoyed the effect she had on his father. Clare, knowing that she shouldn't give in to unworthy feelings, found Sophie intensely irritating, while at the same time trying her best to be nice to her for Matt's sake.

"I hope to goodness he doesn't marry her", she'd said to Simon, after a Sunday lunch in which Sophie for at least the third time had said, "I can't imagine why you don't have a washing-up machine, Mrs Wilson. It would save all this work." Work which Sophie breezily rose above.

"Of course he won't marry her. One doesn't marry girls like Sophie—at least not if one has any sense." Clare had never forgotten the pretty girls in headscarves who, one after another, each envied by her and half the women undergraduates in Cambridge, had sat beside Simon in his Lotus as he shot, showing off, down King's Parade in the early '60s. He was famous in the university. She wasn't, and hadn't yet met him. "Matt's got plenty of sense. He's your son after all."

He hadn't married her, and she couldn't remember how it had ended, but Matt had been quite cheerful afterwards.

It was no doubt unfair on Emma to think of her as another Sophie. For a start, Sophie had been an air-head, Matt's own expression—Clare detected no sign that she had ever read a book—which Matt didn't mind but Hakim certainly would. On the other hand, Hakim might not be able to see that having learnt a little about archaeology and having done a bit of hands-on work on digs perhaps didn't amount to much more than exactly that.

But the poor girl was twenty-three, not even twenty-three, and Hakim was in love with her, so she must be given every possible chance by a critical old schoolma'am who, after she heard about the step-father, realized that she cared most about how this orphan boy so far from home was treated by the British. That was why she'd made sure, all this time, that Charles and Hakim had never met. She must be extra kind to Emma.

Having made this decision and resolved to take an unprejudiced view, she waited for them. They were late, which Hakim never was. Quarter of an hour late. Half an hour late.

Hakim's key in the lock.

"Clare. I'm so sorry we're late."

"Come in, both of you. It couldn't matter less. It's only tea. Nothing to spoil."

She was nervous. Hakim would notice.

"Mrs Wilson, how are you?" Emma shook her hand. "Would you rather I wore a mask?" She had a black mask like Hakim's round her neck.

"O no. Don't worry about the mask. I've had two jabs."

Emma took off the mask and put it in a back pocket of her jeans."I do apologize" she said. "It's entirely my fault we're late."

Nice manners. Clare heard Nanny's voice. Credit where credit's due.

"Never mind. Come into the sitting room while I get the tea."

"Can I help?"

"Absolutely not."

Well. She didn't look at all like Sophie. She was tall, nearly as tall as Hakim, elegant, with longish dark hair, clean and shiny, tidy jeans and a white linen shirt not tucked in. Hakim put an arm round her shoulders and she leant her head towards him as they went into the sitting room.

Clare put the kettle on, again, and went to the sitting room door to say to their backs—they were together looking out of the open window over the square, Emma's arm round Hakim's waist—"What sort of tea do you like, Emma?"

She turned her head to answer.

"O, builder's would be lovely. Thank you."

She made tea in her old Crown Derby teapot, with one ordinary and one decaff teabag, and Hakim's peppermint tea in a mug. Just as she put these on the tray, which was ready on the kitchen table with two cups and saucers, milk, sugar, chocolate digestives, gingerbread which she'd made because Hakim liked it, three small plates, napkins, Hakim appeared to carry it. He looked at her without a word, appealing for her approval. She smiled.

With the tray between them on the table by the fireplace, and Hakim on the sofa between Clare and Emma in the armchairs, Clare said, "Have you just come back to London?"

"Yes, that's right. A couple of days ago. Poor old London. It seems like a hundred years since the first lockdown and I was stuck in Durham, which was fine really, a perfectly good place to be stuck. I haven't been back to London till now. It's good to be here." She looked round the room. "What a lovely flat you have."

She was nervous too, a good sign?

"I like it. It's a fairly standard flat of its kind—these Kensington Victorian houses used to have one family and a lot of servants living in each house. That was another world. But they make good flats."

"I grew up quite near here. In the Boltons."

A famous and very expensive patch of large houses north of the Fulham Road, twenty minutes' walk away.

"Very nice, it must have been. And Hakim tells me you went to St Paul's. Did you enjoy that?"

"I don't know if 'enjoy' is quite the right word. It was jolly hard work."

"It got you to Durham anyway."

"Yes it did. A bit second-eleven they thought at St Paul's, Durham and St Andrew's and Exeter. The brainy girls all got into Oxbridge. But Durham's been fun. And then Hakim turned up when I was being a spare pair of hands at the dig on the Wall."

She looked at him, and he at her, doting, the pair of them.

"Not what I expected at all."

Clare was longing to ask her how much Hakim had told her about himself, but of course she couldn't.

The charge between them was making her feel almost embarrassed. It had been so different, the decorum between Hakim and Ayesha.

She had to say something.

"Have some gingerbread. Hakim likes it."

"It is wonderful, Emma, Clare's gingerbread", he said, and cut her a piece.

She took a bite.

"Mmm. Delicious."

Something else. Anything.

"If your family lived in the Boltons, which primary school did you go to?"

"O, just a state school, in Chelsea, St Joseph's."

This was a surprise.

"Are your family Catholic then?"

"Not really. Not any more anyway. My father—Hakim hasn't met my father yet—was supposed to be a Catholic, went to Stonyhurst and all that. His mother, my grandmother who died a long time ago, was a proper Catholic, quite strict about things, so my parents got married in a Catholic church and my brother and I went to St Joseph's, which was OK, and good enough for me to get into Bute House, that's the St Paul's prep school. But my mother wasn't keen on the Catholic stuff. She never went to Mass, and when—well, when the marriage folded and my father went off, my mother just said 'so much for being a Catholic'. So that was more or less the end of that.

179

I don't think my father's been to Mass for years. O—"

She had caught a look, also caught by Clare, from Hakim.

"I'm so sorry, Mrs Wilson. I'd forgotten you're a Catholic. Hakim did tell me. I probably shouldn't have—"

"Don't worry about it. I know more lapsed Catholics than Catholics. The story of your family isn't at all unusual I'm afraid."

"Really? Well, I suppose that makes it better in a way."

She took another bite of gingerbread.

"What does 'lapsed' mean?"

"O, something like 'dropped out', 'given up', 'stopped functioning'—as a Catholic. There's always the hope that a lapsed Catholic might come back one day."

"Not much hope for my father, I'm afraid. He says things like 'Christianity's a lot of nonsense designed to keep people down'. He's very ambitious, determined—I don't know how to describe him exactly. The absolute opposite, anyway, of what you say 'lapsed' means. He didn't want me to do archaeology in the first place—what's the point? he said—and this last year he wanted me to do an MBA instead of more archaeology. My brother did one at Oxford. Really boring, I thought. The last thing I'd ever want to do, running a business."

"I know practically nothing about MBAs. Since my time, they are."

Another pause.

"I used to be a schoolteacher."

"Yes. Hakim said. I can't imagine anything worse than being a teacher. Annoying kids all day and piles of marking to take home. Year after year correcting the same mistakes—you were a Latin teacher, weren't you?—it must get awfully boring."

"I enjoyed it, oddly enough. If you don't enjoy it you certainly shouldn't be a teacher. I liked the children, specially the teenagers, though one or two were a nightmare, usually because of something bad going on at home."

Not very tactful perhaps. Emma was eating cake and didn't react.

"You must have had a good Latin teacher if you ended up being interested in archaeology."

"O, she was all right I suppose. She was very efficient at teaching us the language. I got an A. Most of the set got A stars. The literature was a real slog. I didn't realize how much we'd have to do when I signed up for the A level."

"What books did you do?"

"Yards of Tacitus. That was quite fun in its way. Such dreadful people. Some Cicero. Really difficult. And Virgil, hundreds of lines of Virgil. She was always telling us how wonderful Virgil was, our teacher I mean, but I never got it. So complicated the rules for getting every line exactly right. How could anyone obey all those rules and write something people might actually want to read?"

"Clare loves Virgil", Hakim said.

"Well there you are. It's a teacher thing, obviously."

"She met him, in the Bardo, didn't you, Clare?"

"What?" Emma looked from Hakim to Clare and back, a little put out. "You mean a ghost?"

Clare laughed.

"Not a ghost. It's a portrait, a mosaic portrait. He's sitting, with a scroll on his lap. There are a few words of the *Aeneid* written on the scroll, and standing each side of him Clio and Melpomene."

"The muses of history and tragedy", Emma said.

Good teachers at St Paul's.

"That's right. It's perfect. He's writing a mythical history for Rome and he knows what he's writing is tragedy."

"What was the date?"

"I can't remember—in the autumn of 2009." She looked at Hakim for his smile.

"I meant the date of the mosaic."

"O I see. I've no idea, I'm afraid."

"Second century, maybe third century", Hakim said. "Someone found it in a garden at Sousse. Imagine: you are digging your garden to plant the onions, the peppers, whatever you are planting, and suddenly there is the face of Virgil."

"Sousse", Emma said. "Wasn't that where a lot of Brits were killed? On a beach?"

"Yes", Hakim said. "It was very sad for Tunisia, mostly a

181

more peaceful country, to have suddenly terrorism. People were shot by a terrorist also in the Bardo, in the same year."

"The poor Bardo", Clare said. "It has the most beautiful, delicate mosaics I've ever seen."

"They are the very best", Hakim said.

But Emma said, "I remember the fuss about Tunisia. A bunch of us at Durham were going there at the end of my first year. Mostly for beaches and clubbing and all that but I was keen on seeing some Roman stuff too. We didn't go. The parents all said terrorism and wouldn't let us. We went to boring old Ibiza instead."

Clare didn't look at Hakim, but said to Emma, "What made you keen on archaeology?"

"I didn't know anything about it really, but I thought it would be less work than history or English, which were my other A levels besides Latin. I don't much like writing essays but I did want to go to Durham, where my best friend at St Paul's was going, to do French and Spanish. I hardly saw her after we got there. She was always working. And then I loved the dig stuff. Out of doors in a trench all day, just looking, sifting earth and looking, and seeing what tiny pieces of this and that can tell you. Pottery's best, and anything with writing on, even one or two letters."

Hakim looked at Clare, now proudly.

"I see", Clare said. "Yes, I can understand the fascination of that. Do you think you'll enjoy looking at the things people bring in to Sotheby's? The work's bound to be different from what you were doing on the Wall."

"Well, it won't be Wellingtons and a sieve in Bond Street, which is a bit of a shame, but I expect it'll be OK. Hakim wants me to make sure things haven't been stolen in Libya. I've no idea how you do that but I expect somebody will tell me. Anyway it's a decent job and it's in London, and with Hakim in the British Museum I had to find something—"

"Of course you did. And it's bound to be interesting."

"Luckily there are quite a lot of jobs around at the moment. Something to do with Covid. Something to do with Brexit. I've no idea what."

Another silence.

"Would you like some more tea Emma? Hakim?"

Hakim shook his head. "No thank you", Emma said. "That was a lovely tea, specially the gingerbread."

She looked adoringly at Hakim, and then smiled across the tea tray at Clare.

"We really should be off. Hakim's going to help me unpack a lot of stuff that's still in my car, and then tomorrow we're going to my parents near Oxford for lunch and leaving the car there. It's a nightmare, according to my brother, having a car in Hackney. Nowhere to park, expensive to be in central London at all, and cheaper and better on the tube or in a taxi. Nice and green, not to have a car."

She stood up, and gave Hakim a hand he didn't need to pull him out of the sofa.

At the door of the flat, Hakim kissed Clare on the cheek and Emma shook hands and said, "It was lovely to meet you. Thank you so much."

They went down in the lift, for proximity no doubt, and Clare watched from the window as they walked away along the square, wound round each other like sixteen-year-olds.

She wasn't another Sophie, which was a good start. But how much of Hakim, of Libya and Syria and the disasters of his world she would bother to get to know or understand, was another matter.

And now they were coming to lunch.

She wished, with painful regret, that she'd managed to organize a meeting between Hakim and Val before it had to be a meeting that was going to be confused by the presence of Emma.

She had known Val now for six months: they were too old, she felt and was sure he did too, for six months to seem a very long time. She was familiar with the thought that the older you get, the shorter each segment of time becomes because each segment of time is a smaller proportion of your whole life. That was fine. Tea in her flat, coffee in his house, on alternate Wednesdays, to be looked forward to without drama as part of the structure of each week, had become a familiar routine.

This was the first time she had asked him to a proper meal. He had greeted her invitation, last week, with his little bow.

"Thank you, Clare. It will bring great pleasure to meet Hakim after so long. I imagine I know him, because of your book, but really I do not. Have you described me to him since he came back from the north?"

"Hardly at all. He knows I met you in the square—he loves the square—after he went to Hadrian's Wall, and that you live nearby. That's about all."

"That is good. We shall find for ourselves who we are."

"I'm afraid his new girlfriend will be coming too."

Val's sharp blue look.

"You do not like the girlfriend?"

"I've only met her once. She's very beautiful. Elegant." She smiled: this was one of Val's words.

"But?"

"She's very English, and rather spoilt I think."

"Spoilt?"

She laughed. "Impossible to explain. It means having been given too much too easily, not being asked to think about other people. There's plenty of money in her background. It's true her parents are divorced. I don't know her well enough even to guess how much that's affected her, but I get the impression most things in her life have gone her way. I suspect there's been more money than love from her family. Her father left her mother for someone much younger, his secretary I dare say, and has given her and her brother an expensive flat. Possibly conscience money? Who knows? But—"

She suddenly felt a little guilty.

"I must try to be fair to her. She's not a bad girl at all. She's an archaeologist, or she's been an archaeology student, which is how Hakim met her. She got an A in A level Latin."

"So that is good? You have Latin in common?"

"Up to a point. She thinks Virgil's boring."

Now Val laughed.

"How will you ever like a girl who thinks Virgil is boring?"

"That's a good question. But for Hakim's sake I must do my best."

"You will do your best of course. As you always do."

"Val! You don't know that."

"I make—what is it called in English? There is a good phrase. Ah. I make an educated guess."

She had telephoned Hakim the next morning, when she knew he would be at the Museum, and left him a message asking him to ring her back when he could. "Not at all urgent and nothing to worry about."

He had rung at ten past one. She imagined him in the Museum café where he used to meet Ayesha. Then she remembered it was probably closed because of Covid.

"Can you and Emma come to lunch on Saturday? I want you to meet the new friend I told you about."

"Of course. I would like very much to meet him. He is the old man from Bosnia who has a cat. Is that right?"

"That's right."

"And he is partly Muslim and partly Jewish?"

"Yes. But he's also mostly Slav, a South Slav he would say, which makes him different from other Muslims and Jews I've known, you, and my father and Dr Rose for instance."

"I will be very interested to meet him. About his country I know nothing."

"He would probably say the same about Libya."

"I have met no person, not one, in London who knows about Libya, unless he is himself Libyan."

"So I'll see you and Emma on Saturday at about one o'clock."

"Yes. That is kind, Clare."

She could tell he didn't want to ring off.

"Is everything all right, Hakim?"

"Yes." A pause. Then he said, "No, everything is not quite all right. Are you hurrying for anything?"

"No. Not at all. Tell me."

"The visit to Emma's mother's house near Oxford was not easy for me. Emma's mother is kind, I think."

She let there be a silence on the telephone while he thought how to tell her what had happened.

"Emma's stepfather asked me many questions which were difficult because I understood he would not like the answers.

Am I a Muslim? Do I go to the mosque? What do I think of IS, of Iran, of Pakistan? Then he asked me, Do I think there are too many Muslims in London or not enough? That is a really bad question."

For a moment she was too shocked to say anything.

"O Hakim. I'm so sorry. What a nightmare for you."

"Clare, this is not your fault."

"How did you manage? What did you say?"

"I told what is true. But I think he was not listening to what I said."

"What about Emma while this was going on?"

"She was not hearing most of the questions. She was talking to her mother in the kitchen about some curtains for the flat."

He stopped. She helped.

"And?"

"She said when we were on the train—her mother took us to the station in Oxford to come back to London—that she did not know I am a Muslim. She had heard the first question."

"You hadn't told her?"

"She did not ask me. I thought she would know because I am Libyan. I said, 'Does it make you worried, that I am a Muslim?' She said—"

Silence.

"What did she say?"

"First she said something like, 'It's fine', or 'It's OK'. Then she said, 'As long as you don't take it too seriously. I don't expect you want to blow us all up or anything?' Those are exactly the words she said. I can't forget them."

"Of course you can't. How could she say that? Though she probably thought it was a joke."

"A joke?" Disbelief in his voice.

"The English are inclined to make jokes about things they don't understand." Particularly English people of a certain class and lack of sensitivity, she didn't say.

Silence.

"And when you got back to the flat?"

"It was all good, as if nothing different, nothing bad, had happened. I don't understand—She said, 'What is the matter,

Hakim?' But I could not tell her."

"I'm not surprised."

Then Clare said, "Where are you, Hakim?"

"I am outside the British Library, with some coffee. Not good coffee. I had to find a book, and also I came because I needed to walk. At my desk I could not concentrate. It is fifteen minutes only."

"I'm glad you're out of doors and you've got some coffee. Listen. I'll try to explain how this happened."

"I am listening."

"This isn't Emma's fault and you mustn't blame her. It's the fault of this wretched country which in a couple of generations has deliberately broken the connection with Christian tradition that lasted for hundreds of years. Hardly anyone of Emma's age, unless they are very fortunate in their family—but even then they may decide that a religious upbringing is only something to be rejected—has any idea of the Christian story or the demands Christian truth makes on people who believe in it. Emma went to a Catholic school till she was seven or eight." The age, it struck Clare, at which children stop believing in Father Christmas. "So all she's known of any religion has been what's suitable for small children. After that she may have been taught a bit about various religions, but all the religions, including Christianity, would have sounded like strange things other people do. If someone isn't brought up with any sense of religion as a deep set of questions, with answers which deserves their attention, they're not going to know what a religion is, any religion. I don't suppose Emma's met anyone she respects who is an adult, intelligent Christian, or Muslim or Jew come to that. Most English people nowadays haven't. And if you're nominally a Christian, living in what is still inaccurately called a Christian country, and you have no idea what Christianity actually is, you'll have no idea what Islam or Judaism is either. So you mustn't feel Emma doesn't care. It's very much more likely that she just doesn't know."

Silence.

"Hakim. Are you still there?"

"I am here. Clare. How can I explain her, I am sorry, how

can I explain to her, anything about Islam, which, as you know Clare, can be so simple and so beautiful, if she thinks only that a person who is a serious Muslim is of course a terrorist? If her stepfather says to her about me this man is dangerous because he is a Muslim, she will have to say—What will she have to say? Don't worry, he is not a serious Muslim, so he is not dangerous. To me, about me, that is not true. That is like saying, Don't worry, Clare is not a serious Christian."

She thought, but only for a few seconds.

"Hakim, this is complicated and very difficult for you, I do understand. But you mustn't let it spoil everything, so soon. What's happened shows really only one thing, that you don't know each other very well yet. It's possible, isn't it, that Emma might learn from you that an intelligent person who takes religion seriously is not the same as being a fanatic. In fact, it's almost the opposite, something which it's perfectly reasonable to be as it always has been." Since Augustine got hold of what was wonderful in Plato or the Arabs got hold of what was wonderful in Aristotle she didn't say. Poor Hakim: the last thing he needed was a lecture. Hold on to what is simple and beautiful.

"How can I do that? She is not interested to talk about religion."

"No. She won't be. But as she gets to know you better, she will perhaps learn what religion really is from your example, from who you are and what you do, not from what you say."

"I do not think she will."

"If you love her, and I'm sure you do, and I can see she loves you, all you can do for now is hope, and pray, that she will discover from being with you that there is nothing to fear, and nothing to joke about, in what is real Islam."

Long silence.

"Hakim?"

"I am sorry, Clare. I will try to hope what you say. I must go now, back to the Museum. Thank you."

She had worried about what to give them to eat. It would have to be a chicken: she was afraid of doing roast lamb not well enough for either Val or Hakim who came from the same, it struck her for the first time, Mediterranean world. Roast beef was a risk, so easy to get it wrong, and too English. An expensive chicken that had had some kind of a life needn't be dull if you cooked it with lots of garlic and tarragon and flambéed it in brandy before making the sauce with some cream: Hakim liked this and Val and Emma almost certainly would. Roast potatoes and spinach and salad. And then three cheeses, one each from England, France and Italy. And at the end a coffee ice cream she'd made herself. Very little could go wrong with any of this.

She was shaking the parboiled potatoes in a sieve to rough them up before putting them in the oven when the telephone rang. She put the sieve over the pan and looked at her watch. Nearly half past eleven: it couldn't be Penny, who always rang at teatime on Saturdays.

"Hallo."

"Clare. I am so sorry."

"Hakim. You can't come after all? Never mind." She did mind.

"It is Emma. Her father has phoned and said she must have lunch with him today, not at his house where the stepmother is, but in a restaurant. I heard Emma say she was going somewhere else for lunch. But the next thing she said was, "Yes, I can chuck. It's not important. See you later, then." I heard her. She told me after the telephone call that if her father wants to see her she must go. She does not see him often, and it is kind of him to arrange to meet her outside his house. I think she is maybe a little afraid of him."

"Poor Emma. I do understand, and she must do what she thinks best. Are you going with her?"

"No. Her father wants to see only her, alone."

"So will you come to lunch anyway?"

"Please. If that is all right."

"O Hakim, of course it's all right. I do want you to meet Val, Mr Radic. And you must try not to worry about Emma's father."

After she'd put the telephone down, she thought she shouldn't have said that. He might not have realized, as she had, that there was cause for considerable worry.

She telephoned Val.

"Clare? There is a problem. You wish me not to come for lunch?"

"No, Val. Please come. I just wanted to tell you that Hakim's girlfriend isn't coming, But he is, and I'm much looking forward to seeing you."

"I will be there."

Tactful Val. No questions.

She went on cooking the lunch, laid the table in the kitchen, put some cheerful flowers she had bought at the supermarket in a jug in the sitting room and opened both the windows. The kitchen was sunnier in the middle of the day because it faced south but she opened the window only a little. Val's cyclamen was struggling a bit on the windowsill. The table looked nice when she'd laid it properly and put her laptop out of sight on a chair at the far end. She hadn't bought flowers for the table: if by any chance one of them came with flowers it would be a shame if there weren't the perfect place to put them.

She had got everything ready and had just finished making the tarragon sauce when, at four minutes past one, the doorbell rang. Val, she thought. Hakim still had a key.

When she opened the door, they were both on the landing by the lift, smiling at each other as they shook hands. "I am Hakim Husain", she heard as Val at the same moment said, "Valerijan Radic", with his little bow of the head. She deduced that Hakim had bounded up the stairs, as he always did, and Val had arrived in the lift.

"Come in, both of you. I see you've met already. Val, these are lovely. Thank you so much."

He gave her the freesias, yellow and white, with some greenery arranged by the flower shop, that he was holding in his left hand.

"You shouldn't have", she said. Freesias were never not expensive. "But they're such pretty flowers. Go into the sitting room while I put them in some water."

She found a small glass vase she was fond of, with a twist to the glass that made any delicate flowers look even better, and put the freesias in the middle of the table facing where she was going to sit at the end, with Hakim on her right so that he could help put dishes on the draining board and Val on her left opposite the window. She took some ice from the fridge and put it in a jug of water on the table. Neither of them, she knew, would drink wine so she hadn't bought any. One last look, and she went to join them.

They were standing, waiting for her. As they looked towards her she realized that to both of them this was a familiar room, to Hakim a very familiar room, and that she and Val could almost be his grandparents. She felt slightly dizzy.

"Come into the kitchen. Lunch is ready."

Val sat down, Hakim carved the chicken, Clare added potatoes, spinach and tarragon sauce to the plates, and when they were all sitting, said, "It's so nice to see both of you here. Do start."

A silence, but a short one.

Val picked up his knife and fork and said to Hakim, "Clare has told me that your country is Libya."

He wasn't going to say that he'd read her book. She'd never told Hakim about the book. It had come, and more or less gone, at least as an object, while he was in the north, and she certainly didn't want him to read her account of Ayesha's death, anyway not for years. She'd forgotten that Val had read the book and Hakim hadn't, until this moment of deep gratitude to Val.

"Yes", Hakim said. "I come from the eastern part of Libya which is called Cyrenaica."

"Like Simon of Cyrene?"

Hakim smiled. "Who helped Jesus to carry his cross", he said. Clare remembered the small, framed, brightly-coloured Victorian picture of Simon of Cyrene, one of the Stations of the Cross, in the little Catholic church in Yorkshire where she had often sat in a pew close to it.

"Yes", Hakim went on. "I am glad he is there, in the story of Jesus. There were many Jews in Cyrene. It was a Greek city, a Roman city, also a Jewish city. There will have been many Berber people also."

Val was eating.

"This chicken is very good, Clare", he said. "Thank you".

Then he said to Hakim, "Your city in the time of Jesus was like my city when I was a boy."

Hakim put down his knife and fork.

"Really? I am sorry. I don't know which was your city."

"How could you know? My city was—really, even now, my city I should say is—the city of Sarajevo in Bosnia."

"I am sorry", Hakim said again. "I have never heard the name Sarajevo. Is it the capital city of Bosnia?"

"It is the capital city of Bosnia. According to the Americans, who stopped the civil war and forced all the people into a strange agreement in 1995, there is another capital city in Sarajevo. East Sarajevo the agreement called as the capital of Republika Srpska. the Serbian Republic which is not in Serbia but is two large and separated parts of Bosnia. But this does not work well so the actual capital of Republika Srpska where they have their parliament and officials is a town called Banja Luka, a name you will not have heard either. Nor has anybody else."

Hakim shook his head. Val smiled at him.

"You are confused. You must not worry if you are confused. It is confusing. Also it will not last. In a year, five years, there will be too many problems with this arrangement. It is the kind of arrangement which does not last. Clare and I have talked about this. In Cyprus, in Ireland, these arrangements have caused much harm. In Israel the arrangement causes even worse harm. In Bosnia the Serbs, who are not the Serbs of Serbia but the Serbs of Bosnia, will not stay quiet. There may be another war."

"In Libya it is different but also the same", Hakim said. "There is war, there has been war, between two parts of what was told to be the same country after the Second World War. The arrangement was made by outside people, as in your country. Libya has never been really a single country, and now after Gaddafi the fighting did not stop, and even now it has not stopped although there is officially a ceasefire."

For a moment Val looked across the table at Hakim.

"Yes", he said. "It is difficult to forget, I know, even for a short time, what has been, and what may be, in one's own country. But we should try, for a while, and for Clare. We are both so fortunate to be here, in London, and in Clare's flat. You should eat your very good chicken."

She could see Hakim making an effort. He looked at her as if he had for a moment forgotten where he was. "Yes, of course", he said.. "The chicken is so good Clare."

"I'm glad you like it."

She was astonished that Hakim, who knew so much, had never heard of Sarajevo. But why would he know the name? Exactly how the First World War began can't have been, in North Africa, an interesting enough story to last, to outlast Mussolini and King Idris and Gaddafi. And during the wars of the 1990s and the siege of Sarajevo Hakim had been a schoolboy in Benghazi.

They ate for a few minutes. Hakim was the first to finish his plateful.

"Mr Radic, I would be very pleased if you would explain how Sarajevo when you were a child was like Cyrene in the first century?"

"I will try." Val put his knife and fork side by side on his empty plate and sat with his fists on the table either side of his plate.

"In that time", he began, "and for hundreds of years before that time, a great mixture of people was there because the city which is in the centre of Bosnia was exactly on the line that had always divided the west from the east, Latin from Greek, Rome from Constantinople. The city had been a Roman town, a market, a trading town because of the valley, the river, the crossing where it is in the mountains. Over the ruined Roman town and after years and years of Slavs fighting each other and occasionally not fighting", he smiled, "some of them Roman Christians and some of them Greek Christians, the Turks of the Ottoman empire built a Muslim city. This was Sarajevo. They started to build nearly six centuries ago. Most of the people in the city have been Muslims, but this Muslim city always had Catholics from the west, Orthodox Christians from the east, and also almost from the beginning Jews from Spain because the Ottomans were kinder to Jews than the Catholics were. More Jews came once the Habsburg empire was ruling Bosnia, Jews this time not from Spain but from the north, from Ashkenazi lands where the Jews were beginning to want to escape from Russian pogroms."

Hakim was listening carefully. Good.

"For all those years in this city between one world and another but inside the Ottoman empire, and then, but not for long, inside the Habsburg empire, people lived side by side and did not kill each other. This was still true when I was a boy and Bosnia was part of Communist Yugoslavia. If you had grown up in Cyrene in the first century, like Simon, who was a Jew I suppose, though perhaps he was a Berber or a Greek—who knows? And perhaps it was difficult to say—it would have been very much the same. Not so? The Roman empire, so terrible and cruel in some times and places, was also not bad at including many peoples, many religions. Like the Ottoman empire. And if you draw a line southwards from Sarajevo across the Mediterranean Sea you will arrive at the coast of Africa not very far from Cyrene. Between west and east, between Latin and Greek, you see. And still in what was for so long the Ottoman empire."

Clare looked at Val, met his blue eyes and smiled. He had done some solid preparation for this meeting with Hakim. Had he guessed that she had been nervous before this lunch, afraid they would have nothing to say to each other? He rarely guessed wrong.

"That's so interesting", she said.

"After lunch", Hakim said, "please can we look at your big atlas, Clare?" He sounded, unusually, about eight years old. "I have not thought enough about this line, which I know very well. It is the line that divides Libya still. It is the line between Carthage and Greece, then between Rome and Greece, then between Tripolitania and Cyrenaica, now between what is supposed to be a government in Tripoli and another one in Benghazi. Soon, if there is real civil war when the election happens and no one agrees about the result, the line may be between Gaddafi's most dangerous son and General Haftar, and there may be more civil war. So always this line, but I never thought about it dividing people, and casting people together also, north of the sea."

He smiled, in his turn, at Val.

"Now I understand that until all the terrible things of the twentieth century the Ottoman empire did hold different people together as the Roman empire, when it was good, also did. I knew this but I had not thought about it."

"The Habsburg empire", Val said, "also did well at holding different people together. The rage of anti-Semitism in what had been Habsburg lands became very horrible only when the Habsburg empire had collapsed. Nationalism has been the wicked thing."

"Yes", Clare said. "Brexit, for example."

Val raised his eyes to heaven.

"But it's almost impossible", Clare went on, "to say anything good about empire nowadays, isn't it? Except among the Brexiteers. Isn't it odd, perhaps it's true only of England, that here nationalism and imperialism are the same thing."

"If you always were the top people, they are the same thing. But everything changes and then there is only a muddle", Val said. "The British have not thought very often or very much about their empire. They did not have to. If they had thought properly, they would have been grateful to be part of the EU. They would not have invented Brexit."

Hakim, looking from Val to Clare and back, perhaps hadn't altogether followed this.

Clare said to him, "The British Empire thought itself so wonderful for so long, alas, when it was, at some times and in some places, as cruel and oppressive as any other."

"In Iraq, for example. Not once but twice", Hakim said.

"O dear", Clare said. "Yes." Then, "But look—you're not eating. There's plenty more. Val?"

"No thank you, Clare. That was so good but enough."

"Hakim? Help yourself."

While Hakim was carving himself some more chicken—he looked at Clare to see if she wanted more and she shook her head—Val said, "Who is the son of Colonel Gaddafi? I have not heard of him."

Hakim turned, still standing, his plate in his hand.

"His name is Saif al-Islam. Gaddafi had six or seven sons. Three are dead. One or two are in prison. Saif was in prison for a time and then escaped or was allowed by somebody to go away. He disappeared for years but he was still in Libya. Now he has reappeared. He says he can unite Libya, which is not true. He is not to be trusted. Not at all. He wears glasses and the clothes of a French intellectual but he is not what he pretends. He had a doctorate from the London School of Economics but somebody else wrote his thesis. Actually he is a criminal. The International Criminal Court want to try him for war crimes."

"Goodness", Clare said. "Then surely he can't be elected President, even in Libya?"

"Who knows? There are people in Libya, I know, who look back to the time of Gaddafi as a good time because there was order on the streets, always fear but order, many people in prison but not fighting. So that seems better than now, when there is much fighting and no order. This election, which is said to be before the end of the year, may be between Saif al-Islam and Haftar. So people will choose Gaddafi's son or they will choose an old man, the age of Gaddafi, who was his favourite general a long time ago. Haftar also has a son who would like to be president. They are all terrible."

Hakim sat down with his plate of food. Val leant forward and said, "What do you think will happen?"

"It is too difficult to think, to guess, what will happen. It is possible there will be no election. If there is an election it is certain it will not be fair. In the end Mr Putin may decide which of them has won."

"That cannot be right. What has Libya for Putin?"

"What had Syria for Putin when he destroyed Aleppo, ancient Aleppo? Only he wants to be the strong man. Syria had chaos in the civil war. Libya has chaos for years, which for Putin is an opportunity for power. Russian soldiers are there. Last year some Russian soldiers saved my life. Like all soldiers they are not all bad men. But they do what Putin orders. I know that Saif and Haftar have both told Putin that if they win the election Russia will be their favourite friend. Both of them before have tried to tell the West they are good democrats. They are not. In Libya there is nobody who has known what is democracy as in the West."

"Is that really true, Hakim, about Putin?" This was Clare. "Do sit down and eat your second helping."

He sat down.

"Certainly it is true. I learn what is happening in Libya from Arabic news on the internet, some of which I know is true."

He started again to eat.

Clare poured more water into her glass, and into Val's.

"Thank you", Val said, and drank half his glass.

"The past", he said, "does not stop because powerful people outside a country that they do not understand say it has stopped. This is true of America—look at Iraq—as it is true of Russia."

Hakim nodded, finished his mouthful and said, "That is exactly right, Mr Radic. In both our countries I think that is right."

After lunch, and when they'd had cups of tea in the sitting room, peppermint for Hakim and Clare, strong builder's with sugar for Val, they talked quietly about Hakim's work and the dating of finds at Vindolanda.

"I wish" Val said, "a scholar as you are had been able to look properly at the Roman things at Sarajevo that were thrown to the surface by the war."

"There is so much everywhere in the empire that wars or storms or the desert or careless builders throw up that nobody who would know what the stones can tell will ever see."

For Hakim the empire was always Rome as the sea was always the Mediterranean. She had just thought this, and smiled at him, when she noticed that Val had fallen asleep. Probably he fell asleep every day after lunch—she didn't know him well enough to know.

"Val", she said, and then, a little louder, "Val."

"It's no good", she said to Hakim. "He's fast asleep."

"You should wake him or he will have a shock when he does wake, in the wrong place."

Kind boy.

She shook Val gently by the shoulder. His shoulder was thinner, more bony, older, than she expected. He woke, looked at her blankly for an instant, and then remembered.

"I'm so sorry, Clare", he said.

"No. Don't be sorry. But I think you need a nap and you'd be more comfortable at home."

"You are right. I must go home. I must see how Ivica is getting on without me. My cat", he said to Hakim.

He stood up, stiffly, for him.

"It has been very interesting to meet you, Hakim. And Clare I thank you so much for my very fine lunch. I am sorry it has sent me to sleep. This is old age."

When he had gone, Hakim having sent for the lift and Clare and Hakim having seen him safely into it, they stood side by side at the sitting room window and watched him walk, quite briskly and securely, across the garden of the square and into the street that led to his mews.

"I think he is a good man, Clare, your new friend."

"I think so too. I'm so glad you liked him."

After a moment he said, "Perhaps it was a good chance that Emma could not come with me today."

"Why? Come and sit down a minute, Hakim. You needn't go yet."

Back on the sofa, he said, "When we were in the kitchen and Mr Radic was explaining Sarajevo—is that the right name?— yes, Sarajevo and Cyrene, I could imagine Emma sitting on the other side of the table, maybe next to Mr Radic, and I could imagine she would be—I don't know how to say—"

"Bored?"

"Maybe she would be bored, yes. She says many things are boring. I did not meet this word much before Emma. She is wonderful, but - It is difficult to explain. It is difficult to understand her. She is so good, so happy, if she finds a coin in an excavation ditch, a little piece of glass, even a clay pipe of the nineteenth century. And she is happy if we go for a walk or sit by a river or watch the sea. But the world, history and politics, they do not interest her. She has learnt some Roman history at her school, but she has forgotten it already. It does

198

not interest her. She does not care about Brexit. She says it hasn't made much difference, has it? How can I tell her it has made very much difference? I am a foreigner. She thinks Mr Johnson is a joke, a good joke. It is a treat not to have a boring prime minister, she says."

He opened his hands in front of him in a despairing gesture.

"She loves me, I think. She shows much love to me. But she is not interested in how different I am, my family, my school, my university, they are all different from hers. My father, and what happened to him; what probably happened to my brother; to her all this is far away, long ago, people she does not know in a history she does not ask me to explain. I told her about Ayesha. She said, 'poor girl. How sad', and nothing more."

"I wonder", Clare said after a minute or two, "what her father said to her over lunch. I hope whatever it was won't make things more difficult for both of you."

"She will tell me when we are both there in her flat." He looked at his watch and stood up. "I should go, to be with her as soon as possible. She will tell me what her father said and I will not understand if it was bad or very bad or perhaps even good."

"O Hakim I'm so sorry. That you're so happy and so unhappy with Emma all at the same time. It will get better, or it will get harder, and then you will know, one way or the other, what you should do."

"I have only this week put my books and my files on the desk in the flat, and my clothes I have put away. I thought, I hoped that Emma and I—that this will be—maybe I did not think enough."

"Hakim, listen a minute. Today isn't an ordinary day. Two things have upset you. First Emma being summoned by her father, more or less ordered to come and have lunch with him. So you think her mother or her stepfather, more likely her stepfather, has made some difficulty about you with her father. You don't know that yet. And even if it is what's happened, Emma seems to be quite a determined girl—look at how she coped with the idea of the MBA. She just refused to do it and her father had to accept that. If she wants to be with you, and after seeing you together the other day I'm sure she does, then she'll stay with you."

He shook his head.

"I cannot tell", he said.

"And the second thing—", she had to try to get him to understand this. "The second thing is your meeting Val here, and talking about so much that you think is interesting. It made you imagine Emma listening or not listening to all that, perhaps finding it boring, and then you wondered whether—well, whether there is enough between you to keep you going. Is that it, more or less?"

Now he nodded.

"Yes, I think that is right. But, really, Clare, how much does it matter, the talk, the history, even Islam, when we are so happy?"

"It may matter, and it may not. You can't know yet. Let me tell you something. I was married for more than forty years to someone who wasn't a Catholic, wasn't any sort of Christian, wasn't interested in Latin, Greek, the ancient world, St Augustine, all the stuff I loved and was teaching. Even Virgil. It was a good marriage and most of the time we were happy with each other, enjoyed being together, and always had plenty, plenty else I suppose you might say, to talk about."

"But your husband was a professor I think? He was very clever. I can see in his study, his books."

"Yes, he was very clever. But also he was very English. There are all sorts of things it's difficult to get the English to take seriously. Religion is the main one. I quickly understood it was something we were never going to share. That could be a bit lonely, but I promise you it was fine once I accepted it."

"You are English, Clare. But about Christianity you are serious I know. Mr Radic is not English—but he is your friend, a foreigner and your friend. So it can be done. And Dr Rose—he was not quite English was he? Maybe he was also a foreigner?"

She laughed.

"There are foreigners everywhere you look in my life. Mr Radic is obviously a foreigner. Dr Rose was a German Jew who was born and grew up in England because of Hitler so he was both English and not. My father was a Czech Jew, not English at all, also here because of Hitler but already grown-up when he came. All of them learnt to manage England quite well. Mr Radic would say he is still learning. And then there's you, also managing England well because you were young when you came and you pick things up quickly. The other thing to remember is that, except for you, all of us are old. I'm nearly eighty, Mr Radic is over eighty, Dr Rose was even older. From long lives we have discovered and remembered a good deal. Emma is very young. But she's not stupid and she has a mind of her own. If both of you can learn from each other, even learn each other, as you go along, there will be a future for you together, I'm sure."

"I am not sure. I hope", he said.

"Now you must go or Emma will be wondering where you've got to."

At the door he kissed her goodbye, easily and naturally, like an English young man kissing his mother or his grandmother. At least Emma had done this for him.

"Thank you, Clare, for lunch and for everything."

As he reached the top of the stairs, she said, "Hakim" and he turned.

"Good luck. And if you think I can help, let me know. Any time."

"Thank you."

He waved before turning back and running down the stairs.

She washed up and tidied the kitchen without noticing what she was doing. It was good that Hakim had more or less demolished the chicken and eaten the last roast potatoes with his second helping. She thought he and Val had both enjoyed what she'd cooked for them. Later she would have the rest of the spinach, the rest of the tarragon sauce and a poached egg for her supper.

When she'd put the last things away and wiped the table and the draining board she sat facing Val's freesias and felt old, tired and sad.

For months she had looked forward to introducing Val to Hakim, Hakim to Val, and it had been a joy to watch them warming to each other, interested in each other, across an age gap of almost fifty years and what she had assumed would be an even greater gap of languages, worlds and experience. One of them, after all, was so very European, and other not. They did have important things in common: each of them by quite different routes had found a refuge, a place of safety and affection, in England. A series of chances had brought each of them, after all, to her kitchen table on a summer Saturday. And each of them had his work, a firm base in knowledge and love, Hakim in his stones, Val in his books.

She had hoped for these connections to be made, but she had failed, thinking about them together, to think enough, to imagine enough, of the loneliness they also had in common, the loneliness that perhaps had been there under the surface of what they said to each other. She was sad, now, for both of them, for their loss, the loss they shared. Neither of them had any family, anyone close, left alive after the random killings of civil war in both their countries.

Loss, her own also after the memories brought to the surface of her mind by the old recording on the *Today* programme, was actually what bound the day together.

She had lost Matt, not in a civil war of course but far away in a war which no one had thought through before it or during it, and which was now ending only in betrayal and deadly danger for thousands of innocent people. Hakim and Val had each lost everyone in wars of hatred, ambition, cynical manipulation.

She very much hoped they would meet again. But was this only selfish, since her wretched lunch had so much upset Hakim? She hoped it hadn't upset Val, but of that she couldn't be sure. Perhaps Hakim had reminded him too much of the sons he had lost.

How different would their conversation have been if Emma had been there? Probably very different. Hakim's anxiety and Val's courtesy would have produced what? More constraint, more polite chat, less real connection. But it was the connection that had shown Hakim how great a distance there was between him and Emma, to whose flat in Hackney he was rushing back to see what her father had said, or demanded, in the restaurant he had arranged in order, no doubt, to give her an undisturbed talking-to.

Clare felt to blame for Hakim's complicated distress, although she could see that Emma's absence had been no one's fault, an accident that couldn't have been predicted, and also that Hakim was going to have to face, sooner or later, what had just struck him for the first time. She couldn't help him to negotiate the collision between Emma's obtuse Englishness and his own inner loyalties which he wouldn't be able to describe to Emma in words she would understand.

She sighed, letting out a long sad breath, remembering Ayesha. Why did Ayesha, kind, intelligent Ayesha, a faithful Muslim who understood Hakim, have to die? It wasn't fair.

She dimly remembered reading somewhere something like: "God made the world beautiful and good. Who said it had to be fair?" Probably some old rabbi's saying.

Sex, which may have been a revelation to Hakim, and probably hadn't been to Emma, would no doubt keep them together for a bit, as long as Emma had the courage to resist what might be a campaign by her father and stepfather—Clare knew she might here be putting two and two together and making five—to persuade her to give him up. She seemed like the kind of girl who would almost on principle do the opposite of what the grown-ups wanted. That might well be good enough. For a while. But Hakim wasn't Matt, who had dispensed with Sophie after at least several months without, as far as she could remember, noticeable heartache.

She must have fallen asleep at the kitchen table because when the telephone rang she came to with a start, uncomfortable and stiff, her head on her folded arms. She got up, looked at the clock, almost five it said, so this was Penny, who usually rang after tea on Saturdays. Groggily she went to the counter by the toaster and picked up the receiver. She sat, in a different chair, as she answered.

"Hello."

"Mum. It's me."

"Yes of course, darling. I'm sorry."

"Are you OK, Mum? Did I wake you up? Surely you weren't asleep. at five o'clock? Not like you at all."

"I wasn't asleep. Not really. I'm so sorry. I had rather a bad night." And an exhausting day, she didn't say.

"O well. No reason why you shouldn't go to sleep in the afternoon. Loads of old people spend half their time asleep."

"I suppose you think there's not much point in being awake where you're as old as me."

"No, Mum. Don't be cross. I didn't mean that at all. Is everything all right, in the flat and so on??

"Yes. Everything's fine. Just the same as usual. How are you? Have you heard from the children this week?"

"Not a word I'm afraid. I suppose no news is good news."

"I wish Carrie would come home. It would be so nice to have her back, safe and sound."

"Yes, wouldn't it? I'm sure she'll come back as soon as she can."

What could she think of to say to Penny?

"How's Leckenby? The garden must be looking lovely."

"It's pretty good, though the roses have been a bit rubbish this year, and a few things got completely done in by the cold in May. Wicked frosts for several nights. There won't be any plums or pears."

"I would love to come some time".

It seemed suddenly so long since she had been in Yorkshire, probably the longest time she had been away in her whole life. She was nearly crying.

"Well, you must. We'll try and arrange something as soon as all these wretched rules are scrapped and things get back to normal. Charles could bring you up in the train one weekend when it's safe."

No. Not two hours on the train alone with Charles.

Silence.

"Mum. Are you still there? Are you really all right?"

An effort, to make her voice sound ordinary.

"Yes darling, really I am. Don't worry about me. I'm just a bit tired today."

"Well. If you're sure. Ring up if you're feeling ill, won't you?

And I'll ring again in a day or two to check you're OK."

"Thank you, darling. That's very kind."

Probably she wouldn't, ring in a day or two, but that didn't matter a bit.

She put the kettle on, changed her mind, switched the kettle off, and, taking only her keys in her pocket, left the flat and walked up to Kensington Gardens past the end of Val's mews, through the expensive streets that were quiet on an early Saturday evening, their inhabitants no doubt in the country for the weekend, and went as far as the Round Pond before turning back. Almost in the square, looking along Val's mews, she wished she had a cat to go home to.

Walking is supposed to help one to think. It doesn't always work.

Back in the kitchen she did make a mug of tea and put her laptop back in its place on the table. She opened the drawer at that end of the table to look at the message she had stuck inside the drawer. She couldn't remember where she'd found it, or more likely heard it on the wireless.

> *Make the sign of the cross.*
> *Forgive your enemies.*
> *Say a prayer.*

CHAPTER 10

TUESDAY 24 AUGUST 2021

A few weeks later, on a Tuesday afternoon towards the end of August, she had given up fighting with a paragraph that wouldn't come right and was sitting in the kitchen listening to the last episode of a detective story on Radio 4 and doing a bit of her protracted embroidery project, a new cover for the seat of an eighteenth-century chair that had belonged to her mother. This sewing, although she never actually undid any of it, was almost Penelope-like in the time it was taking—time until what? She had no idea.

The bell of the street door rang.

She got up with some difficulty—she had been sitting, stupidly, too long without moving—and went to the intercom beside her front door. Probably it was somebody selling something, quite likely to push all six buttons on the intercom one after another.

"Hello."

"Gran. It's me."

Carrie's voice. After all this time.

"Carrie, is it really you? I didn't know you were even in England. Come up. How lovely."

One minute later—she bounded up the stairs as Hakim always did—Carrie was hugging her in the doorway of the flat.

After the hug Carrie, who seemed to have got taller, held Clare's hands and looked at her, looked down at her—perhaps it was she who had got shorter—for a long moment.

"Gran, you look terrific, just the same as ever. It's so brilliant to see you after such a long time, two whole years."

Still holding one of Carrie's hands in one of hers, Clare led her into the kitchen, and then let go of her hand, opened the drawer for a tissue and sat down rather quickly.

"Don't cry, Gran. Look. I'll put the kettle on."

Clare sniffed hard and blew her nose.

"I'm so sorry, darling. It's wonderful to see you. But I wasn't at all expecting—It's just a bit of a shock."

"I should have rung. Silly of me. But I wanted to give you a surprise. Mum said you're always here."

Not absolutely always, but never mind. Thank goodness it wasn't Wednesday or Saturday.

"Decaff tea?"

"Please."

"This tin's still got builder's in, hasn't it?" An ancient china jar from Fortnum's that had had Stilton cheese in it when her father had given it to Simon and her for Christmas. Probably thirty years ago. "Dear old builder's", Carrie said, "so nice to get back to. And you haven't changed anything in the kitchen. Thank the Lord. Mum can't talk about anything except all the improvements she's going to do in David's house."

Carrie was giving her time to get over the shock of seeing her after so long.

Clare blew her nose again, shook her head to banish her reaction, and looked up at Carrie as she got the milk out of the fridge.

"It's lovely to see you, darling. I can't tell you—When did you get back?"

"I arrived yesterday. We arrived yesterday. I've brought Bill with me."

"Goodness—is he here? Have you left him downstairs?"

'No, Gran, don't worry. He's got terrible jet lag. He's fast asleep in Barnes."

"You must bring him here. I'd love to meet him. How's it going, Bill and the parents?"

"O, fine. He's not at all surprising, my Bill, just what you'd imagine a nice American college boy to look like. Short haircut and new white sneakers which he bought in Delhi. Both his parents are doctors, couldn't be more respectable. And he calls Dad 'Sir' which goes down a storm."

"I bet it does. What about all the Covid rules? Did you have a difficult time getting back to England?"

"It's so complicated you wouldn't believe. But Bill's parents sent us some money and that was a big help. We got jabbed in India and had to get tests there, and then there were tests waiting for us here. I don't think I'm supposed to leave Barnes but I was longing to see you. You're not scared are you? Of seeing me, I mean."

"Certainly not. I've had both vaccinations and seeing you - well, it's the best treat I could possibly have. What's the point of being alive, after all, if one can't see the occasional person one's fond of?"

"Tea", Carrie said, putting her mug and Clare's on the table. "Have you got a biscuit, Gran? I'm starving. I think it's the jet lag. My system's got no idea what the time is."

"Of course. The big tin by the kettle."

Hakim's chocolate digestives, not that she'd seen Hakim since the complicated lunch with Val at the beginning of July.

"You look well, Carrie, in spite of everything. You must have had a dreadfully sad time in Nepal, with Covid and no vaccines and all the things you told me about. And frightening as well as sad."

"Yes. It was really grim for a month or two. But the people up in the mountains are so patient and good, you wouldn't believe. They don't expect help to come from outside so when it doesn't that's quite normal. It was us, the NGO workers, the foreigners, who were so ashamed of their countries, of the whole of the rich world, doing nothing, absolutely nothing for the poorest people. Nepal was like the poorest African countries still are, no vaccines and not enough doctors and nurses at the best of times, let alone now. And we weren't trying to cope with a war at the same time. Imagine Sudan, or Yemen, or Syria still, or Afghanistan now. Do you know that thousands and thousands of people in Afghanistan are likely to die this coming winter of simple starvation because all the money's left the country with the useless government running away, and America won't let the Taliban have any if they're going to be running the country?"

"Please darling, don't let's talk about Afghanistan."

"O gran, I'm so sorry. Uncle Matt. I'd completely forgotten. These last few weeks must have been particularly rotten for you."

"Well—"

But Carrie in full flow couldn't be stopped. Obviously it was impossible for her to say all this at home when she hadn't seen her parents for so long.

"Isn't it all a dreadful mess, though? And how much does anyone care? The government here's an absolute disgrace. You know, when I went to Nepal none of the worst of it had happened. It seems about a thousand years ago, and I've only been watching from the other side of the world because of brilliant stuff in the *Guardian* online and the *New York Times.* Boris Johnson winning the election by so much—I could hardly believe it—and Dad and all his chums gloating—you should have seen the email he sent me after his majority went up—as if all the Labour voters who thought they were voting for Brexit because they were voting Tory hadn't actually been done in by years of Tory cuts. And the House of Commons was so feeble and the Brexiteers and the DUP so awful that the poor old country got a much worse Brexit than it need have after that wretched referendum—I'll never ever forgive myself for not bothering to vote—what was I thinking of?"

"That seems such a long time ago now. Nothing happened for ages. And then there was such a hopeless muddle in the House of Commons where a majority of MPs were in favour of Remain but couldn't persuade themselves to vote with each other. That was partly the fault of Corbyn. What with all that and the time it took for Boris Johnson and the dreadful Lord Frost to negotiate a bad, hard Brexit, it wasn't till this year that the consequences started really to kick in. Now more and more people can see what a disaster it's all been but of course it's too late to do anything about it. Maybe after I'm dead"—she had caught "maybe" from Hakim and was pleased when she found herself saying it—"this country will see sense and ask the EU to have us back. But it won't be straightforward. Why should they make it easy for us, for goodness' sake? The only good thing you can say about Brexit is that it's such an obvious disaster no other country is likely to copy it. A warning and not an example as my nanny used to say."

"But isn't it rotten to have so many other countries in the

world either hating us, or despising us for being so stupid, or just thinking we can't be trusted because we break our promises?'

"Don't. I know. I do know. A couple of months ago I had a proper row with your father when they'd kindly asked me to Sunday lunch in Barnes where I hadn't been for ages."

Carrie took another biscuit out of the tin.

"Goodness, Gran. Did you really? Good for you. Poor Mum. And I wasn't even there. What was the row about? Though I can probably guess."

"In the end it was about Brexit and also about the aid cuts, though it began when I tried to have a go at him about vaccines for Nepal because I promised you I would."

"O dear. I shouldn't have badgered you into that. I'm so sorry."

"Don't be sorry. Of course you should've. You were entirely right to try to persuade your father to take a real moral stand for a change, and what you wanted him to do wasn't even at all left-wing, and I was right to support you. It didn't help that Gordon Brown, good old Gordon Brown, was the person making most noise about the rich countries needing to send vaccines to the poor. In any case, neither you not I got any-where with Charles and a few days after the argument we had, when there was the big vote in parliament over the aid cuts, naturally he voted in favour of the cuts. Then I had a nasty feeling you and I had probably only confirmed him in his views by trying to talk him out of them."

"Probably we had. You know Dad: *Telegraph* readers right, *Guardian* readers wrong, full stop. Whatever the issue. The thing about Dad is that actually he isn't terribly bright."

Clare laughed. "Well—"

"You've noticed? The Tory party actually likes stuffing not very bright cannon-fodder MPs into safe seats. As long as they do what they're told, the fact that they haven't much of a clue what's going on is OK by the top brass. MPs like Dad are much less trouble than the clever ones and seats like Dad's are so safe there's no danger of their being lost however hopeless the MPs."

"O dear, I'm afraid you're right."

"By the way, what exactly happened in that vote? I know the cuts ended up being confirmed. It was topic A with the NGOs, you can imagine."

"Well, the cuts went through, naturally. But the government majority was right down, from eighty to thirty-something, and more than twenty Tories voted against the government. All the Tory MPs who'd been soldiers voted against the government, and so did Mrs May herself. God bless them, but it wasn't any use."

"Of course. Boris Johnson's huge majority."

"You said you'd seen some effects of the cuts already in Nepal."

"Yes, we have. It's bad enough there but it's much worse in other places. And what a moment to choose to cut aid, in the middle of a pandemic. You know, in Afghanistan, and look what's happening there, our aid has gone down from eighty million pounds to twenty. O sorry, sorry, I shouldn't have mentioned Afghanistan again."

"Don't be silly darling. Goodness knows, I haven't been able to think about much else in the last couple of weeks, but I'm used to thinking about it now. And it helps to talk about it."

She'd been careful not to tell Val on Saturday how miserable the news of the chaos in Afghanistan made her feel: he had so much more experience of war than she had, and had lost so many more of those he loved. She had lost Matt. He had lost everyone.

Was she going to tell Carrie about Val? Today? Later?

"The last few days", Carrie was saying, "seem to have been an absolute shambles. I've missed quite a lot of it because we were travelling but when I looked at all the news I could find on the internet last night I could hardly believe what I was seeing. The airport in Kabul with people throwing their babies over the wire at American soldiers to save them, and people climbing onto American planes and falling off them as they took off. Really really awful."

"Yes." Clare couldn't stop remembering Matt's interpreter in the team photograph: what had become of him, and his family? Were they in those desperate crowds at the airport? She couldn't face the pictures on the television: the *Today* programme she had several times in the last few days had to switch off. Had he struggled to the British embassy to find the consulate closed and the staff gone, while young soldiers with no experience of anything were trying to deal with hundreds of visa applications? Anyone producing enough proof of working for the British even to get into the visa queue was producing, for the Taliban, evidence of guilt.

"We shouldn't be doing this", Clare said. "We shouldn't be abandoning people who worked for us because they hoped for better times in Afghanistan and expected to be rescued by us if the Taliban came back. Now they'll be killed. And why were the Afghan army so pathetic when they've had billions of dollars of training and kit all these years? And the Afghan government?"

"Bill says the Americans always think dollars are the answer, dollars will fix anything, and at the same time they trust all the wrong people. The president—what's his name? Ashraf Ghani - has buzzed off to Uzbekistan, no doubt, Bill says, heading for the Gulf with suitcases full of dollars. The Gulf Arabs are beyond everything awful but the Americans love them because they don't like Iran. And another thing Bill says because he's talked to American aid people who've worked in Afghanistan for years is that great chunks of the Afghan army never even existed. The generals have taken the money that was supposed to go to lists and lists of soldiers, and they've kept the money because the soldiers were never anything but names. Invented names. Can you beat it? Bill says these corrupt generals were often being paid both by America and by the Taliban. I expect they're on their way to the Gulf as well."

"Goodness, darling. Can that really be true?"

"I'm afraid it is. It's a specially bad corruption story, but if you do aid work in chaotic countries you run into any amount of corruption. We all do our best, or almost all of us do our best, to make sure the people who are supposed to be being helped get the help, but it isn't always possible. This ghastly government abolishing DFID, which always had some brilliant people in it, isn't going to make anything any better anywhere."

"I'm sure you're right. And there's nothing any of us can do. It's years till the next election, and I can't see the Tories in the House of Commons chucking out Boris Johnson while they think he's still popular enough for them to keep their seats. O dear. Not much of a country to welcome you back to."

"Dead right, Gran. But we're not going to stay long. I haven't told Mum and Dad yet so don't breathe a word, will you?"

Hold the right thought, stay calm, Clare told herself, and, as with Matt, and Hakim, "never let the children see that you think you can't manage without them."

"You know I won't. I am the grave. But what's your plan, darling?"

"Not quite fixed yet. Bill's applied for a job with the International Rescue Committee in New York. They sound quite interested in him, and he's got really good references from the outfit he's been working for in Nepal all this time— also, you know, he's clever and he did a master's at Columbia after his degree at Tufts."

"I thought he went to a liberal arts college in Vermont."

"That was Paul, who was my boyfriend for a bit when I was first in Nepal. You have got a good memory, Gran. Bill arrived about six months ago, when the epidemic was beginning. Paul went home long before that. He was a nice chap too but he always seemed much younger than me though he wasn't. Bill's quite different. Tougher. More—more definite, somehow."

"What was his subject? At Tufts?"

"O loads of stuff—American universities let you do much more than English ones do. But his main programme was international relations. He could probably get into the State Department but he says he wants to be in the field and not sitting in an office in a suit, so the IRC looked like a good option."

"Isn't that the thing David Miliband runs?"

"That's right. You're amazing, Gran, at keeping up. I don't know how you do it."

"O, just Radio 4 and the *Guardian*. David Miliband should have been Prime Minister. He should still be Prime Minister now."

"Do you think?"

"I certainly do. Maybe you weren't bothering much with politics then—I think you were still at school—so perhaps you've forgotten that Ed Miliband did in his brother to be leader of the Labour Party when Gordon Brown packed it in though David was much the better bet, more weight, more brains, more seriousness. He'd been Foreign Secretary for years. And then Ed Miliband lost the 2015 election, to David Cameron. And Brexit. If David Miliband had won that election, and he might well have, we wouldn't have had a referendum at all, and none of us would have heard of Corbyn."

"O Gran, that's awful. What an awful thought. What must Ed Miliband think when he wakes up in the middle of the night?"

"Or David Cameron, worse. Who knows? Perhaps they think it's all fate and not their fault. Anyway, bother politicians. Tell me more about your plans."

"Well. Bill has to be interviewed in New York, for the job. And he wants me to meet his parents."

"What do you gather about his parents?"

"They sound great. They both work in a hospital on the upper east side. I've no idea what that means, but you've been to New York, haven't you Gran?"

"For five minutes years ago, yes. I loved it. The upper east side just means the top right-hand quarter of Manhattan. Mixed, very posh and then much less posh."

"I can't remember the name of the hospital but I think it's quite famous. They've got an apartment in the city—I'm quoting Bill—so a flat in New York, and a house in the country, in the Catskills, mountains I think, not too far from New York, where they go for holidays."

"Has Bill got brothers and sisters?"

"Two sisters, younger than him, one at college, one still at school. Bill says I'll like them and they'll like me because I've travelled and done the sort of stuff they'd like to do. His parents might be trickier. They're terrific Democrats and Bill says they think Boris Johnson is practically the same as Trump. So they won't be all that keen on the idea of a Tory MP's daughter."

"I'm sure you needn't worry. They'll only have to talk to you for ten minutes to see how unlike a Tory MP's daughter you actually are."

"I hope so."

"When do you think you might go?"

"As soon as we can get it organized. There are terribly complicated US Covid rules and we may not be able to go until we've had our second jabs."

"And how long will you stay?"

"It depends. I'm hoping to get a job in New York myself, perhaps even a job in IRC too. If Bill gets the job and is sent somewhere I'll probably go with him anyway. He's talking about the DRC, sorry, the Congo, where IRC does a lot of work. Endless initials. You get used to them in the aid business."

"Darling. The Congo—it must be one of the most dangerous countries in the world."

"Probably it is, but Bill has very good French and only a bit of Arabic from Tufts, so he sees himself being brilliant in a French-speaking African country. Fascinating, it would be, don't you think, even if a bit scary? But we'll see. He knows that if he gets the job it could be an office and a suit in New York, at least for a bit. Though at the moment everyone's still at home in pyjamas, working through Zoom and stuff. Not doctors, obviously, like his parents."

Clare could only think she didn't want to lose Carrie again.

"So what d'you reckon, Gran?"

"What do I reckon? It's all very exciting, and I've no doubt you will love New York, and the pair of you—you must be a pretty solid pair by now after all you've coped with in Nepal—will have an interesting time and do lots of good wherever you find yourselves."

"But?"

"But nothing. I've missed you all this time, that's all."

"I've missed you too, Gran, of course I have."

Carrie stood up and picked up both their mugs.

"I'm going to make us some more tea, and then you must tell me how you've been really, through all these lockdowns and everything?" She filled the kettle and switched it on, still talking. "I did love your book, by the way, and as I was reading it I could tell how well you were doing, just sitting at the kitchen table and writing, a whole book. Fantastic, at your age, to have the concentration."

"Years of practice. You have to be good at concentrating to mark thirty A level Latin unseens when you're already knackered by a long day in the classroom and cooking the supper for Grandpa when you got back from school."

"I bet you do."

She rattled about with mugs, teabags, the fridge, milk.

"There. More tea. Now. The news. How's Hakim?"

"O dear, Hakim. A bit of a saga there. He went up to Durham and Hadrian's Wall in the autumn, I think I told you, and that was fine. He loved it. Freezing Northumberland all through the winter but really interesting archaeology. And a girl."

"A girl? A girlfriend? About time."

"Yes and no. I see what you mean but—"

"So he's got over—what was the Indian doctor called?"

"Ayesha. Poor Ayesha. She was a lovely girl and suited Hakim really well. It was the saddest thing that she died."

"And the new girlfriend? You haven't met her?"

"Yes, I have. He came back from the north a few weeks ago and she arrived a few days later. He brought her to tea."

"And?"

"I don't think she's a bad girl, quite clever, quite independent-minded. She wouldn't do the MBA her father wanted her to do—her parents are divorced but there's obviously lots of money about—because she wanted to do archaeology instead. That's how she met Hakim, in a trench in the snow on Hadrian's Wall. But now she's got a standard Sloane job in Sotheby's."

"All that doesn't sound hopeless. Did you like her when she came here?"

"Not very much. Difficult to explain. I'd probably have thought her a reasonably friendly, if spoilt, posh girl with some things to be said for her if I'd just met her, if she'd had nothing to do with Hakim. As it is, I'm afraid it'll end in tears. She's too English for him, too set in privilege and ignorance. I don't think he has the foggiest idea what makes her tick. And I doubt if she's bothered to find out anything at all about Libya, or come to that about Islam, which matters a good deal to him. Let alone death: you know he lost everyone in his family one way and another before he came to England."

"Goodness, Gran, you can be fierce. I'd forgotten. 'Set in privilege and ignorance'—that's quite a condemnation."

"I'm very fond of Hakim."

"I know you are. But he's been living in England for years now. He's likely to have to cope with an English girlfriend at some point. I expect he'll manage fine. He's not living here at the moment is he?"

"He's living with Emma, that's her name, in the flat her father bought for her and her brother in Hackney. Spoilt, you see. The brother is conveniently in New York."

"Perhaps we'll meet him."

"Darling, I doubt it. He's a banker."

Carrie laughed. "Probably not, then."

Then, after drinking some tea, she said, "So what else is new? I'm so glad you didn't let Mum and Dad bully you out of the flat. It's so much yours, so much you, I think you'd have been really sad anywhere else, even in David's house. That'll suit Mum and Dad perfectly well once they've tarted it up, jolly lucky for them that it's there."

"I'm glad you think that's a good plan. I thought perhaps you might have liked David's house yourself?"

"O Gran, what a sweet thought. But I can't imagine me and Bill living in a bijou house between South Ken and Chelsea. We need to be in the field, working, that's what we love. That's what we hope IRC will send us off to do."

Clare, in her turn, drank some of her tea.

"There is one other bit of news."

"Really? How exciting. What?"

Clare picked up a biscuit and put it down again.

"I've made a new friend", she said, realizing as she said it that she sounded like a child coming home from school to report a playground triumph.

"That's brilliant, Gran, specially in lockdown. Where on earth did you manage to meet her?"

"Him."

"Him? Even better. Honestly, you are a one, Gran. Fancy scooping in a boyfriend at your age. So what's the story?"

"I met him in the garden, the square garden. I'd seen him a few times and thought he looked a bit scruffy, as if his wife had died and he needed looking after. Then it turned out—well, he came and told me one day when I was sitting on a bench in the garden—that he'd read my book."

'How on earth—?"

"Mr Clements in the pub."

"You're not telling me Mr Clements has read your book?"

"No, of course he hasn't. But the Taylors, the old couple upstairs, told him about it. Gossip, you know, happens even in South Ken, and the square is a village in its way."

"So does he live in the square, your boyfriend?"

"No, but he has a key to the garden because he used to help the old gardener."

"I see. Small world."

"Exactly."

"So is he a widower, like you thought?"

"Yes and no." She smiled.

"How d'you mean?"

"He is a widower because his wife is dead, but he's not a recent widower as I guessed, because she died nearly thirty years ago, in the siege of Sarajevo."

"Where's that?"

"Carrie—haven't you heard of Sarajevo?"

"I've heard of it, yes. Wasn't it where somebody was assassinated which started World War I?"

"I always forget how young you are. When were you born? 1997? So you weren't born when there was a terrible civil war in Europe, mass murders and all sorts of horrors, and the siege of Sarajevo, the capital of Bosnia, which lasted nearly four years. No wonder you've never heard of it. Not the sort of thing they teach in schools."

"So he must be quite old, your friend?"

"Yes, he's three years older than me."

"Very respectable for a boyfriend."

"Carrie—don't tease. I'm fond of him and we like chatting. That's it. Some nice company that doesn't involve either of us travelling anywhere."

"It sounds perfect. Well done you, Gran."

Carrie ate another biscuit.

"Does he have children, grandchildren, this old boy?"

"He had two sons. The older one was killed in the war in Bosnia, still very young, twenty-two I think. He was a soldier, or a fighter anyway, fighting against the Bosnian Serbs—it was all extremely complicated. The second boy was still a student, or would have been if there'd been anywhere to study, and he was killed with his mother by a Serb bomb."

It had taken months of quiet conversations about all sorts of things before Val had told her how they had died, and even then he had told her only the bare facts she had given Carrie.

"Goodness how sad. I'd no idea—about this war, I mean. I don't think I could find Bosnia on a map."

"Everyone's forgotten about it now. It was horrible. There was an actual massacre of Muslim men and boys, in a place called Srebrenica, seven or eight thousand of them shot, I can't remember the number exactly, like the Nazi massacres of Jews. Not long after that the Americans finally stopped the war, or more or less stopped it, and your uncle Matt was sent to Bosnia to help make sure the peace treaty wasn't broken."

"I never knew that."

"Why would you? It wasn't Iraq and it wasn't Afghanistan. I don't think he had to do any fighting there, and he loved the country, really beautiful he said, though there were burnt houses and new graves and awful stories in practically every village. What he told us, Grandpa and me, when he came home on leave, and it wasn't much, was all I knew about Bosnia really, before I met Val."

"Val? Is that his name, your friend?"

"Valerijan, with an extra j. Val is easy, and I've got used to it."

"Surname?"

"Radic."

"Like radish?"

"Almost, yes. That's annoying for him. It's what his colleagues in the bookshop called him when he first arrived in England."

"How often do you see him?"

"Twice a week. On Saturdays we go for a walk. On Wednesdays we take it in turns to have each other to tea, or in his case coffee."

"So he's been here?"

"Certainly he has."

"Does Mum know about this?"

"Carrie, don't. You sound more schoolma'amish than I ever do. 'This' isn't anything, or isn't any more than a couple of old people, each living alone, finding someone else, with a quite different past history, interesting and sympathetic to talk to. That's all. Val means a good deal to me. I've got used to him and he's a very nice man. But there's nothing to it, I promise, nothing that would mean anything to anyone else, and I can't face explaining another foreigner to your mother. Let alone your father."

"Has Hakim met him?"

"Yes he has. I had them both to lunch a few weeks ago."

"Did they get on?"

"They did. In some ways they got on too well."

"Wasn't it good, that they got on, nice for you, I mean?"

"Yes, it was. They had more in common that I'd realized and they seemed to like each other. But—complicated again. Emma, the girlfriend, was meant to be coming to lunch too but she cried off. An order from her father to have lunch with him, and that may be turning into another set of problems for Hakim. More disapproval of the foreigner, the Muslim. But what was sad was that Hakim, after talking happily to Val all through lunch, said to me after Val had gone that if Emma had been there, she'd have been bored, wouldn't have seen the point of an elderly refugee from a country she'd never heard of with a history she knew nothing about. And I think Hakim understood that what he'd guessed about what Emma's reaction to Val, perhaps not so much to Val himself as to Hakim's conversation with him, was a bad sign for the future."

"Couldn't he have been wrong? Supposing I'd been there instead of Emma? I expect I'm about the same age as her and I know nothing at all about Bosnia either. I don't think I'd have been bored. And if I'd been nuts about Hakim, as presumably Emma is, wouldn't I have been pleased to see him interested, engaged, talking to this old man he'd never met before? Obviously enjoying himself?"

"Darling Carrie, all that's quite true, but Emma's, alas, not at all like you. She's a completely different kind of girl. What I thought myself, though Hakim didn't say this, was that her nose would have been out of joint because she wouldn't have been the centre of attention. Perhaps, now I come to think of it, that's only a different way of putting what Hakim was saying about her being bored."

Carrie thought while she finished her biscuit. She tipped up the tin.

"Sorry, Gran. I've eaten the lot."

"That's all right. Why not? I don't expect there are many chocolate digestives in Nepal."

Carrie looked as if she were thinking.

"Poor old Hakim", she said. "If this is his first—you know, his first real relationship, which I bet it is—he'll be properly miserable if it all goes pear-shaped. Which it sounds as if it easily could."

"Exactly. His relationship with Ayesha was as real as anything, but I'm sure you're right. I don't think it was a physical affair. That's why I worry about him now."

"He'll manage. He's pretty strong, isn't he?"

"Very strong in some ways, but I'm afraid clueless about the kind of tough, complacent English girl that Emma is. I can see he's besotted with her, and it's that together with the cluelessness that make him vulnerable. So unlucky that he's got himself attached to her."

"Gran, you're not responsible for Hakim, you know. He's a perfectly capable grown-up. It's you yourself you're responsible for. And while we're on the subject of you, how much do you really know about your friend Val? Do I get to meet him, now I'm back?"

221

"I'd love you to meet him. I missed you so much when I first started talking to him. I wanted you to inspect him for me, to see if you thought I should trust him. I decided I could, all by myself, months ago, and I've never doubted I was right. But you must meet him before you go to America. It'll make him more real, somehow, knowing that you know him, that you can occasionally imagine me and him chatting away while you and Bill are being wonderful in New York or the Congo. O dear—I do hope not the Congo."

"You must remember, Gran, that aid workers are almost always all right everywhere. People need them. Now—"

She looked at her watch and stood up.

"I really must be getting back to Barnes. I told Mum I was coming to see you but she's asked a few people for drinks in the garden at half past six—outside, so it's allowed apparently—to say hello to me and Bill. She says they're keen to see me after such a long time, which I very much doubt, and Bill is a curiosity I suppose. Anyway she'll kill me if I'm late, and Barnes is such a pain at the moment because of Hammersmith Bridge. At least you can walk over it now and it doesn't take long to get to Hammersmith from here on the tube. When can I come to meet Val?"

"What about Saturday teatime? You'll still be here then, won't you?"

"That sounds perfect. Do I bring Bill or would you rather not? Just say, Gran. He won't mind and nor will I, and Mum's bound to ask you to meet him in Barnes anyway."

Clare thought.

"If you really don't mind, I think I'd rather you came by yourself, honestly. I'd like to be able to observe properly how you and Val hit it off or fail to hit it off, and if I were at the same time being nice enough to Bill, who's a total stranger after all, I wouldn't be able to. Or something like that."

Carrie laughed. "That's what I thought you might think."

"It's wonderful to have you back, Carrie. I've really missed you all this time. I do hope you'll be around at least for a few weeks."

"Goodbye, Gran. See you on Saturday."

She was almost through the front door when Clare called her back.

"Carrie. Not a word to Mum about Val. Promise?"

"My turn to be the grave. Of course, Gran."

The next day they decided to walk before tea as the sun was shining. While they were ambling along the Flower Walk where the asters and dahlias were showing off their garish heads as big as saucers, she asked Val if he'd like to meet Carrie on Saturday.

He stopped and smiled his blue smile into her eyes. "How wonderful, Clare, she has come back from Nepal. You must be delighted. And I would be delighted to meet her. Carrie is good, you told me, and I have not forgotten that."

"Don't expect too much, Val. She's young and—well—quite straightforward. She hasn't read many books."

"How could this be important, how many books she has read? She is your granddaughter. It will be an honour for me to meet her."

CHAPTER 11

SATURDAY 28 AUGUST 2021

On Saturday Carrie arrived first.

"I brought a cake", she said, putting on the kitchen table a square white cardboard box done up with a pink paper ribbon.

"O darling you shouldn't have. That's a terribly expensive shop."

"It makes terribly good cakes. Anyway I'm rich. You can't spend any money in Nepal. Nothing to spend it on."

"I hope Bill didn't mind you leaving him behind?"

"Not a bit. He's gone for some enormous walk all along the river. You know Americans, bonkers about exercise and fitness and all that. How many thousand steps a day. He has a watch that counts. And Mum and Dad have gone to Leckenby for the bank holiday weekend so we've got the house to ourselves for a few days, which is lovely. I'm very fond of it, after all, dear old house, and next time I'm in England they're bound to have sold it. So it's a treat, Bill and I being there while the cat's away."

"I do understand. Very nice for you, both of you."

"Mum said to tell you she won't ring today. She knows I'm coming to tea so I'll be responsible for making sure you're OK."

"That's fine. I am, as you see, perfectly OK."

"Tea in the sitting room? You've done a lovely tray. Let's put this cake on a plate and I'll take the tray."

"Thank you darling. I'll make the actual tea when Val gets here. Any minute, that'll be. He's very punctual. Old people are punctual because of nothing much going on in their lives."

The bell from the street door rang as Carrie came back into the kitchen.

"There he is. What did I tell you?"

She was nervous, again, this time for no reason.

She opened her front door as he closed the old iron gate of the lift. As he came in he took her hand and kissed it: this was as much a surprise as Hakim kissing her cheek had been when he brought Emma to tea. Even more of a surprise. Was he showing Carrie something? What? Probably he hadn't thought what.

"This is Carrie", she said, in as ordinary a voice as she could manage.

"How do you do, Carrie", Val said, shaking her hand.

"Hello, Mr Radic. Can I call you Val, like Gran?"

"Of course you can. It is a great pleasure to meet you."

"Go into the sitting room while I make the tea", Clare said to them both.

They did, and when, four minutes later, she carried the Crown Derby teapot in both hands into the sitting room, Carrie, sitting on the sofa and leaning forward towards Val, was talking about the complications of the journey back from Nepal. Val was listening affectionately as if he'd known her for years.

"You were sad to leave them, the people you have been caring for?"

Carrie looked more closely at him, and smiled. "I was, yes. No one else has thought I might be. It was sad. I may never go to Nepal again, and they're such lovely people, specially the children and the old people. Lots of the old people have died of Covid. No one complains. Everyone was terrified to begin with—it was all so sudden and so unexpected. But they accepted it after a bit, as fate or something, and we couldn't persuade them not to sit with the people who were dying."

"You were fortunate not to catch the Coronavirus yourself. As your grandmother was fortunate, when she was so brave."

Carrie turned to Clare.

"Gran? I hope you haven't been being brave. You swore you were being careful and obeying all the rules."

"I was careful. I am careful. Val just means I was lucky not to catch the virus when Ayesha was here, Hakim's girlfriend."

"O yes, of course. It was all in your book. Poor girl. And poor Hakim. But she didn't die here, in the flat?"

"No, no. She died in hospital, near the beginning of the epidemic, in May last year. It was the worst patch of all, for deaths."

After a moment of silence, almost of prayer, in memory of Ayesha whom neither Carrie nor Val had known, Clare said, "Have some tea, both of you."

They took their cups of tea, and Clare cut Carrie's cake.

"Carrie", Val said, "May I ask you where you will go to next? I cannot believe you will be happy to stay in England, which is not—how may I say this when your father, Clare has told me, is a member of parliament—which is not at present at its best."

Carrie laughed.

"It's OK. Don't worry about Dad. I disagree with him about practically everything and so does Gran. You're quite right. Not at its best is putting it mildly. I wouldn't want to stay here for long at the moment with this dreadful government and the way people are being treated when they've had to go through God knows what to get here. But my boyfriend is American and he's hoping to get an aid job in New York, so we'll be going there soon and then probably to some country somewhere where the west is actually doing some good."

"What would be an aid job in New York?"

"Sorry. There's a heavyweight outfit, I mean a big organization, in New York called the International Rescue Committee. They run programmes to help people in poor countries, with food and medicine and so on, and specially they help refugees. My boyfriend has applied for a job with them, and if he gets it he could be sent anywhere in the world and I'd go with him. The head of the organization is that chap called David Miliband who used to be Foreign Secretary in the days when we had foreign secretaries who knew anything about anything. Gran thinks David Miliband would be Prime Minister now, a proper Prime Minister instead of ridiculous Boris, if a whole series of things hadn't gone wrong in politics."

"I heard him on the wireless just the other day", Clare said, "talking about Afghanistan and the appalling time people are having, with our aid cut by three quarters, and failed harvests as well. He's very impressive and if he'd been leader of the Labour Party", Clare said, "and if he'd won the 2015 election, we wouldn't have had Brexit and everyone would have forgotten about it by now."

Val had been listening more carefully to Carrie than to her.

"I remember the name David Miliband", he said. "But do you think who you call a proper Prime Minister is what English people want? They seem to love Mr Johnson."

"They love him because he told them lies and made them promises he can't keep. It'll all go belly-up for sure and then they'll want to dump him a.s.a.p. Crash and burn."

Val looked puzzled again. Clare wished Carrie would speak English.

Carrie, knife poised, asked Val with a look if he wanted another slice of cake. He shook his head and Carrie cut another piece for herself. "Gran?" "No thank you darling—but it's a lovely cake. So kind of you to bring it."

"It is sad", Val said, "for a foreigner like me, coming from a country where democracy has only so short history that no one knows how it should work, to see in England, such an old democracy, with deep roots like an old tree you could imagine, that people do not care to choose a good government. They could but they do not."

"Try Nepal", Carrie said through a mouthful of cake.

"Alas, I know almost nothing about Nepal. Only Mount Everest."

"It's very poor. That's the main thing about it, really. While I was there we discovered that people were leaving the villages to work in factories in Malaysia, specially, once the pandemic got going, making protective gloves, PPE you know, for practically every country in the world. They thought they'd make their fortunes and send money home but actually it was slave labour, only debt for a whole year—a year's wages to get the job—and there were awful accidents all the time on production lines."

"Goodness, Carrie", Clare said. "How dreadful. Was there anything you could do?"

"Practically nothing. We made a fuss, got the story to the BBC, but nobody much cared. And it's such a shame that they feel they have to leave their villages. It's so very beautiful, you can't imagine—"

"You did send some lovely pictures", Clare said.

"Not good enough. The foothills of the mountains and then the Himalayas, jungle turning into snow, it's absolutely stunning. But the country's a real mess, the politics, I mean. There were kings, pretty good shockers, and now there's supposed to be a republic, democratic elections and all that, but actually the powerful people are like powerful people in most places, only wanting to hang on to power and they're mostly corrupt as well. Like Boris, but at least we'll be able to get rid of him eventually. I've no idea how, but we don't have Prime Ministers who last for ever, thank the Lord."

"It only needs the Tory MPs", Clare said, "to decide he'll lose them votes, even lose them their seats, in the next election, and that'll be the end of him. They're very good at blood on the carpet."

"Roll on the day", Carrie said.

Val wasn't listening.

"My country also is very beautiful", he said. "We also had some terrible kings. And now we have a kind of double republic which the Americans invented for us and it will not last."

"I don't understand", Carrie said. "What's a double republic?"

"That is a good question because it is an arrangement that sounds to be nonsense because it is nonsense. I will try to tell what it is. There was a country called Bosnia, always until after the death of Tito—have you heard of Marshal Tito? He was for a long time the president of Yugoslavia."

"I think so. He was neutral in the Cold War. Is that right?"

"More or less. He was a clever man and we owed him much in Yugoslavia although of course he was also a Communist. What was I telling? Ah, yes. Until Tito died we in my country, Bosnia, were always part of someone else's something, an empire, not always the same empire, or a kingdom, or at last communist Yugoslavia. Over some years, because only Tito had held it together, his Yugoslavia broke into pieces. The Serbs and the Croats and the Slovenes said they were separate countries. Outside countries said all right, we agree that they should be. Bosnia is in the middle. The Serbs and the Croats decide to divide Bosnia between them so that it may not any longer exist. You must understand that most people in Bosnia are Muslims, not Croats who are Catholic, not Serbs who are Orthodox, although there are many of both. Then there was a war, a terrible war, thousands of people were killed. In this war all sides had some cruel fighters, even the Muslims, but the most cruel were Bosnian Serbs. And most of the people they killed were Bosnian Muslims. Like me. Or like I might be. My grandfather was Muslim."

He paused, perhaps to decide whether or not to go on.

"When were you born, Carrie?—I am sorry, you are not so old as to mind that I ask you?"

"I don't mind a bit. I was born in April 1997."

"So. You were not born when all these things were happening. But, you understand, for an old person, as I am or your grandmother is, it is not so long ago. And now I hear—I had a long letter some weeks ago from my last friend in Sarajevo, the city where I was born, my city—I hear that the Bosnian Serbs do not accept that their politicians and generals who organized massacres and bombed Sarajevo for nearly four years were criminals, war criminals who have been convicted by international courts so that they are in prison or dead. No. Now they are heroes. And Serb children and Serb soldiers in Bosnia are being taught that the massacres never happened, that the war crimes were invented. This is lies instead of truth, propaganda instead of history and it is very dangerous for the future."

"Alternative facts. Like Donald Trump saying the election was stolen, and millions of people believing him."

"Exactly so. And Putin has now made Stalin a hero in Russia."

"But what about the double republic?" Carrie said.

"I am sorry. It is confusing, the story, and I am confusing the story more by telling it badly. Forgive me, Carrie. The double republic is like this. There is a country called the Federation of Bosnia and Herzegovina. Never mind Herzegovina, it is always part of Bosnia. Suppose this country is this big." He raised his hands and shaped a country with his hands a foot apart and then a foot between the top and the bottom hands. "Then suppose another country is inside the first one, a piece in the north-west and a piece in the south-east, just joined together by a thin piece at the top." He demonstrated with his right hand while his left stayed still as the south west boundary of Bosnia. "These pieces, inside the Federation and not much smaller than itself it is, make a second country."

His hands were back on his knees as he leant towards Carrie.

"This second country is called Republika Srpska. Most, not all but most, of its people are Bosnian Serbs. They are the ones who have the children and the young soldiers being told that the murderers of the war, Mladic the murderer general, and Karadjic the murderer politician, should be their heroes. But the families and the friends of the people they murdered, most of them Muslims, are there, close by across the frontier that is not a frontier. How can these people live together in a country that is both united and not united? It will not survive, Bosnia will not survive, Sarajevo will not survive as it now is, for very long."

"I'm so sorry", Carrie said. "What a mess, what a terrible mess. It must make you miserable, thinking about it, from so far away, when there's nothing you can do."

He looked at her for a moment or two.

"You are kind. Like your grandmother."

He looked at Clare and smiled. "Carrie is good", he said. "As you told me."

He turned hack towards Carrie, sitting on the sofa between them like a child trying to follow what two old people were saying to each other. Clare smiled at the thought.

"You know", he said to Carrie, "I would go, even now when I think the peace is again in danger, to my city, to Sarajevo, if I thought there could be something useful there that I would be able to do. The war is now a long time, many years, past, and I have—how can I say?—I have in a safe place in my mind the ones I lost, a safe place perhaps in God. But I do not go there because there is nothing I could do. I am too old, as you see, to be useful anywhere, so I must only wait for what I am sure will be bad news from Bosnia before too long."

"Poor you", Carrie said. "I do understand. It must be really difficult. But you know something? You're useful to Gran. You're a good friend to her, I can tell, and she hasn't had a good friend for a while."

Although he was in a comfortable armchair, the one he always sat in in this room if he came to tea and they moved out of the kitchen, Val was sitting upright to talk to Carrie.

He looked down at his hands on his knees. Clare saw the hands stiffen. For a moment he said nothing.

Then he looked at Carrie, perhaps with tears behind his eyes, tears Clare had never seen before.

"Thank you, Carrie." He cleared his throat. "I shall not forget that you have said this."

Suddenly he stood up.

"I must go home now. I have talked too much. If I have talked too much you will forgive me, Clare. I will leave you, Carrie, with your grandmother because you have not for so long been able to talk to her. Goodbye."

Clare, who was sitting back in her armchair and always took longer than Val to move, was still getting painfully to her feet when he turned in the sitting room doorway and raised his hand.

"Thank you, Clare and Carrie."

Then his little bow and he had gone, shutting the front door of the flat gently behind him.

Clare sank back into her chair.

"O dear", Carrie said. "I frightened him away, didn't I? Opening my mouth and putting my foot in it as usual. I'm so sorry, Gran."

"Don't be sorry, darling. He doesn't do showing his feelings. It's about the only way he's quite English. I'm sure that's all it was. I'm so glad you've met him. It makes him more real somehow."

"Gran, honestly! You couldn't have made him up. No one could. Such a story—and a whole country I've never even heard of. He's as real as anything. In fact he's an absolute duck. It's so brilliant that you've found him—and it's obviously brilliant for him too. What a terrific stroke of luck."

"Well, yes, it was, it is. Darling, I'm sorry. I need some more tea. Would you be an angel and put some hot water in the pot?"

While Carrie was in the kitchen, Clare did get out of her

chair, went to the open window and looked out over the dusty, sunny square. He'd disappeared. He could walk quickly still, as she couldn't, and he didn't have a stick.

"Sit down again, Gran. Here's some more tea. I'm going to have another piece of cake. English cake with cream and jam is the sort of thing you never have in a poor Asian country and when you get home you don't realize how much you've missed it."

"Victoria sponge", Clare said. "What a name when you come to think of it."

"Listen, Gran. When did you last have a holiday?"

"A holiday? Darling, what do you mean? I haven't had exactly a holiday for years and years. But what's sad is that I haven't been to Leckenby since the Christmas before last. Leckenby's not exactly a holiday. In some ways it's more like going home. But I do miss it. The Christmas before last is so long ago. It must be the longest time I've not been in Yorkshire in the whole of my life. Sometimes I'm sure I'll never see it again. After all, I could die any day, any hour, like David, couldn't I?"

"Gran, you're not going to die. Well, of course you are, in the end, but I'm sure you're not going to die any time soon. Look how well you are. And look how much there is to stay alive for. I bet you're writing another book."

"Well—"

"You are. I knew it. How cool is that, at your age?"

"No one may want to publish it."

"Of course they will. Look at your first one with the lovely Libyan ruins on the front for Hakim. I wonder how he's getting on with the dodgy girlfriend. Has he said anything?"

"Not a word. He notices things, Hakim, and I expect he feels that she and I make a kind of collision it's difficult for him to cope with. I just hope it's going all right."

"More tea?"

"No, really. Thank you. Even I have had enough tea for one teatime."

"The reason I asked you about a holiday is that I think you should go to Leckenby. Soon. Before the summer's completely over."

"But darling, I can't. Your father and I are on such terrible terms. Your mum comes to see me every so often, and that's fine. She checks I'm OK and we don't talk about politics. She'll be full of news about you and Bill next time I see her. But Charles and I are bound to argue, unless we say nothing at all to each other, and I really can't bear what the government is doing, or not doing, particularly in Afghanistan, so it's better if we don't meet, and easier for Mum."

"I do see. I expect you're right to stay out of his way for the moment. But I've just thought of a plan, while I was in the kitchen after Val left so quickly."

"A plan?"

"Mum and Dad are going to the south of France, some fancy villa belonging to another MP, on Tuesday."

"O yes. I vaguely remember Mum saying something about that."

"They're coming back next Sunday for the House starting up again and Dad says Mum must stay in London for two or three weeks because they've got to do networking, having the right people to dinner and all that stuff, because nothing's been possible for so long. And she's got to be in Barnes while the house is on the market because of viewings and making sure there are flowers in the drawing room and the kitchen's tidy. So she says, anyway."

"I don't see what any of that's got to do with me having a holiday—which I'm not at all sure I want in any case."

"You'll want this one. I want to show Bill Yorkshire before we go to New York. We can go up on a train, take you with us, and stay in Leckenby for a few days. No danger of Mum and Dad showing up."

It took a minute or two for Clare to grasp, to imagine. this.

"Darling Carrie, what a perfectly wonderful idea. I'd love that. You know I would."

"Have you still got your driving licence, Gran?"

"I suppose so. I haven't driven a car, obviously, since that Christmas, the Christmas before last. But—yes, now I come to think of it, I had to renew it earlier in the year, because I'm so ancient. There was a form to fill in. Could I still see properly.

Was I going dotty. That sort of question. Though how they find out if you tell them a pack of lies I've no idea. Eventually a new licence came back. So, yes, I'm still allowed to drive."

"That's good because we can share using Mum's old car. Bill and I can set out on huge walks, which is what he'll want to do, and while we're doing that you can take the car and do whatever you want."

"It all sounds perfect."

Carrie let a moment go by.

"And there's another thing", she said, "which I think would make it even better."

"What's that?"

"Suppose we tell Mum about Val—I'm sure I can do it so she thinks it's good news, and we can leave out anything that might rattle Dad—and then you ask Val to come with us to Leckenby? There's plenty of room. Bill and I can have the spare room and you and Val can have my room and Daisy's room, all very proper and respectable. And think how you'd love to show him Yorkshire."

Clare's turn for some silence.

"Darling. Do you think you could—I could? Wouldn't Mum be horrified?"

"Why on earth should she be? Obviously we'd have to pitch it right. 'Gran's got a boyfriend. He chatted her up on a park bench.' I don't think that would go down very well."

"Though true", said Clare.

"Come on, Gran. Diplomacy. You can tell the truth without telling all the truth. That's why they make you swear in the witness box to tell the whole truth, though no one ever does. 'Gran's got an old friend'—he is old, after all—'He's a widower so he's lonely, like her, and he's been stuck in London for months, like she has. Wouldn't it be good to give both of them a little holiday? Bill and I could go up to York on the train with them and look after them for a few days at Leckenby. What do you think?' Something like that should do the trick nicely."

"'Who is this friend? What's his name?' Your Mum would say next."

"'He's called Val, Val Radic', I say. He's a refugee who

234

arrived in England a long time ago. He lives near Gran, in Kensington.'Where did he come from?' Mum would say. 'Somewhere in eastern Europe. I'm not sure where. Like Gran's father, you know.' Mum always forgets she's a quarter Jewish."

"So, luckily, does your Dad. I remember brushing the Jewish refugee element in my family rather under the carpet when your mother said she wanted to marry Charles. His parents—you didn't know them very well, did you? Your other grandfather died years and years ago and your other grandmother didn't much like children—were on the stuffy side. Not very keen on the idea of foreigners. Luckily Grandpa was as English as could be."

"Thank goodness for foreigners. I like being a bit Jewish. And look at Val—so nice, and not at all English." Clare for an instant remembered him kissing her hand as he arrived for tea. "I'm glad we were still being quite decent to refugees when he arrived. Very different from now."

"O Carrie, don't. When Val arrived, fifteen years ago, he'd been working in Poland for ten years so he didn't even have to say he was a refugee, though he was one. He was just a person in the European Union who could live anywhere inside it. And now look at what's happening with the people crossing the Channel in those leaky boats and the Home Secretary wanting to push them back towards France so they drown. If they get here she wants to ship them off to some Devil's Island place in the middle of nowhere like the Australians did with people struggling in boats to get to Australia. They're called 'illegal', though there's no legal way for them to apply for asylum, and 'criminals' though they've done nothing wrong. And now, just this week, thousands of terrified Afghans who we promised to look after because for years they've worked for us have been left behind for the Taliban to kill. They'll try to escape. A few will get out, to Pakistan or wherever, and some of them may end up trying to get across the Channel in a boat no more substantial than a paddling pool. It's dreadful even to think about."

"I know Gran, it's awful, the whole thing. I can't talk to Dad about it, obviously. He still goes on about immigration all being the EU's fault and people voting for Brexit because they didn't want England overrun with Muslims—I ask you."

"There you are. One of the worst lies of the Brexit campaign was that Turkey was about to join the EU which would let seventy million Muslims into England. The appalling Cummings said afterwards that without the Turkey threat and the other big lie, about three hundred and fifty million pounds a week for the health service, the Brexit vote wouldn't have been won. He wasn't apologizing. He was gloating. So without those lies we'd never have had this prime minister or this home secretary. Sometimes I despair, I really do."

"Gran, you mustn't despair. It's not like you. How about my plan? I tell Mum about Val. Bill and I take you both up to York on the train, masks and distancing and all, we get a taxi to Leckenby and then stay a few days and use Mum's car. What do you think?"

"Well—I suppose—it sounds almost too good to be true. But why not? Darling, I think it's a lovely idea. Let's see what Mum says before counting our chickens, but you are so kind to think of it."

The next day was Sunday. She'd taken a long time to get to sleep, remembering bits and pieces of what Val and Carrie had said over tea, and rattled rather than pleased by Carrie's plan—she didn't want Penny to know about Val, and the idea of Carrie and American Bill, who she hadn't even met, together with Val and her on a train and then in a taxi seemed, in sleepless imagination, somehow dangerous, even doomed, Wouldn't Val in Leckenby be the kind of collision that Hakim had found even the idea of Emma and Val together in her kitchen to be? Two ways of being that couldn't be united, couldn't be held together by, in, the same person. When eventually she slept, a confused nightmare came back and back. Every time it returned it woke her and every time she managed to fall asleep, there it still was, David in York station asking her about a lost child but she couldn't hear what he was saying, and there were soldiers in strange uniforms talking a language she didn't know and not seeing her when she tried to ask them for help because she wasn't tall enough. All the station, its dozen platforms, the stairs, the bridge, the lifts and the tunnels underneath the railway lines had to be searched and searched again. She couldn't escape and couldn't find the lost child. The dream had her more than once in tears as she woke.

In the morning when she got up to go to Mass—plain and brief and distanced nowadays in the Carmelite church the other side of Kensington High Street where she had been to Mass for decades—she felt, after her bad night, stiff and a bit shivery, and a hundred years old.

In the fresh air, walking steadily with her stick up the Gloucester Road towards Kensington Gardens, she wondered why she couldn't decide what to hope for. She was used to being able to think quite clearly but now, as she walked, she could only muddle her way from one conclusion to its opposite so quickly that they were almost simultaneous: it would be lovely beyond anything she had allowed herself to imagine to be in Yorkshire with Val, to take him to the moors, to the ruined abbey of her childhood and all her life, to the quiet graveyard where Matt was buried; at the same time she was certain it would be a terrible mistake, it might easily wreck whatever there was between her and Val and she would most painfully and for ever regret it.

She even heard Simon's voice: "You're being totally ridiculous, love. If you'd like to go to Yorkshire with this chap, just go. Nice place, nice chap. What's not to like? You're making a fuss about nothing." It was the sort of problem that to Simon simply didn't exist. David, on the other hand—But if David were still alive, Val wouldn't have become her friend. QED she thought, and, again, wasn't sure why.

In Mass she tried to clear her mind of all this, and to pray, for peace and hope, and couldn't. At the consecration she looked up at the priest, who seemed far in the distance over mostly empty pews, though it wasn't a very big church, and couldn't regain even the sense of the presence of Christ that she had been so moved to come back to when it was first possible to go to Mass in a church again. She received communion and knelt afterwards. God be merciful to me a sinner. Before she left the church, she had decided that she would ring Carrie when she got home and tell her to forget the whole plan. What had made up her mind? She had no idea. But she walked home more briskly.

She was making strengthening coffee, real coffee which she allowed herself in the mornings, when Carrie rang.

"I've done it Gran. It was a breeze. Mum thought it was a really good idea. About time you had a few days in Leckenby, she said. Being in the country would make a change and do you good. And bring Val by all means. If he's from eastern Europe probably just as well Dad won't meet him. You know Dad, she said. Yes I do, I said. That was about it. I got her at a good moment—she's thinking about nothing except what she should pack for the Riviera. Will it be black tie for dinner? Do I think she's too old for that stripey bathing suit she's had for years?"

"Goodness, Carrie. You're very brave. Well done."

"Aren't you pleased, Gran?"

"Yes, but—"

"You mustn't worry about Covid. We'll do everything we're supposed to and it'll be fine. Bill thinks it's a brilliant idea. So far he's only seen bits of London. He hasn't realized England does country too. Rather well, if it's Yorkshire, as we know. Leave it all to me. I'll get the tickets online."

"Hold on a minute, Carrie. I should ask Val first, before you get the tickets I mean."

"O yes of course. Ask him today and let me know."

As she put the telephone back on its rest she realized she'd been half, perhaps more than half, hoping that Penny had vetoed the plan.

She looked at the kitchen clock. Twenty past eleven. She had no idea what Val did on Sunday mornings. A tradition had developed between them that they always met on Wednesday and Saturday afternoons, and they didn't communicate either by telephone or by email. Eccentric no doubt, for nowadays, but it suited them both. She had his landline number and his email address, and he had hers. They had very seldom used either. She didn't want to make any sort of a drama out of this

238

invitation. She would go and see him, and hope he was in.

At his house in the sunshine of the mews she rang the bell. After a minute or two he opened the door, in the old panama hat he always wore in hot weather.

"Clare. How very good. Come in."

His house was fuller of light than she had ever seen it.

"Come into my so small yard. There is space for another chair."

Through the kitchen, out of the French window, into the yard, with one climbing rose, now over, on the wall and some geraniums in pots.

She saw he had been sitting in an old canvas folding chair, the kind advertisements called a director's chair. The *Observer*, open at a middle spread, was beside the chair where he'd dropped it. She could see that while Val was opening the front door for her Ivica had jumped into the chair and was asleep, pretending he'd been there for hours. Val picked him up and put him gently on the ground.

"Foolish cat. We have a guest. Sit down, please, Clare. Do you like some lemon and ice?"

"That sounds delicious."

He went into the kitchen, opened the fridge, then a drawer, did one or two things she heard but didn't see and reappeared with his tray. Two glasses with lemon juice that presumably he had just squeezed, some ice in the glasses, a little jug of water, some sugar in a bowl and two spoons. He put the tray on the ground, went back, and returned with a kitchen chair. He sat opposite her.

"Perfect", she said. "*Citron pressé* like in France."

"My grandmother used to make it in the summer, though she was by no means a Frenchwoman, only a Croat. She had been to Paris once, very long ago."

"There you are. It's a very French thing. Or was."

"Why do you come on Sunday, Clare? You have been to Mass? Is everything OK?"

"I have been to Mass, yes, and everything's fine. I'm sorry. I hope I didn't startle you?"

"Startle?"

"Surprise you too much?"

"No, not at all too much. It is good to see you."

She sipped her iced lemon.

"The thing is, Val, Carrie has made a suggestion. She was so pleased to meet you—"

"I also was pleased, to meet her. Good Carrie. She is intelligent and—how to say?—She is alive, lively. That is attractive."

"I'm glad you liked her. Well, the thing is"—stop dithering, she said to herself; get on with it—"she's going to Yorkshire next week, to her parents' house in the village where I always stayed in the holidays when I was growing up. Her parents are away. She asked me if I would like to go with her and her boyfriend on the train to York and then stay a few days in the house."

"That is excellent. You have said how sad you have been through the coronavirus time not to be able to go to Yorkshire. So I will not see you on Wednesday and Saturday. But soon you will come back. This is a good invitation. Not so?"

"Very good, yes."

She paused, feeling shy. As if she were sixteen and finding herself at a party asking a boy to dance. Another sip of lemon.

"She also suggested that you might like to come too. What do you think? A holiday in the country after all this time? Perhaps enjoyable? I could show you—"

He stopped her with a blue look. He said nothing for a few moments. Then he shook his head.

"No, Clare."

Again nothing. He put his hands on his knees and bent his head, then looked up, and directly at her.

"It will be—" He hesitated, searching for exactness? "It will be too close. It is your own, this place, your childhood place. I am only a foreigner. It is too early for me to come in to this place. It is too early in your life."

He stopped, but then said, more easily, "Also I cannot leave Ivica by himself. It is not possible."

How stupid of her not to have guessed that he would say no.

"Of course", she said quickly. "Of course I understand. It was just a thought—of Carrie's really."

After a minute or two he said, "Will you go? To Yorkshire with Carrie and her American friend?"

"I hadn't—Yes, I think I will go. It's sweet of her to have asked me."

"That is good. You will tell me, how it has been, when you come back to London?"

"Yes, Val, I will tell you."

She thought she was going to cry, managed not to, and finished her *citron pressé*.

He put his glass, still half full, on the tray and picked up the paper, restoring it to its proper shape. She had been too distracted to collect her *Observer* on the way back from Mass.

"You must be very careful when you travel. The coronavirus is getting worse all this time. Look." He gave her the paper and pointed to a piece on the right of the front page. *Covid cases,* the headline said, *are 26 times higher than a year ago.*

"O dear, yes. But the vaccinations we've had should make all the difference, shouldn't they?"

She was answering automatically, her attention caught and held by the big headline and the main piece on the front page: *Ministry ignored frantic pleas to help Afghans.* She read the first few lines of the report, which said that thousands of emails from MPs and charities begging for help for Afghans trying to get out of the country hadn't even been read.

She gave him back the paper.

"Have you read this, Val? About Afghanistan. What has happened to this country? Once we were good about refugees, and about people who worked for us abroad. I'm sure the Foreign Office used to be careful and efficient. Now it seems to be incompetent and cruel. If the Foreign Office is as bad as the Home Office, it's because this government itself is incompetent and cruel. It's very hard to bear."

"I know", Val said. "What is happening in Afghanistan is very bad. And I understand that for you it is worse, because of your boy."

"There was a young interpreter with my son's squadron. He was very useful, and cheerful. The soldiers loved him. Perhaps it's for him and his family that someone is asking for help.

241

Perhaps he's asking for help himself. And no one even reads the message."

Now she was crying.

Val put down the paper and took both her hands in his as they sat. "Clare. It is war. I know what is war. The young men die, and it is for nothing. And other young men are lost. We are old. We can do nothing now."

She took her hands from his, opened her bag which she had propped beside her chair, and took out a tissue. She blew her nose firmly.

"Thank you, Val. You're quite right. We can do nothing but be sad, and ashamed."

She blew her nose again, put the tissue in her bag and stood up.

"Thank you again—for—for everything. I must go home. I promised to telephone Carrie this morning to tell her—"

"You will go with her to Yorkshire?"

"Yes. I'll go. I'll see you when I get back."

"Of course."

He went ahead of her, through the kitchen, through his sitting room, and opened the front door for her.

"Goodbye, Clare. For today."

"Goodbye, Val. I'll be back on Wednesday week."

In her flat she rang Carrie.

"Darling, I'm afraid Val can't come."

"O never mind. I'll go ahead and get three tickets then. I'll let you know the train. Bill and I can pick you up in a taxi on the way to the station."

"No need for an expensive taxi. Very easy to get to King's Cross on the tube as you know."

"Not with a suitcase, Gran, and not with Covid either. We'll pick you up. I'll get back to you. Probably it'll be Saturday morning."

"All right, darling. That'll be lovely."

She went out again to get her *Observer*. As she walked, seven minutes to the newsagent, seven minutes back, she felt lighter, younger, happier, despite the news about the Foreign Office and Afghanistan.

"It is too early in your life": whichever he meant, or both, he understood. Already she was looking forward to seeing him again when she came back.

CHAPTER 12

THURSDAY 9 DECEMBER 2021

Those days in Yorkshire were a gift from God. She couldn't write them down, not yet.

Three months since then had gone by. Three months in the life of an old person is an almost negligible amount of time, and in these three months almost nothing, in any case, had happened to her. But she was sad and tired, perhaps mostly because she had thought of attempting something that she should have known was too much for her, and had probably abandoned the idea sooner than she need have.

Someone, she couldn't remember who, a priest in a long-ago confessional, or a teacher when she was an earnest school-girl, or most likely her father, had said to her once, "There's never nothing you can do", and it was because she believed this was true that she had decided that she should rescue at least one family of Afghan refugees from one of the hotel bedrooms where even the few who had been brought to England when so many had been left behind had been parked and apparently more or less forgotten.

What prompted her actually to try to do this herself was four or five minutes of conversation she'd heard on *Woman's Hour* a few weeks ago. She knew which day it had been. In the morning of the feast of All Saints, the first of November, she had just come back from Mass, as usual nowadays quiet, cool and distanced. The priest had delivered a homily about saints not just being the those approved by the Church with familiar names and dates for them to be remembered and stories that could be looked up, but anyone, everyone, their names known not to us but to God, who in their lives had managed to travel so far towards a life with, a life in, God that when they died they were there or practically there. This wasn't the first All Saints homily on these lines she had heard, but it had got her down as she recognized it shouldn't have.

Walking home she felt far far away from God, even far away, in this cruel and untruthful world, from Jesus, whose presence in the reality of his time she remembered detail by detail every evening before she got into bed. At Mass she had received communion, as she always did, but as the wafer melted in her mouth she felt in communion with nothing, with no one. What had become of that sureness, that delight, in the presence of God that she had known in those blue and gold days in Yorkshire in September? She knew perfectly well, of course, that the perception of God in the beauty of his created world was something that came and went, that couldn't be relied on, that might strengthen faith but wasn't itself faith. But in the last few weeks, particularly since Carrie and Bill had left for New York, she had lost her grip, her hold, on what had for years kept her upright, kept her walking forward. Where was her certainty that it was in the presence of God that she lived and breathed, slept and woke, tried to write, went out to meet Val, came home to her warm flat and the armchair where she was reading *The Brothers Karamazov* every evening? Instead of feeling safe with God she felt confused, afraid of dying, though she wasn't ill, before she could regain her balance as a human being, and above all ashamed to be, without ever having intended to be, a responsible person in a country that was heartless, thoughtless, and dismissive of the needs of so many people who might, who would, die because of our carelessness, our refusal to care.

Where was the answer to Ivan Karamazov's fury—a passage of the book she'd never forgotten since she read it when she was sixteen or seventeen—with a world in which the torture of children was only the worst kind of vicious human behaviour unexplainable except by the absence of God? Or the answer to her fury with the rich countries, specially those which had undertaken to support Afghanistan, that, never mind the menace from the Taliban, were leaving millions of Afghans close to starvation when basic supplies or just their own money to buy food could help them?

Was there anything she could do, an elderly widow, comfortably off, living in South Kensington as she had for decades, to redress these wrongs, these terrible wrongs? Of course there wasn't.

Then, back in the flat, she turned on as she always did, without thinking, the kettle and the wireless. A woman was being interviewed, an intelligent, articulate woman whose accent Clare couldn't identify. After a few exchanges with the interviewer it was clear that the woman was an Afghan journalist, and perhaps also a teacher, who had been for two months, with her children, in a hotel in Kingston where between two hundred and fifty and three hundred other Afghan refugees were also living. The woman wasn't even sure of the number. The two months meant she had been rescued towards the end of August, the last week when it was possible for anyone to leave on a flight for Europe though others had since struggled to the border with Pakistan or Tajikistan. The woman wasn't complaining. She and her children were alive and safe, although she didn't know whether or not her husband had survived the triumph of the Taliban: telephone contact was patchy and also risky because calls from or to the UK might be incriminating. She was hoping that soon someone would be able to produce a flat or a couple of rooms where she and her children could live, could escape the confinement of a hotel where everyone else was also an anxious refugee worried about those left behind. She didn't say what her husband had done in the past or did for a living. Saying on the BBC that he had helped the British might be the death sentence Clare remembered hearing it had already been for many who had had to declare what they had done to try to get a visa. Irrespective of whatever her husband might have done or not done before the collapse of the government and the army, as an educated professional woman with good English she might well have been killed on her own account if she hadn't managed to leave the country. Now, presumably among the five thousand who had been rescued, she and her children were stuck, almost as if they were in prison.

After the interview was over she turned off the wireless, made her coffee and sat at the kitchen table, pleased, even excited at the idea of being truly useful to someone. It was obvious what she should do. For weeks, months really, since the collapse of everything in Afghanistan at the end of August, she had wished she could find a way of helping, helping Matt's interpreter, though of course she didn't know even his name, helping anyone who had helped British soldiers or doctors or aid workers like Carrie and had been abandoned to the Taliban. She had sent some money to the UN refugee agency, and some more to Médecins Sans Frontières but that had seemed too easy, hadn't cost her enough: she was ashamed to think that a hundred pounds would now buy in England eight packets of cigarettes, the amount she used to smoke in a week, though she had given up smoking years ago. Two hundred pounds to reliable charities might make a small difference to a few people in Afghanistan, but she needed to make some kind of reparation for the dereliction of responsibility that haunted her days, and particularly her nights. There was a debt: couldn't she repay a tiny part of it?

Here at last was something she was able to do that would cost her, would cost her, above all, her contentment at being alone in her flat except for when Val came to tea and Penny's occasional visits. This would be an actual sacrifice, even if only of calm, of habit, so not of much, but a sacrifice nonetheless, something real to set against the desertion of a whole desperately poor country for no good reason.

She decided that she should offer to have this woman and her children to stay in her flat until they could find a proper place to live. Very quickly she was imagining the woman in Matt's room, where scrupulous Hakim of course had left no trace of his recent brief stay. And she could at last, which in itself would be a good thing, clear out, clean and tidy Penny's room for the children: she remembered the dead spider and its dead victims caught in the curtain on the night of *Doctor Zhivago*, and realized she'd hardly been into the room since and certainly hadn't washed the curtains. The woman in the interview hadn't said how old her children were. Perhaps they would enjoy the rocking horse, the doll's house. Perhaps one of them was still young enough for the cot, the playpen—couldn't it be like having in the flat the great-grandchildren Carrie and Daisy showed no sign of producing? And if the woman needed some peace and quiet in which to write, since she was a journalist, she could use Simon's study. She found herself beginning to wonder about local primary schools, and how old the children would have to be to walk to school by themselves, when she shook her head and pulled herself together.

This was a daydream, improvised in a few minutes to console her for the guilt she felt about Afghanistan, mixed up with the grief for Matt that never left her, and to counter her sense of uselessness. Perhaps she could after all do something, not nothing, be of some help, even if only to one family who were already in England? Put like that, her dream seemed reasonable, moderate, achievable. But could she make the dream come true, for the woman and her children in the Kingston hotel, and for herself? Should she even try?

"Not a good idea", she heard Simon say in her head as he certainly would have said had he been in the room. "Unrealistic. So like you to think you should spoil your orderly life, which you're quite old enough to deserve, because giving yourself a hard time would somehow make up for a tiny fragment of the world's injustice. And it would be hard. Imagine."

She wouldn't let herself imagine how difficult it might be. She shut down Simon's voice from the long past of her marriage, but not before he said, "You're being ridiculous even to think of doing this. So like you, to be carried away by an idea that would for sure be too much for you."

"For sure": Simon, and no one else she had ever known, often said this.

She could at least find out about the possibilities. Simon hadn't always been right.

How should she set about volunteering to give the journalist and her family a couple of rooms in her flat? She had no idea. Should she telephone *Woman's Hour*, or Kingston council? Probably not. There would be long waits on the telephone, a lot of Vivaldi, and the impossibility of reaching a person who could tell her what to do next. Was there a London charity in charge of finding temporary homes for refugees who had arrived with nothing? She tried the internet, which she wasn't good at. There seemed to be a charity in Wales which arranged for people to have refugees staying with them for a week or a month or more until something better was found for them. But not in London. She probably wasn't looking in the right places or with the right words.

Suddenly she panicked, as if she had already irrevocably given up the quietness and undemandingness of her flat to children she didn't know and a formidable woman she might not even like. It took her a minute or two for her to remember that she hadn't in fact done, or even decided, anything.

She needed help with the internet. Hakim? Certainly not. She was worried about him: she didn't know how it was going with the girlfriend, Emma with her low boredom threshold, and she hadn't heard a word from him for weeks. She definitely couldn't bother him over nothing. Carrie? She couldn't bother her either for help with the internet, but she saw that she needed her more for advice. And that perhaps wouldn't be too tiresome?

Carrie had been in New York for a little over a month. The day before she left, she came, without Bill, though Clare had become fond of Bill after her few days with both of them in Yorkshire, to say goodbye. Clare had felt real despair as she watched Carrie from her sitting-room window, striding to the end of the square and disappearing towards the Gloucester Road. With the possibility, or threat, of the Congo or some equally terrifying country awaiting Carrie and Bill, would she ever see her again? She herself would, even if Carrie stayed safe, most likely be dead before they came back to England. That afternoon, really for the first time, she had felt properly old. Usually, though knowing perfectly well that she was old, it wasn't how she felt. A little stiffer getting out of bed or out of an armchair, a little slower up the stairs so a little more inclined to take the lift if it was working, a little more careful to plan how she was going to get up again if she had to go down on her knees. But after she reached the kitchen table when Carrie had gone she felt truly old, spent, finished, as if she had no more energy or strength for anything. What was the point of her still being alive? This hadn't lasted, thank God at least for that. But her autumn of unhappiness and distance from God had probably begun that day.

Carrie meanwhile was fine. In a couple of emails she'd reported that Bill's family were wonderful—"You'd love them, Gran, you really would, specially his father, Southern and silver-haired with a voice like James Stewart's"—and that New York was "fantastic, just like everyone's always said". A couple of weeks later Bill had got his job at the International Rescue Committee—"of course he has, good old Bill, they'd be nuts to have turned him down"—and was, thank the Lord, for the time being in a Manhattan office in a suit. Carrie had applied for an internship in the same organization: they didn't need another salary while they were living, quite happily as far as Clare could tell, in Bill's parents' spare room. Knowing Carrie and her powers of persuasion, Clare thought she was as likely to get it as Bill had been to get the job.

It seemed more possible, less intrusive, to ask Carrie for her advice from the streets of New York than it had been to email her about nothing much in the Covid-stricken mountains of Nepal, which Clare had never done.

Darling Carrie,
Can I bother you for some advice?

You know I've been getting more and more miserable about the terrible plight of people in Afghanistan, not just because of Uncle Matt and his wasted death, but because what we've done, as a country, by abandoning Afghanistan is unforgivable and the situation there is getting worse and worse. Today I heard on the radio—no use talking to Carrie about the wireless, to her a joke word—*an interview with a woman, an Afghan journalist with very good English, who's been marooned for two months with her children in a hotel in Kingston, her husband's fate unknown. I thought I should find a way of offering her and the children a couple of rooms in the flat until they can be given somewhere of their own. It would surely be much better than a grim hotel full of other refugees? What do you think?*

(I imagine this is the sort of thing the IRC deals with several times a day.)

　　　　Lots of love, and to good Bill,
　　　　　　Gran

That was enough.

Not till after lunch, wondering why Carrie hadn't answered, did she remember that she'd forgotten the time difference. When she sent her email it was still so early in the morning in New York that Carrie wouldn't have been even awake.

Just after two, so just after nine in New York, Carrie's answer came.

Hi Gran,
No bother at all—always great to hear from you.

Typical Gran, to have such a kind and generous idea but honestly I don't think you should do it. You do love the flat after so many years, and you do have your own way of doing things which another woman in the kitchen—think of that, Gran— might drastically upset. Not to mention children racketing about which is what children do. They might stay for ages and you wouldn't know how to ask them to go—and suppose Hakim wants to come back if the girlfriend situation ends in tears?

Another thing I've just thought of. If you try to fix this through a charity they're likely to ask your age and then they might think you really wanted some free help in the flat. I'd hate you to have to cope with that sort of conversation with some snotty social worker on the phone.

So I think you should forget about filling the flat with Afghans—since this family have made it to England they'll soon find somewhere proper to live I'm sure. Probably dozens of people listening to the radio at the same time as you have already offered spare rooms, student flats, whatever. Time to be pleased with being old—you can always say prayers and send some money to one of the charities still battling on in Afghanistan, the usual good stuff I'm sure you do anyway.

Don't say anything about your idea to Mum—I'm sure you won't. Imagine what Dad would say.

Give my love to Val next time you see him.
Love you
C xxx

So that was that. She was grateful to Carrie for answering so quickly and for being so direct and so sensible, particularly about the possible reaction from a charity, something that hadn't crossed her mind.

But she was irrationally disappointed as well, as if there had been something new and satisfying to look forward to which had been taken away from her. As if the cheerful presence of children in the flat, coming into the kitchen to tell her things, had been a real possibility. This was nonsense and she knew it.

After a day or two she had set herself to write a couple of pages about this non-event, but it turned out to be too complicated to put down when she hadn't yet overcome the sense of unreal hope and so of unreal loss which had muddled her, and she gave up.

And now more than another month had gone by. Still she'd heard nothing from Hakim. She reminded herself from time to time that after all he wasn't actually one of the children and she couldn't expect him to check in regularly to see if she was all right. At the same time she suspected that he had, obviously without saying anything and probably without any conscious thought, resigned some of his instinctive responsibility for her to Val. But she did recognize that his silence was one of the things that were emptying her days of light, and it was impossible to tell whether the silence meant that things with Emma were going very well or very badly. She was sure, after seeing them together just once, that it would be one or the other. The contrast between Hakim and Emma as an infatuated pair and Carrie and Bill, who had behaved during those few days in Leckenby like a slightly scratchy but very fond married couple, had been striking, and had much cheered her when she thought of Carrie and Bill supporting each other in whatever suffering country they might be sent to.

Suffering countries. While she plodded through her eventless days, looking forward only to her gentle conversations with Val, the news from Afghanistan was getting worse and worse, and we, the British, seemed capable only of a careless sloppiness that in its effects amounted to actual cruelty.

She remembered so many stories she had heard on the wireless or read in the paper. There was the story of a chef who had worked in the British Embassy in Kabul for thirteen years: he reached the airport with great difficulty at the end of August to be told that he couldn't have a visa or a passport because his employer was a contractor and not the Foreign Office. So that was probably the end of him. "A contractor" meant people making undeserved money out of doing things the government should be doing itself, as in G4S, whoever they were, who had sent three hundred security guards at the embassy not the exit visas they had pleaded for but redundancy notices that were actually death sentences. While all these people were failing to reach the flights that would have saved their lives, Boris Johnson, prompted no doubt by his sentimental wife, got a planeload of cats and dogs to jump the queue.

Then there was the terrible report by Antony Loyd, a very brave journalist whose book on the Bosnian wars, lent her by Val, had appalled her. He had found, after the last escape flight had left Kabul, papers scattered on the floor of an office in the abandoned embassy with the names and details of Afghans working or offering to work for the British. More and more of the truth about what had happened as the Americans and the British left the country went on emerging. The day before yesterday a junior official in the Foreign Office who had resigned in despair told the parliamentary select committee for foreign affairs that he'd been left alone for days on end to cope with thousands of desperate emails from Afghanistan at the end of August and into September, with the Foreign Secretary deciding nothing and thousands of emails every day not being even opened. The senders of emails that were opened were told that their messages had been "logged", but in fact nothing whatever had been done with them. A hundred and fifty thousand Afghans had asked for help to leave the country. Five thousand - that figure again, sometimes actually boasted about—had been got out. Even Boris Johnson had managed to sack the Foreign Secretary shortly after this dreadful fortnight, but there was no reason to suppose that his successor, the tough, ambitious, unprincipled Liz Truss (she had been a remainer on Brexit until that looked like a career-breaker) would do anything to help unlock the money, nine billion dollars of Afghan money someone on the wireless had said, that is frozen in the west by disapproval of the Taliban when it could be feeding the starving in Afghanistan.

On the *Today* programme she'd heard Rory Stewart say "DFID—sorry, the Foreign Office—is doing nothing to save Afghanistan from famine". That sentence said a great deal. Rory Stewart knew Afghanistan better than any other English politician and had worked for Theresa May as the secretary of state for international development before the department was abolished by Boris Johnson. More recently he'd written that if America and Britain had left just a few troops in Afghanistan (perhaps indefinitely but look at Korea, where American troops were still holding the line seventy years after its war), the Taliban would have been unable to take complete control and mass starvation could have been avoided and perhaps even the education and careers of girls and women saved.

She was having nightmares almost every night. Often she dreamt about telephone calls, and her dreams were so vivid that she would wake convinced she had heard, could still hear, her telephone ringing, but always it stopped before she reached it. Twice she had got out of bed and, cold in bare feet, stumbled almost to the kitchen before she realized there was total silence in the flat. She was haunted by the knowledge that, now that practically everyone in the world had a mobile telephone, people in all sorts of terrifying situations were desperately appealing for help, to Britain, to London, to the government, in her nightmares directly to her, for help, and getting no help. Telephone numbers abounded, numbers everyone knew, numbers no one else knew, numbers given out for use in emergency, like those, no doubt, given to Afghans working for the British. They called and no one answered. Last week somewhere in the Channel, twenty-seven people had drowned when their inflatable boat sank in the freezing dark. They had mobile phones. They rang the French emergency number and were told to ring the British; they rang the British emergency number and were told to ring the French. They were dead. One of them was an Afghan; no one would ever know the story of the last two months of his life, which had taken him somehow or other, across which hostile countries one could only guess, from the chaos in Kabul to the French coast. Telephone calls into the night of indifference, or, worse, the night of cruel Home Office policy: these were the telephone calls of her nights, mixed up with the fear that Hakim had tried to reach her and she'd failed to answer the telephone in time or at all.

Every morning, with a cup of tea, she tried to banish these miseries, and later tried on the internet to discover whether there was any better news. There wasn't. The Afghan Resettlement Scheme, announced with a characteristic Boris Johnson flourish of boastfulness was still said to be "not yet open", while the World Food Programme was constantly appealing for money for Afghanistan which it obviously wasn't getting.

Yesterday, Wednesday, had been a complicated day. In the morning she went to Mass, more to banish the anxieties of the night than because it was the feast of the Immaculate Conception, which she thought she remembered as a holiday of obligation but which didn't seem to be one any more. There were a dozen people widely scattered in the church. She'd always found the feast problematic, not because it was difficult to believe that Mary, having to be worthy of bearing the son of God, was uniquely without sin, but because the Church's insistence on this as a dogma, and hence a feast, declared so recently and in a manner so unnecessarily irritating to Protestants, seemed somehow legalistic, almost chilling. Poor old Augustine was ultimately responsible. Since she first heard the phrase she had always thought original sin not just an idea but an absolutely evident fact. But the pinning of original sin to the moment of conception, instead of, for example, to the first moment of disobedience, the first defiance of goodness or truth, on the pattern of Adam's, was what had made possible the forbidding theological label for Mary's sinlessness, though Augustine himself was never either legalistic or chilling.

But she swiftly dismissed this familiar grumbling. A weekday Mass was always good and she walked there and back, with her stick, not fast but steadily. There were not many people about, those that were in the streets were mostly in masks and mostly careful to give each other plenty of space. It wasn't yet cold. The winter seemed to be arriving as late as the spring had done, and the summer had been only rarely warm and sunny: climate change seemed in London only to have muddled the seasons, not, or probably not yet, to have made them extreme or frightening, though there had been a few hours of flooding in July, with people's basements and bits of the Tube filling with water, and another brief flood in the middle of September, after she got back from Yorkshire and as if those magical days had brought a nemesis storm to wipe them into the past.

After lunch and a nap in her armchair, with the day still grey but mild for early December, she put on her old coat and her babushka headscarf and went down the stairs. As she unlocked the garden gate she saw that Val was already sitting on their bench, reading something that looked like a couple of pages of typescript. When she was a few yards away, he folded the pages as he stood up to greet her.

"Clare. I am so happy to see you. This morning this email came", he tapped with his right forefinger the pages he was holding in his left hand, "and I thought how good that it is Wednesday so that I may tell Clare the news of this email, really a letter."

She could see the news was not good.

"Do you want to walk to the park? Or shall we sit on the bench while you tell me about it?"

"It is not too cold for you in the garden?"

"No it's not cold. Sit down, Val, and tell me what the letter, the email, says."

She sat on the bench, putting her hand on the place beside her, until he also sat.

He unfolded the letter and smoothed out its two pages, each with text on one side, on his lap. He sat looking down at his hands on the paper.

"I would ask you to read this, but it is written in Serbo-Croat, so this is not possible."

He didn't move or speak. She could tell he didn't know how to begin.

"Who is the letter from?" she said.

He looked up, and nearly smiled.

"It is from my old friend, who is now my only friend still living, still alive, in Sarajevo."

"That's good anyway, that he's in touch when you've been away so long."

"Yes. It is good. He sends me an email every few months, and I reply, so we know we are not dead. But this email of today is not good. Sarajevo is worried about the future, my friend is worried, very worried. He is afraid that—Do you know who is Milorad Dodik?"

She thought. The name meant nothing to her.

"No, I'm afraid I don't."

"*Voilà*, my grandmother would say. In English I think you would say, there you are, or that is what I thought. No one in UK does know who Milorad Dodik is, though he has been for years the most powerful man in Republika Srpska, the prime minister, one of the three joint presidents, one Serb, one Croat, one Muslim, who all the time quarrel, of Bosnia arranged by the Americans in 1995, arranged and then forgotten. Bosnia has been forgotten in UK altogether, even if it was because of the wars well known not long ago. Your brave son was there, before Afghanistan of course?"

"He was, yes, but when the war was over."

"Over, yes, for the time. Over truly, no. You remember I have told you Republika Srpska?"

"Yes, Val. Of course I remember." More than once he had told her, and he had told Hakim, and Carrie.

"It's a large part of Bosnia", she said, "that doesn't want to be part of Bosnia? Is that right?"

"That is correct. But all is much worse than that. I will tell you some examples. There is a joint army, for the defence of Bosnia, according to the American arrangements. But Mr Dodik does not approve of a joint army, so he does everything possible to him to undermine this army and at the same time he carefully chooses the Republika Srpska police and organizes them so that they are becoming themselves an army which they should not be. He trains these policemen like soldiers, and gives them machine guns so that they will be stronger than the

Bosnian army. This means he is imagining, he is encouraging, a civil war. Again a civil war.

"Another example is that he teaches these soldiers, and orders the teaching of schoolchildren in Republika Srpska, that there was no massacre at Srebrenica in 1995. He proclaims that this is a story only. He calls it—I am thinking of the English words for the words of my friend in this letter—he calls it an invented myth, a myth that has been fabricated, perhaps that is a better word. He has even told that the siege of Sarajevo was an invented myth also, that the Bosnian Serbs did not sit by their guns in the hills round the city and fire their shells into the city for almost four years, destroying so much and killing—" He stopped. She knew why. But she couldn't interrupt.

"This terrible man wishes to break Bosnia. He wishes Republika Srpska to leave Bosnia altogether. To become part of Serbia? Perhaps. To become an independent country where he can be another corrupt dictator? More likely this is what he wants. Will he succeed? Who can tell? I don't think he can really succeed. Republika Srpska will not be recognized as a country, except by Putin. But new civil war on the way to his failure would again be horrible. And again, like Karadzic and Mladic, he cannot be stopped unless by outside people. Sanctions might stop him. Soldiers, planes, bombs, will better stop him. But now the west does not care. The Americans left, the British left, as they all now have left Afghanistan, and there is no outside country to stop Dodik, only outside countries to help him. There are good countries who are not trying to stop him, and there are bad countries who are succeeding to help him. Russia of course always helps Serbs, Serbs in Serbia and Serbs in Bosnia. In 1914, and now. China more and more will help any people which is not the west. His friends, they are terrible people, as terrible as he is, more terrible. Listen—" He turned over the top page of the printed-out email, read a few lines, and prodded the end of the first paragraph of the second page with his finger.

"Listen to this. In September Mr Dodik went to a meeting, a forum with a grand title in Budapest. There is one of his friends, whose meeting it is, Victor Urban, the Hungary prime minister, who is almost a fascist. Other friends at the forum were the Poland prime minister who is not actually more than a little better than Urban, also Mr Mike Pence who is almost worse than Mr Trump because he is more clever. Also this Algerian Jewish French hater of Muslims, M. Zemmour, who hopes to be the next president of France. God forbid. And behind them all are the plans of Mr Putin to disturb and disrupt anything in Europe that might be going well, to show that democracy does not work. He wants chaos, as Hakim told us, about Syria and Libya. In Bosnia his chaos will soon come."

"O dear, Val. And the best we can do to show that democracy does work is Boris Johnson."

He looked at her blankly as if he'd never heard of Boris Johnson.

"In Pale", he said, "where Karadzic ruled all through the siege of Sarajevo, sending the bombers over the city—it is a Serb town in the hills—they have called a college building the Radovan Karadzic building, as if he is a hero. He is a criminal. He is in prison, here, in England. But the truth of him they do not accept."

He picked up his letter with both hands and put it down again in a gesture of despair.

"And more", he said. "My friend's sister died. I remember her when we were all young. She married a Croat, an engineer, a good man I think. He was killed in the first war, so by Muslims, in 1993. A few weeks ago she died. My friend travelled north to go to her funeral, in a Croat town near the border. What is happening there is now terrible. There are many refugees, from Syria, from Afghanistan also. They are trying to reach the EU. Croatia is in the EU. Bosnia is not, and—because of these things I have told you—will not be. The refugees have crossed already Turkey, the Afghans even have crossed Iran. The Greeks, also in the EU, do not allow them, so they chase them into Serbia where no one wants to stay, so they go into Bosnia which also does not want them. They try to cross the border to Croatia but the Croats beat them back with clubs. These beaters, they are not official soldiers, not official police. They do not wear uniforms but black disguise with black balaclava masks so that no one can say who they are, who they were, even if they kill people. They have no names because they obey orders to have no names. The refugees have no names because nobody will give them papers to say they exist. They cannot go forward; they cannot go back. So they are living in camps that are not even camps, plastic and rusty iron, in the dirty field and the cold."

"I didn't realize that the EU border was like that", Clare said. "I suppose I should have. How awful. It makes you wonder what has happened to people who are supposed to be Christian—the Croats say they are Catholics, don't they?—that they can treat refugees so badly?"

"The Croats said they were Catholics when they were keeping Jews in camps for the Nazis to murder. The Serbs who are denying truth and bullying Muslims say they are Christians also. Muslims in Bosnia have been only a little more kind, a little more generous, although Islam teaches that you should always do good to the traveller and the foreigner. And Catholic Poles—I have known some very kind and some very cruel Catholic Poles—are no different to the Croats. With clubs and also with guns they are chasing back over their border refugees who have been brought from Africa by the terrible Lukashenko, another corrupt dictator, to invade the EU. Putin loves Lukashenko, naturally, because he is causing trouble for an EU country."

"I see. The EU border again. I don't understand about Poland", Clare said. "It seemed so hopeful twenty years ago. And now such bad things one gathers—"

"Ah, Poland. It is sad, the story now. Twenty years ago I was there, you know."

"Of course. I remember. And it seemed good, then, didn't it? Hopeful for the future?"

"It was good. For me it was very good. Sarajevo I could not bear then. Too much, too many, were lost. And Wrocław, where I had nobody and nothing, but books to care for in a city that, like Sarajevo, had very much suffered but many years past, was happier and a good place for a foreigner."

"Val, you've never really told me about your time in Poland.

I know so little about the country and nothing at all about— how do you say it?"

"Wrocław. Never mind. Breslau, the German name is easier."

"Look. It's getting cold, sitting here, isn't it? And your letter has made you sad. Let's go up to the flat and have a cup of tea. I know it's the wrong day, but it doesn't matter that we haven't been for a walk, and this morning I walked all the way up to Kensington Church Street for Mass."

At last he smiled.

"Did you, Clare? How Catholic you are. I do sometimes not remember. The Immaculate Conception."

"Fancy you knowing the date of such a Catholic feast."

"You must not forget my grandmother and the nuns of my childhood. I am a lot of things in religion, fused but not confused as we know, and always I have hidden among the religions, perhaps even from God, but I am not a Protestant, not at all. Feasts are good, Catholic, Jewish, Muslim, let us all celebrate when we can. So yes, please, tea. It is cold, and it is getting dark."

He folded his letter and put it in his pocket. Then he stood up, easily, and, as she put one hand on the arm of the bench to press down and help her stand, he took her other hand in his and pulled her up gently. In a whole year he'd never done this before.

"Thank you", she said. "I can't sit for too long without moving or I get stiff."

"This is my fault for too much talking."

"Tea", she said.

At the kitchen table over mugs of decaff tea, and no cake because they should have been for a walk but a plate of chocolate digestives—she always had some in the tin for Hakim, in case—she said, "Now. Tell me, Val, about Breslau."

She was holding her hot mug in her hands to warm them. His hands, closed fists, were on the table either side of his plate as he sat still, looking down.

"I will try", eventually he said, without raising his head.

Then, "I will tell you a tale of three cities", he said, looking across the table at her and smiling.

"One is Sarajevo I have told much about, so you know what it was, my city of all my life until it was impossible for me to stay. The next is Wrocław, Breslau, where I went at the new year of 1996 and lived until 2006 when I came as you know to London. And the third is Lviv, Lwów, Lemberg, a beautiful and tragic city where I have never been, even as a visitor or for a holiday. What do they share, these three cities, one in Bosnia always, one in Poland but once in Germany, one in Ukraine but once in Poland?"

He paused, sipped his tea, put down his mug.

"All three were Habsburg cities, Sarajevo not for long, Wrocław and Lviv for many hundreds of years. All three had long Communist times, very bad in Lviv, bad in Wrocław, less bad in Sarajevo. All three had great and famous libraries. Libraries were my work, my life, except for my family, my wife, my boys."

He stopped. More tea. He straightened his shoulders.

"All three libraries had catastrophes. This is why I know them as one story. I have told you the catastrophe of my library in Sarajevo. It was after this, and the deaths, that I could not stay. The job at the university library in Wrocław was good and they gave it to me, I have told you, for my long time as a librarian and for looking after the German books, and also I think because I was not German. I went to Wrocław on many trains and with one suitcase. I was a refugee. The station was big and grand. So were the buildings of the university. Old but new, if you can understand. I did not know when I came to Wrocław that the Russians had sieged Breslau, for only a few weeks so not like the nearly four years of the siege of Sarajevo. But the Red Army on its victory march towards Berlin was much more terrible than the Serbs in the mountains of Bosnia. The city gave up the fight six days after Hitler died. Then it was destroyed. There was chaos for weeks, wrecking and looting and the Russian soldiers fighting each other for German stores of food, German bicycles, German pianos. They threw petrol at buildings and burnt them to piles of rubble. At the beginning of the siege, with the Russians already surrounding the city, the librarians of the university library, which had a very precious and ancient collection, the best library in Germany they said, moved all the books to be safe in a church. It was the church of St Anne. No one did forget. On the tenth of May 1945, the date that the old were still every year not forgetting when I lived in Wrocław, the church of St Anne was burnt with all the books to ash, as in Sarajevo. This was the end of German Breslau. Out of the ash came Polish Wrocław, a new old city."

He stopped, calmer now, for a proper drink of tea. He even took a biscuit from the plate and ate it. She waited until he'd finished it.

"And the third city? With its different names?" which, never having heard them before, she had already forgotten.

"Is this boring, Clare? Does my tale of three cities"—he was enjoying this phrase—"seem to you interesting?"

"O Val, do go on. It's as interesting as can be."

"Thank you, Clare. I will try. When I started to work in the library—there was very much work because the German books had not been well catalogued even since the war—I heard for the first time of this city, this third city. I might have heard of it because on the map it was not so far away from Sarajevo, a little beyond Romania. But the map is not how people know things and a little beyond Romania was a different world. This city was, in German, Lemberg, a Habsburg city in the kingdom of Galicia after the Partition of Poland, Austrian, Polish, Jewish, Ukrainian, as Breslau before Hitler had been German, Polish and Jewish. Lemberg also was Lwów in Polish, and a Polish city again, as really it always had been, after the Great War, in free Poland. It has been a most civilized city, most tolerant, with many Jews in the university and the hospitals. It was in this way like Sarajevo but without Muslims, and it was more famous and more important. Then was Hitler's war. The Russians came in 1940 and murdered Poles. In the university many. The Nazis came in 1941 and murdered Jews. In the university all. Then the Russians came again and in 1945 was Lwów's last catastrophe. Now you are a Ukraine city, Stalin said, not Polish. The Poles will leave or die. The Poles left and from the university they took with them as much, as many, as they could, of the books and manuscripts and other things in the library, which was a great library, and from the Ossolineum Institute which was the largest collection in the world of Poland's history and books and other precious things, made by a Polish nobleman to save Polish past after the Partition had abolished the country. All this they took to the west, to Breslau, the old German city that now was the new Polish city of Wrocław, and of course they took themselves, the scholars, the doctors, the lawyers, the scientists. This meant that the contents of a university, the people and the books and the history, were moved to a place where the buildings and the books of another university had been destroyed and many of its people were dead or pushed to more to the west, to Berlin or to Hamburg."

"What a story, Val. I'd no idea—well, absolutely no idea, since I didn't know anything about either of these cities. But how wonderful that these Polish professors could start all over again in a new Polish city."

"Yes. For the Poles who had lived, it was wonderful. Half the scholars in Lwów university before the war were Jews. They were dead. But, as you see, the future for the Polish university was good. And they have, or they had when I knew Wrocław, kept a—what is the English word?—continuity, that is it, they have kept a continuity with the German past, which is very good I think. They did not deny that Breslau used to have a most distinguished university even if it was German, and they wished to carry the tradition. The German books I cared for in the library might say the University of Breslau on the plate inside the binding, or they might say the University of Lemberg. They had deep in the past also a shared history. The Habsburg emperor Leopold founded the university in Breslau. Once upon the time Habsburg Lemberg was called Leopoldstadt. And the universities of Breslau and of Lemberg, both, were very long ago planned by the Jesuits in what then were two Catholic cities. You see—"

"Goodness. The Jesuits were everywhere. One forgets."

"It is important, not to forget. There was one day, in the university at Wrocław, that was for not forgetting. I must tell you this day, so that it is not forgotten. Is it possible to have some more tea first, please?"

"O Val, I'm so sorry. I'll make some of course. I'd love to hear about the day."

"Excuse me, Clare, while you make the tea."

He left for the cloakroom. She made more tea. He came back, sat down, smiled at her.

"Thank you, Clare. You have helped me not to think about this letter. I will ask you for your advice. About the letter. But first I will tell you the one marvellous day in Wrocław."

She took the teabags out of the mugs. Milk. Sugar for Val.

"There. Now, this marvellous day."

"The year was 2002, nearly 20 years ago, in the middle of November, so it was cold. The winters in Wrocław were very cold. The day was exactly three hundred years since the university was founded, a German university founded by an Austrian emperor in a city in which Catholics and Protestants and Jews already were living. On this day I watched and I heard. There were celebrations. There was a grand procession, of doctors and professors in velvet gowns, velvet and fur and square black hats, into the Leopoldina—there he is, Leopold, I told you him—which is a great baroque hall full of statues and marble columns with curly carvings and gilt everywhere. You can imagine. I suppose this hall was put again together from rubble after the war. On this day, the president of Poland and the president of Germany were both in the Leopoldina and both of them made speeches—you understand, how remarkable this was already—but the best speech was from an old American Jew, a professor who was born in Breslau in the 1920s. His name was—"

He looked at her as if she might know. She shook her head. With his eyes tight shut, he thought for a moment, and then shook his head.

"No good", he said. "I cannot get it back, his name. Certainly he is now dead. His parents and his grandfathers were educated in Breslau university but not himself because he was too young when Hitler came. He was like me, a refugee. He was lucky. He escaped to America. He called his speech 'The Recovery of Europe', you understand why. It was very clever, the title, which I have not forgotten. Europe is recovering. We are recovering Europe. Both. I did cry, listening to this speech. He said after the terrible century of Stalin and Hitler, and this university had much suffered from both of them, there was perhaps a new hope, even certainly a new hope. One quotation in this speech I never forgot. It was from Gandhi. Someone asked Gandhi what he thought of western civilization and he said it would be a good idea. The speech, you see, was in English, for these Germans and these Poles. Gandhi's saying is very English. Not American, but English although of course he was an Indian. The audience enjoyed this quotation. After this speech, we all went to the university church where there was Beethoven's ninth symphony and Polish choirs sang the Schiller Ode in German, and again I cried."

At last he stopped, and smiled his blue smile across the chocolate digestives. "So you see, I have not forgotten how that day was, and how good Poland could be. Ah—his name, the old American Jew, was Fritz Stern. I think he was a good man. Two years later Poland was allowed to join the EU, which is why I am able to be here in England, free and with the correct papers. Poland is not so good now. England is not so good now because of Brexit."

"Talk about England being not so good—I read somewhere that cathedrals and concert halls here are nervous now of performing the ninth symphony because the Ode to Joy is the anthem of the EU so there might be demonstrations. Can you believe it? Now Beethoven is a dangerous composer."

He wasn't listening. His smile had disappeared. His face clouded, he bent his head and hid his face in his hands.

After a minute or two, as if rubbing away tears, he pulled his hands down his face, clasped them on the table and said, without looking at her, "England chooses to leave the EU. Or it is tricked into leaving the EU. This is stupid. But England has a history that is its own, and it does have also an old democracy, even if now it has Boris Johnson. Bosnia does not have its own history, and it cannot make a democracy because it is too divided and too full of lies and hate and it will never be allowed to join the EU. My friend asks me to go to Sarajevo for a visit, to see him before one of us is dead. Should I go? Shall I go? This is what I must ask you, Clare."

At last, the reason for all this remembering of Poland, all this displacement.

"Ah", she said. Please don't go, she didn't say. She said instead, "How long is it since you have seen Sarajevo?"

From the long past she remembered a senior figure in some school, she couldn't remember which figure or which school, telling her, "If you don't know what to say next, ask a question."

"It is twenty-five years, Clare. A quarter of a century, so long it has been. I was very unhappy to leave Sarajevo and also I was very happy. It was a city only of ghosts and echoes. I could not there breathe. I could breathe better in Poland, as a foreigner in Poland. And better in London than in Poland. And best now, with you, Clare. Only to breathe like a normal person. I have not thought, not expected, that I would see Sarajevo again. It was like another death, to leave. And I have thought I should be allowing the good memories of the past to defeat, no, not to defeat, but to replace, the bad memories, as when there is a death. To forget the fear and the pain, and remember what was good in the life. This is what to do after a death. So I was safer not to go back, not to allow the fear and the pain to return, perhaps to after all win, you understand. This I have decided for so long. But perhaps it was a wrong decision?"

Clare drank a little of her new, hot tea.

"I think perhaps you are making the question too complicated", she said.

He looked at her now, surprised.

"How, too complicated?"

"Don't think, just for a moment, about Sarajevo. Think about your friend. Would it be good to see him again? Would you enjoy that?"

"Enjoy? I don't know. Is it possible to enjoy anything in a country so unhappy?"

"Of course it is. Perhaps 'enjoy' isn't the right word. But your friend is asking you to come because it would be good to see you, comforting perhaps in difficult times, a consolation? Mightn't that be even a pleasure, for both of you? Is he alone, as you are?"

"Yes. No." He smiled. "Yes and no." This was by now an old joke. "His wife has been a long time dead. He has two daughters. One married an American who was a soldier with the NATO army that came after the Bosnia war. She lives in America. He visited her once. She has some children. She wanted him to stay, not to return to Bosnia, but he did not very much like America and he chose to stay in Sarajevo, where he has many pupils who are now friends."

"He is a teacher?"

"He is, he was—naturally he is retired by now—a teacher, a teacher like you, in the first gymnasium which means the oldest gymnasium, which was bombed in the siege but afterwards mended. This is a Habsburg gymnasium as there is in every Habsburg city. He is also like you a Catholic. We were boys together in the nuns' school I told you, naughty boys probably, so long ago. My grandmother loved him because he was a clown. He pretended to be an old nun or the music teacher with his glasses coming down his nose and he was very funny."

"His other daughter?"

"She is in Bosnia still. Her husband is a school teacher in a village in the mountains. He is I think a Muslim. They have two children, maybe three, and my friend travels sometimes to their house. Maybe—"

He stopped because, she could see, he was imagining the village, the mountains, a visit.

"Maybe you could go with him to see his daughter, to meet the children, in the countryside which is so beautiful? You love the mountains, I remember you told Carrie, when she was talking about Nepal."

"Yes. You understand, it is home, Bosnia is my home, not only the poor damaged city with its politics and its troubles, but the mountains where my grandmother took me in the summers, to her friends, her family, when I was a boy. The flowers, the kind donkey, the clear streams, the cherries and the plums I loved—and later, with Lejla and our boys, we had summer times, summer weeks, with her family in the mountains. So beautiful also—"

He stopped again, swallowed, wiped the back of his hand hard across his mouth.

"I am sorry, Clare. It is because of you, your telling to me your holiday in Yorkshire, that I have remembered—"

He couldn't go on.

"Because of me, Val? How because of me?"

Had she been tactless, too enthusiastic when she came back, trying to tell him of a place, places, he couldn't possibly imagine, just because she loved them and wanted him to be able to share, a little—Which of course he couldn't, so he had been reminded of places of his childhood and his children's childhood which he hadn't seen for decades. It wasn't fair. She could go to Yorkshire any time, just by getting on a train, and when she got there she would find that no one had spoilt, never mind bombed or burnt, the cottages, the churches, the lanes, the fields and woods and stone walls of her childhood, let alone killed all the people in a village and left it without a roof on any house, without a window unbroken, a room unransacked. He had told her enough. It would never be the same for him, so far away from his mountains and with a war, three wars, between him and his childhood. And Mostar: she remembered seeing pictures of a wonderful ancient bridge, its perfect stone curve over a river flowing between two sides of a town bombed to rubble in the war.

He leant back on his kitchen chair and spread his hands wide. She saw he knew she had understood.

"I am so sorry", she said. "I talked too much when I got back." This is what happens, she didn't say, with the old who haven't enough people to talk to: they lose such judgement as they ever had about what to say when and who they should say it to. She could have told Hakim about Yorkshire if he hadn't disappeared from her life, but he wouldn't really have been interested except in what was left by the Romans, especially now that he had learnt Northumberland for himself.

Where was he? How was he? Without him, and without Carrie, she had talked too much to Val.

"No, Clare. Not too much. Really not too much. And it was not the words you said, the places you told me, that made

269

me think, made me imagine, even before this letter of today arrived, that maybe I should try, one time, once I should say, to go home. It was your love for what is home that I understood."

"I see."

Of course she saw. She had lived contentedly in London for almost all her life, as a child because her father's work was in London, after Cambridge because she married Simon and his work was in London, and so, when Penny and Matt went to school, was hers. But Yorkshire, where her grandparents lived, where she went only for holidays, but all through her life for holidays, was home in a way London had never become. Was it only because it was beautiful? Or was it something deeper-rooted than beauty? She remembered reading somewhere that every Frenchman wants to live in Paris and every Frenchman wants to die in his village. Something like that, was it? The place where you have felt the land, the trees, the stone of the walls and the village streets where valerian grows, all-heal, the water in the rattling becks, the clay in the red pantiles. Romantic nonsense, Simon would have said, did say, every so often, about Yorkshire which he thought cold, unfriendly and uncivilized because he couldn't cope with her mother's hunting and shooting relations and they couldn't cope with a left-wing professor of economics. And Simon was impervious to the countryside. "I don't see the point of walking."

"So you must go", she said.

"Really? You think so? Is this your advice, Clare, that I should go?"

"It is. Yes, it is. Really. If you decide not to go you won't forget the idea. It will grow and grow until you change your mind. And by then—"

"By then it may be too late? You are saying? I might be dead, or my friend might be dead? Or there might again be a war in Bosnia. So while we are both alive and there is not a war, I should go?"

Or I might be dead before you come back, she didn't say.

"That's right. One never knows at our age."

He looked at her with some fear in his eyes.

"You will not die, Clare. If I go to Sarajevo, you must not die."

She laughed, which was easy.

"I'll try not to. No. Seriously, you mustn't worry about me."

Had he even heard this? He was looking down again, at his clasped hands, not seeing them.

"I thought for so long", he said, "that back is where no one can go."

"I know you did. I haven't forgotten. You said that to me when I hardly knew you."

"It is true. To go back, to get back the time, is not possible. And Bosnia is now so unhappy, so full of people who more and more hate each other, and where the truth is destroyed every day. People say England is like this, with Brexit and Boris Johnson, but it is not. It is much much better, even now. If I could help Bosnia, Sarajevo, if I could do something good—of course I cannot, do anything good. I have been too long away and I am too old."

He stopped, and then picked up what he had dropped.

"It is almost right, that back is where no one can go. But when you told me your days in Yorkshire I understood I had not been quite correct. It is possible, it is good, sometimes to go back, if it is to go home. Not so?"

"Yes, in a way it is possible. It will also be painful for you, Val, to be in Sarajevo again."

She mustn't try to change his mind, but this at least was obviously true.

"Of course. But maybe this also will be good. I went to Poland, I left Bosnia, too soon, too quickly, after they were dead. Maybe I did not allow the pain its time. If I am in Sarajevo I will visit their graves. The grave of Osman, my first boy, is far away on the edge of a Muslim village which the Serb soldiers burnt down. I have not seen his grave. Maybe there will be some time to go there."

This was the first time Val had told her his son's name.

"What is the name of your second boy, Val?"

"Niko. Nikola. You see, one Muslim name and one Christian name. We agreed. But always we agreed, I and Lejla. Almost always. Sometimes about Lejla's mother we did not agree."

Clare smiled.

"Mothers-in-law", she said. "They are difficult everywhere. If you asked my son-in-law, Carrie's father, about me, he would say 'She's quite impossible, always has been, always will be.'"

"No, Clare."

"Yes. He thinks I am almost a Marxist. And he doesn't like Catholics much either. And my father was a foreigner. He isn't keen on foreigners."

"How does he think you are a Marxist when you are a Catholic? No person can be both."

"Well—they can, but not often in England. And, as you know, I'm definitely not a Marxist, only what my son-in-law would call a woolly liberal."

"Woolly?"

"Soft, generally quite harmless, but confused."

"I do not understand England."

She almost reached out a hand to lay it on his hands on the table, but didn't.

"The English don't understand themselves very well. Why did you disagree about Lejla's mother? Did she disapprove of you?"

"Disapprove?"

"Did she think you should be better, different in some way to deserve to be married to her daughter?"

"Actually it was the opposite. She was always kind to me. She liked it that I was a librarian, that I went every day to the library in my suit and a tie. She thought I was very well educated. All this annoyed Lejla. Lejla's father was dead, not in the war, in any war, but in an accident with a tractor. Lejla loved her father. Lejla's brother was a farmer. Like her father he had a suit only for a funeral or a wedding."

"I see. Lejla's mother was a snob."

A questioning look.

"Sorry. An untranslatable English word. It means someone who overrates, thinks too much of, position or status, where a person stands in society, how much money or education they have, and underrates everything else."

He still looked puzzled. Too elaborate an explanation.

"Does it mean that the signs are more important than what is real? A suit is a sign only. A tractor is a sign only. The man in the suit or the man who drives the tractor is real? Is this correct?"

"Exactly. You've put it much better than I did. I'm sure there are snobs everywhere, always. I remember my father saying that in Jewish Prague mothers wanted to be able to say 'My son the doctor' or 'My son the lawyer'. 'My son the printer'—that's what my father was—didn't quite cut it. Sorry. Wasn't quite good enough."

"*Voilà*—the same."

He smiled his blue smile, and spread his hands above the table.

"They are all dead now. But I shall go to Sarajevo. Clare, you have given me the courage. Thank you. Now—"

He stood, with resolution, and pushed his chair tidily up to the table.

"I shall go, and discover on the internet if there are flights and tickets and terrible coronavirus rules."

"Good luck with that. I haven't bought a ticket to anywhere for years, but I do remember trying to on the internet and it was really difficult. I think you're better at it all than I am."

"I can try. Sometimes I can succeed. I had to make my book-shop catalogue into digital, the list of second-hand books you understand, when the internet was new. I was too old but a good Italian girl taught me. I know how to bring up to date my little list of books I can sell. But for buying anything, a ticket or anything, It is all more complicated now. I will do my best."

He went out, fetched his coat and came back.

"Will you be in the square on Saturday as always, Clare?"

"Of course I will."

"I shall report my research."

She heard the lift come up, its doors open and shut, and the lift go down. She just, because she was listening for it, heard the front door of the house close behind him. From one of the windows in the sitting room she watched him cross the square garden and disappear into the street that led to his mews.

If he went to Bosnia when would he come back? Would he ever come back? He couldn't possibly leave before Saturday. Could he?

She went back to the kitchen and Googled flights from London to Sarajevo, hoping there wouldn't be any or that Bosnia was forbidding entry to travellers from the UK because of Covid. There were plenty of flights, not even very expensive, Val had for years, since long before Mrs May's "hostile environment", had a British passport and he could stay in Bosnia for as long as six months without a visa. The whole thing was not much more difficult than going to Yorkshire on a train.

She shut her laptop and allowed despair, beyond tears, to bow her down until her head rested on her folded arms on the kitchen table. She didn't think she could cope, now, if Val went to Bosnia and didn't come back.

Then she remembered Ivica. She raised her head and looked round the consoling kitchen, which was the same as ever.

He won't leave Ivica. He said he couldn't leave him when I asked him to come to Leckenby. He'll change his mind. He won't go. She looked at the telephone as if at any minute he might ring and say he wasn't going.

CHAPTER 13

THURSDAY 3 FEBRUARY 2022

For no reason, or, more accurately for no reason she could identify, and so for a reason known to God, something to do with grace that can't be predicted and can't be accounted for, yesterday had been quite different, so much better that she felt it already as a turning-point, perhaps even a point of no return. How deeply she hoped, and prayed, that it would somehow become exactly that, a point of no return to her sadness, her sense of absence and loss, which had been bad when Hakim left to live with Emma, worse when Carrie and Bill left for New York, worst, dreadful, when Val left for Bosnia.

She wasn't poor, she wasn't ill, no one had died. But for months, really since the brief flood in London in September after she came back to the flat from Yorkshire, she had felt deprived, without, without something essential to her, which she couldn't define except by calling it the presence of God. Wasn't it what Val had long ago, on account of *Doctor Zhivago*, told her was called *Taqwa* in Arabic? She knew perfectly well that it was actually wrong to allow the absence of people, however closely attached to them she was, to become the absence of God. She had been to confession to ask for absolution for what in these attachments was sinful, but the priest, a stranger to whom she tried to describe what she was feeling, had told her that to miss those she was fond of was natural, and if she prayed for them to be safe in the hands of God she would soon feel more hopeful. She did try. She didn't feel more hopeful. Awake in the worst of the nights, between three and five in the morning, she feared, between dreams and anxieties she couldn't tell apart, for Hakim unable to cope with Emma, for Carrie in some terrifying country, for Val most of all.

Yesterday was Candlemas, the day once officially called the Feast of the Purification of the Blessed Virgin Mary, a chill title suggesting that even Mary needed to be cleansed after the pollution of childbirth, but now called the Feast of the Presentation of the Lord, much better. Mary and Joseph take the baby to the temple to be consecrated to God. They also take a pair of turtle-doves or two young pigeons to be sacrificed, birds, Clare had always understood, that are also emblems of the youth and innocence of both the baby and his mother, who will be offered, like them, to God. "A sword will pierce your soul": Simeon's words to Mary. Candles held by people in the church, as perhaps the candles of the menorah were lit for the people in the temple in Jerusalem, were, are, emblems of the light of the world shining in the darkness which didn't, doesn't, understand it but couldn't, can't, extinguish it, the light of God for Jews, for Christians also the light of the child who was given by, and is being given back to, God.

She had stood in the church with her candle, the people still thinly spread, partly because some were still nervous of getting at all close to anyone else, partly because, she could see, a number of people who had given up coming to Mass when they were ordered to, in the first lockdown, had never returned.

Every twenty days when she reached this story in her regular prayer of the Rosary just before she got into bed, she would put her right hand on her left shoulder, imagining the baby, not quite six weeks old so still not heavy to hold, with his head needing a hand to support it, asleep on her shoulder before she gave him into Simeon's arms. Perhaps the baby woke and looked up at the old man, with a baby's gaze, before Simeon spoke the words of the *Nunc dimittis*.

The story was in Luke's gospel, and it had always seemed to her, because of this and, even more because of other events that Mary knew as no one else did, particularly the message of the angel that she was to conceive the son of God, that Luke must have heard about them from Mary. So perhaps old Simeon really did say the words with which Clare ended her prayer every night, the English words she had first learnt before she was even a Catholic.

Lord, now lettest thou thy servant depart in peace, according to thy word. For mine eyes have seen the salvation you have prepared before the face of all people, a light to lighten the gentiles, and the glory of thy people Israel.

And surely what he then said, astonishingly, to Mary, that the child would be rejected so that—so that?—the secret thoughts of many would be laid bare, must have been reported by Mary. By Mary herself? To Luke himself? Meanwhile Anna, the prophetess who lived in the temple fasting and praying, and who by chance saw there Mary and the baby with Simeon and Joseph, and in her turn praised God for the baby's arrival, was very old. Luke says she was eighty-four, so she and Simeon were both close to death. No wonder his prayer was about death and about hope, not just for Israel but for every human being, in the coming of the child who was God and was and is the candle in the night of the world.

At Mass yesterday she had prayed for herself and for Val, almost as old as Simeon and Anna, that they should be allowed to depart in peace in the light of Christ, perhaps not too far away from each other. Val had promised that at least once while he was in Sarajevo he would go to Mass in a Catholic church, perhaps even in the Catholic cathedral, and pray for her and with her. Had he done this? Would he do this? She didn't know. She believed. She had had two brief emails, one saying that he had arrived safely, and, two weeks later, another telling her that he was about to travel to the mountains with his friend to visit the friend's daughter and her family. So would he go to Mass while he was away? Of course he would. The Mass, after all, was also part of his childhood, and he had promised. And there had been Christmas Day.

For the first two or three weeks—he had left in the end in the first week of January, when the flights became cheaper after the holidays—she had missed him so badly that she couldn't imagine why she hadn't tried to stop him going. "Don't let the children see that you think you can't manage without them." Val wasn't a child; couldn't she have said, "Please don't go. I shall miss you too much"? She could have, but she was right, really she knew, not to have.

The days, without Wednesdays and Saturdays to look forward to, were exactly the same as each other except for Sundays, with Mass always and a different and better newspaper than on weekdays. Penny rang every Saturday, at six rather than at five as she used to: Clare had invented a reason in the summer for getting Penny to ring later and the habit had stuck. Penny had asked her to come to Leckenby for Christmas, and she'd said she didn't feel up to the journey—that unassailable excuse for the old—because she didn't want to miss the last few days of Val being in London, and also because she couldn't face Charles. How could she possibly get through meal after meal during several days chatting to Charles about this and that, as she had managed to three or four times at lunch in Barnes, still unsold, in the last few months? The last thing she wanted was to have to try to keep this up for a whole Christmas visit when the behaviour of the government about Afghanistan and refugees from everywhere was actually getting worse and worse, and the frivolous carelessness of Boris Johnson himself was making all reasonable people more and more miserable, furious and ashamed. Parties at Downing Street when people weren't allowed to meet even outside, and thousands of people were dying without their husbands, wives, children, to see them out of the world, were only the last straw. Ministers keen to hang on to their jobs went on defending Boris Johnson—you heard them practically every day on the *Today* programme— sounding less and less convincing, even less and less convinced. It was obvious that the Tory party would turn on him, get rid of him, as soon as they saw him as more of a liability than an asset. She couldn't understand the spell he had cast on so many ordinary people that the majority of Tory MPs still saw him as an asset: they must, or he would have gone by now.

Christmas had been quiet, warm, friendly. They remembered that on Christmas Day last year they had had their first proper conversation, in the cold, on their bench in the square, so that the day was almost like an anniversary though neither of them would have got anywhere near the word. And they had been, together, to Mass.

Val had said, as they walked back, in their usual companionable silence, from the Albert Memorial on the Wednesday before Christmas, "May I come, please, to Mass with you, Clare, on Christmas Day?" She was so surprised that she stopped and, as he also stopped, looked up at him—he was a little taller than her, several inches shorter than Simon—and said, "O Val, of course you may. It would be wonderful."

He only smiled.

They walked on. A few minutes later, still walking, and not looking up, he said, "You understand, Clare, I am far away, still I am far away, from the little boy whose grandmother taught him to pray beside his bed, or the naughty schoolboy who accepted what the nuns told him about God because he accepted what they told him about arithmetic or about a caterpillar becoming a butterfly. But because of knowing you and learning how it is possible, which I did not ever know, for an intelligent and old person, who has also suffered as I have suffered, to be a good Catholic, and because I am soon going back to the city of my grandmother and the nuns, it would be right for me to come to Mass in your church, most of all on Christmas Day. By Easter Day, who knows?"

She let the shiver this question caused her go by, and said, "I'll come to your house at half past ten. We can walk up to the eleven o'clock Mass, and then perhaps you'd like to come to lunch in the flat? It's a Saturday after all."

"That would be so good, Clare. Thank you."

She could tell he wanted to say something else and didn't know how to. They had almost reached the gate out of Kensington Gardens when he said, "Will you—Will it be necessary for me to talk to the people in the church?"

Was that all?

"No, Val, absolutely not. I don't know them really, just to say hello, no more than that. 'Happy Christmas' will do nicely."

"That is very good."

After supper when she was sitting by the fire with her rug over her knees—she was reading *A Nest of Gentlefolk* because she'd wanted to stay in Russia while needing something easier and shorter after too much Dostoyevsky—she put the book down suddenly when she remembered him saying, "By Easter Day, who knows?" What did he mean? Did he mean he might not be back before Easter? She knew he hadn't got a return ticket with a date. "It is not possible to decide now when I shall leave." There were weeks and weeks after Christmas before Ash Wednesday, then all the weeks of Lent. Easter seemed a long, long way away.

Or did he mean he might be feeling differently, one way or the other, about the Church by Easter? More drawn towards it, more repelled by it? All this was only speculation of course. It was something, even a good deal, and entirely unexpected, that he'd asked if he could come with her to Mass. She must be only pleased, and must try not to think at all about what he'd said.

Over the whole year she'd known him she'd gathered from fragments of his story that he'd picked up and dropped here and there as they talked that he'd never altogether lost a kind of loyalty of the heart to the figure of Jesus, the figure of Christ that he'd remembered for so many years. It was not only what had stayed with him from his childhood, his grandmother and the nuns. He had remembered exactly, for example, the Christ Pantocrator at the end of Dr Zhivago's poem called "Gethsemane". He thought he had, lost, irrevocably lost, this loyalty. "I don't believe any of the Christian teaching, you understand, Clare. Maybe God is somewhere, somehow, so that we are not one and one and one alone in our lives that will stop in death. That God is, even that God does care for us, human souls, that we should try not to do wrong, do harmful things, this Jews and Muslims believe as Christians do. But that God came to this world and suffered with us and for us so that we are forgiven, this I cannot, really I cannot, believe."

And now he wanted to come to Mass, on the feast of his coming to this world.

They sat side by side like a couple—they were after all a kind of couple—in the church, which was quite full but with one half of the congregation distanced and even the other half, where they were sitting, fairly spaced out. There were a few children, one or two with new toys. A three-year-old sat on a kneeler at his parents' feet playing quietly with a shiny red tractor. Clare was impressed. Matt at that age wouldn't have been able to stifle tractor noises even in church. She was so pleased to have Val sitting beside her that she failed to listen properly to the homily. It was short and sensible, not, as sometimes happened at Christmas or Easter, the priest making the most of the presence of people who practically never came to Mass by trying to say too much. Jesus, a defenceless new-born baby coming into a dangerous world, should remind us that every new-born baby is defenceless, that the world is always dangerous, and that all babies and their mothers need the protection the world can afford and too often fails to give. Clare thought of the mothers in Afghanistan who couldn't feed the children they already had, and couldn't produce enough milk for a newborn baby because they had themselves been hungry for months. A couple of days ago John Simpson, back from Afghanistan and after fifty years of war reporting, had cried on the *Today* programme for a widow whose husband had been shot and who had nothing to give her five children to eat. They would die. Perhaps they were already dead.

She tried to pay proper attention to the Eucharistic prayer, the heart of the Mass, but was too acutely aware of Val kneeling beside her, his eyes closed, his concentration absolute, to pray herself. She had no idea how long it was since he had been to a Mass.

She went up, in the orderly distanced queue, to receive Holy Communion. As she stood waiting she wondered if she should have explained that he could have come up, with his arms crossed over his chest, to receive a blessing, and then was glad she hadn't presented him with a choice there was no need for him to make. She went back to kneel beside him. As she did he looked at her for a moment. There were tears in his eyes. After the blessing—he didn't cross himself—and a moment of stillness, side by side, they turned together to leave the church. People were quietly greeting each other, smiling, saying "Happy Christmas", "Merry Christmas". "What a good boy", Clare said to the parents of the tractor-enthusiast. Just as they were about to go through the door from the church into the porch he turned back so that he was facing the altar and the tabernacle with its light for the Blessed Sacrament. She thought he was going to genuflect, as, without thinking, she already had. Instead he knelt down on both knees, bent his head and crossed himself, and then held on to the back of a chair to stand up. He smiled at Clare. They walked back to the flat without exchanging a single word.

In the kitchen she produced a bottle of what, judging only by its price, she hoped was a reasonably nice Burgundy, and gave it to him, with her corkscrew, to open. When he'd poured some wine into the two glasses ready on the neatly laid kitchen table, she raised her glass and said "Happy Christmas, Val". "Thank you, Clare", he said, raising his towards her.

Over their lunch, a spicy chicken casserole she had made on Christmas Eve, they talked about his expedition to Bosnia, how pleased he was to have decided to go, how pleased his friend was that he was coming, how complicated it had been organizing his ticket.

"You know, I had to buy one of these." He took out of his pocket a smartphone, as used by Penny, Hakim, Carrie and most of the human race, and put it on the table. "I promised that never I would be made to get one. I do not like to be connected to too much. I do not need to be connected to many people. I have lived in two countries with spies. But now you must have one of these to show you have been three times vaccinated, to show even your ticket at the airport. So I did buy one. I went to a telephone shop in Kensington High Street. It was complicated even to buy it, questions of contracts and applications I did not know how to answer. I had to let the girl in the shop answer for me. 'Very simple I prefer', I said several times, but very simple it seems they cannot be."

"Well done, Val, for coping with that. I'm afraid we can't for ever pretend the modern world doesn't exist."

"We can, nearly always we can."

She smiled.

"If I never go abroad again", she said, "and I don't expect I will, I can probably manage not to get a smartphone. I can go on pretending the modern world doesn't exist. I think the old deserve the privilege of turning a blind eye to some things, don't you? Even if the young think they're mad."

"I talk to no one who is young", Val said.

"O Val, I'm sorry." Careless of her.

"No", he said. "Be sorry for nothing. Maybe I shall meet some young people, my friend's family in the mountains. That will be good." He smiled. "Have you had a message from Carrie for Christmas?"

"O yes. Both the children sent emails, Daisy's was just saying Happy Christmas and she hoped I was still well and being careful. Carrie was surprised I hadn't gone to Yorkshire, but I'd told her you were going to Bosnia in a few days so she understood—she sent best wishes to you—and anyway she knows I can't do very much time with her father while he's so stupidly loyal to this dreadful government."

"Clare—are you saying to me that you decided not to go to Yorkshire which you love because I am going away?"

Damn. Even more careless. One glass of wine.

"No. Well, partly I suppose. I'm so glad now, today, that I'm here and not there."

She saw him decide to let it go.

"And Carrie, how is she?"

"Carrie's very well. She's working at the International Rescue Committee office in New York where her boyfriend Bill has a job. She was being an intern, a volunteer, you know, working for no money to learn, and I'm sure also to show them how useful she could be, and now they've promised her a proper job. I'm not surprised. She's bright and competent and has her couple of years aid experience from Nepal."

"That is good."

"It is good, yes."

He looked at her, his head on one side, like, it struck her, an inquisitive bird.

"But. Clare? You do not say your 'but', but there is 'but'. I understand that you are sad she has again gone away. But also I think you have said that you are afraid that she, maybe she and Bill, will be sent to some difficult country where this charity does its work? So they may be in danger? Is this your 'but'?"

"Yes. Both those things. It's very brave and generous of them to do the kind of work they were doing in Nepal, and want to go on doing. But I can't help remembering Matt, also brave and generous, being a soldier to make the world a safer, fairer place. And look—"

"I understand. He died for these good things and where he died, the country is less safe and less fair."

He stopped and looked at her from the depth of his eyes. "It is like my Osman. He died fighting against the Bosnian Serbs, for safety and fairness in Sarajevo and all of Bosnia, and look, as you say—But this I must see for myself, if there is still any hope, when I go there."

She saw he wanted to say something more. After a minute or two of him looking down at his hands, he raised his eyes to hers and said, "They died, our boys, both our boys. It appears they died for nothing. But they died for what is good. Even if what is good never did come. That is not nothing. It is held for ever—"

By now, and after kneeling beside him at Mass, she could say, "In the hands of God?"

"Even in the hands of God. This we should say, on Christmas Day. As also must be the lives, the goodness, of Lejla and Nico, even if their deaths were only the chance of where a shell did fall, and they had no brave idea of dying."

"Of course, Val. They are also in the hands of God. As are you and I, whatever happens."

He nodded, just.

She let a moment or two go by, and then said, "Would you like some more chicken?"

"Thank you. No. It is very good."

She got up, cleared the plates, and took off the foil cover she had left on two kinds of cheese. Crisp water biscuits on a plate. Butter from the fridge, and some short lengths of celery she had washed and left to be cold. She put all these on the table.

"There", she said, "Do have some cheese. And a little more wine?"

"Thank you."

He poured himself half a glass. She shook her head when he offered to fill her glass.

"Are you pleased with Bill", he said, finding an easier subject. "this young man for Carrie? You have told me nearly nothing of him."

This was quite true. When she came back after those few days in September she had tried to tell him about what she'd felt at finding herself back in Yorkshire, with consequences she was trying not to regret. And he hadn't asked her about Bill.

"I think so, yes. Certainly not worried, anyway. It isn't a passionate love affair"—she thought of Hakim—"which is probably a good thing. Carrie seems contented and settled with him. And I do think he's brave and generous, like our boys, though he's a little dull which Matt never was and I'm sure your Osman wasn't either."

"Contented and settled, you say. And he is even a little dull. Does this mean she is happy? Is this enough? She is very young."

"I do hope so, I really do. The key to it all is that she admires him, perhaps in a way that's a kind of opposite, a kind of positive for a negative, of what she's felt for a long time about her father. The parallel, the echo, has only this minute struck me, but it could be so. For instance, Bill says that bright, well-educated young Americans like him have a duty to go to parts of the world which have been damaged by American foreign policy mistakes, or by European imperialist exploitation, which have left poor people having a desperate time just trying to stay alive with not enough food, often no medical help within reach, and sometimes all the dangers of civil war to cope with as well. All this is music to Carrie's ears. She's inclined to think foreign policy mistakes, like Iraq and this dreadful withdrawal from Afghanistan, and old imperialist attitudes, are all summed up in her father. And here's Bill, coming along to help put the wrongs to rights, and she can work beside him. Does he love her? Hard to tell. He's patient with her—she can be very argumentative, always sure she's right—and I think he'll take care of her if they have a difficult time, which is all good. I just hope it isn't a case of St John Rivers."

"Of who?"

"Jane Eyre. I'm sorry, Val. So English, Jane Eyre. She almost goes to India with a serious-minded missionary who wants her to marry him because she would be useful."

"Ah. I know, of course. I have read this book, so long ago, in which language I have forgotten. I thought the missionary was called St John like the writer of the gospel. I could not understand why."

"St John pronounced Sinjn. It's a first name, not unknown but not at all common. English is impossible. Never mind. I think Bill will be kind to Carrie. So he won't be like Mr Rivers. But he's a very serious boy, and he is a little bit preachy—"

"Preachy?"

"Sorry again. In Yorkshire, the only chance I've had to get to know him, in just a few days so I don't know him well, he sometimes talked as if he were addressing a hundred people in a church when he was only talking to me and Carrie in Penny's little sitting room by the fire. Very American. Also, now I've thought of the parallel, the opposites, he was a little like Carrie's father talking to a Tory party meeting—though of course what he was saying was quite different. Anyway, Carrie thinks he's wonderful, which is all that matters."

Once or twice, listening to Bill, she had thought of Simon, who would have said, "He's not a fool but he's terribly pompous. Not a joke on the horizon. Get him over here to do another degree at LSE and at least we'd knock a bit of irony into him." When she vividly remembered Simon, she was glad that he wasn't still alive to see what had become of English politics. He would have been made miserable by Brexit and by the spectacle of Boris Johnson as prime minister. And much that was happening would have made him furious, almost to the point of throwing something at the television which once or twice, over lesser irritations than Boris Johnson, she'd thought he was going to.

Bill. Yes. "And he is a nice boy. According to Carrie since she's been in New York he has a very solid family, which matters a lot, and in Yorkshire he was sweet to me. He might easily have thought the presence of Carrie's old grandmother was ruining their romantic holiday in the country. Though somehow the young don't seem very romantic nowadays."

"Maybe they should read *Doctor Zhivago*. Alone in the snow."

She looked at him for a moment, but hurried on. "I wonder if they'd see the point of it, if they could be bothered to read such a long book."

Val shrugged. "Maybe not."

"You know what it is, the reason I mean, for them not understanding romance. It's all too easy for them. They get together. They split up. Nobody is in despair. Where are the obstacles, the disapproval, the secrecy, the danger that used to make for romance?"

Across the table, his blue smile.

"They are left for the old", he said.

She had gone with him to the airport, almost a month ago now, because she couldn't bear not to, although she knew perfectly well that it would have been more sensible to say goodbye in his house or in her flat.

"What about a taxi?"

She looked at his luggage, ready in his sitting room. One old canvas bag, quite big, with two handles, several zips and straps round the whole thing. If it had been made of leather it would have been at home in a nineteenth-century novel, but it would also have been much heavier. He did have a shoulder bag too, equally old, equally foreign-looking, but not heavy either. She knew what he was going to say.

"Clare. Certainly not. A taxi is too expensive. There is nothing I have that is heavy, and there is a good tube to the airport."

What Hakim always called the dear old Piccadilly Line because it took him, when he was living in the flat, from Gloucester Road to the British Museum in half an hour. Hakim. Alas.

"All right. Well, perhaps we'd better go."

He looked round his sitting room. It was tidier than usual, with nothing on the table he used as a desk.

"Your laptop?", she said.

"I have put it upstairs in the cupboard with the towels. I have my famous telephone so it is not necessary for me to take it."

That meant he was expecting to be back before too long. Didn't it?

"And Ivica?"

"He will be very well looked after by Muhammad's daughter. I asked Muhammad for his advice about Ivica and he said his daughter, her name is Fatima, has wanted for a long time a cat."

"Where does Muhammad live?"

"Across the river, in Battersea, in a basement flat—with four children, can you imagine?—so he has made a cat door for Ivica in his back door, like the one here in my kitchen door."

"I hope Ivica will be all right there."

"He has been with Fatima already for two days. Muhammad told me yesterday he is happy. He will be spoilt, as you say. I do not worry about him. Muhammad took also my plants to Battersea. He drove a cat in a box and my plants in another box, in the Bentley, which has white leather seats. What would the rich Russian say? But Muhammad is very careful. He arranged a rug and a lot of newspapers on the white leather."

He looked at his watch.

"We should go, Clare."

At Heathrow they walked from the tube station for what seemed like several miles. She was glad of her stick, and of the moving walkways, some of which were working. She wanted to stay with him as long as she could, and after the check-in queue, where they slowly shuffled forward without saying anything, and the bumpy passage of his bag to the conveyor belt, there was time for a cup of coffee before he had to disappear into the other side of all the doors, where only passengers are allowed, to deal with everything else.

"Sit here", she said, beside a little table, "while I get the coffee. Would you like anything to eat? A sandwich?"

He shook his head. Suddenly he was looking old, sad, even afraid.

She brought two espressos from the counter and sat down.

"Clare", he said, looking down at his hands clasped on the table. "Why am I going away?"

She stopped herself saying how much she wished he weren't, and instead said, "There are very good reasons for going, you know. You'll remember them, really you will, probably as soon as you get on the plane and—well, and as soon as everything seems quite different from usual. Then it'll be an adventure, and you'll begin to think how good it will be to see your friend, your city, your mountains, after so many years, and—"

He wouldn't look at her but she pressed on.

"Lejla's grave, and Nico's, and perhaps Osman's in the village in the hills. It will all be good, I'm sure."

He looked up.

"Yes", he said, without conviction. "I hope. And it is too late to not go". At last he smiled, "Also too expensive."

"Quite right. Of course you must go."

She drank her coffee, which was neither good nor hot enough. "Your coffee?'

But he shook his head again, not so sadly, and she drank his coffee too.

"Now", he said, picking up his shoulder bag.

"Have you got something to read on the journey?"

He patted his bag. "*Ravenna*, the book you gave me. Towards Ravenna I am travelling."

"Very good."

"Also your book. To read again."

He stopped, undid a pocket on the outside of his shoulder bag, and took out a small padded envelope, sealed with sticky tape.

"This is for you, Clare. Open it when you are in your flat. You will take care of what is here, please."

He gave it to her. She put it in her bag.

That was all.

They crossed a wide space full of people queuing, or standing about, staring at information boards or just waiting, some sitting on suitcases, some pacifying toddlers, one or two old people with sticks looking round, in vain, for a chair, and reached the gate for departures.

He put down his bag, took both her hands in his and kissed first one hand and then the other. Then he hugged her, long and close, and left her without looking back.

He vanished, the finality of his going reminded her, for one moment only, of the finality of the curtains shutting on Simon's coffin as it slid into the depths, presumably the fiery depths, of the crematorium. Nearly thirteen years ago.

Very slowly, more tired, she thought, than she had ever been before, she walked all the miles through the tunnels lined with advertisements back to the tube station. She waited with the crowd on the platform; most of the people were not wearing masks, which after all this time of taking care made her feel nervous. In the train she sat absolutely still, without opening her bag to get out her paperback copy of *On the Eve*, the Turgenev novel she had started a few nights ago and had nearly finished, let alone Val's envelope. After the lift at Gloucester Road she emerged into the sunless daylight. It was very cold. At last in her flat she took off her gloves, coat, hat, boots, and went to the kitchen to make a cup of tea. While the kettle boiled she fetched her tartan rug and when she sat at the table with her tea she pulled the rug round her shoulders to stop herself shivering, and took Val's envelope out of her bag. She felt it. There was something hard there, not the pages of a letter as, she realized, she had been hoping. But he wouldn't have asked her to take care of a letter, unless it were for someone else. His will? No. Whatever he had sealed up for her wasn't paper. She turned the envelope over and over. It was soft, lined with bubble-wrap. A new jiffy bag, not used before. He had bought it specially. There was nothing written on it, not even her name, and a lot of sticky tape. She had to get up to find a knife to open it.

Inside, further wrapped in tissue paper, which she unfolded very gently, was a crucifix, an extraordinary crucifix like none she had ever seen before. It was about seven inches high and made mostly of silver, badly tarnished but so elaborately worked, with semi-precious stones in the silver curlicues, green and red and orange, and some very small stones, white with scarlet crosses, and a number of little pieces of lapis lazuli, that it was impossible to imagine trying to clean the silver. Particularly as a few of the stones, and some of the bits of silver at the edges of the so-complicated cross, were already missing. Most astonishing of all, on both sides, front and back, of the cross were tiny carved panels, pictures but carved in relief, for which all the silver and inlaid stones were only the frame. These panels, so small, so finely carved, that she had to find the spectacles she used for sewing and the big magnifying glass from the drawer in Simon's desk to look at them properly. She thought at first that they were carved of wood, but the fineness, and the minuteness of the detail, and the fact that they had survived in such a perfect state for, probably, many centuries, made her think that they must be carved of ivory, their colour, a pale brown, the result of age.

Under the light in the middle of the kitchen table, with her sewing spectacles pushed up her nose and moving Simon's magnifying glass nearer and further from the panels as she tried to see as clearly as she could, she looked at them very carefully. The central panel on the front showed Christ on the cross, with four figures, two of them perhaps Mary and John, at the foot of the cross. The panel on the back of this one—each small piece of ivory, if that was what it was, had a front and a back—was carved into what looked like a depiction of the Holy Spirit as rays of light coming from above, with below the rays a standing figure who was perhaps the resurrected Christ. On each side of the whole astonishing object were four smaller panels, each nearly square and half the size of the two rectangular central panels. One was above, one below, and one at each side of the Crucifixion on the front and of the Resurrection on the back. A presiding figure, obviously God the Father, was carved at the top on each side; there was an angel in each of the panels beside the Resurrection, and on the front a male figure at each side of the Crucifixion. Perhaps these were two of the evangelists, because in the lower panels on both the front and the back of the crucifix, beneath the feet of Christ, were two more male figures, each sitting with a book or a scroll on a lectern or a desk. Each of these eight panels was less than half an inch square.

She had no idea of how old this crucifix might be—she thought it must be Byzantine - but the longer she looked at it, the more she marvelled at the carving, the workmanship. The work in this, she thought, remembering the filigree decoration and the delicacy of the calligraphy in the pages from the Lisbon Bible in Val's sitting room. This ivory carving was even more remarkable. Behind Christ on the cross and in the panels to each side with the evangelists were a Roman colonnade so perfectly carved that each minute round arch seemed to have beyond it the darkness of a stone building. She tried to imagine the smallness and sharpness of the tools, the chisels, that had been used to make these images.

She picked it up and held it in front of her, perhaps a couple of feet, and of course could see nothing but the elaborate silver and the inlaid stones, with the carving no more than faint lines in the tiny panels. What, who, where could it have been made for? Surely not for a church, where it was too small to be properly seen except by one person at a time, very close to it. For someone's oratory, someone's desk? It couldn't have been on a wall or flat on a surface because then only one side would have been visible. She looked at the base. Below the panels was a round handle, again of elaborate inlaid silver, extending for about three inches, so that you could hold the crucifix in one hand—heavy to hold, it was—or perhaps it was fixed to the top of some kind of pole or staff, because the handle was hollow, with a round hole at the bottom. Might it have been carried by a priest in a procession? Then almost nothing of the work would have been visible as it went slowly past the congregation. But that never mattered in churches. She remembered in the splendour of Chartres sitting on a stone bench at the side of the nave and reading that the backs of the statues, so high up that they were difficult to see anyway, were as perfectly carved as the fronts.

She was guessing. To find out anything about the cross and its carvings she would have to take it to the V and A, or Sotheby's. She thought of Emma. Absolutely not. She wasn't going to take it out of the flat until Val came back. What had he said? "You will take care of what is here." Because he expected to come back? Or because he expected not to come back?

"Please", he had added, as if she needed him to ask.

He loved this beautiful thing. He had brought it, no doubt, all the way from Sarajevo to Wrocław and from Wrocław to London, and he wanted her to keep it safe. Was it perhaps his grandmother's? Or had he saved it from the library in Sarajevo, or the museum, because it was too damaged to be exhibited?

She took it into her bedroom and propped it with great care against the mirror on her dressing table, illogically because she couldn't see the other side, the back, the Resurrection, even though she knew it was reflected in the mirror, but it seemed the right place to put it.

She looked at her watch. He was in the air now, flying towards Sarajevo and she hoped feeling much better, remembering why he had decided to go, pleased to be going to arrive, soon, in the city of his childhood.

On the way home, in those long tunnels at the airport, and then in the Tube, she had been so tired that she was sure she was ill, or was going to be ill. What lay ahead, life without seeing him on Wednesdays and Saturdays, without seeing him, perhaps, ever again, was beyond her strength. She was too old. If she got really ill and needed looking after, she would have to leave the flat for a care home or get someone to look after her, neither of which she could even think about now, though she had thought about them sensibly in the past. If she had to do either, Val would come back, if he came back, to find her life, and therefore his, not the same as they had been now for a whole year. She had just wanted to go to bed when she got home, and not to have to decide even when to get up. But his crucifix had braced her, made her feel that there must be hope because there was faith. And love.

It was Wednesday the fifth of January, Wednesday, usually the day for their walk. She ate some bread and cheese for lunch, didn't go out again, and did go to sleep for half an hour in her armchair. She read the paper, still mostly about Covid, risks, plans, conflicting views of what was likely to happen in the next few weeks. After supper she spent a few minutes looking for *On the Eve* before remembering—old age—that she'd left it in her bag, and settled into her armchair by the fire with her rug over her knees to read the last two or three chapters.

She'd read the book, as she'd read most of the important Russian novels, years and years ago when she was young. This one she'd almost entirely forgotten: a brave impetuous girl who had defied her conventional parents—her father who addressed her as if she were a political meeting reminded Clare of Charles—and married a romantic revolutionary who wanted to throw imperialist Russians and Austrians out of the Balkans. How lucky for Charles and Penny that Carrie, at least for the moment, had settled for Bill. So this was a Balkan story of a century and a half ago, and also a very Russian domestic drama like lots of Chekhov. Almost at the end of the book the young couple, poor and full of urgent idealism, had reached Venice, on their way to the Dalmatian coast from where they were to travel to Bosnia, and then perhaps to Serbia, and on to Insarov's Bulgaria, to lead a revolt. Venice was still in the Habsburg empire: arrogant Austrian officers pushed mere Slavs out of their way. She had completely forgotten the end of the story. Insarov, having recovered once from pneumonia, becomes very ill, and dies, with Elena beside him, on a sofa in their lodgings in Venice. A death in Venice before Wagner's, or Aschenbach's. Elena manages to get his coffin onto a boat to cross the Adriatic so that he can be buried in South Slav land where he belongs. There is a storm at sea. Perhaps the ship is wrecked. She has written to her mother saying she is going to be a nun in Bosnia, but nothing definite is ever again heard of her.

Clare finished the book with tears in her throat, tears in her eyes. Venice. Hadn't Val said, only this morning though it already seemed days ago, "towards Ravenna I am travelling"? Wasn't Venice, Ravenna's successor fifty or sixty miles up the coast, the second great Byzantine city on the Adriatic shore? Mightn't Val's crucifix have reached Sarajevo from Venice like the Haggadah? And Elena taking Insarov's body across the dangerous sea to bury him at home, when he should have been fighting to free the South Slavs—it was all too close to what had happened today, to what had happened to Val all through his life.

She prayed as usual, and went to bed as usual, but couldn't sleep properly. After long confused hours when anxieties and nightmares, the neon-lit tunnels at the airport and Insarov coughing and coughing and Val hugging her as if they were never to meet again, were so jumbled together that she felt by five o'clock in the morning that she'd hardly slept at all, she got out of bed, cold and shaky, and made a new hot water-bottle and a mug of tea in the kitchen before she thought of the crucifix.

Holding her hot water bottle, comforting already, under her arm, and her mug in her hand, she went back to her bedroom and sat down at her dressing table to make sure it was real, that she hadn't dreamt it, the silver, the stones, the tiny carved scenes. She hadn't. There it was, and Val had left it for her, not just so that she could look after it, but so that it would look after her. Because he expected to come back? Because he expected not to come back? She couldn't get the question out of her head. But she got into bed, sipped her tea, prayed for Val and for Carrie and for Hakim, and slept with no more nightmares until almost eight o'clock.

Over her breakfast coffee, without turning on the wireless because she needed to think, she decided, because there was no alternative, that, with Val's crucifix on her dressing table to help her, she had to pull herself together. She winced at the cliché, but at the same time recognized it as an exact description of what has to be done when one is scattered by unhappiness, and unless she managed to do it, how could she get on with the rest of her life? After all, a little over a year ago, when Hakim had already gone to Hadrian's Wall, and the old man she occasionally saw in the square was no more than that, her days and what she found to do in them had seemed of course not wonderful but ordinarily acceptable. The boring routine of her life. That was what she must find, now, to be as all right as she had found it then.

In this spirit of resolution she set off in the freezing morning to walk up to Kensington Church Street for Mass because it was Epiphany, a holiday of obligation being celebrated on the right day (they weren't always: eliding the great feasts with a nearby Sunday was a concession to laziness she thought feeble of the Church), and also because it was a good way to begin.

This was a feast she loved. The wonder of the wise men following the star to find the newborn child who would be the king of the Jews made her think, every time she reached it in her nightly recitation of the rosary, of Hakim's gentle inclination of his head, between a nod and a bow, with his hand on his heart, with which he had greeted her until the irruption of Emma into his life had made it possible for him to kiss her on the cheek. It was with this reverence, she was certain, that the wise men greeted Mary and the baby. Perhaps they came from Persia. Of course there were no Muslims yet, but the teachings of the Zoroastrians were already ancient and surely this sign of respect and awe was the habit of the east. They must have bowed, with their hands on their hearts, before they knelt to present their gifts as in all the paintings.

The story of their journey and their visit was in Matthew's gospel, not in Luke's, so perhaps didn't come from Mary herself. But everyone in Judaea must have remembered the horrifying killing of babies and toddlers that followed the wise men's visit. And this year she could think only, as she knelt for the Eucharistic prayer, that it was because of what they told Herod about the king of the Jews, and therefore because they came, that all the boys up to two years old in Bethlehem and the neighbourhood were killed by Herod's soldiers. The massacre of the innocents, terrible phrase. And it wasn't unlike the massacre of Muslim men and boys at Srebrenica in 1995. Rachel weeping for her children.

Val had gone to Bosnia to pray at the graves of his boys, who, like Matt, had been killed in a war that achieved nothing.

She left the church feeling sadder, more muddled, than when she'd arrived. The feast was about the epiphany, the showing forth, of Christ to the world, the world outside Israel. He was the light of revelation for the gentiles, as Simeon was a few weeks later to say in the temple. The wise men had taken their discovery of the child home to Persia. And then the king of the Jews had massacred Jewish children. At Srebrenica Christian Serbs had massacred Muslims. In Sarajevo Serb bombers had killed anyone who had the bad luck to be hit by a shell.

Back in the flat she went to make sure that Val's crucifix was still there, propped against her dressing table mirror, and then pottered from room to room trying to reassemble her resolution. She was also trying to make up her mind what to read next. She had read four Turgenev stories after she finished *The Brothers Karamazov*. They were all of his books that she had in the flat, and anyway she needed something longer and heavier to keep her going while Val was away. Perhaps he might even be back before she finished it. She didn't want to leave Russia, where all her reading had been since *Doctor Zhivago*. She looked along the Russian shelf in the sitting room, and, bracing herself a little, took out *The Devils*. She had read it once, so long ago that she'd probably been too young to understand it, though she did remember that it was terrifying and shocking. Putin's aggressive, truthless Russia, threatening Ukraine with armies and lies, was being no less frightening than Stalin's Russia, or even Hitler's Nazi Germany in the years before 1939. If Russia invaded Ukraine, the misery of Afghanistan and the fears for Bosnia, let alone the continuing shambles in Hakim's Libya, all of them already remote from most people's attention in England, would fade from the news altogether.

Would it be good for some time each day to quieten everything else in the confused noise of nineteenth-century Russia? Perhaps.

She had written nothing for weeks.

She decided to write about her days at Leckenby in September. Hadn't they, after all, been magical days that were like a gift, that were a gift, from God, and Val hadn't even been with her?

At the kitchen table she opened her laptop. No emails. Make the sign of the cross. Forgive your enemies. She didn't have any. Say a prayer. She had. She did. She always did. But she couldn't even begin.

Val hadn't been there and now she was sure he never would be, never beside her to walk along the lanes, through the sloping field by the river when it was no more than a beck, high in the dale, with oak trees that were ancient but had never become tall, in the sheep-cropped grass, thin over the limestone bone of the dale.

There was no reason, really no reason she told herself, to think that he wouldn't come back. His house, his laptop in the airing cupboard, even Ivica with Fatima in Battersea, were waiting for him. He hadn't, or as far as she knew he hadn't, made any of the kind of arrangements a prudent person would make if he weren't intending to come back. But she was convinced, most of the time, however irrationally, that she wouldn't see him again.

And how could she write about those days if he weren't even going to read what she wrote?

CHAPTER 14

TUESDAY 1 MARCH 2022

She was sitting in the kitchen in her dressing gown, as usual listening to the *Today* programme. A forty-mile long convoy of Russian tanks, armoured cars full of soldiers and who knew what outlawed and terrifying weapons, was approaching Kiev. The courage and resolve of the Ukrainians, in the five days since Putin's unprovoked, savage and irrational attach on them had begun, had moved the rest of the world. Now was Kiev, Kyiv as the BBC were learning to call it, going to be smashed to pieces with thousands of dead as Grozny in Chechnya had been twenty years ago? Someone was already reporting that Chechens were beginning to arrive in Ukraine to help the resistance.

It was all dreadful to listen to, just to listen to. She thought and therefore prayed for the people in Kyiv and Kharkiv in cellars and basement car parks, in the dark, in the cold—in Ukraine it was snowing outside this morning—trying to comfort children, trying not to remember bow hungry they were, waiting for the kind of attack not suffered by these cities since Hitler's advance through Ukraine in 1941, slaughtering the Jews as the German soldiers terrorized Ukraine.

As she listened she heard Afghanistan, which she had not forgotten for a single day since the end of August, mentioned three times. In the report on today's papers she heard one sentence about a photograph in the *Telegraph* of Afghan men with scars from operations to remove their kidneys to sell so that they could buy food for their families. Then she heard a brief interview on the street in Philadelphia with an ashamed American shopkeeper who had been asked what he thought of the invasion of Ukraine: "Putin wouldn't have done this if we hadn't cut and run from Afghanistan in the summer. No fight left in the US. That's what we showed him." And then Dominic

Raab, who had been the useless Foreign Secretary lying on a beach as the British also bolted from Afghanistan, when asked what we were doing for Ukrainian refugees, blandly said how well we had done with Afghan refugees. "We have responded in Afghanistan", he said.

We hadn't. Because of Matt's interpreter and her own failure to help any actual Afghan people who had managed to reach England—but really, she knew, because of Matt's death—she had noticed every bit of news about the refugees.

In August, even before the last British soldiers left, Boris Johnson's government announced, with, as far as she could remember, the usual fanfare about leading the world, something called the "Afghan Citizens' Resettlement Scheme". Then far too few, but about fifteen thousand, people, were taken out of the country in time to save them from the Taliban—many ending up, like the journalist on *Woman's Hour*, dumped in hotels. Every time all through the autumn that Clare checked on the government website, the Resettlement Scheme "hadn't yet opened". When, finally, it was declared to be open, in January so more than four months later, its beneficiaries turned out to be five thousand people who were already here. So its opening was a lie. And only ten days ago she had heard on the wireless that the six-month visas these same people were given in August were beginning to run out, and that the Home Office was failing to send them renewal documents. In a few days or a few weeks they would become illegal immigrants, with no proof, no papers, to show they have permission to be here. The result would be the slamming doors familiar to refugees since the 1930s: no bank, no GP practice, no possible employer, no landlord, no insurance company, will count you as existing once you can't produce the right papers. And these are the Afghans who are here. Not long before that she'd heard, or perhaps read in the paper, that Biden was "retaining", whatever that meant, billions of dollars of what were called "Afghan assets" in America for the families of victims of 9.11. These families were surely managing all right after more than twenty years, and 9.11 in any case wasn't the fault of the Afghan people. Now, of course, with the crisis in Ukraine, invented by Putin and turned by Putin into all-out war waged against a country guilty of nothing more than preferring democracy to Russian-imposed tyranny, everyone would forget, if they hadn't already forgotten, about Afghanistan where the suffering of equally innocent people was at least partly our fault.

Yesterday the Home Secretary was refusing to allow Ukrainian refugees instant asylum unless they had immediate family already here: a widowed Ukrainian with a daughter in England didn't count as immediate family and had been prevented by the Home Secretary's Border Force from catching the Eurostar to take her to London from Paris: what had this old woman, perhaps Clare's age, already been through to get as far as Paris?

Meanwhile the government's dreadful borders bill, making all asylum-seekers criminals, was on its slow way through parliament though parts of it were known by everyone to be illegal.

She groaned, as she often did at the ghastliness of the news, which at the moment was more appalling every day than it had been the day before. As she got up, to put the kettle on again for more tea, she heard Hakim's key in the lock. He'd left only fifteen minutes ago, as he did every day: twenty past eight was plenty of time to get him to the Museum by nine. He must have forgotten something important.

"There is no Piccadilly Line today", he said, putting his head round the kitchen door. "The whole Tube is on strike."

"No—what a nightmare for everyone. It would have been on the news if it weren't for—"

"If it weren't for President Putin. Of course."

"What are you going to do?"

"I will not try a bus. The queues are already too long. It is no problem for me. I shall stay and work, if that is all right for you. I tried to call the department. There was no answer. So I have texted my boss. I expect he is not able to travel to the Museum himself."

"More coffee?"

"Please. A moment."

She made real coffee instead of tea—Hakim had made himself a mug of instant coffee before he set off for work—and he reappeared.

"I collected your newspaper."

"Thank you."

Bombed out buildings on the front of the *Guardian*, and as she turned the pages, waiting for the coffee to brew, she saw headlined both the hard-heartedness of the Home Secretary and the embarrassing incompetence of the Foreign Secretary, the result in both cases of Boris Johnson appointing people to jobs that could hardly be more important not because they would be any good at them but for their loyalty to him.

"It's all dreadful", she said.

"President Putin", Hakim said, "has been always a terrible man. He has brought destruction in Chechnya and in Syria. He is too powerful in Libya as I do know. Why does the West not notice until now?"

"Hubris", she said.

"The hubris of the West?"

"Yes. The end of the Soviet Union was called the end of history. You won't remember. You were a schoolboy in Libya. The Americans, and perhaps the English as well, assumed that as the USSR had collapsed, all we had to do was to wait patiently for the victory of democracy and the triumph of liberal, tolerant values everywhere in the world. That was hubris, or at any rate dangerous complacency. We patted ourselves on the back."

"What does this mean?"

"Sorry. It means we told ourselves how splendid we were, how we deserved everything to go our way. I remember George Bush, the first President Bush, saying that America by the grace of God had won the Cold War, and I remember my husband, who knew much more about recent history than I did, saying that was nonsense. The USSR crumbled because practically no one in Russia, let alone in the satellite countries, really believed in it any more, and America hadn't needed to do much to help. He also said, now I come to think of it, that it was clever Ukrainians in Lwów, Lviv, who had thought about Ukrainian independence from Russia for years, who had manoeuvred Yeltsin into dissolving the USSR. That's interesting now don't

302

you think?"

She remembered, for the first time in the less than a week since this war began, what Val had told her about Lviv, the old Polish city of Lwów, the old Habsburg city of Lemberg, and its library, some of the remnants of which he had looked after in Wrocław.

"Of course. It is very interesting but also it is probably very sad. It is not looking possible for Putin not to win this war. But the hubris?"

"What I meant was that we have been too careless, too optimistic all this time, too sure that democracy had won, and where it hadn't it soon would, to notice what was actually happening. We didn't notice, and Putin did."

"Yes. Now I understand. I understand from Libya. The Arab Spring—even the name, the spring for the Arab countries, was full of hope. I think the West understood that hope to mean democracy for all of us who had suffered the dictators, Ben Ali, Mubarak, Gaddafi—they went, and where are these countries now? Are they peaceful and democratic? By no means. And Syria, where the dictator has not gone, is the worst of all, with Putin making everything worse, very much worse, in Syria, where he bombed and poisoned people for Assad."

"That's right. We did nothing in Syria. We did nothing when he invaded Crimea. He said he would invade Ukraine again. We weren't paying attention to what he was saying, and he has invaded Ukraine again, this time all of it. The last straw was probably the way we treated Afghanistan in the summer. We showed we couldn't be trusted and we showed we didn't care. Hubris, you see, and the poor Ukrainians are having to face the nemesis, which is not their own."

"Yes. Other people pay for the pride of the west. The Palestinians for example, and many Iraqis. And the countries where there are many refugees from Syria."

He got up, and filled his mug with more coffee. Clare shook her head when he lifted the cafetière in her direction.

Standing by the door, mug in hand, he said, "Clare. I am sorry to see you are so sad. You are sad also about Mr Radic. I know."

"Yes, you're right. But there's nothing I can do about Ukraine, or about Val. And there's not much I can do for you, poor Hakim. You've got plenty to be sad about yourself."

"It is already not so sad for me, because you are so good. And also because I understand maybe it has been an escape. Now, I must do some real work."

"Of course you must. See you at lunchtime."

He raised his mug in farewell, and went off to his desk in Simon's study.

Nearly two weeks ago, on the Wednesday in the middle of February that was six weeks after Val left for Sarajevo, she had been sitting by the fire after supper, reading *The Devils*, which was appalling and gripping—surely Dostoyevsky was the first highbrow thriller-writer?—as she had found *The Brothers Karamazov* this time, but *The Devils* was both more appalling and more gripping, when the telephone rang. She looked at her watch. A quarter to nine. Penny never rang in the evening. Unless something had happened to Carrie or Daisy? She pulled herself out of her armchair as quickly as she could, which wasn't quickly, and went to the kitchen.

"Hallo."

"Clare."

"Hakim. How wonderful. Where are you?"

She hadn't heard his voice for months.

Because of all that had happened two years ago when he had been for weeks unreachable in Libya she stupidly thought that he might be there, or in Egypt, or stuck in some airport.

"I'm in Chipping Warden."

"Goodness. Where's Chipping Warden?"

Obviously, anyway, it couldn't not be in England.

"It is nowhere. A few miles from a place called Banbury. There is here, beside Chipping Warden, a new Roman town with no name."

Naturally there would be a Roman town.

"Can I please come to the flat, Clare?"

"Of course you can. When would you like to come?"

"Is it possible I come tonight? It will be late. I am sorry.

There is a train from Banbury that will arrive at a station called Mary- something at twenty past ten. I will get a taxi. It is not too far I think."

"Marylebone. Not far, no. It shouldn't take long at night. I'll expect you at about eleven."

"This will be late for you. I am sorry."

"Don't be sorry. It'll be good to see you whenever you get here."

It was as if the sun had come out after weeks of grey skies and rain.

She hoovered and dusted Matt's room, turned on the radiator though there wasn't much heating time left in the evening, and made up the bed, and then made sure that Simon's study, which she looked after regularly, was clean and tidy, and turned on its radiator too.

Still there was at least an hour and a half before he could possibly arrive. She had a long bath, and curled up in her armchair with Dostoyevsky. Hakim was used to her dressing gown.

It was impossible to concentrate on the complexities of the group of revolutionaries round the terrifying figure of Stavrogin, who, as the menace to Ukraine seemed to be getting worse and worse, she couldn't help imagining as Putin with his cold eyes. Instead she sat, warm and comfortable, nearly asleep, wondering what had happened to deliver Hakim to her so long—how long? Almost six months it must be—after Emma had swept him off to Hackney. It couldn't be good. Or perhaps it could, at least eventually.

She wasn't too fast asleep to hear the bell from the street door. It was ten to eleven.

He came, as always, up the stairs. He had his shoulder bag but not his enormous rucksack. In the doorway, he kissed her on the cheek, and then stepped back to look at her.

"Clare. It is so good to see you. I am sorry it is—"

"Don't be sorry about anything."

When he'd put down his bag and taken off his coat, which was a Barbour she'd bought him for Northumberland, hanging it up on one of the four hooks by the door as if he had left that morning, she said, "Come into the kitchen. What would you like? Have you had any supper?"

"I did not have supper. But before I left the pub in the village I was so happy to be coming to you that I bought a cheese sandwich. I ate it in the train, and it was the best cheese sandwich I ever had. I would like please some mint tea if still you have some."

"Yes, I have some." I had a feeling you might come back before too long, she didn't say.

She made him his tea, and a mug of camomile tea for herself. She didn't want to ask him anything.

After a few minutes he said, "Clare. Can I come back to stay in the flat please? For a short time, until—until I am not sure when."

"Of course you can. You can stay as long as you like, you know that."

"Thank you. As I thank you for all the years."

"It's all right, Hakim, as you know. I like you being here. Now I think you should go to bed. You look very tired."

"Yes. For some weeks it is not easy. I was happy to go to Chipping Warden for two days. I will tell it all in the morning."

"Off you go. I hope you sleep well."

"I did not understand. Perhaps from the beginning I did not understand. I thought because she was very passionate with me—it was so good, you see—she would want to learn—"

He stopped. He kept stopping. His very good English wasn't up to describing what would no doubt have been hard to put into words in his own language.

"You thought she would want to discover who you are, what has made you who you are, your country, your religion, your family. Is that what you thought, you hoped?"

"Yes. That is what I hoped. Now I see that I did not think about it but it was what I expected. I expected this because I was interested, really interested, in her, in her family and how she might think. But it was so strange. She was not herself interested to tell me even about herself."

"Perhaps that was because the story of her family is difficult? A divorce is always difficult for the children of the marriage."

306

"She would not say to me even that it was difficult. I thought one day she would maybe cry, about her father and her stepmother, who she does not like, so almost never she sees her father. But she does not cry, about this or about anything. I do not understand a girl who does not ever cry."

"What did you talk about, in the evenings, at the weekends?"

"At first we talked about work, or maybe the news. She watched all the television news because she was always hoping that the Covid rules would be taken away so that we could be out in the evening, at the cinema, with her friends, at a restaurant. And then when we were allowed go to these things she always wanted to. She liked to go our nearly every night. She does not like to cook. She does not like me to have work I must do in the evening, for a meeting the next day for example, and even more she does not like me to go to Friday prayers in the mosque. She says that Friday prayers are like having to go to Mass on Sundays for Catholics. Silly, she says. What is the difference between Friday or Sunday and any other day? But I do, I did go, to Friday prayers. There is a big mosque with its Islamic centre in Hackney. Most of the people are Indian or Pakistani, but they are friendly to Arabs. There may be some extreme Islamists. I have not met this there."

She didn't interrupt.

After a moment he went on.

"Emma thinks that all Muslims would be terrorists if they are brave enough."

"Surely she doesn't think you could be a terrorist?"

"I don't know. Maybe. One time she asked me why I did not try to convert her to Islam. 'You are supposed to try, aren't you?' She said she could become a Muslim like Jemima Khan. Then she said, 'My parents would love that, wouldn't they?'" It was not kind to say that, I think."

Another pause.

"A few weeks ago, after Christmas—"

Here was an easy question.

"Where did you go for Christmas? Or did you stay in London?"

"We went for two nights to the house of her mother and her stepfather. Her brother was there, from America. No one had seen her brother for two years because of Covid."

"What was he like?"

"I did not find out. He did not speak to me. He spoke to his mother and to his stepfather, and also to Emma, as if I was not in the room."

"O dear. Poor Hakim. What a horrible Christmas. Did any of them bother to talk to you?"

"Only Emma's mother. She tried, I think, to be kind. She asked me when I was going back to Libya. 'You must want to see your family', she said. I said that my family had died because of Colonel Gaddafi and the war to get rid of him. She said she did not know that Colonel Gaddafi was in Libya but surely now that he has gone it would be good to go home. I said there had been more or less a civil war for ten years and when I went there to look at the Roman stones for the Museum I was nearly killed. 'O, your eye', she said. 'How tactless of me. I'm so sorry.' I think that was the only kind talk in those two days. Emma's stepfather said 'Why are you celebrating Christmas when you are a Muslim?' and Emma did not help me with the answer."

"I'm so sorry. It all makes me ashamed to be English."

"I think it is not their fault. They do not know any foreigners, maybe. They are not interested to find out what is the same, what is different, in a foreigner like me."

"Well. They should be."

Obviously he needed to get to the end of the story.

"And now?" she said.

"Since Christmas it is only a few weeks, but it was worse and worse with Emma. She has a new job."

"What? I thought she was so pleased to be working at Sotheby's."

"She said it was boring. That is the worst thing, the worst word, for her, boring. Now I understand that she was never much interested in stones, or even in the Romans. The archaeology was something for a degree. Nothing more. And at Vindolanda it was me she—It is not me any more. Her father has found her a job in the City. She does not want to talk to me. She does not want any more—"

He couldn't say it.

"I understand."

"I thought she is maybe ill. But she said no, she was fine. I thought even she is maybe pregnant. I did not ask her, and now this is not possible. Then five days ago on Saturday I told her the Museum has asked me to go to Chipping Warden on Monday until Wednesday, yesterday, yes, to look at what has been found at a new Roman site that the engineers for HS2 have discovered. I would stay in a pub for two nights. The Museum had arranged this. Before Christmas she would be sad if I told I would be away. But on Saturday she looked happy and she said, 'Good. Then I will be out all day tomorrow'. She came to the flat very late on Sunday night and would not speak. She looked—I could see she had been with someone—someone else. I had to go to Chipping Warden on Monday before she was awake. Yesterday she sent me a text on my phone. Look."

She had to put on her sewing glasses to see the message.

It's over. You won't be surprised. Come to the flat for your things when I'm at work Thursday. Sorry. It was good for a while. Leave the key. Emma.

She replaced the sewing glasses with her ordinary ones and gave him back his phone.

"That's so unkind. How could she? How could she just send a text? And how could she not see how lucky she was, to have you in her life?"

"No, Clare. For her I was not good luck. I was bad luck. At the beginning, in the mud and the cold of Northumberland, I was interesting for her, a foreigner who she did not expect to meet on Hadrian's Wall. But when we came to London it was not the same. She wanted to talk to her friends, not to me. It was difficult with her friends. 'This is Hakim', she said, and then nothing. She did not explain me to them. With other people I was a stranger. At home in her flat I was very close. I thought I was very close. But there was—"

Again he stopped, searching for the right words.

"A distance between you? A space you couldn't cross?"

"That is right. A distance. But was this distance because I am a foreigner? Ayesha was a foreigner to me. She was Indian. And we never did—"

"I know."

"But there was not the distance."

"Ayesha was a Muslim."

"Of course. But it was not only that."

"No. It wasn't. Ayesha was far from her home, like you. You were a friend in a country that was foreign for both of you. Also she'd chosen to be a doctor, to care for people, to listen to people. She had already been looking after patients for years when you met her. She was here in the flat such a short time, but it was as if even I had known her for much longer. Emma is very young which has been perhaps part of the problem, but also she is spoilt—too much money and not enough love in her family—and selfish."

"Selfish?"

Could he not have heard the word before?

"She thinks about what suits her, what is good for her, and not very much about what is good for other people, even people as close to her as you thought you were."

With his one dark, troubled eye, he looked at Clare over the cold remains of their breakfast on the kitchen table.

"No. It is not, as you say, not very much, that she thinks about other people. It would be more true to say not at all. I should have more quickly understood this."

He stood up and cleared the breakfast things, putting them in the sink and turning on the tap.

"Don't wash up, Hakim. Shouldn't you be going to the Museum? Just leave all that."

"Yes." He turned off the tap. "I should go. I will go. And can I—"

"Yes, You must come back tonight with your things. You know you can stay as long as you like."

He went to collect his laptop in his shoulder bag. From the kitchen door he said, "How is Mr Radic?"

"O". But of course he couldn't have known. "He's gone to Sarajevo, the city where he was born, you remember, to visit old friends in Bosnia."

"Will be come back to London?"

"I hope so."

"That is sad for you. He is a friend, I saw. He also is a foreigner, but there is not the distance. Is this right?"

"Yes, Hakim, quite right. Now go and get on with your day. This evening you can tell me about your new Roman site. Take your key."

On the evening of the same day, she heard him come in. It was just after *The Archers*, so it was a quarter past seven. She was in the kitchen chopping an onion. She switched off the wireless. He appeared in the doorway with his shoulder bag, his rucksack stuffed full, and a large Sainsbury's bag full of books and papers. He looked miserable.

"Good evening, Clare. I will put down these things."

He went along the passage to Matt's room, and then across to Simon's study, and came back after hanging up his coat.

"What happened?"

"Nothing. There was nothing for me. No letter—I imagined maybe—But—"

"But?"

"A man was in the flat with her last night. It was easy to see. Some clothes. My clothes were on the floor by my rucksack, all my clothes, so quickly. But now I understand that the weeks since Christmas—this was why she would not tell, she would not say to me anything."

"Sit down Hakim. I'll make you some tea. I'm so so sorry."

He stood at the other end of the table from where she always sat. Three times he banged his clenched fists on the table, after the third bang leaving his fists pressing down on the tablecloth.

Not looking at her, with his head bent, he said: "Ayesha and Samira are dead. Both of them are dead. Samira died because Libya is a terrible country. Ayesha died because she was a good doctor who did more than she needed to do. And now I found an English archaeologist, not a nurse, not a doctor, not in Libya, not in danger. I found her, or so it seemed in the spring and the summer in those green hills. I thought—But I did not think. She is not even an archaeologist and she does not care. She does not care for stones and she does not care for me. First and second, Samira and Ayesha, it is fate, bad fate. Anyone might be dead in Libya. Anyone might be dead because of Covid, most of all at the beginning. But third it is that I am a fool."

"You're not a fool. Absolutely not. This can happen to anyone. A mistake, so easy to make, when you're carried away."

"Carried away? What does this mean?"

"I'm sorry. It means when a feeling, an emotion, is like a river flowing so strongly that you're carried along by the current. The river takes you downstream, on the flood. It's not possible to swim against the force of the water. It's not possible to think clearly. The other person has carried you away. She seems like everything that matters in the world, but at the same time you don't know her well enough to see who she really is. This is the excitement, the danger, how you are carried away."

He sat down, at last, and looked at her.

"Clare. This is like Virgil. I understand. You are right. Yes. But when the river throws you on the bank, you are cold and wet and you know that you were a fool."

"But as I say, you're not alone. It's an old story, and there are lots of poems. There's a famous English one that starts 'They flee from me that sometime did me seek', which means she seemed so keen, that girl, and now she runs away, like Emma. But the girl in that poem had deserted the poet for Henry VIII, which I expect was a very bad exchange."

She was talking for the sake of talking, and he wasn't really listening.

"There are beautiful sad poems in Arabic also."

Or perhaps he was. He recited what must have been a couple of lines of an Arabic poem.

He stood up. "I must not think too much. I have promised to give a first report in three days on what is found in the new town. I should start, only to sort out my notes, before supper."

"Of course. Do some work for half an hour. We'll have supper at eight, and then I want to hear about what they've discovered."

It was good that he had straightforward work to do. After supper they sat on each side of the fire, as they had done on and off for years, before Ayesha, after Ayesha, before Emma, and he talked, every so often stopping and sitting for a moment still as he remembered that he had lost Emma, about the dozens of archaeologists working in the damp Northamptonshire fields to find as much as they could before the site had to be buried again for the railway that was costing so much and was going to do so little good.

"There is everything there. Everything of a middle Roman town on an important road and a river, with an important market, for maybe hundreds of years. The coins, a lot of coins, and the different burials. different kinds over many years, so different religions, show—"

He lost for a moment what he was going to say.

"I am sorry, Clare. The coins and the burials show that this was a British settlement, already quite big, and it became gradually Roman over the times. So we find no violence, no killing of the people, but it was a better life to be Roman. People could see. At the late third and in the fourth century the rich people in this town had things that were expensive, Samian pottery with paintings of figures, from Gaul, some jewels, some glass. There were craftsmen, always craftsmen in Roman towns, metalsmiths—what a good English word—and potters, bakers, leatherworkers no doubt like the leatherworkers in Vindolanda although there is not peat to preserve the leather. Weights and measures for the market they have found." She remembered for a second the almost still usable Roman market stalls in Leptis Magna, in Libya, where Hakim should be. "There are no mosaics found yet, and because of the railway the archaeologists will maybe not have enough time to dig for them where the rich people lived."

He stopped again.

"The rich people. How cruel were the rich people."

"O, Hakim. Rich people aren't always cruel."

"The archaeologists have found a shackle, which was not in a burial. So there have been slaves in the town. In Roman Britain there is almost no evidence of slaves. Somebody rich was cruel. Also they have found, which is rare and interesting to archaeologists, some galena."

"What is galena?"

"It is what is left from melting lead. It is very white. The rich Roman ladies used it for their faces."

"For their faces? O I see. Make-up. Not very good for them, I imagine. Lead is poisonous."

"Exactly."

"Hakim. Listen to me. You mustn't mix up what may or may not have gone on in your Roman town with poor Emma."

"Poor Emma?"

"Yes. She's lost you, you know, as well as you losing her, and that's a serious loss which she'll perhaps understand one day. But at the moment she's only a careless girl with a lot of growing up to do. That's all."

"Yes. Yes. You are right. Always you are right."

"Not always, but possibly this time."

After a minute or two he said, "Clare, I am very tired. I shall go to bed if that is all right."

"Of course it's all right. Tomorrow things will look better."

They did, as far as she could tell, or at any rate in the days that followed he was never again so cast down. He didn't say anything more about Emma, and nor, naturally, did Clare.

And now that evening, not yet two weeks ago, seemed much further in the past. Hakim had settled back into the flat almost as if he had never been to the north for a whole year and to Emma's flat in Hackney for six months after that. Not quite, of course. He was quieter, more self-contained, even more polite and careful of her feelings, than ever. Older and wiser was perhaps what the change amounted to. He was a comfort in the absence, and unbroken silence, of Val, and nightly she thanked God for his safe return.

CHAPTER 15

10 MARCH 2022

The nights lately had been bad.

The photographs she'd seen in the paper, the stories she'd heard on the radio, of exhausted and frightened children, mothers, grandparents, struggling in stations among crowds to get on a train, any train, that might be going westwards, walking along roads with pushchairs, wheelchairs, plastic bags and little else, roads that the Russians might shell at any moment, and the husbands, fathers, sons saying goodbye because they were staying in Ukraine to fight—it was almost beyond bearing just to know that this was happening, while she was safe, warm, and above all at home.

There had been photographs too of captured Russian soldiers, boys of eighteen or nineteen, terrified, cold, trying to telephone their mothers. She had read in the paper of the desperate women all over Russia trying to discover, from the Committee of Soldiers' Mothers, which had begun during Russia's last disastrous war, in Afghanistan, and which even Putin couldn't abolish, where their sons were, whether they were alive or dead. "It's just a sea of tears", the head of the committee said, sitting at her desk in Moscow taking the telephone calls. Clare thanked God for the careful soldiers who had come to tell her and Simon of Matt's death.

The pictures and the voices of refugees came and went in her dreams, or in her sleepless hours, or in the confused patches between memory and imagination when she was neither quite asleep nor quite awake. And when she was thoroughly awake, she was more ashamed and furious than miserable because every day for days and days she was hearing how the British government was failing to help.

However, the haunted nights had unlocked the days.

With her laptop as always on the kitchen table and a mug

of tea beside her, she found that, as soon as Hakim had left for the Museum, she could write, in clarity and anger, so that she wouldn't forget what was happening now.

All the EU countries were allowing refugees from Ukraine to come in from the war they had left, often in great danger, to be welcomed, fed, given clothes and shelter, without questions, without visas, without bureaucratic obstacles and incomprehension. Only the British were bullying already traumatized people with conflicting instructions, an appointment system that sent them back to roads and trains they had already travelled on, sometimes to find there was no appointment or not even a person to talk to where they had been told to go, and above all with visa requirements that included so-called biometric tests, meaning fingerprinting and the kind of photographs you have on a passport, that couldn't be carried out at the border, and forms of many pages for each refugee, including each child, that had to be filled in online, taking hours for each form, by people who had no money to charge their phones let alone pay a taxi, and often didn't have enough English to understand the questions on the forms. As if these exhausted women and children were likely to be a danger to anyone.

In the House of Commons the Prime Minister and the Home Secretary said one thing one day and another the next, pretending, as they had over Afghan refugees, that we, the British, were offering a generous welcome to despairing people. We were not. Yesterday's process was today described as new when it wasn't; offices in Calais, and then in Lille, were said to have been set up to help people with visas when they didn't exist; and the numbers of people to be helped into Britain—"hundreds of thousands" said Boris Johnson—turned out to have been, so far, a very few hundred. And today's near-lie was that from next Tuesday Ukrainian refugees could get their visas on line instead of booking interviews in offices: this turned out only to apply to Ukrainian passport-holders with family already here. The most depressing underlying fact about all this was that a new and cruel maze of bureaucratic walls to keep people out had been made possible by Brexit.

Would it be possible now to write about her few days in Yorkshire, six months ago, because her understanding that those days had been for her a coming home had been made all the more acute by the faces of the Ukrainian children the other side of the windows of trains as their fathers waved for what must have seemed like the last time and might well turn out to have been exactly that?

She prayed at night and often during the day that these children would see their fathers again.

A refugee was a person who was forced to leave home, and who might never return.

What was happening in Ukraine had made her realize, nearly thirty years after his death, that she had failed always to imagine what it had been for her father as a young man, not a child but only twenty-five or twenty-six, Carrie's age, much younger than Hakim, to leave Prague, to leave also the cottage in the country where his grandmother lived and where he had spent summers as a boy. Why hadn't she ever asked him to tell her, to tell her properly, about the prosperous flat in Prague where his parents lived, his father a lawyer in moustache and stiff collar, his mother a lady of the Habsburg empire—the empire of Val's Sarajevo and Lemberg and Breslau—in black silk with her hair in an elegant chignon? This was the one photograph she had seen. There was no photograph of his grandmother's house in a village with geese and storks and beehives painted blue—that was all she could remember him telling her—and, no doubt, plum trees like the trees Val remembered from childhood holidays in the Bosnian mountains.

Home is where you remember the creak of the garden gate and the patch of nettles where an old bucket with no bottom has rusted for ever.

Where had this sentence come from? She had no idea.

Because of the trains and the children's faces and the crowds trying to escape, and because the Russian army was behaving like the armies of Hitler's war, it was impossible not to think all the time of the Nazi massacres of the Jews. Lviv was talked about every day, for the first time for decades. The Russians hadn't yet reached it and it was full of refugees from further east. Val had told her about the beautiful city that at the beginning of Hitler's war was mostly Polish and Jewish. Thousands of refugees had reached it before the Russians arrived in 1939: these had been Jews from Germany travelling east. When the Nazis invaded in 1941 there was nowhere for them to go. Before the Russians retreated from the invading Germans they killed hundreds of Poles, doctors, lawyers, teachers, professors, priests, to weaken Poland later, and, with the Russians gone, the Jews were trapped with the millions already in Ukraine: in the west the Poles had been for generations reasonably tolerant and the east had been for more generations in the Russian Pale of Settlement, where the Tsarist empire ordered the Jews to live because they weren't wanted in Russia proper, unless they were rich. Hitler tried to kill them all. More than thirty thousand Jews had been shot in two days at Babi Yar on the edge of Kyiv in 1941 and as many a little later in Odessa. The Russians had hidden the facts for decades because they wanted all those killed by Hitler to be called "citizens of the USSR". Free Ukraine had built a memorial at Babi Yar. Last week the Russians bombed it.

She thought of the letter from a mother in Ukraine to her son in Russia in Vasily Grossman's *Life and Fate*, a book Val had given her last year. The letter was her last greeting: she knew the Nazis would kill her, and they did. Grossman was the son.

All this suffering and sorrow, then and horrifyingly now, would not leave her memory, her imagination. It was difficult to collect the bodies of the dead in besieged Mariupol, and they were having to be buried in mass graves, like the Jews in Babi Yar, buried where they had been killed, heaps of bodies under slung-in earth. There were no names of the dead.

When she couldn't bear to think about it all any longer she went out to fetch the newspaper and buy something to give Hakim for supper.

The sun, almost springlike, was shining after a shower, and she went into the garden with her shopping for a moment, to look at the daffodils, most of them out, fresh and encouraging, and to remember Val. Their bench was too wet to sit on so she walked through the garden, out of his gate and along the street to his mews. Several times during the weeks he had been away she had done this, to make sure his house was as he'd left it, but really just to put a hand on his red front door as if it could promise her that he would come back.

While her soup was warming up she looked through the *Guardian*. Here was something that would upset Val: Russians were circumventing the fierce sanctions that were supposed to stop them travelling anywhere by flying to Belgrade, and then on to wherever they chose. The Serbs had doubled the regular number of flights from Moscow, and had, of course, not joined any of the European sanctions. Last week she had heard on the *Today* programme—on Saturday she thought—that there had been demonstrations against the Russian invasion of Ukraine in practically every European city, including several in Britain, but in Belgrade the demonstration, of several thousand people, was in support of Putin. What was happening in Sarajevo?

She had just taken a plate and a bowl out of the plate rack on the draining board for her lunch when something made her open her laptop: she rarely opened it unless she were about to start work.

An email from Carrie. There. Lovely. She hadn't heard from her for nearly a month, since Clare had told her that Hakim and Emma had fallen out and he'd come back to the flat, and Carrie had replied, more or less, hooray.

She decided to keep the email until she'd had lunch because it was a treat. She had her soup and some bread and cheese and an apple, washed up, made some decaff coffee, and sat down to read it.

Hi gran

How are you? I'm sure you're doing OK and not getting COVID or Mum would have said. Good for you. It must be nice for you to have Hakim to fuss over again. I hope he isn't too miserable. Perhaps he's even relieved? At least if you've been dumped you don't have to feel guilty as well as sad.

This is to tell you Bill and I are off to Afghanistan! The boss is desperate about Afghanistan because he thinks the world, all the funding countries etc etc, will be so distracted and scared by what's happening in Ukraine—absolutely dreadful, isn't it?—that they'll forget that millions of people are starving in Afghanistan. So he's sending a team out, particularly to help with the children, the girls not allowed to go to school etc etc. I hope you'll be pleased. I know how miserable you were when everybody ratted in the summer. So if we can do something to make things a bit better it'll also be in memory of Uncle Matt. A couple of years in Nepal probably quite good prep for Afghanistan—mountain villages, very poor people, impossible languages.

I've told the parents. Horrified of course, but I'm used to that and I know you won't be.

I'll keep you posted. And DON'T WORRY. I'm sure we'll be fine.

> *Love you*
> *Carrie*

Wonderful Carrie, so brave and good. But how dangerous might it be for them in Afghanistan? She remembered Carrie saying something about aid workers being safe because people needed them and why should they be hated? But Bill? Gangling, serious Bill so unmistakably American? Couldn't he be hated by anyone who felt let down by Americans making promises that were broken? And Carrie with her posh English voice? British promises had been broken too.

She must ring poor Penny, who wouldn't be getting much support from Charles.

She looked at the kitchen clock. Just after two. Worth a try.

"Mum? Are you all right?"

"I'm fine, darling, absolutely fine. It's about Carrie—you must be—"

"I'm sorry Mum, this isn't a brilliant moment. I've got some people for lunch, and bridge and so on. Can I ring you back—after tea, say?"

"After tea would be fine. Talk to you later."

"Bye, Mum."

She sipped her decaff coffee, now not hot enough. Then

she did a bit of internet searching. The government said on no account should anyone travel to Afghanistan. The International Rescue Committee website was asking people not to forget Afghanistan while appealing for money for Ukrainian refugees. It said it had been working in Afghanistan since 1988 and almost all its staff were Afghans. A charity called Afghanaid was appealing for funds but sounding as if the big NGOs were still getting aid through to desperate people.

She sent Afghanaid a hundred pounds and decided to go out for a walk until teatime. She couldn't go on writing. She couldn't listen to any more news. The shambles the government was making over Ukrainian refugees only reminded her that she'd failed to offer a room to that Afghan woman she'd heard being interviewed months ago, who was most likely still stuck in a hotel.

She walked all the way to the Albert Memorial, quite fast, with her stick. When she got there she realized that it was because of Val that she loved the extraordinary mixture of statues and symbols that made dutiful, German, Prince Albert the very centre of imperial, industrial, powerful and prosperous Britain, all that it no longer was. Perhaps above all confident. Instead of just emptily boastful: Boris Johnson always talking about world this and world that, while no one in the actual world listened or cared any more.

Val had found something new, usually something to smile at, not with mockery but with affection, almost every time they'd walked this far. The memorial represented, of course, a pride well lost, a hubristic over-reaching that deserved to end in tears, but the greed, cruelty and carelessness that had made possible and then sustained the empire could for a few minutes be forgotten here. She was sure Victoria's beloved Albert had never been personally cruel to anyone.

A century and a half after his memorial was made, Carrie was going to try to help the oppressed and hungry people of a country that had been a victim for two centuries of imperial enterprises and rivalries run from capital cities thousands of miles away. Britain and Russia, Britain and the Ottomans, Russia again, America and Britain. And now Putin's invasion of Ukraine would mean that there would be even less concern, even less money, even less food and medicine and help, for Afghanistan.

More slowly, old and tired, and glad only that Hakim would be back for supper, she walked all the way through Kensington Gardens and along the Gloucester Road to the flat. She was tempted to get a taxi, which would take five minutes, but decided it was good for her to walk.

Penny rang at five thirty.

"Mum. You mustn't worry about Carrie, you know. Charles says she'll be quite safe, probably sitting in an office in Kabul, and it's a very responsible charity."

Carrie obviously hadn't said anything to her parents about mountain villages, and what had happened to "horrified of course"? This was Penny being soothing because Clare was so old.

"Anyway better to help the Afghans in their own country than have any more of them pouring in here when there are going to be thousands of people coming from Ukraine any minute."

"Is that what Charles thinks? That Afghans have been pouring in?"

"Well, perhaps not pouring. But thousands of them, Boris says."

"Boris makes things up as he goes along. Far too many Afghans were abandoned in the summer. Left behind to be bullied, or tortured or killed for all we know, by the Taliban. People like Matt's interpreter who they all loved."

"You don't know that Mum."

"No I don't. But I do know we did badly in the summer, and we're doing badly again with the poor Ukrainians. Visas, for goodness' sake, for babies and toddlers whose fathers are likely to be killed by the Russian."

"Mum. You won't go having Ukrainians in the flat, will you? You might never get rid of them." Clare thought for a second of *Waiting for Godot*, a play about, among other things, refugees. "You want to get rid of him?" Vladimir says to Pozzo about Lucky, over and over again.

322

"In any case", Penny was still talking, "one refugee's quite enough to be going on with. We thought Hakim had finally gone, but he always seems to come back."

"Hakim's hardly a refugee any more. He's been in England for nearly eight years. He'd never be allowed in now."

"Quite right, Charles would say. Never mind Hakim. Are you really OK yourself? You don't sound brilliant."

"I'm perfectly all right, darling. I shall be anxious about Carrie whatever Charles says. But there's nothing to be done, I see that." Prayer, she thought but didn't say, can always be done.

"By the way, Mum, we've had a decent offer for the house at last."

"O, that's good. Has Charles organized getting rid of Mr Steinberg?"

"Not difficult as it turned out. Rather a peculiar set-up I gather, but he's gone already, I think, so if we really are selling this house we can get cracking on my new kitchen."

"That all sounds very good."

"I must go, Mum. There's an actual cocktail party, would you believe, so old-fashioned, the Richmond Conservatives are having this evening, so I must go and have a bath. Lots of love, and try not to worry about Carrie."

"All right, darling, I'll try. 'Bye."

When Hakim had taken off his coat and taken his computer bag to Simon's study, she said:

"Hakim, I had an email from Carrie in New York. She's going to Afghanistan."

Hakim looked at her carefully.

"Does she go with her boyfriend?"

"Yes."

"Clare. That is good. He will look after her. She will be useful, and you have suffered so much because your son's death was not useful. And they will be safe. There is no war now in Afghanistan."

Then she cried, as she hadn't all day, in gratitude.

CHAPTER 16

WEDNESDAY 23 MARCH 2022

She closed her laptop, stood up, stiff because of sitting still for too long, and put on both the kettle and the wireless.

It was nearly nine o'clock in the morning. Hakim had long gone to the Museum. He was in good spirits these days. He was writing a paper presenting to his boss a case for sending him back to Libya to look at the Roman sites two further years into sporadic fighting and patchy government control since he last went, and since he lost his eye when the Russian jeep he was in was mortared. She remembered every time she heard on the news that Putin's Wagner Group—terrifying Russian special forces mercenaries—had been ordered to murder heroic President Zelensky, that three or four of them had saved Hakim's life.

"Do you really want to go back, Hakim?"

"Of course. It is my home. I know you understand this. It is where I am responsible, not responsible by myself. There are archaeologists and scholars working in Tripoli and in Benghazi although it is very difficult, and more difficult because Tripolitania and Cyrenaica are not closer together but more apart. If I can come from London it is helpful for them, to find some support, even some international money."

"But how safe is Libya at the moment?"

"When is Libya ever safe since 2011? When is it ever safe since Mussolini? But it is better than two years ago it was when I was there, and it may get again worse. There now should be an election in June, the election that did not happen in December, which may cause much trouble, so it is better to go before the election."

"Well, you know best of course. And going home—it's so important."

She thought, as so often, of Val, but didn't say anything. She also saw that Hakim was filling the space in his life that his loss of Emma had left by turning all his attention to Libya.

This conversation had taken place two days ago, and she had tried, all over again, not to worry about Hakim setting off. Why did everyone she cared about have to go away? Foreigners—serve you right, Charles would say—and the pull of home.

And Carrie was in Afghanistan: she had had an email saying she and Bill had arrived safely and everything seemed fine, not hostile in Kabul, and brave women were still working, able to meet them and speaking English. It was all right to be out in the street without a man to keep an eye on you, and it was all right to wear a hijab—plenty of local women in hijabs, she said, though some were in burqas. So that at least was a reassuring start.

But early this morning she had heard that the Taliban had changed their minds about girls going back to secondary schools, which had been closed to them since August. They had been told that they could start school again today and at the last minute, when many were actually waiting at the gates of their schools, they had been told they couldn't, a cruel disappointment for thousands of teenage girls looking forward to classrooms after nearly seven months of being cooped up at home, looking forward to an interesting life as an educated, perhaps a professional, person. She thought that Matt's interpreter, who'd become for her a figure representative of the suffering of so many, might well have teenage daughters with ambitions ordinary in the West. The Taliban had produced a feeble excuse about uniforms: this probably meant there'd been a row at the top of the government, which the more moderate had lost. Telling half the population of the country that they weren't worth educating—no doubt partly because some of the Taliban were afraid of competent independent-minded women—was appalling. But few people in the world would have spare sympathy for these girls because of what was happening in Ukraine.

Carrie would have been miserable for them, and no doubt furious with the Taliban. Clare hoped Bill would restrain her from any kind of dangerous demonstration. She imagined her consoling tearful girls; perhaps she'd been able to get near enough to a few of them to give them constructive support. She was glad she and Bill were there.

There were just a few minutes of the *Today* programme left. Before seven o'clock when she was making her first cup of tea there had been a report of a bad-tempered debate last night in the House of Commons. The Home Secretary's dreadful bill, called the Nationality and Borders Bill to make it sound as if it were protecting us—from what?—had been given nineteen amendments by the House of Lords, making it more liberal, more civilized, kinder, and more legal. All Labour and Liberal MPs were in favour of all the amendments, and the government, with their large mindless majority, Charles and his friends who thought wrongly that all immigration was unpopular, threw out every single one, so that the bill was now exactly the same as before it went to the Lords. In spite, for example, of more than sixty Tories joining the opposition to plead for asylum-seekers to be allowed to work, for everyone else's sake as well as theirs, the government refused to consider this, ignoring the hundreds of thousands of unfilled jobs in the country, and the extreme poverty or even, quite often, slavery into which asylum seekers disappear.

She thought of the black boy at the petrol station who had appealed for help to Penny years ago, before the pandemic, and had vanished into God knows where before anyone could rescue him. As for sending asylum-seekers abroad, to be "processed", horrible word, which was another provision in the bill, no other country, however remote or poor, has agreed to take them. But the bill stands, in all its hostile detail, though it breaks human rights law and every decent precedent concerning asylum-seekers and refugees, and was called by a Lib Dem MP the worst bill in his seventeen years in parliament.

But now, as she switched on, she heard a woman in Kyiv laughing, actually laughing, as she talked about the orchids she was growing for her balcony because she hoped this nightmare would be over by the summer. She said she had seen and heard the lies about Ukraine on Russian television every day for twenty years. In Ukraine no one believed them. Flowers and the spring were signs that life in Ukraine will win.

How could she feel sorry for herself for a single instant, even if Val had gone and Carrie had gone and Hakim might soon go, when this woman and so many, many more were being so brave, with their whole beloved country under terrifying attack, and children, she had heard last night, in Mariupol dying of hunger and thirst, and a theatre with hundreds of people sheltering in its basement bombed days ago with rescuers unable to reach it? How could Russian soldiers, who had mothers and brothers and children themselves, shell the convoys taking supplies into Mariupol so that children without food or water would die, and shoot people struggling to hear signs of life in the ruins of the theatre?

It was the same question as always in the cruellest wars: how had ordinary Germans, and, come to that, ordinary Ukrainians and Lithuanians, who at home wouldn't have hurt a child or, very likely, drowned a kitten or shot a rabbit, become the people who ordered old women, old men, mothers carrying babies, children holding toddlers by the hand, into gas chambers in Sobibor, Belzec, Treblinka, pushing them in, bolting steel doors behind them, hearing their cries?

Hitler, Stalin, Putin: *libido dominandi*, identified by Augustine as the root of human evil, and lauded by Nietzsche as the will to power. There you have it.

It was more than she could bear to think about. So she walked, as briskly as was now possible, which was not as briskly as Val, up to Kensington Church Street for Mass and prayed for them all, and for Val, wherever he was. It was a most beautiful early spring day, sunny, even warm, and after Mass she went into Kensington Gardens and sat on a bench among the daffodils, thinking of the woman in Kyiv with her orchids and praying, again, that she and her orchids and her balcony and the block of flats where she lived would all be there, flourishing as they should be, in the summer.

Heaven and earth are full of your glory, however much we spoil, neglect, fail to be grateful for it, she thought, prayed, as she watched the girls pushing babies, old people walking as slowly as she did, toddlers wobbling on scooters. Children older than three or four were in school on a Wednesday morning in March, in Lent. The sunshine and the flowers and the greenness of the grass did lift the spirit: even the most horrible wars do end, or always have ended.

After lunch, and after *The World at One*, which was all about what the chancellor of the exchequer had decided to do—not nearly enough, she gathered, though she understood the implications of his statement very little—about the rapidly rising cost of everything, giving, naturally, the poor the worst of it, she wrote three or four paragraphs. Then she cut, pasted, added, took away, until she was moderately pleased with what she'd done, though she knew it might not survive the scrutiny of tomorrow morning.

She had left the kitchen and was comfortable in her armchair in her sunny sitting room, knowing she would soon fall asleep, but resolved that a nap—she was nearly eighty after all—would not be for long, when the telephone rang. She struggled to her feet and hoped whoever it was would have the patience to let her reach the kitchen before giving up. She looked at the clock. Nearly five to three. She had been asleep for some time. This was probably a scam.

"Hello."

"Clare."

She sat down. She couldn't believe it.

"Clare?"

"Val. How wonderful to hear you. Where are you?"

"I am in my house. It is Wednesday afternoon. Do we meet in the garden?"

"Of course, of course. When?"

"Almost now, maybe? Soon it is three o'clock."

"O, Val. I'll be there. Five minutes."

Thanks be to God, she said to herself, aloud, as she put the telephone on its rest. He's back. He's safe. He's himself. She had been quite sure she would never see him again.

He was already sitting on their bench when she unlocked the gate on her side of the garden. He got up and came towards

her, his hands spread in greeting. They hugged, and he kissed
her on both cheeks, and then held her shoulders for a moment
to look at her properly. She thought he looked thinner, a little
older.

"Clare, You are well. And it is the summer in London."

This was easy.

"No it isn't. It's March. It's a little patch of spring and soon
it will get cold again. But how lovely, how lucky, that it's a
beautiful day today."

Side by side they walked to their bench and sat down, with,
as always, a decorous distance between them. For some time
neither of them said anything, and she recognized something
she had so badly missed, the quality of silence between them.

He was sitting still, looking not at her but, his head bent, at
his hands, relaxed on his knees.

Eventually she said, "When did you get back?"

He looked up and smiled. His smile.

"Yesterday, late in the evening. It was good."

"How is your house?"

"Ah, my house. My house has become a reason, not the
most important, to leave Sarajevo, to return to London. I did
not know it would be a reason."

"Is it all right, your house? I've been to check the outside
once or twice"—more like a dozen times—"while you were
away."

"It is good. A lot of dust, and one mouse I think has been in
the kitchen. Ivica would not have allowed this mouse."

"Ivica—he certainly wouldn't. Have you seen Muhammad?
How is Ivica?"

"This morning I talked to Muhammad. He took the Bentley
to Battersea to collect my geraniums and my orchid. Ivica is
very well. Fatima loves him so much he sleeps on her bed. I
must leave him there. It would be unkind now to take him from
Fatima. She is eight years old."

"Of course. A happy cat, a happy child. But sad for you."

"Yes. But Ivica is not the problem."

"The problem? Is there a problem with the house?"

"It is impossible to know if there is a problem or if there is not. Muhammad is worried. Last week one day two men came. Muhammad does not know what sort of men. They did not say. They had no badges with their names. They were wearing suits, not uniforms, but Muhammad thinks they were police-men, some kind of policemen. They asked him questions, the questions policemen ask. Where is the owner of the house? What is his name? How long did he go away? When does he come back? Have you telephone calls from him?"

"Those aren't difficult questions for Muhammad, surely?'

"No, Clare. They did not ask about me and my little house. These questions were about the Russian owner of the very valuable house with gold taps—and of my house too. This is because of the terrible Mr Putin, you know, these questions." He looked at her with unhappy eyes. "I leave Sarajevo, this time I know it is for ever, because the terrible Mr Putin is getting too close to Bosnia and Dodik, and soon there may be again a civil war in Bosnia. And I come back to London and I find Muhammad afraid that he will be sacked from his job. And perhaps I will be told I must leave my house. Because of Mr Putin again."

"O I see. Val, how awful. It never occurred to me—the Russian, of course. Everyone's trying to clamp down on the famous oligarchs, though London was pleased for years to have all their ill-gotten gains pouring in. How stupid of me—I never thought of your landlord. Do you know his name? We could look him up and see if he's on the list of bad Russians."

Val shook his head.

"I have never known his name."

"But you must pay your rent to someone?"

"The bank does pay—a direct debit it is called—and the name of to whom the rent is paid has changed, three or four times. A letter comes to say there is a change of this name and I need to do nothing. So I keep the letter and throw away the letter that came before this one."

"What about Muhammad? How long has he worked for the Russian? Does he know who pays him?"

"He has worked for him since the Russian, or maybe the mysterious company, made all the improvements to the house,

330

five years ago, six maybe, it is difficult to remember exactly. And the Bentley was bought, and needed, more than the house needed, to be looked after."

"And who pays Muhammad?"

"They are called Something Holdings. Muhammad when I ask him cannot remember the name. They do not fail to pay his wages into his account in the bank, but he forgets their name which does not mean to him anything. He says only it is not Russian."

"Surely he's met the actual man he works for?"

"Of course. Many times. When this Russian is in London he lives in the mews with his wife, or his new girlfriend—there have been different ones—and drives his beautiful car to racing places, Newmarket, Cheltenham, Ascot. In those English clothes, you know, to look like an English gentleman, with the wife or the girlfriend in a marvellous hat. Muhammad thinks he owns some horses for racing. The races at Cheltenham while coronavirus began is the last time Muhammad saw him. That is two years. And Muhammad is sure that the name he is told to call him, Mr Chekhov, is not his real name. I'm sure Muhammad is correct, even if he does not know the writer. Sometimes mail does come for Mr Chekhov, but not for any other Russian name."

"Goodness, how complicated. But I wonder if really there is a worry? If Mr Chekhov is an oligarch, and he's quite likely to be - I heard on the wireless that fifty-one oligarchs have been sanctioned, whatever that really means—he can't come back to England, and I think he's not allowed to buy or sell anything here. So you should be quite safe in your house. Frozen assets, they call it."

"Frozen assets: what an expression. If I am a frozen tenant in an asset, what does this mean? Will the Holdings people still pay Muhammad? Is the Bentley frozen also? And what about the policemen? The questions?"

"They might not have been policemen. They might have been insurance people, or tax inspectors, or lawyers."

"I hope this does not mean there will be some change. I hope not very much, for poor Muhammad, who takes care of the car and the house for two years since the coronavirus started with the Russian never coming. None of this could be the fault of an honest Syrian doing the job he is paid to do. And he is good, and careful. All my plants are alive which he brought back today."

She thought for a moment.

"There weren't any sinister letters waiting for you?"

"Letters?"

"From the police, the bank, insurance companies, lawyers. Letters about your house I mean?"

It took him a minute to process this question.

"No. There was a pile, a small pile"—he demonstrated with one hand an inch above the other—"of the papers the postman had brought. Muhammad had put them on the kitchen table. There were some advertisements for takeaway food and mini-cabs and flowers to order to be delivered for a lot of money, also some papers from politicians wanting to be voted for in the London election, two from the Conservatives. They must worry they will lose this election. Do they think, who will vote Conservative when Conservative means Mr Johnson? So the Conservatives spend money—they have much money—on shiny photographs and posters to put up in my window, which I will not do of course. But here people will vote Conservative even with Mr Johnson because always they do. There was no letter about my house."

She could see how much he was enjoying talking, even if he was anxious about Muhammad and his house.

"Well, in that case, I don't think you need to worry at all. Bad news about things like houses always comes in letters."

"Do you think so? Good. That is very good. But—"

He raised both hands in a gesture that she thought meant there was something he wanted to say that was too complicated or too difficult to explain.

"But?"

He shook his head.

"You didn't come back to London because you were anxious about your house and your Russian landlord, did you?"

He shook his head again.

"So it was Sarajevo, Bosnia, something that happened there that made you decide to come back?"

"Yes. Yes and no."

They both smiled.

After a moment she said, "I'm so glad you did decide, to come back."

"Clare, I am glad also."

She must wait for him to tell her what he wanted to tell her. Asking questions, she could see, wouldn't help him.

They sat for a few minutes in silence, The odd small bird was singing, too early but encouraged by the warm sunshine, against the constant dull sound of traffic in the Gloucester Road, the Cromwell Road, and the occasional roar of a motorbike or an impatient souped-up car showing off. Two nannies or au pairs with five small children, one a toddler in a push-chair, came into the square. They made for a bench and the children started arguing about what they were going to play. "OK hide-and-seek", one of the nannies said. "We'll count to ten and then come and find you." the four children scattered, shrieking, into the shrubs and trees.

"—Nine. Ten. We're coming!"

The girls put up a convincing show of having no idea where the children, three of them clearly visible, had hidden. Once they'd been found the fourth child, really hidden, started to cry. A wail of "Nobody found me" led the seekers to the fourth child. "It's all right, Nicky, you won, you know. We couldn't find you." "But I was lost."

"I know, once I did know, how he feels", Val said.

The little boy sobbed until the other nanny said, "All right, guys, let's call it snack time", and the children gathered round the bench where the nannies were taking packets of crisps and little boxes of apple juice with straws out of a sensible hessian bag.

"Val", Clare said. "Come to my flat and we'll have some tea."

At the kitchen table—"It is so good to be here, Clare. So good."—with mugs of peppermint tea and Hakim's chocolate digestives on a plate, she must let him decide whether or not to talk about Bosnia.

She chose what, from the little she knew of his trip, was likely to have gone best.

"Tell me about your friend's family in the mountains."

He put down his mug and smiled.

"Ah—I did not understand until we were there, for nearly two weeks, with snow most of the days, how much I did love the true Bosnia, the hills, behind each other you know, the fir trees high up and in the village gardens the plum trees and the apple trees, cut back with care for the flowers and the fruit that will come, waiting for the spring. I watched my friend's son-in-law—he is a teacher in the village school so this was a Saturday or a Sunday—when he split logs into pieces for the fire with an axe, the chips—chips, is that the word?"

She nodded.

"The chips flying"—his hands flew apart and came back to rest on the table—"and the scent, the pine scent, of the wood like warmth in the cold air. And by the fire in the evening, the wood burning in the stove and the plum brandy from the trees —It was as it was when I was a child, sometimes, in holidays far from Sarajevo."

"Lovely, it sounds."

She let the picture settle for a minute or two.

"Are they worried? About the future?"

"They do not say until the children are asleep. They have two girls, nine and seven years old, and a boy, who is younger, three years old I think, so the children have known only peace, and new houses. The village was a Muslim village. It was destroyed in the war. The houses were burnt and most of the fruit trees. But the Serbs did not want the village, only to destroy it. So after the war the people who were still alive came back and built again the houses, and planted the trees. There was a small mosque, damaged but made of stone, so it is built again, and a small church, Orthodox of course, which of course was not damaged. Children come from the farms and the smaller villages to the school where the young man, my friend's son-in-law, is a teacher. Some are Serbs, because Serbia is not far, but now they learn again together as before the wars."

"That all sounds as good as it could be?"

"It is possible, in a village in the mountains, for people to try to forget and for children not to know, or not yet to know, what happened in the war. Even the parents, the grandparents, my friend the grandfather, do not say the names."

He stopped.

"The names?"

"The names of the killing places. To say them there is like to say Chelmno or Treblinka in Wrocław, but in Poland the killers came from Germany. In Srebrenica and Višegrad the killers were known people, neighbours for all the years, even friends. Civil war, you see. That is more terrible. Also not so far in the past. There are people remembered."

"Višegrad? I don't know that name."

"No. The name has been lost outside Bosnia because Srebrenica was more terrible and also it was later in the war and so many Muslims were killed that America at last did bomb, to stop the war."

He sipped his tea, deciding whether to tell her. He put down his mug, and, looking at the table, said, "Višegrad is a town, not a large town, a few miles down to the river from the village where I was. It has a bridge, a famous bridge, one of the most beautiful bridges in the world I am sure, not one great arch like the bridge in Mostar, but many arches, eleven arches, over the Drina, the river. I counted the arches. I stood at the centre of this bridge. I had not before ever seen it. It is an Ottoman bridge of the sixteenth century and by the goodness of God it has not been destroyed in any war. But—"

She saw it was difficult for him to go on. More tea.

"In 1992, at the beginning of the Bosnia war, the Serbs decided to cut off the head of the Muslim people in the east, near Serbia."

"Cut off people's heads?"

"No. They shot them. But to take away the leaders of the Muslims, the doctors and the teachers and the lawyers, the richer people, the people with more education, the leaders in this town, Višegrad, and even in the villages, so there would be no one left to manage, to organize, resistance. It is exactly as the Russians did to the Polish officers at Katyn, and to the

Poles in Lviv also. Everyone who has glasses they think has been to a university or a high school so everyone who has glasses must die. They killed also hundreds of women and children. Altogether three thousand people. So many bodies were thrown into the Drina that the lake and the dam below the town were blocked."

"Val—how dreadful. I had no idea—"

"Excuse me, Clare—"

He had his hand to his mouth and left the kitchen quickly. After a few minutes she heard the plug pulled in the cloakroom. He came back.

"I am sorry."

He sipped a little more tea and wiped his mouth.

"No. Even I, in Sarajevo, sixty or seventy miles away, did not know the numbers who were killed in Višegrad. Friends and some family of my friend's son-in-law were killed then. His father was killed. He was a doctor in the town. It was what is called genocide, because only Muslims were chosen to be killed, as was so with the eight thousand men and boys in Srebenica, which is to the north and also close to Serbia but three years later. You know, when the United Nations told that Serbia had committed genocide in these places, Russia, Mr Putin's Russia of course, vetoed the—whatever it would be called, the definition, the declaration."

"The resolution, I think."

"So it could not be made. These terrible things my friend's son-in-law does not tell to the children, his own children and the children in the school. Višegrad for them is only a town for shopping, and to be shown the wonderful bridge, and Srebrenica, a name famous in the world, is a name they do not know. They do not know yet, poor children. When they are older, they will know. These things have been examples to Russia, which always has been on the side of Serbia in any war, in every war, examples of killing ordinary people, examples of lies. And Russia now is being an example to Mr Dodik."

"Examples of lies, Val? I don't understand."

"The war in Bosnia, the wars I should say, began with lies. President Milosevic told the Serbs, the Serbs in Serbia and of course also the Serbs in Bosnia, first there was a Croat plot, a Ustache plot, so a Nazi plot, to take the government of Bosnia and kill Serbs in Bosnia. Mr Tudjman in Croatia was not a good man but this was a lie, the same lie that Mr Putin tells of Ukraine: the government of Ukraine is a government of Nazis, he says, and they will kill the Russians in the east of Ukraine. It will be genocide: he uses even this terrible word. No word of this is true. These lies of Milosevic and Putin are to put new life into old bad memories of Hitler's war, when Croatia was Nazi and helped Hitler, when some Ukrainians also did help Hitler, to kill the Jews for example. Does Mr Putin notice that President Zelensky is a Jew? He does notice, so he bombs the memorial at Babi Yar."

"Goodness—history can be so dangerous. Unscrupulous people can do what they like with the past, Boris Johnson for one. But I do understand. These lies are almost the same."

"And under all there is the bigger lie, also the same. First in Bosnia and now in Ukraine it is told that this is not a country. Bosnia is not a country. It is an invention. It must be part of something called Greater Serbia, which is a kind of lie in itself. In Bosnia, the Serbs say, the Croats must go to Croatia, there are not so many of them, but the Muslims—there are many more Muslims in Bosnia than the Croats and more also than the Bosnian Serbs—where are they to go? Perhaps they make a plot to kill Serbs, an Islamist Jihad. This is another lie. So they must go to the grave. So there is Višegrad, and there is Srebrenica.

"In the same way now Mr Putin says that Ukraine also is an invention. It must be part of something called Greater Russia, which is also a kind of lie. Ukraine was Polish for hundreds of years before it was Russian. Unfortunately this lie of Greater Russia is blessed in Moscow by the Patriarch of the Russian church who tells of 'the Russian world', Russia, Belarus, Ukraine, all one. Of this Russian world Mr Putin is the saviour. He is almost the Messiah for the Patriarch who has said Mr Putin was sent by God."

"Really? That is dreadful. O dear, I wish I understood about the Orthodox. How can Russian Orthodox soldiers be fighting against Ukrainian soldiers who are also Russian Orthodox?"

"Ah, it is more complicated. Always more complicated with the Orthodox. In Ukraine there are three kinds of Orthodox."

"Three? Can there be?"

"The Orthodox who obey the Patriarch in Moscow, fewer and fewer, even fewer now that he gives a holy icon to Putin's most cruel soldiers to protect them; the Orthodox who obey the poor old Patriarch in Constantinople, Istanbul of course, where he is but he has no power; and the Orthodox, in the west, the most Polish, part of Ukraine who obey the Pope."

"And they are all being killed by Putin?"

"That is right. This war is bad for many people, many things. It is very bad for the Orthodox Church."

"But surely this war can't affect Bosnia."

He nodded slowly, solemnly.

"Can it? How can it?"

"Mr Dodik can copy Mr Putin as Mr Putin has copied Mr Milosevic. The idea, Greater Serbia, has not died. Mr Dodik is trying already to undo the connections between Muslims, Croats and Serbs that were arranged by America to hold Bosnia together. The arrangement was to honour, to remember, to respect—which is the English word? perhaps all—the past of Bosnia, the Ottoman, even the Habsburg past, of a place between west and east, of Sarajevo where all the religions were allowed to be neighbours, even friends, even marriages as in my family. *Komšiluk*. I have told you this word. Even Hitler did not destroy it although he destroyed the Jews. Now it is weak and the Serbs would destroy what there is of it that is left. The lies are told every day. Mr Dodik tells that there was no killing at Srebrenica: the story is a lie invented by Muslims. In Serb places, in Banja Luka where is the government of Republika Srpska, there are posters and even T-shirts with the face of Mladic—he was the general, you understand, who ordered Srebrenica—here he is the hero. There in the shops are the face of Mladic and the face of Putin, side by side. I saw these terrible signs of the future. There will be civil war again if Dodik makes Republika Srpska a country to attack what there is left of Bosnia. I must go back to London, I decide. I am too old and there is nothing I can do in Sarajevo."

"But why now, after so long since the war? Nearly thirty years, it must be."

"Now because now the West, the US, the UK, Europe, does not any longer care. But Putin does care. If Bosnia is lost again in civil war it will be another defeat for the West so another victory for Putin. So he will do everything to help Mr Dodik. The worse Mr Dodik can make everything in Bosnia, the further away Bosnia will be from being allowed to join the European Union or NATO. Putin will be pleased. He attacks Ukraine so that Ukraine will not join the European Union or NATO. In Bosnia Mr Dodik and Serbia will do this work for him. On the second weekend of the war in Ukraine there were demonstrations all over Europe, and here in England, in many cities, against Putin. There was one only demonstration in favour of Putin. It was in Belgrade. You understand?"

"Of course I do. I did. When I heard about that demonstration I thought of you."

He wasn't listening. He leant forward, as if to make a concluding point.

"And now", he said, "of course the whole world is looking at Ukraine, and saying there has not been a war in Europe since 1945, and Bosnia is even more forgotten."

"O dear, Val. I'm sure you're right. We can only look at one thing at a time. Afghanistan—"

"Exactly. Afghanistan, so soon, is also forgotten. The West lost, gave up, in Afghanistan—so did Russia of course but before Putin. And in Iraq, in Syria, the West lost, and Putin or Putin's friends have won."

"And in Libya. Ask Hakim."

"Ah. Hakim." He smiled. "When I—when I had to go to your toilet, I saw Hakim is here again. His coat is here. Not so?"

"Yes, he came back. Poor Hakim. The girlfriend didn't last. His heart was broken—but not too badly." She'd never tried to explain Emma, incomprehensibly English, to Val.

"How is the heart not too badly broken?"

She laughed. "Well. Passion—and not enough else. They didn't really know each other when they decided to live together—"

"And when they did live together, what they found was not so good?"

"That's right. Anyway, he's fine. He wants to go to Libya again, to see what two more years of trouble have done to his stones."

"He has much courage. And maybe it is instead of the lost girl?"

"Partly, I'm sure it is. But courage he's always had. And he minds about his stones more than anything." She thought of Ayesha. "Almost anything."

"And how is Carrie in New York?"

"O Val. Carrie and Bill, her boyfriend, have been sent to Afghanistan by the charity they work for. Hakim says I shouldn't worry because there is no war in Afghanistan. But it's impossible not to worry. The Taliban, you know—And Carrie isn't very tactful."

"Hakim is right. Afghanistan needs help so badly. They will be pleased to see people to help, even the Taliban will be pleased."

"I do hope so."

Then she said, "Prayers, as usual, all one can do."

He smiled.

"I did go to Mass, Clare. In Sarajevo. It was the Mass for Ash Wednesday, ashes for sins, my sins, and the sins of the world."

"Yes. I was there too. I'm so glad you were."

Silence for a moment or two.

"You must be happy", Val said. "That Hakim is here. I should like to see him again. He is a very intelligent young man, I think. And he knows what is civil war."

"I'm sure he would like to see you too. Why don't you come to lunch on Saturday—Saturday's our other day, after all— and Hakim should be here. If he isn't, come to lunch anyway and we could go for a walk in the afternoon, specially if this weather lasts."

"That would be my great pleasure, Clare. It is so good—"

He didn't finish the sentence.

As he was going, she said, "Val."

He turned in the doorway.

"Would you like me to give you back your wonderful crucifix? Now you're here in your house again?"

He looked at her for a long minute.

"No, Clare. The crucifix is yours. It suffered in the fire. We did our best with it but some stones were lost, the silver was damaged and the ivories were not any more white. It could not be shown. They said I could keep it, to know it was safe. Now it will be safe with you."

CHAPTER 17

SUNDAY 27 MARCH 2022

On Friday, two days ago and two days after Val's reappearance, it was the Feast of the Annunciation, perhaps, after Easter itself, the day of the Church's year that she most loved, and year after year found the most moving, the day remembering a mystery more wonderful by far than the birth of the baby at Christmas.

When, in her prayers before she went to bed, she reached, every twenty days, her return to the beginning of the Rosary for her ten Hail Marys, she paused in awe, almost in fear, at the scale of what this moment meant. It was the beginning of the saving of the world, and yet it was a moment of apparent insignificance, of almost nothing. She thought of Mary as a young girl, far away and long ago, caught by an angel into a story of which she could have had only the vaguest idea. St Luke gives the angel a name, Gabriel, presumably because the messenger who brought from God news of such supreme importance must have been one of the greatest of the angels, rather as this angel is always given stature and beauty and wings, even when he is kneeling, as he should, before Mary. The painting she always remembered was a Piero della Francesca panel, that crowned an altarpiece in Perugia she had once seen with Simon. The angel knelt; Mary looked not at the angel but down, head bent in obedience; between them an empty colonnaded passage stretched into the long future.

But Mary perhaps saw no one, saw nothing, only heard, somehow, that she had attracted the attention, the favour, of God, which was frightening enough, and then that, although she was a virgin, she was going to conceive by the power of the Holy Spirit and give birth to a son who would be called the son of God, which was very much more frightening, and impossible to understand. She doesn't have to understand; she has only to consent. She does consent and the angel leaves her. No wonder she goes as quickly as she can, to find some support, to visit her cousin Elizabeth, much older—Clare had read somewhere that she was Mary's aunt—but also pregnant.

At Mass on the morning of the feast, so full of light and promise—lilies on the altar in the middle of the plainness of Lent, and, as it happened, on another day of sunshine and warmth—she thought, not for the first time, that it had to be so. There had to be a moment when Mary understood that the child she was carrying, miraculously because she knew no man had made her pregnant, was a child whose father was God, a child unique in the history of the world, and that she was asked by God to allow herself to be this child's mother. Luke's description of this moment as the visit of an angel had only fixed what had to have happened as a story that everyone who heard it would remember for ever.

Wasn't it like the story of Adam and Eve? In the time before sin there had to be a moment when a person was able to hear and understand what God was commanding, and was also able to choose to disobey God. In the understanding and the disobedience was the line drawn between him, her, them, humankind, and the rest of creation, which is innocent of sin and innocent of the knowledge of God. Hence the other story to be remembered for ever.

Today as she thanked God for the coming of Christ into the world, and for Mary's consent to his coming, she prayed for the people of Ukraine suffering now for a whole month the cruelty of a wicked, a truly sinful, onslaught. And also, so small a thing but to her so precious, she thanked God for the safe return of Val.

On Wednesday evening she'd told Hakim that Val had come back to London. He said, "Clare, that is very good. Now, if they will give me permission, and some money, to go to Libya, I shall not leave you alone."

"You are very kind, Hakim. Do you think they will? Give you permission?"

He shrugged. "It is possible. My report on the new town

they liked." He smiled. "Partly because there is really nothing of high enough interest for the Museum that has been found, so all they need to do is to place my report in the correct file for information that may be useful one day. They like that."

"Of course they do." File and forget, she didn't say. "How soon do you think you'll know, about Libya?"

"In a week I should know. There is a meeting—"

"There's always a meeting. Meanwhile—"

"Meanwhile?"

"Might you be here for lunch on Saturday? Or have you another plan?"

"I have no plan, Clare, you can imagine."

"Val said he would like to see you again, so I've asked him to lunch."

"I will be here. Thank you. It will be interesting to hear how it has been, his visit to Bosnia."

"Difficult, and worrying I'm afraid."

"Which place in Europe, or in the Mediterranean, that has been always difficult is not more difficult now?"

When Val arrived, as always punctual, Hakim opened the door of the flat and waited for the lift. Clare watched from the kitchen door as they shook hands, warmly. She realized she had never shaken hands with either of them. Something to do with the caution with which women are treated by Muslims? Though now, with both of them having lived in England for years, a very occasional hug had turned out to be possible.

Today Val, with his familiar little bow of the head, said only, "Clare. How kind of you to ask me to lunch, and how good to meet again Hakim." He presented her with a bunch of yellow tulips: she'd thought he might bring flowers, so she'd left the kitchen table without any.

The day before, after the Mass for the Annunciation, she had bought and roasted the best chicken she could find. Hakim had carved it this morning, and washed lettuce and peeled hard-boiled eggs, and sliced tomatoes which weren't going to taste of much in March, while she carefully cooked some new potatoes which even said they were British, and made an aioli,

344

as a gesture of confidence in the spring weather. She'd cleared the table of notes for her book and cuttings from the *Guardian*, and sent Hakim out, while she laid it, to buy daffodils for the sitting room. Hakim and Val went into the sitting room while she put the tulips in a jug and arranged some anchovies and gherkins in a little Moorish dish Hakim had bought in London and given her years ago.

"Lunch is ready", she said to their backs: they were looking out at the square, one at each window. Hakim gestured to Val to go ahead of him.

At lunch they talked about Val's time in Bosnia. He gave Hakim a shorter and less anguished version of the account he had given Clare on Wednesday. Over their pudding, Clare's home-made vanilla ice cream and hot gingerbread, Hakim's favourite, Hakim asked Val if he thought that a country divided against itself could ever be sorted out and made to work by people, however well-meaning, using pressure from outside the country.

"You ask me this because Bosnia at the end of the war was divided and America arranged the country with Republika Srpska a different country inside it? And now it does not work. Could it ever work? You ask me because of Libya?"

"Yes. But I think Bosnia has a better history of unity than Libya has? Is that correct?"

"The history of Libya I do not know well. Libya and Bosnia, both were peaceful, usually peaceful, in the Ottoman empire, I think. But now this is long ago. Then, and even in the Habsburg empire, the people in Bosnia, different religions but the same people, lived in some unity. But Bosnia has a worse history of civil war, recent civil war, than any country maybe, at least any country in Europe, until now, these few weeks in Ukraine. What happened in Bosnia thirty years ago cannot be forgotten, although it is already forgotten here, for example, and in America."

"Memory is short", Hakim said. "But history is very long. Rome—"

"Hakim, honestly, Rome—", Clare said, laughing.

"No, Clare. Rome is never too long ago to be—what is the

English word?—relevant. That's it. Rome is always relevant. Look at Northumberland. Both our countries, Mr Radic's Bosnia and my Libya, were quite peaceful in the Roman empire for hundreds of years. Peace can be done."

"But Hakim", Val said, "—and please now to call me Val— you ask me if the American arrangement, or the UN arrangement, or NATO's, whichever it was, of Bosnia can support the peace it was designed for."

He thought for a moment, eating a piece of gingerbread.

"The answer, I think, is that it is too difficult to support, to hold together is maybe a better description, this peace without good intentions of all the people who must try. Often your Romans did terrible things, but after the terrible things the intentions for the people were good. Usually good. Peace, justice, a respect for the law, even if mostly because it is easier to collect the taxes from people if there is no war. The Bosnian Serbs do not have good intentions. They were given their Republika Srpska, inside Bosnia and not even in one joined-together piece, and they want it to be an independent country. This independence will destroy Bosnia. If the Bosnian Serbs will not do their part in Bosnia, it will fall into pieces. There is an international person called the High Representative who is appointed to keep the arrangement to stick together. When this person was an Englishman, very strong, a politician who was also a soldier—" He looked at Clare for help with the name.

"Paddy Ashdown."

"Yes. Thank you, Clare. Mr Ashdown did well, but then there were still in Bosnia European and American soldiers, and there was some international money. Now there are no soldiers except the Bosnian army which is not properly Bosnian but Serb, and there is no money and the High Representative is not strong. Also the economy is poor. I think there will be civil war in Bosnia soon again."

"In Libya", Hakim said, "really, civil war has not stopped since our Great Leader Gaddafi was killed." For an instant he met Clare's eye and she smiled: he was, no doubt very riskily, mocking the Great Leader when she'd first seen him, as he was taking her group of elderly English cruise passengers round the sites in Cyrene. "It is sometimes better, sometimes worse, but it is always a chaos because it is not one side against the other side, like the Serbs against the Muslims in Bosnia—is that right?"

"There are also the Croats making complications. The Serbs do not want Croats because they are Catholic. And some Croats in the wars were as cruel as the Serbs, actual neo-Nazis as Putin accuses in Ukraine, where it is a lie. But in Bosnia it is usually clear who is against who."

"In Libya nothing is clear. There are militias who really are gangs of soldiers, or often not soldiers but only gangs of men with guns—there were too many guns in Libya when Gaddafi was defeated and there are many more guns now—and at the top there are bad people who want only the power, some in Tripoli, some in what should be Benghazi but now is actually Tobruk. The worst of them are still left behind by Gaddafi. The Great Leader's most clever and most dishonest son, Saif al-Islam, wants to rule all of Libya. So does Marshal—he calls himself Marshal—Haftar, who was Gaddafi's friend in the army coup in 1969. Can you believe he is even still alive? One official from the United Nations, strong like Mr Ashdown although she is a woman, tries to get these bad people and the others who have had some power since Gaddafi to agree to manage, together, proper elections, because the elections at the end of last year were cancelled. She may be able to. She may not. If I can be sent there, I will go to Libya soon to inspect the stones, before the election in June does happen and makes things worse or does not happen and also makes things worse."

For a moment Val looked at him.

"You have much courage. It was in Libya that you were injured?"

"Yes." He touched the black patch over his eye: he had a false eye but he hated it and always wore his patch. "Two years ago." He looked at Clare again. "I shall be more careful."

"Good", Clare said.

After lunch they sat in the sitting room, a tray on the table by the fireplace with cups and saucers and mint tea in her best teapot. She'd long ago abandoned giving Val coffee hopelessly inferior to his.

"Does the war in Ukraine seem close in Bosnia?" Hakim asked Val.

"Yes. It is confusing for the Bosnian Serbs. They mostly like Putin, because all Serbs always have thought Russia will protect them. But also Serbia itself wishes to join the EU, so it watches carefully what will happen to Ukraine. I think the Bosnian Serbs who are old enough to remember the wars in Bosnia, and so who know that denying Srebrenica is a lie, are surprised now at all Europe condemning Putin, when thirty years ago all Europe did not condemn them. There were in England even politicians who said, 'The Balkans. What can you expect? There are ancient ethnic hatreds.' This is quite untrue. And the issues in Bosnia are not ethnic. Islam is not a race."

"Goodness", Clare said. "Is it really thirty years?" She thought of Matt setting off for Bosnia, it seemed not long ago at all. Old age, and the elision of time.

"It is thirty years. April 6th 1992 was the beginning. April 6th is next week. Bosnia voted to be independent. Yes, said the EU—which Britain was at that time part of—and yes, said America. The Serbs refused to vote. The next day, actually the next day, which shows that they were ready to make the war, the siege of Sarajevo began. The Bosnian Serbs and the Serbs in Serbia were bombing the city and shooting the people. Also the torture began, the killing, and the rapes."

Clare winced at the word, as she always did if she read it in the paper or heard it on the wireless. In the plural it was dreadful.

"As now in Ukraine", Val went on. "And it is wrong to be said that Ukraine is war that has not been seen in Europe since 1945. It has been seen, in Bosnia, thirty years ago, and then there was no help, no weapons coming for the Bosnian Muslims who were being bombed and killed. Sarajevo has been fortunate in one only difference: the Serbs did not have the terrible guns and bombs of the Russians. If they did have these guns and bombs Sarajevo would have been as is Mariupol."

"Or as Aleppo", Hakim said. "Aleppo has been also forgotten. Aleppo is not Europe but Aleppo is in civilization, it is in Roman Syria. We have in the Museum the photographs, the lists of the destruction. Aleppo is one of the great cities of the world, a city of all the histories, of even before history, all the empires, Babylonian, Assyrian, Greek, Roman, Byzantine, Islamic, Persian, Ottoman—every sort of ancient building, temples, churches, mosques, synagogues—they were bombed by Putin. Also he bombed hospitals as targets. There were thousands of dead people. As now in Ukraine."

"Why, why did we let Putin get away with these crimes? War crimes they're talking about, in Ukraine. But Aleppo was a war crime, surely?" Clare said.

"So was Grozny", Val said. "The first city destroyed by Mr Putin. He was allowed to destroy these cities. The West did not do anything to stop him. So he despises the West. It is in decline, he says. There was Mr Trump. There is still Mr Trump. There is Brexit and Mr Johnson. Is not all this the West in decline? And Mr Putin watched America and England invade Iraq. So the answer is two answers, what we did not try to stop, and the example of what we did ourselves."

"Of course", Hakim said. "The example also was important. America and the UK invaded Iraq for an invented reason, the weapons they knew Saddam Hussein did not any more have. Putin has invaded Ukraine also for an invented reason. The Nazi government that does not exist."

A silence, between them.

Was there anything positive that could be said? She tried. "At least people are being generous about the refugees from Ukraine."

"But here in England", Val said, "there was not the sympathy for Syrian refugees that they are showing for Ukrainians, not the thousands and thousands of people who offer to help. Why is that?"

"Syria is far away", Hakim said. "And it was Muslims who suffered, as Muslims also suffered in Grozny and in Iraq."

"Also it's the pictures", Clare said. "The refugees, the trains, the children—it looks to people here like films of World War Two. Putin reminds them of Hitler. So they want to help. As they haven't wanted to help not only Syrians but Afghans, even the Afghans who managed to get out, never mind the thousands who helped us and are still there. We find it easier to be kind to Putin's victims than to victims of our own broken promises."

"Afghanistan also is far away and those who suffer are Muslims", Val said.

"But really", Hakim said, "Britain is not having the refugees, even though people are kind. I do not understand that so many people, two hundred thousand, have offered a house, a flat, a room, to the Ukrainians, but almost no Ukrainians are allowed to come. This is the government, Clare, isn't it?"

"It is. The wretched government. Every other country is letting Ukrainians come without visas. We won't, so we say yes, Ukrainians can come and then we say no, you and you and you can't come. It's beyond belief cruel. It's our old friend the hostile environment, Mrs May's hostile environment, only Priti Patel is ten times more hostile than Mrs May."

"This is not strange. That is, it is not new", Val said. "When— when my family were killed in Sarajevo, I tried to find the way to come to England. It was my first idea, England. But a visa was necessary. To be given a visa it was necessary to go to a British consulate. There was no British consulate in Sarajevo. To find a British consulate it was necessary to travel to another country. This country, whichever it was, was safe enough to have a British consulate, so it was safe enough for a refugee to stay. So there was no visa. I will tell you a number. From Bosnia Germany did take a quarter of a million refugees escaping the war. England took four thousand."

"O Val", Clare said.

He put his cup and saucer on the tray, and after a moment said, "How did you get to England, Hakim, and even from an Arab country?"

"It was impossible. It would be, it would have been impossible without Clare. She found for me a job which I was able to do. And she—and I stayed here in Clare's flat. Without her I would not be in England. Without her I might have been myself dead. The Home Office did give a few hundred visas to Libyans after the end of Gaddafi."

He put down his cup and saucer beside Val's.

"But they give none now. The refugee camps in Libya are probably the worst in the world. People who have crossed the Sahara to escape wars or terrible hunger are in these camps because the European countries bribe Libya to keep them there. And Libyans also want to leave and cannot leave."

"O dear", Clare said. "Every day there's something worse one didn't know about before. And nothing one can do. I wanted to help an Afghan woman and her children in the autumn. She was stuck in a hotel. A clever woman, a lawyer I think, or a journalist. I thought I could offer them two rooms in the flat because Hakim had gone. Carrie told me not to try because I am too old and social services would think I was trying to find a cheap servant. I couldn't face that conversation. So I didn't try. I've been ashamed ever since of what was actually cowardice. And now, when so many people are offering to take Ukrainians the government are making it impossible for them to get here."

"It is bad", Val said. "The Home Office now is very bad. Hakim and I must be thankful that we could escape from civil war when we did escape. Civil war is always the worst. Ukraine is a civil war as well as the attack of one country on another country. Both of us did escape and we have been lucky, even blessed by God."

Val, on the sofa, and Hakim, leaning back on the armchair opposite hers, looked at Clare, and smiled.

"I'm the one who's lucky", she said.

It was impossible to say anything else so she got up, put her cup and saucer on the tray and was about to carry it to the kitchen when Hakim took it from her.

Val said, "How good that you could help him to come from Libya to England."

"It wasn't difficult then. I'm sure it would be impossible now."

"Was he in bad danger in Libya?"

"Yes, I think so. His father and his brother had both been killed. Also his girlfriend. And his education—two degrees— people wearing glasses, you know."

"I see. That is bad danger. And you were able—Whoever saves one life—you know the saying from the Talmud?"

"Saves the whole world. Yes I do. It's wonderful. I just wish—"

"You wish to save more people, more worlds. But Carrie was right I think, about the Afghan family."

"Perhaps. I don't know."

"And Hakim came back. Something else", Val said. "The saying from the Talmud is also the same saying in the Koran. That is good, not so?"

"I didn't know that. Of course it's good, very good."

"Is Hakim a Muslim who believes?"

"O yes."

"I would like to show him my pages of the Lisbon Bible? Would he be interested to see them?"

"Of course."

She heard sounds of Hakim in the kitchen starting to wash up.

"You're not to wash up", she said at the kitchen door. "You've done quite enough helping today already. Walk back to Val's house with him. He's got something to show you which he thinks you might find interesting."

Hakim looked from her to Val, who nodded, and back to Clare.

"With pleasure", he said, sounding like Val, and turned off the tap.

She watched them walk side by side across the garden, stopping to say something, probably how nice the daffodils looked, and was cheered.

When Hakim reappeared an hour later, he said, "I was so pleased to see his beautiful pages. They are the story of Mr Radic's life, Muslim and Jewish and Catholic. So strange to think of now. And he told me that his story is also the story of Sarajevo."

That was yesterday. And this morning at Mass, the glow of her simple lunch for the three of them, and of how well Val and Hakim had got on, and how touched Hakim had been that Val

352

wanted him to look at his pages, seemed to be matched by the glow of the day. *Laetare* Sunday, the Sunday of rejoicing in the middle of Lent, with the lilies of the Annunciation still in the church: she had forgotten that it would be today, and that the Mass was all about forgiveness. She was early for Mass—she had walked up to Kensington Church Street faster than usual in the sunshine—and there had been time for her to follow another old lady into the confessional before Mass. She hadn't prepared her confession but she knew she should make it some time in Lent, and she said she was sorry for losing hope over the last weeks, for being sad almost to the point of despair over Afghanistan and Ukraine and refugees suffering so much, and for not being able to see God anywhere in what was happening, and for not even being grateful for all that God had given her. What she said was incoherent and she wondered if it was a proper confession, but when she stopped talking the priest, after a silence when she thought he was waiting for her to confess some proper sins—she knew how childish this was—said, "You are here. That means you still have your faith in God and in his loving forgiveness. If you feel you don't deserve his forgiveness, that's fine. None of us does. In any case when you pray don't worry about what you feel. What you feel doesn't matter. You are there, you are here, only to pay attention. Try to keep yourself out of the picture. Now, your act of contrition."

The gospel reading was the story of the prodigal son. When you have nothing left you come back to God and he forgives you. That was all she could think through the homily which she wasn't listening to, and after receiving communion she knelt, with thanks.

Penny was coming to tea.

She'd telephoned earlier in the week and said, "You know it's Mother's Day on Sunday, Mum."

"O is it? Mothering Sunday. I always forget when it is."

"I'd ask you to lunch only Charles has got some Tory Wives coming—he's supposed to charm them into organizing fund-raising bridge parties or tennis tournaments at Hurlingham or something. Not really your cup of tea. I've got a brilliant girl coming to cook and wash up, so shall I come to tea after it's over? We're off to Leckenby for a couple of weeks on Thursday and it would be nice to see you before we go."

"Yes, of course, darling. It'll be lovely to see you."

Hakim had said at breakfast, leisurely on Sunday with a lot of good Italian coffee, and croissants that he'd bought when he went to fetch her *Observer*, that he was going to be out all day. "I don't think your daughter is very approving of me. I could work in your husband's study so that she does not see me, but maybe she does not like it that I am sitting at his desk. I emailed a friend who is a ceramics curator at the Victoria and Albert, a junior curator, and we will have lunch in the café. He wants to show me some conservation work in his department."

"Are you sure, Hakim? I don't want you to think you can't be here because of Penny."

"It's good, Clare. He is a nice boy. I met him at a conference on Roman pottery. You must have tea with your daughter and I will come back at six. Will that be OK?"

"Totally OK. Thank you."

Penny came in with a Peter Jones bag full of shopping. She dumped it on the floor with her handbag and kissed Clare in the hall.

"Hello, Mum. Nowhere, absolutely nowhere to park. I had to walk miles. And Sloane Square was just as bad. At least in the new house we'll get a Kensington and Chelsea parking thingy."

She took off her coat, an old cream waterproof jacket, and hung it on a hook beside Hakim's navy blue trench coat which Clare had given him years ago when he was first in England.

"Whose is that? You haven't got someone else for tea?"

"That's Hakim's coat. He's out."

"Hakim? He's back? I thought he'd gone. Some girl?"

"It didn't work out, so he's back."

"Really, Mum, you are hopeless. Anyway, tactful of him to go out. I won't tell Charles he's back."

"Don't be cross, darling. Tea, that's what you need. I'm sorry you couldn't find a parking place, but not so bad, a bit of a walk on such a lovely day?"

"I suppose. No. You're quite right, Mum. It could have been tipping it down."

Clare made a pot of decaff tea—Penny wasn't fussy about tea—and put it on the kitchen table. Cups, plates, a jug of milk, the other half of the gingerbread, chocolate digestives.

"Gingerbread—delicious. I wish I could make cakes."

Clare as always didn't say why don't you try?

"How's the new house going?"

"Well at least it is, going I mean, at last. Swarming with builders, ghetto-blasters, mugs of tea, beer cans—huge skip outside which looks as if it's got half the house in it. Very unpopular with the neighhbours in such a small street. The whole house is a tip at the moment, but they are getting on with it."

Clare thought sadly of David's little house where nothing had changed for decades, but it was so much better for Penny and Charles to be doing what they wanted with David's house rather than making her leave the flat.

"It's all slower and more expensive than they said—but that's always the way with builders, isn't it? They keep finding horrors nobody knew were there."

"When do you think you'll be able to move?"

"Some time in the summer, maybe June, more likely July. At least in decent weather."

"It's all very exciting. I'm sure you'll make it really nice."

Penny cut herself another piece of gingerbread, and looked across the table at Clare, knife poised.

"No thank you, darling."

With her mouth full Penny said, "What about you, Mum? How are you?"

"O, I'm fine, you know. Plodding on. I'm very glad to have managed not to get Covid all this time. Lots of old people are getting it I gather. The jabs wear off apparently, but I should be getting another one soon. April, they said, for people over seventy-five."

"We were wondering if you'd like to come to Leckenby for Easter? We'd love to have you and everything's allowed now."

Absolutely not. After her days in September at Leckenby without Penny and Charles, she could face Charles at every meal even less than she would have been able to then. And the government were doing worse, even worse, about so many things, while trying to con the country into thinking they were doing brilliantly, which would make talking to Charles more difficult than ever. Also she didn't want to be away if Hakim were going to Libya. Also there was Val.

"It's a lovely thought, but no, darling, I don't think it would be sensible to travel on a train at the moment. No one is bothering with masks any more and you can't open windows on trains, which are bound to be very full over Easter. But it's very kind of you to ask me, specially as Charles and I—well, we don't get on brilliantly, do we?"

"You and Charles would get on perfectly OK if only you wouldn't talk about politics. But I see what you mean about the Covid risks, until you've had your next jab anyway. Let's hope we can get you up to Leckenby in the summer."

"It should surely all be over by then, Covid I mean. Any news from the children? I do worry about Carrie."

"They're fine. Daisy rings up every three or four weeks. She says she's working very hard on her master's course, though Charles thinks whatever she's learning—I can't remember what it's all about—is pretty much a waste of time. She's coming home in the summer. It'll be fun to have her in the new house. Carrie doesn't email very often but she sounds cheerful, and they're quite safe thank goodness, at least she says they are, up in the mountains helping with what food and medicines they can get for the villages."

"Carrie is wonderful."

"Of course she is, though Charles says where is all this do-gooding going to get her? What she needs is a career."

She nearly said Charles doesn't think do-gooding is doing good but managed not to. Instead she said, "There's plenty of time, don't you think? She's not twenty-five yet, is she? And what she's doing is something I wish we could all do more of, properly helping some of the most desperate people in the world, when the state they're in is partly our fault. I'm very proud of her."

"We are too of course, although—Do you think she'll marry Bill? You saw them a bit, didn't you?"

Penny had forgotten they'd taken her to Leckenby.

"She might. But she easily might not. He's a bit of a lecturer, isn't he? Not very many jokes."

"Well, he's American. Quite rich they are, one gathers, his family, a big flat in New York and a house in the country. Could be a lot worse."

Jane Austen, Clare thought.

"We'll see", she said.

When Hakim came back at six Penny had gone, and Clare had washed up the tea things and was looking vaguely out of the kitchen window deciding how to turn the rest of yesterday's chicken into something a bit more interesting for supper than another cold meal.

"I hope you had a nice time at the V and A?"

"Clare, it was wonderful. They have a ceramics collection which Philip Jones, the curator who showed me the collection, says is the best in the whole world. I was surprised when he said this. But maybe he is right. I saw many many beautiful and interesting things, very old beautiful things from China I did not know there were. This collection is fifteen minutes walk away and I did not know."

"Hakim. How lovely. But how hopeless of me. I didn't realize—I've lived here all these years and been in and out of the V and A since time began, and I've never looked at the porcelain so I didn't know."

"Next time you go to the museum, you should look."

The future still held the possibility of something worthwhile she hadn't done before and could easily do, even if it was only looking at objects she knew nothing about without David and without Hakim. That was good. And because Val was back, was alive, was himself, she could perhaps now write about Leckenby in September because he would be able to read what she wrote. Though she had asked herself several times whether, if she ever managed to finish this book, she should ask him to read the whole thing before it was published, supposing anyone were to be kind enough to publish it. He might be upset by the idea of his very private life becoming public, if the number of readers likely to come across her book could be described as public, a public, the public. Her public, perhaps. Once the book was finished she would ask him.

CHAPTER 18

SATURDAY 4—WEDNESDAY 8 SEPTEMBER 2021

The question was: could she do them justice, those few days?

There were so many things that went right. How rare it is to be able even to think this, so much more often is it a case of how many things go wrong.

Val deciding it would be better if he didn't come; the early September beauty of the weather, the late summer gold and blue; instead of Charles and Penny, Carrie and Bill in the house for company, and that only for breakfast and in the evenings, because Bill was keen on long walks and Carrie wanted to show him that she was as good at walking as anyone. On all three of the whole days they had, Carrie and Bill were out for lunch because, after his first experience of a village pub, Bill wanted to repeat it so on the next two days they planned their walks round friendly pubs and Clare drove them to the start of a route that would, having taken in a pub in the middle, eventually bring them home. Carrie, in charge of a battered old Ordnance Survey map, was enthusiastic about bits of local country she'd never seen before.

On their first night they ate a basic spaghetti, all that was needed for which Clare knew they would find in Penny's larder. On the next two nights Clare cooked the supper, soon after which, tired and pleased with their day, Carrie and Bill went to bed. "Sorry, Gran, we're knackered." On their last evening her cousin Michael asked all three of them to dinner in the big house, the house of Clare's childhood holidays, and her mother's home until she left it to do war work in London when she was eighteen, and met Clare's father, the Czech Jew who had fled Hitler's Europe. Bill thought the house and the children and Michael's golden retriever and the grouse Michael's wife Sarah gave them for dinner, in their proper dining room with silver cutlery and candles on the table, all perfect. "England is great, Carrie. You never said. It's like a movie."

So she was alone each day, with Penny's old car to go wherever she liked.

She remembered each sunlit day, clear and distinct, like illuminated pages in a medieval manuscript, pictures in red, green, gold, blue, and words yet to be read, with a decorated initial to begin each page.

S for Sunday. In the morning she went to Mass in the nearest Catholic church, a few miles away, the modest Victorian building with plaster saints, which might have held fifty or sixty people, and which she'd never seen full except on her wedding day when she couldn't see much because her mother wouldn't let her wear her glasses with her wedding dress. Today it wasn't even half full, the congregation masked and spaced out for Covid, but the Mass was lovely, quiet, without any music because of Covid, and with a gentle middle-aged priest. As she left the church an old woman, probably older than her, put a hand on her arm and said, "Aren't you Clare Wilson?"

"I am, yes—I'm afraid I—"

"I thought I recognized you. Mary Redmond. There's no earthly reason why you should remember me. Our children used to play together while we had coffee after Mass, fifty years ago I should imagine. I used to do a Sunday school in the first half of Mass for the little ones. So sad there don't seem to be any little ones in church nowadays, do there? Penny and Matthew, is that right?"

"O yes, of course I remember". She didn't.

"How nice to see you again. Are you living up here now?"

"No. I'm afraid I'm still in London. I'm only here for a few days."

"I must fly—there's my son." A middle-aged man in a tweed cap waved from the window of a Range Rover. "He's come to collect me. I can't get him to Mass however hard I try. You should go to Stanbrook you know, if you're here for a visit. Nuns. Terribly holy, they are. And their church is quite extraordinary, very modern. It's not far. They have Vespers at six. I might see you there. I try to go on a Sunday. 'Bye for now."

She had heard before that a community of nuns had several years ago left a huge Victorian convent somewhere in the south, now far too big for them, and had built a new monastery on a remote hillside. She might have a look, but not at six today. Three minutes of Mrs Redmond was plenty.

She bought the *Observer* in the small town where the church was, took it back to Penny's house and sat in the garden with some coffee, reading the paper. The cabinet were squabbling over who was to blame for the betrayal of Afghanistan while hundreds and hundreds of people in danger from the Taliban, probably including Matt's interpreter—this was when she started worrying about him—had been abandoned.

She remembered, too, that she'd heard on the *Sunday* programme, on Penny's kitchen wireless while she was making eggs and bacon for Carrie and Bill, Gordon Brown saying that this country would have a billion spare Covid vaccines by December even if everyone had had boosters and everyone over twelve had been vaccinated. Almost all these vaccines would become out of date and go to waste unless we started giving them away now. Two per cent of people in Africa had had one jab. She had listened in the kind of despair she so often felt these days: there was no chance of the cabinet or the wider Tory party represented by Charles taking the slightest notice of Gordon Brown.

She closed the paper to enjoy, simply to enjoy, being alone, in the sun, in a basket chair with cushions, on the warm flagstones outside Penny's kitchen door, the climbing roses still with flowers and white butterflies dancing over the lavender. It would have been peaceful but for the ordinary village noises of one person mowing and another, further away, trimming a hedge with a chainsaw. The sun or the hum of machinery or both sent her into a doze. She woke after what must have been more than a few minutes, the newspaper dropped beside her and her coffee almost cold. Bother old age.

After eating for lunch some bread and cheese and an apple she drove, through a golden afternoon with the moorland hills to the north navy blue in the harvest-time light, to the Saxon church in a dale far from any village where Matt was buried, near her parents, other members of her family, and more people she had known. Not Simon: he had told her several times to be sure to have him cremated and that he didn't want a memorial of any kind, not a service, not a stone, nothing. When they asked her at the crematorium about the ashes and she shook her head, she'd felt she was consigning him to oblivion, but she knew that was exactly what he wanted. "All flesh is grass: that's Christian isn't it? As well as true, for once. So there you are."

It was quieter in the graveyard than it had been in the village, almost silent but not quite because traffic on the road half a mile away was just audible. A couple of other people came with flowers for a recent burial, replaced some dead flowers, and went away. There were pigeons. She stood for some time at Matt's grave and his memory was very close. So was Simon's whatever he himself had believed or, of course, not believed. She thanked God for their share, her share, a fragmentary temporal share, in eternal memory, as at the beginning of *Doctor Zhivago*. The memory of God.

She walked over lumpy grass through the graveyard and spent ten minutes on her knees in the little, cold, ancient church, with its Saxon window and its Saxon sundial in the porch saying that the church was rebuilt in the days of Tostig the Earl, so before 1066. The first church had been knocked down by the Vikings. It was so very long, the story of this holy plot in its obscure dale. In the church she remembered, as she always did when she was able to come, that it was kneeling here, alone as now, more than sixty years ago, thinking of a beloved teacher who had recently died, that she realized that he had not gone, he was not snuffed out like the flame of a match, so he was with God, in God, so God must, somewhere, somehow, in some way she couldn't begin to understand, be there. At the time she was perhaps seventeen—she knew she had come to the church on a bike—and only very recently more uncertain than the precocious schoolgirl who had announced she was an atheist. Now she thanked God for that moment, and for all the sureness of the faith, both complicated and infinitely simple—she thought, as so often, of Augustine - that had, over so many years, gradually followed.

She went outside into the warm late-afternoon sunshine, heavy with the scent of the yew tree by the gate, and with clouds of tiny insects hovering in the air, and turned to walk a little way up the dale, old meadows, old woodland above the river which in early September was dry, its mysterious stream hidden underground beneath the cracked limestone pavement of the river bed. She remembered a walk with Simon up this dale, thirty or forty years ago, in May, with bluebells and cowslips and wild garlic in the woods and bright new leaves on the beeches and oak trees. And in the meadows buttercups and dandelions, dandelions to tell the hours that never are told again—the line, with its modesty and its huge melancholy, slipped into her mind like Virgil's *lacrimae rerum*.

But when she reached the gate into the first meadow she saw that the trees on the long hill behind the river bed had been felled, recently felled, and only lines and lines of white tree guards protecting from rabbits and deer dozens of newly planted saplings rose almost up to the skyline. Otherwise an empty hillside with scrub turning brown in the sun and the odd tree still standing for no apparent reason, as on a battlefield. She didn't even open the gate but went back to her car by the churchyard gate and drove for fifteen minutes to where, along a lane, she knew she would find woods and above them the heather on the moor still just purple and the gold of bracken not yet tawny brown.

As always when she had left the car and the woods and come out onto the moor, it was the smell, like the smell of nowhere else, heather and peat, bog myrtle and tiny yellow flowers in the sheep-cropped grass, and the sound of hidden water running softly under the black heather stems, that reminded her of moments, patches of time like this one, scattered through all her life. She walked a little, stopped for longer, listened for a curlew and did, after a bit, hear one, put up two little groups of grouse which flew low over the heather with, today, no one waiting to shoot them, and watched the sheep here and there, white, shorn, with their lambs grown fat. They were still here, in spite of Brexit, and there being no market for their wool. Would they be here next year? The year after? Would she be still on this planet the human race was failing to rescue from what the human race had done to it?

She walked back to the car, drove slowly to Penny's house, collecting some shopping on the way, and when Carrie and Bill appeared—"We walked for absolutely miles Gran. I've got to have a bath. Did you have a nice day?"—she was making the supper. They were already going upstairs, slowly, when she said, "Perfect, darling, thank you."

M for Monday. When she'd delivered Carrie and Bill to the beginning of their walk, she drove to Rievaulx and parked her car in the car park, always empty on weekdays, belonging to the Methodist chapel at the top of the village. She hadn't been here for many years, probably since Penny and Matt had been bored teenagers she'd failed to interest in the twelfth-century Cistercians. "Mum, why do you always like ruins best?" "That bridge in France was good, though"; this was Matt remembering the Pont du Gard, which she had persuaded Simon to make a detour for them all to see when he'd been keen to get to a two-star restaurant where he'd booked a table. Even Simon had been impressed by the Pont du Gard, and they weren't late for dinner.

She'd remembered the Methodist car park, and a few minutes later, when she saw that the abbey was closed—why? The school holidays over? Covid probably—she remembered a way into the ruins of the cloister, the refectory, the chapter house, the long, wonderful church in which dozens of monks once sang in the choir and on Sundays hundreds of lay brothers stood in the nave and listened, or failed to listen, to the Mass being celebrated far away at the high altar. She wandered through the fallen stones and looked up, up, at the choir arches, which hadn't fallen. There was no one in this house of so many except her, and she very much hoped that no cross custodian belonging to English Heritage would appear and tick her off for being there when what they would no doubt call "the site" was closed. None did.

She walked along what would have been the north wall of the cloister if anything here faced in the proper liturgical direction, and thought of the monks who sat at their desks, sheltered and with plenty of light, copying or even writing books of their own, as Aelred had. She had loved Aelred since she first heard about him, in a lecture on medieval Latin in Cambridge. He was the third abbot here, and he had written some readable, moving books, and was never parted from his copy of Augustine's *Confessions*, which made him a man she felt she knew. The stones of the wall were warm to her touch. She went back up the wide steps from the cloister into the church, and ran her hand down the carved surface of a pillar in the choir. Stones, out of the ground from nearby quarries and placed to last. The stones in the aisle, more ruined than the choir, had lasted nearly nine centuries where the first monks had put them. Stones. She wished Hakim were beside her: about medieval Christian stones he knew almost nothing, though he'd loved Durham cathedral.

Almost there was silence but again, as yesterday in the graveyard, not quite. A tractor towing something that rattled came down the village street; a tanker delivering oil somewhere trundled slowly, too wide to pass anything coming the other way in the narrow road between cottages; now and then there was a car; once a motorbike; worse, several times aeroplanes, small aeroplanes, not jets, circled above the valley where the abbey had been built on the slope of a hill terraced so that the church, the cloister, lesser buildings were on successive flat levels going down towards the river. She thought of this terracing, of the huge labour that achieved it, lines of monks and lay brothers with picks and shovels and barrows, nothing noisier than these, and the aching backs and blistered hands at the end of each day. To the greater glory of God.

She returned to the cloister and sat on a wooden bench, like the bench she and Val so often sat on in the garden of the square but newer and more comfortable, against the wall of the lay brothers' range and facing, across the empty grass where once no doubt there had been apple trees and a herb garden, the broken stones of the chapter house.

Because of the bench she thought about Val. He had been right not to come. She needed to be by herself in these unchanged places of her childhood. She needed to look for blackberries where they had always been, in the long hedge outside the village, and find them, as she had yesterday when she got back from the moor. Val had understood this, because understanding was what he did. The world was so terrible, and she had been so upset by the abandonment of Afghanistan, that she needed the sustenance of these things that felt like a return home, though she had spent much more of her life in London than in Yorkshire. And Val himself—could he ever go home? He had left Sarajevo so many years ago, and now he felt that the brittle peace in Bosnia might easily fracture. And Hakim? Going home two years ago had nearly killed him.

As she sat on the bench she remembered, not in detail or one by one, the many conversations she and Val had had as they sat in the garden. It was the ease, the undemonstrative warmth, the relaxed silences that didn't matter, that she remembered, not what they'd said, or not much of what they'd said. Memory, although it is who we are, perhaps is less important than we often think. When Penny and Matt were little she remembered—remembered, there you are, she thought now—thinking how sad it was that the laughing baby, the happy toddler on the swing, wouldn't remember the summer day in the park, or the picnic by the river where an hour throwing pebbles into the water, and counting how often Simon could get a flat stone to bounce, was enough. But it wasn't sad. The happiness was what counted, what meant what it meant, not the memory of it. Years later she came across the phrase "the sacrament of the present moment". Exactly. Known to God. Eternal memory again, in other words, other thoughts.

She watched a small flock of pigeons, perhaps twelve or fifteen birds, wheeling above the choir of the church, forming and re-forming in a changing pattern as they flew, bright when they flashed into the sun, dark, mostly, against the light, until for no reason she could see they all flew away, towards the trees that lined the river, and out of sight. Soon, in the midday heat, she fell asleep.

She slept for a long time. When she woke she was stiff and a little shivery and it took her a minute or two to remember where she was. She looked at her watch. Almost three o'clock. With the help of her stick and the arm of the bench she got to her feet and looked across the cloister. Still no one. Still, more or less, silence except for the pigeons she could now hear rather than see, and one or two pheasants calling their clanking call from the woods above the abbey. The tractor with the rattling trailer came up the village.

It was long past lunchtime. Was she hungry? No. Thirsty? There was a perfectly good river. She left the abbey, walked a little way down the road, through a five-barred gate and across a field where two horses raised their heads and looked at her without moving, and down a bank, with wild roses long over, to the river. The water was icy, and it was surprisingly difficult to cup enough at a time in her hands for a drink. Having got close enough for this, she also splashed her face to wake herself up properly, and managed, with her stick and the help of a large rock wedged in the bank, to get to her feet and climb back up the bank. Such a nuisance, old age.

Then she walked, slowly and still entirely alone although it was such a lovely day and this was such a famous place to visit, upstream, along the river, quiet pools where there might have been trout—her Czech father had who had fished as a boy in the Tatra mountains, loved fishing in these little Yorkshire rivers—and then rapids with the water chattering over stones. She came, staying close to the river bank, to a small field which had at its back an ancient quarry, cracks in the old vertical surface, marked by centuries of weather, were now home to ferns much smaller than bracken and pink Herb Robert. Long ago someone had told her that this was the monks' first quarry where they had cut the stone for their church, the stone that was now those great bases of the fallen columns of the nave, dark stone, not high quality for carving. That had come later with the white stone of the choir, from a quarry down the dale, and professional masons which the abbey could afford by then. She stood in the grassy space with the river behind her and imagined the heavy labour of cutting the stone out of the hillside, and hoisting squared chunks of it on to wooden rafts to be floated and prodded to the abbey, still a building site, along a canal the monks had had to dig to avoid the rapids. This canal was always visible, though dry at this time of the year. She walked through some trees, crossed to the side of the fields opposite the river and walked, more and more slowly, back towards the abbey. A group of hikers came towards her, half a dozen people kitted out with proper walking boots, serious socks, and two sticks each though they were at least thirty years younger than her. They smiled and nodded. "Afternoon. Lovely day."

When they'd gone she stood still and looked at the abbey, perhaps two hundred yards away, with the reddish pantile roofs of the cottages low beneath it, and the ruined walls, the ruined arches, facing west, the pale stone now golden in the afternoon sun. She took her glasses off and watched the fallen buildings of the abbey blur until they became much as they would have looked to a traveller approaching down the dale in, say, the thirteenth century, not ruined at all and deeply impressive, the buildings looking something like a Cambridge college and something like a large farm, with a cathedral at their back. So it must have seemed to someone plodding, with a stick, eight centuries ago, beside the canal, dry at the end of summer as now, and with the trees by the river and up the hill beyond the abbey so dark green as to be almost dark blue. Gold and blue. She put on her glasses and saw a ruin. What Henry VIII wanted he usually got.

She drove slowly back to Penny's house and the bars of shadow cast across a sunlit uphill road lined by an avenue of massive trees were more blue and gold.

She put on the kettle for some tea, made a cheese and chutney sandwich, didn't turn on the wireless, and sat on the terrace outside the kitchen door for an hour thinking that the day had been a gift from God, and from those long-dead monks who had been presented, by a Norman baron, with the dale to build their abbey in so very long ago.

T for Tuesday. Her last day, and partly because of Rievaulx and its bare ruined choirs, and partly because they were going out to supper so there was no need to shop or cook, she decided to go to Vespers at the nuns' monastery. It would be good to hear them singing. It hadn't seemed likely that Mrs Redmond would be at Vespers on a weekday. And before that? Perhaps an ancient church that wasn't ruined, and another walk on the heather. She decided to go to Lastingham and bought on the way some prawn sandwiches and two little boxes of apple juice with straws, the kind you give children. And no *Guardian*. For this day only, she would forget about the news.

In Lastingham, a village as small as the village of Rievaulx and much older, she parked at the side of the little road by the church and walked uphill to the gate into the graveyard and round the west end to the door into the nave, hoping the church was open. It was. She closed the door behind her and breathed in the familiar smell of old hymn books, old kneelers, snuffed candles, dust and polish. Polish in vain: there would always be more dust on the lectern, more wax on the candlesticks.

There was no one about.

She sat for a few minutes on a chair with a rush seat and a hymn book speckled with mould in the back of the chair in front of it, and looked about, dimly remembering that some monks had come here soon after the Conquest and started building a new church where there had been a Saxon monastery recorded by Bede. The lawless wilds, also recorded by Bede and not improved in the four centuries since the Saxon monks arrived, were too much for these Normans and they retreated to York, leaving this half-finished, wonderfully vaulted church that had ever since been here in the village as its parish church. Dust danced in shafts of sunlight gilding the air and here and there the stone. This church was built forty years before the Cistercians came from Burgundy to Rievaulx, another revival, like the one recorded in the Saxon sundial she had been looking at the day before yesterday. The monks from Lindisfarne who had set up the first monastery here had arrived in the seventh century, and the community survived until, probably, the Vikings smoked them out after something like two hundred years. The founding abbot, St Cedd, had died here and was buried under the crypt.

The crypt. It was for the crypt that she'd come. For a few more minutes she collected her memories—it was a long time since last she came here—and then, awkwardly and very cautiously, having switched on a light, she trod, one foot joining the other on each step, down some narrow stone stairs to the crypt.

She'd forgotten how big it was, as long, as wide, as the church above, but low and dark with thick short columns, their capitals simple and solid with carved leaves, an aisle to each side, and at the east end an apse with a small window and an altar. Pieces of Saxon carving stood in the shadows against the walls. She knelt and prayed for the world, for Afghanistan, for Libya, for Bosnia, for all the frightened and hungry people in these countries and everywhere that had refugees on the roads, in camps, with no prospect of reaching safety that they could see or afford, and the homes all of them had once had destroyed or abandoned because of war and danger.

After some time, because it was difficult to leave, she went back up the stairs as carefully as she had come down, and switched off the light. In the church she read that the crypt had not been altered since it was built in the 1070s. This place was nearer in time to the Romans than to us, much nearer if you remembered St Cedd coming with his monks in the seventh century, and she knew that a mile away there were traces of a Roman military camp. She thought as she had in Rievaulx that she would try to bring Hakim here one day.

She drove for twenty minutes on smaller and smaller roads first west and then north—there was almost no traffic—until she reached a place, near the top of the most beautiful of all these dales, that she had seen only once, decades ago with her parents, and never forgotten.

Leaving the car on some grass just far enough off the road for a tractor to get by, she walked through a gate in a stone wall, up a hill, feeling the spring in the cropped grass that was never completely dry, towards the moor and the heather but then—she had remembered the way—over the brow of the hill she found what she had hoped to find, a grassy dip, more than a dip, a bowl, almost circular, as wide as she imagined a Greek theatre to have been, with small, ancient oak trees here and there, as if the blind Oedipus, led by Antigone, were about to stumble through the trees onto the stage, leaning on his staff. She stood on the edge of the green bowl in the moors, alone in the sunshine. On the slope the other side of the trees were a few scattered sheep. The silence, as not in Penny's garden, as not quite at the ruined abbey yesterday, here was absolute.

She found a fallen tree to sit down beside, so that she'd be able to lean on it to stand up, and ate her sandwiches and drank one of the boxes of apple juice. She stuffed the two empty packets in her bag and sat with her back to the fallen tree, in the gold of the light and the blue of the oak leaves so late in the summer, thanking God that nothing here, nothing yesterday, nothing the day before except the felling of some trees—all flesh is grass - had changed since she was a child, until she fell asleep.

She got back to Penny's house in time to change out of old corduroy trousers she would never have worn in London into a respectable cotton skirt, and set off for Vespers. Carrie had looked up the nuns on the internet and found her the way, which was simple and only a few miles, and she arrived just before six at an extraordinary place, at the top of an uphill road through fields with sheep safely grazing. She stopped beside one other car, with a forest through a gate ahead of her, and turned towards a modest low range of buildings with at their back a tall stone tower, not exactly a tower but a building high and pointed like the prow of a ship, which must be the nuns' church. The door into the church, past a welcoming statue of St Benedict, was open, with a notice inside asking that visitors wear masks and sanitize their hands. Then there was another door, and then the inside of the church, the ship, a blaze of golden light through the tall, tall windows on her right, with the blueness of the sky and the distant view beyond, and the pale golden stone of the altar, and the pale golden wood of the nuns' choir stalls and the few chairs for visitors, comfortable with cushioned seats and kneelers. There were two other visitors, an old lady like her, in corduroy trousers, and a young man with a backpack propped against his chair. She knelt until at six exactly she and the other old lady and the young man stood as the nuns, about twenty of them, processed past her in silence to their places in the choir and began to sing.

Their singing, the sunlight, the goldenness of the church—she listened and watched and wished the dark discordances and untidiness of her self would melt into what she was seeing and hearing until she was no longer—what? Anything but a peaceful soul being carried by the ship that was the church. Was this how a person was led to become a nun? It was more complicated, she knew perfectly well, than this, but just for a few minutes she deeply regretted how much and in how many ways it was, for her, too late. But at least she was here, in this ship with its sharp prow sailing through the stormy waters of the world. She remembered Hakim's ship on the chalice that had been found close to Hadrian's Wall. "A boat like the church, to carry people over the sea."

As the nuns sang, a hymn, psalms, responses, she looked at the altar, creamy stone, with a plain cross carved on its front, a line down, a line across, at the left of the horizontal line a plain Alpha, at the right a plain Omega, so the horizontal line was time, and the vertical line crossed time as the coming of Christ from eternity intersected time. On the wall above and beyond the altar there hung a tall icon of the crucifixion. Timeless, placeless and styleless, as an icon should be, it powerfully brought into the church the presence of the crucified figure hanging on the cross. Above his head was the familiar notice, fixed on the cross on the order of Pontius Pilate, governor of Judaea, Iesus Nazarenus Rex Iudaeorum, INRI. She must have seen the notice hundreds of times in a long life of visiting churches and galleries, full of images of the crucifixion. But here, now, in the prow of this pale golden ship it was as if she had never before really seen it. Pilate had said to Jesus, "What is truth?" perhaps because, like almost everyone nowadays, he thought no answer was possible, perhaps because he actually wanted to know. And then, though he would have preferred to save Jesus from the death of a criminal, he was persuaded to have him crucified because he was told that Jesus's claim to be a king, the king, made him an enemy of Caesar, an enemy of the empire. But his notice called him king of the Jews, the people of Judaea Pilate was appointed to rule. Why? To show that anyone claiming to be a king Rome would nail to a cross? Or to show that Pilate had been sufficiently impressed by this man who told him his kingdom was not of this world to call him king of the Jews and to insist on his notice remaining when the Jews wanted it taken down? Whatever the reason it had stayed for ever after, and Jesus was and is the king of the Jews as of the world that is not merely this world.

When she got back to Penny's house Carrie was sitting at the kitchen table with a cup of tea.

"Hullo, Gran. Thank goodness you're back. We wondered where you'd got to. Are you OK? Tea?"

"Yes, please, decaff would be lovely. How was your day?"

"A bit of a flop actually." She was on her feet, making Clare's tea. "The pub was a dud, and the walk was too long. Silly of us, and we got a bit lost as well. I've got awful blisters on my heels. Bill's having a shower. I'm quite glad we're going back to dear old Barnes tomorrow honestly."

"O dear. Never mind. It'll be nice to see Michael and Sarah tonight anyway."

"O Lord, I'd forgotten about them. Never mind, they're so nice and it'll be educational for Bill to see the Yorkshire gentry in their native habitat. Your day all right, Gran? You didn't get lost or anything?"

"Absolutely not." More like found, she didn't say. "No. It was—it was really good. Thank you darling, for asking me to come up here with you. It's been lovely."

CHAPTER 19

MONDAY 25 APRIL 2022

That was then, more than seven months ago. Looking back to those days always cheered her, but so much since then had been only sad that most of the time the late summer blue and gold had seemed unrecoverably far away and long ago.

In the autumn the worst, the haunting worst that got her out of bed at three in the morning to turn on the World Service and make camomile tea, was what was happening in Afghanistan. She still kept hearing and reading that Afghan judges, for example, and they were only one example, who had helped the British for years were being refused visas although the Taliban would kill them if they could find them. But now the worst, and it was much worse, was what was happening in Ukraine, the flattening of Mariupol where, shut in the steel works, mothers and babies and old grandmothers like her were hungry and thirsty and ill and terrified, and wounded soldiers were dying of gangrene, while thousands of Ukrainians were being taken to Russia where some were so badly treated that they were sent home to have limbs amputated. We weren't even making it easy for desperate refugees to come here: yesterday a report in the *Observer* said that the Home Office was refusing visas to one child in a family so that the whole family, even if the mother and her other children were granted visas, wouldn't travel. This was horribly devious and cruel, inflating the number of visas issued, keeping down the number of refugees able to arrive.

And now these blessed months of her own life, her delicately balanced life of Wednesdays and Saturdays talking to Val and, when she could, gently writing and editing and rewriting her book, were over.

She needed to try to write down what had happened in the few days since she'd got home from a quiet Easter weekend in Yorkshire.

The phrase "the sense of an ending" wouldn't leave her alone. She knew it was the title of two famous books, one, a fascinating and difficult work of criticism by Frank Kermode she'd read when it first appeared, a thousand years ago, and not understood; the other was a much more recent novel which she hadn't read.

But it wasn't the sense of an ending that had knocked her down last Wednesday so that she wasn't sure if she would ever be able to get herself upright again. It was an ending.

She'd gone after all to Leckenby to stay with Penny and Charles for Easter, not, really, because she wanted to—she knew that those days in September were for all sorts of reasons unrepeatable, and she was pleased that in the two weeks before Easter she had at last managed to make a start on writing them down—but because Hakim wasn't there, Val was safely back, and Penny had perfectly reasonably said, "Look, Mum. You've been here all winter, mouldering in your flat. You do need a change. I'm sure you'd enjoy a bit of country air, and the journey won't be at all bad if I come with you in the train. We can let Charles drive himself up as fast as he likes." She'd also said, in the train, "You know, Mum, there's really no need for you and Charles to talk about politics, is there?"

There hadn't been. She'd managed a cheerful, "Catholics, you know", when Charles said on Good Friday, "seems peculiar, going to church in the afternoon", and she'd driven Penny's old car to her usual Yorkshire church where a reasonable number of still masked and spaced people stood, in the tense silence unlike any other in the year, to listen to St John's account of the Passion, the trials, the crucifixion. He was there.

For the rest of the weekend she'd avoided topics likely to cause an argument, except once when Charles said over Easter Sunday lunch, "I keep seeing Ukrainian blue and yellow bunting everywhere, by the church, over the door of the town hall, even in the villages. It's rather splendid, isn't it? And terrific numbers of people are volunteering to take in refugees."

Clare failed to resist saying, "It would be splendid, if the Home Office weren't making it practically impossible for people to actually come."

"What do you mean, Clare? I suppose this is the *Guardian* talking as usual. You can't really want to us to let in Russian spies who might be poisoners like the ones in Salisbury, pretending to be Ukrainian refugees? If nobody knows any English how are the border guards supposed to know the difference if you let people in without visas?"

"Most people can tell the difference between a Ukrainian toddler and a Russian spy."

"Mum, do have some more lamb", Penny said, and Clare let it go.

She came home by herself on the train on Easter Tuesday— "You'll be all right, Mum, won't you?" "Of course I will, and I'll wear my mask all the way."—and was so pleased to be back in the flat that while the kettle boiled that she went from room to room happily checking that everything was as she had left it, specially Val's crucifix which she took out of her dressing table drawer and put in its place against the mirror.

Hakim was in Libya. The Museum had given him a month to find out as much as he could about the state of the Roman sites, the degree of care for them that the authorities, insecure and faction-ridden as they were, were able to provide, and the fate of statues, marbles and mosaics in the two years since he was last there, especially in Cyrene. In one of the two reassuring emails he'd sent—*I'm very busy, Clare, and very well. Do not worry*—he'd said that the Tobruk so-called government in eastern Libya seemed to be less capable of protecting his beloved stones than the people in Tripoli. He hoped the Museum might use his report to back an international appeal to help the World Heritage Sites, Leptis, Sabratha, Cyrene, strengthen what they could do against developers and looters. She thought of the dazzling sea and the fallen stones where she had first met Hakim: more blue and gold.

He had left his room and his desk in Simon's study as neat as he always did. He wouldn't be back for another three weeks.

She was looking forward to seeing Val tomorrow, Wednesday, to wish him a happy Easter, though she knew that without her he wouldn't have been to Mass, and to report that she'd had an uneventful time in Yorkshire, agreeable but nothing like those September days, and that she'd managed not to quarrel with Charles. The week since their last Wednesday walk seemed much longer than a week because she'd been away. And the sun was shining as it had shone on Penny's daffodils, dying back, and the bluebells almost at their best in the woods above Leckenby.

She unlocked the gate of the garden at exactly three o'clock. He wasn't sitting on their bench. This was surprising. He was always there first. She sat down. He wouldn't be long.

Five minutes went by, ten minutes, a quarter of an hour.

She looked at the second hand ticking forward on her watch. She couldn't hear a tick from her watch but—she hadn't brought anything to read—she made herself remember something that had from time to time frightened her as a child: listening to the ticking of a clock and thinking, tick by tick, that that tick, that second, had gone and would never happen again. Like Housman's dandelions.

He didn't come. Children were playing at the other end of the square. She gave him five more minutes. She watched the children. "Nobody found me." There was no hide-and-seek today. Still he didn't come.

At twenty past three she crossed the garden to his gate and three minutes later was in the mews.

There was blue and white tape, saying Police Line Do Not Cross, fixed from one side of the mews to the other. Beyond the tape were two cars, one of them a police car. She had to stop at the tape. The door of the Russian's house was open. Val's door was also open. So was the garage door. The garage was empty. A man she'd never seen before was standing on the cobbles talking to Muhammad whose hands were spread in disbelief or helplessness. There was no sign of Val.

"Muhammad", she called, interrupting. "Where's Mr Radic? Is he all right?"

Muhammad and the man took a couple of steps towards her. While Muhammad was saying, "Mrs Wilson. Mr Radic is not all right. He is in the hospital", the stranger said, "Excuse me, madam, are you local?"

"Why in the hospital? What's happened? Yes, I'm local. I

live in the square. Does it matter?"

"Metropolitan Police CID", the stranger said. "Are you a relative of Mr Radic?"

She looked from one to the other. Muhammad was looking down at the cobbles.

"Muhammad, for goodness' sake—what's happened?"

He shook his head and wouldn't look at her.

"No", she said to the policeman. "I'm not a relative. I'm an old friend." This was true in one sense, if not in the other. "Mr Radic has no family in England. My name is Wilson." She gave him her address and he wrote it down. "Can you tell me what's happened?"

"You're not press by any chance?"

"For heaven's sake, do I look like a journalist? I'm nearly eighty."

"It's sensitive information on account of the Russia connection at the moment. The ultimate owner of these houses—"

"Please tell me what's happened to my friend."

"There's been a major break-in. Overnight apparently. They forced the French window at the back of the extended house and loaded up a van probably, parked in the mews. Seems to have been a lot of expensive kit, state-of-the-art electronics as well as valuable pictures and that, according to this gentleman, Mr—" He looked down at his notes.

"My name is Muhammad Ibrahim."

"Mr Ibrahim, who seems to be some kind of caretaker, but not living in. Lives in Battersea, he says. And they took the car, a very pricey Bentley Mr Ibrahim says. This seems to have upset him more than anything. The owner's one of these Russian oligarchs, you see, on the list since the war in Ukraine. It's easy to find, this list. Easy to spot the empty luxury properties. Open door for criminals. This isn't the first and most likely won't be the last."

"But Mr Radic?"

"Ah. I'm sorry, Mrs—" He looked down at his notepad. "Mrs Wilson, if he's a friend of yours. When Mr Ibrahim got here this morning and found the doors open he went in to the smaller house, where Mr Radic lives I believe, and found him on the floor, in pyjamas and dressing gown he says. He must have heard something next door, or even in his own house, and disturbed the villains."

"Did they attack him? Did they shoot him? Was he injured?"

"Not as far as I know. I gather he was just unconscious."

"The men with the ambulance", Muhammad said, "came very quick, before the police. They took him away. They were very careful to carry him. They said to the policeman, the first policeman, this morning, it is heart attack or stroke, I think it was the word, stroke. He has a bad shock. No blood. There is no blood."

"Do you know if he's still alive?" she said to the detective.

"No idea, I'm afraid. We'll have to get a witness statement off him when he comes round. If he comes round. Any next of kin at all? Next of kin would have been informed if he carried a diary, a passport."

"You said he was in his dressing gown."

"So I did. Sorry."

"I told his name", Muhammad said, "to the men with the ambulance."

"Which hospital?" Clare said.

Muhammad shook his head but the detective said, "It'll be the Chelsea and Westminster. Fulham Road. Bound to be. Nearest hospital with A and E."

It was this that made her cry. Not yet three years ago her old friend, really her old friend in every sense, David Rose her GP for forty years and then her friend, had died in the Chelsea and Westminster and she hadn't been with him, though for reasons of chance and kindness Hakim had. Then, early in the pandemic, Ayesha had died in the Chelsea and Westminster where she'd been working, and Hakim who loved Ayesha was in Libya, and Clare couldn't be there with her because of the Covid rules. Now it would be the same. Val might have already died. She couldn't bear it. She must. And again Hakim was in Libya.

She swallowed her tears, blew her nose, mopped her face, sniffed hard.

"I'm sorry", she said to the detective. "Is it allowed for me to go into his house? He—he hasn't got anyone else—" She was thinking what might he need in hospital?

"It's a police crime scene. You can just have a look, I suppose, poke your head round the door. Don't touch anything. Evidence."

He lifted the tape so that she could stoop under it.

She went in. Two men in overalls were kneeling on the floor of the sitting room. One was photographing something on the carpet. She saw that Val's laptop had gone from his desk, and then, although the photographs over the fireplace were still there, she saw that the framed pages from the Lisbon Bible had also gone, leaving pale rectangles on the wall where they had hung for years. The burglars, after finding so much loot next door, must have imagined they might be worth a lot of money. They were wrong, but the thought didn't cheer her.

She wanted to go upstairs—she had gone upstairs only, ever, to his bathroom—and find perhaps a sponge bag, shaving kit, clean pyjamas, a towel, for the hospital, but the policeman had told her not to touch anything, and she would have to search for these things. She realized how little, really, she knew him after the sixteen months, only sixteen months, of what now seemed like their life together, their talking and their silences. How careful the distance between them had been.

Still in the doorway she shook her head and turned back to the mews.

"Thank you", she said, for no reason, to the detective. "I'll go home and ring the hospital."

He lifted the tape for her and gave her a kind of sloppy salute. Muhammad followed her so she stopped for him.

"Mrs Wilson. What shall I do?"

"Muhammad, I'm so sorry. What a dreadful thing, and such a shock for you as well as for Mr Radic. When the police have finished, they'll tell you to lock up, I'm sure, and then you must go home. But you must tell the people who pay you for this Russian man what's happened, and that they need to deal with the insurance and all that. The insurance people will need to come here and talk to you, and probably the police will be back."

"I am the caretaker. I have not taken the care. They will tell me I have no job now."

"I'm sure they won't. This isn't your fault, Muhammad. No one could think you are to blame. They'll still need you. The Russian isn't allowed to come here because of the war, and he can't sell the house. So the people who pay you will need you, and go on paying you. You must try not to worry."

He looked at her, trying to believe her.

"Thank you, Mrs Wilson."

"Another thing. The police may well catch the burglars because of the Bentley. It must be very difficult to hide a car like that."

Muhammad's face crumpled and he put a hand to his mouth.

Damn. She shouldn't have mentioned the wretched car.

"Have you got a mobile telephone, Muhammad?"

"Of course." He patted the back pocket of his jeans.

"Can you give me the number? I'll need to come back to find things for Mr Radic while he's in hospital, and if I can ring you we can make a time for you to let me in."

"I can write you the number if—"

She found a pencil and the little notebook she always had in her bag, and he wrote down the number. In return she wrote her number on another page, tore it out and gave it to him.

"One more thing", she said. "Did Mr Radic have any other regular visitors, like me? Anyone who often came to see him?"

He thought, and shook his head.

"He was too much alone, I think. It is good you come."

She swallowed more tears.

"Ring me if you need help with anything here."

"Thank you. One thing I am pleased—"

"Pleased?"

"I am pleased that Fatima looks after Ivica since Mr Radic went away. These robbers could kill him."

"Back you go, Muhammad, and do what you can to tidy up when the police let you."

When she got home she rang the hospital and asked for A and E. Eventually she was put through to someone on the desk.

"An elderly man was brought in by ambulance this morning. Mr Radic. Valerijan Radic. There was a burglary and he was found unconscious."

"Address?"

She gave his address.

"Are you a relative?"

"An old friend. He has no relatives in this country."

"Asylum seeker, is he?"

"Certainly not. He's lived here for fifteen years."

"Bear with me."

She waited.

"Found him."

Nobody found me, she thought.

"O. Cardiac arrest. He passed away in the ambulance, I'm afraid. They couldn't get him back. I'm sorry."

"Thank you", she said. She didn't let it reach her. She wasn't ready.

"What—what will happen to him?"

"If you're the next of kin—or the closest person I suppose—you need to inform an undertaker. There are several local—"

"I know. I've done this before."

"As soon as possible, please. There's always pressure on the mortuary."

"I'll do my best."

She sat at the kitchen table, still and quiet. Who could she tell? Who knew him? Who would be sad with her? His friends in Bosnia? She didn't know even their names.

Hakim, and Carrie? Hakim was in Libya. Carrie was in Afghanistan. Each of them was coping with goodness knows what difficulties and even dangers. How could she bother them with the death of Val because of a burglary? Why was there a burglary? Because of Putin's war in Ukraine.

She was suddenly furious, uselessly furious. That sinister, cruel man with his pale eyes and his pretence of being a faithful Christian was killing Ukrainians every day. There were still women and children and old people shut in the steel works in Mariupol dying while every day they were lied to about a possible rescue. What was the death of one old man in Kensington compared to the terror of missile strikes and murders and rapes in a whole country that had done nothing to provoke this war? But Putin had killed Val as surely as his soldiers had killed the thousands of Ukrainians who had already died in the war, and the thousands of wretched Russian soldiers dying because they had been carelessly sent to fight for Putin's lies, and the lies of Patriarch Kirill. Putin the man of God. Trump had been the man of God. She groaned, alone at her kitchen table.

Val's death was also the death of a world, as in the Torah and the Koran. She remembered all he had told her of his childhood, his family, his work among the books of the complicated past, but above all of Sarajevo, the city in the bowl between the mountains where the people and the religions had lived side by side for so long, the air full of the bells of the churches and the calls of the muezzin and before Hitler the quiet pull of the synagogues, Sephardi and Ashkenazi. And then civil war and all that Val had lost, his wife, his boys, his library, his life. Milosevic and Mladic and Karadzic had always had Russia behind them; the Serbs had had Russia behind them for centuries. Miloran Dodik has Putin behind him. And Val is another victim of Putin's war because Putin's oligarch friends, given "golden visas" by careless British governments to sink billions of crookedly earned dollars into London, were now on a sanctions list anyone could read, not allowed to come here, not allowed to sell their yachts and mansions, leaving their houses empty for criminals to loot.

Steadied by a cup of tea but still, she knew, not allowing Val's death into her soul, she walked to the Brompton Road to the undertakers who had organized David's funeral, and asked them, saying she would pay, to deal with having Val cremated in the simplest possible coffin and ceremony.

"Would you expect many mourners at the crematorium, Mrs Wilson?"

"Very few, I'm afraid." She would tell the people in the bookshop where he'd worked. She knew it had moved from off the Charing Cross Road, and was now close by, in the Gloucester Road; there might be one or two still there who remembered him.

"Any religion at all, Mr Radic?"

Yes, yes, she thought. Yes and no. Perfect. She remembered him saying once, "All my life I have hidden between religions". She saw his blue smile.

"No", she said.

She would ask for a Mass to be said for him in the Carmelite church where they had, at least, knelt side by side on Christmas Day.

At home she rang Muhammad and told him Val had died. She said, "I'm so sorry" into his silence on the phone, because he couldn't manage to, and arranged to meet him in the mews the next morning, to sort out what she could for him and for Val. Then she emailed Carrie.

Darling Carrie,

I'm so sorry to bother you. I hope you and Bill are safe and well. I'm sure you're doing good work, and I'm very proud of you. Afghanistan doesn't sound all that peaceful—I hope you're very far away from IS bombs.

This is to tell you that Val has died. He had a heart attack last night caused by the shock of a beastly burglary in the house next door and then in his own little house in the mews. The posh house belongs to a Russian oligarch, sanctioned because of the war in Ukraine, so it was wide open to criminals. All the fault of horrible Putin.

I'm sad because I was fond of Val, a new friend in my old age which doesn't often happen, and also because it all reminds me of David's death which I realize I've never altogether got over. I thought you'd understand, and no one else met Val except Hakim who's away in Libya, I hope safer than last time he went.

Much love to both of you—let me know you're OK from time to time—

  Gran

After sending this she ate a honey sandwich, a consoling childhood treat occasionally produced by her nanny, and slept, lying on her bed, for an hour. She woke to the desolation of loss, with, in her head, the words "like a thief in the night". She couldn't remember whether it was Jesus or death who would come like a thief in the night. Both, perhaps.

Without thinking she made a mug of decaff tea.

There was already an answer from Carrie. She looked at the kitchen clock. Nearly six. Half past nine in Afghanistan, so not too late for Carrie.

Poor Gran. Another death, and too like David's. I'm so very sorry. He was such a nice man and it was so lucky you found him—you might easily not have.

I'm sure you'll bravely keep going because you always do, and perhaps Hakim will be back soon.

Don't worry about us. We're fine, and doing what we can with the children, particularly me with the girls. In the villages everyone's hungry. The US has got to let the Afghans have more money. There's enough food but people have no money to buy it. The US and probably the UK as well don't realize the Taliban aren't the same as they used to be. Not loads better but at least a bit. The country's changed a lot in 20 years and that's good— part of what Uncle Matt was here for. I think it will sort out in time.

Love you lots and love from Bill he says,
    Carrie

The next morning in the mews Muhammad, without saying anything, greeted her with Hakim's bowed head and hand to the heart, and unlocked Val's house where the police had left every cupboard and drawer open. She found nothing helpful among his things, no will, no name of a solicitor, nothing about his funeral. No passport: the police must have taken it. A file of bank statements which showed rent going out on a monthly banker's order, and two pensions coming in, one from Poland. At least the statements gave her the bank and the branch, which should be told that he'd died. There wasn't much money in his account, not quite four hundred pounds, not enough to pay for his funeral. Thank God that didn't matter. She knew his belongings were worth almost nothing except perhaps for his books. She would get his bookshop to take them—few of them were English and the bookshop was European—or to tell her of a dealer who might be interested. She couldn't find any trace of his friends in Bosnia. Their emails would have been on his laptop, but there was no laptop.

"Where do you think he kept his mobile phone?"

"The policeman took it away", Muhammad said.

Why? Did the police think Val might have tipped off the burglars?

They'd never let her have his telephone. She wasn't his next of kin, or an executor since there was no will. She so wished he had been as efficient, as provident and as English, as David had been. But David, completely a foreigner, was also completely English, and he knew he was ill. Val, as far as she'd ever discovered, wasn't ill and was afraid of dying, though not afraid of death. She did remember him saying, the second time they met, "it would be better to die quickly". So perhaps he hadn't been able to face any planning for his death. At least he'd died with no dying having had to be suffered, or so she hoped and prayed.

Then, in the kitchen, in a drawer with knives and wooden spoons and a potato peeler and a ball of string she saw an envelope addressed simply to Clare. She couldn't open it with Muhammad there so she showed him the envelope—"for me" she said—and put it in her bag.

As she left his house she looked sadly at the patches on the wall where the pages of the Lisbon Bible had hung, and, saying to Muhammad, "I'll take these to keep for him", she put, beside the envelope in her bag, the photographs of his parents and of his wife with their little boys.

At her own kitchen table with a mug of coffee so much less good than his thick, sweet coffee which she would never taste again, she opened the envelope. She had never before seen his handwriting.

Dear Clare,

Thank you for the light you are in the shadow of my life. If I die please say a prayer for me every day. God will hear your prayer. He found you for me.

Here is for you a quotation from Ibn Arabi, who was a faith-ful Muslim a little younger than Abelard:
"Yes and no; between yes and no, spirits take flight."

Valerijan Radic
Christmas Day
2021

Milton Keynes UK
Ingram Content Group UK Ltd.
UKHW011813130923
428619UK00001B/69